Four Steps
to the
Perfect
Fake Date

OTHER TITLES BY LILIAN MONROE

For all books, visit:
www.lilianmonroe.com

Stand-Alone Novels

Four Steps to the Perfect Revenge

The Four Groomsmen of the Wedpocalypse

Conquest
Craving
Combat
Calamity

Manhattan Billionaires

Big Bossy Mistake
Big Bossy Trouble
Big Bossy Problem
Big Bossy Surprise
Forbidden Boss

The Heart's Cove Hotties Series

Dirty Little Midlife Crisis
Dirty Little Midlife Mess
Dirty Little Midlife Mistake
Dirty Little Midlife Disaster
Dirty Little Midlife Debacle
Dirty Little Midlife Secret
Dirty Little Midlife Dilemma
Dirty Little Midlife Drama
Dirty Little Midlife (fake) Date
Filthy Little Midlife Fling

The We Shouldn't Series (Brother's Best Friend Romance)

Shouldn't Want You
Can't Have You
Don't Need You
Won't Miss You

The Protector Series

His Vow
His Oath
His Word

The Love/Hate Series

Hate at First Sight
Loathe at First Sight
Despise at First Sight

The Unexpected Series (Surprise Pregnancy)

Knocked Up by the CEO
Knocked Up by the Single Dad
Knocked Up . . . Again!
Knocked Up by the Billionaire's Son

The Royally Unexpected Series (Surprise Pregnancy)

Yours for Christmas
Bad Prince
Heartless Prince
Cruel Prince
Broken Prince
Wicked Prince
Wrong Prince
Lone Prince
Ice Queen
Rogue Prince

The Mr. Right Series
(Football Romance / Fake Engagement)

Engaged to Mr. Right
Engaged to Mr. Wrong
Engaged to Mr. Perfect

The Clarke Brothers Series

Lie to Me
Swear to Me
Run to Me

The Doctor's Orders Series

Doctor O
Doctor D
Doctor L

Four Steps to the Perfect Fake Date

LILIAN MONROE

 Montlake

Text copyright © 2025 by Lilian Monroe
All rights reserved.

Published by Montlake, Seattle

www.apub.com

Amazon, the Amazon logo, and Montlake are trademarks of Amazon.com, Inc., or its affiliates.

ISBN-13: 9781662526565 (paperback)
ISBN-13: 9781662526558 (digital)

Cover design by Letitia Hasser
Cover images: © Regina Wamba; © Runrun2 / Shutterstock

Printed in the United States of America

Four Steps
to the
Perfect
Fake Date

STEP ONE: IDENTIFY THE EVENT . . . AND FIND A DATE

CHAPTER 1

Daphne Davis was a good girl who followed rules and ticked boxes. She flossed daily and preened when the dentist noticed her absence of plaque. She kept on top of her finances, her health, and her chores in a way that lifestyle influencers only pretended to do when the cameras were rolling.

Life was better when there was order. Safety. Stability. When items had homes in labeled boxes and every commitment was immortalized in a color-coded calendar.

But even good little rule followers like Daphne sometimes went bad.

As she drove home from the party at her parents' house with a tub of mint-chip ice cream sandwiched between her thighs, Daphne felt like a rebel. From the outside, her revolt was laughable. But on the inside, the core of her was turning brittle. Everything that made Daphne *Daphne* felt like the faded garments on an old scarecrow, only a few bits of fraying thread keeping her together while crows circled overhead.

All she'd stolen was a container of ice cream—and a spoon—from her parents' kitchen, and then she'd sneaked away from the party through the back door. She hadn't said goodbye to anyone, but none of the partygoers had seemed to notice or care when she'd made her bid for freedom.

The ice cream chilled her crotch as she tore off the lid and flicked it onto the passenger seat, and Daphne ignored the little voice in her head that told her she should at least wait until she was home so she could use a bowl. Who needed a bowl when you had desperation?

She drove with one hand on the wheel, the other digging her spoon into the pint with the single-mindedness of a toddler who knew she had only a few minutes to get away with something naughty. Creamy, mint-flavored ice cream hit her tongue, and she let out a moan.

It was ice cream from a local shop that was only open during the warmer months, which meant that this deliciousness had survived the fall and half the winter in her parents' freezer yet still tasted like heaven. Sorcery. If there was one thing she'd missed when she'd been away from Fernley Island, it was Rhonda Roberts's ice cream. Her mint-chip deliciousness was one of the few truly good things about the small tree-covered patch of land in the middle of the Salish Sea.

Things that weren't so good: the incessant gossip, the lack of privacy, the stagnancy, and the fact that somehow, on an island of misfits and weirdos, Miss Goody Two-Shoes Daphne Davis, who did exactly what she was supposed to do all the time, was the odd one out.

Figured.

Unfortunately, doing exactly what she was supposed to do all the time hadn't led Daphne down the path of success these last two years. She'd failed to foresee a few things, even with a comprehensive, color-coded schedule and a bulletproof routine. Like her ex-fiancé telling her he wasn't in love with her anymore. Or the sale of the forever home they'd purchased together, which turned out not to be forever at all. Or the layoffs at her steady accounting job.

Jobless, homeless, near broke, and alone. Just the triumphant return home every eldest daughter imagined for herself.

Squeezing the steering wheel with a bloodless grip while she scooped another mouthful of minty ice cream into her gob, Daphne pushed down memories of everything that had gone wrong and focused on keeping her car between the lines and her speed under the limit. These were rules she could follow. Rules that made sense. If she followed the rules, everything would be okay.

After swerving slightly as she tried to angle the spoon to a particularly chip-dense patch of ice cream, Daphne jerked the wheel to right the car, flicking some of her snack on her sweater in the process.

"Crap," she said, glancing down at the dribble of melting ice cream drawing a line down her front. Gritting her teeth, she ignored the mess and went for another spoonful.

If she'd been able to think clearly, Daphne might have wondered why she was seeking solace in a pint of cream and sugar. Or why it felt so imperative that she eat as much ice cream as possible before she got back to the little one-bedroom apartment she'd rented for a six-month term. She might have wondered why she was planning, without consciously deciding it, to throw the pint out before she went up to her apartment, as if she'd need to hide the evidence. Evidence of what?

If she'd felt like herself, Daphne could have set the stolen spoon aside and focused on the road, using the quiet of the car to sort through her chaotic thoughts. She could have embraced the darkness of the forest on either side of the road, watching the way her headlights carved moving shadows between the trunks.

Was it being back on Fernley Island that was putting her on edge? Did she feel like a failure because she was supposed to be the successful sister, and yet she'd had to come back to this small island in the Pacific Northwest out of desperation after her string of recent misfortunes?

Or, more shamefully, was it the fact that the party at her parents' house had been a celebration of her sister Ellie's engagement to Hugh Hartford, and Daphne couldn't quite swallow the acid taste of her own envy?

A few splatters of rain fell on the windshield, and Daphne let out a sigh. That was as familiar as the rest of the island where she'd grown up, though she hadn't escaped the gray skies and wet weather during her time in Seattle. She passed a soggy-looking sign made of an old sheet of plywood spray-painted with the words **PRIVATE: KEEP OUT** in drippy black letters, and she knew that the intersection where she'd turn left was coming up just over the crest of the next hill.

She wrapped her fingers around her spoon and jabbed it at the ice cream between her legs with the kind of urgency that hinted at an unwell mind.

Soon, she'd be in her small, tidy, impersonal apartment she'd rented in Carlisle, the largest and only town on the island. The ice cream would be dispatched into some public trash can down the block from her building. She would take a shower and wash off the effort it had taken to keep her smile hooked high on her cheeks all evening, get a good night's rest, and prepare for her first day of work on Monday.

Everything would be fine. All she had to do was eat as much ice cream as possible and not think about the stomachache to come.

That was her plan, at least, until headlights appeared behind her. Whoever it was had their brights on—or maybe those horrible white LEDs that made her eyeballs ache. They were high enough that Daphne knew the vehicle was a gigantic truck. She slowed as she came to the intersection, indicating left, hoping whoever was driving behind her wasn't heading into town.

But the truck followed her at the turn, and Daphne settled in for a squinty drive home, cursing the driver, who probably had no use for a huge truck to begin with. She'd bet every dollar in her fastidiously managed savings account that the truck bed remained empty at least 95 percent of the time.

She ate more ice cream and stewed in her own resentment. Her inner thighs were wet from the condensation beading on the container, but even the discomfort of wet, cold jeans couldn't clear her head.

Then more lights appeared above the headlights. These ones were red and blue, and they flashed ominously in the dark. A loud *whoop* cut through the night, and Daphne's entire body clenched. The ice cream container collapsed, and melty mint-chip cream oozed from the top.

Daphne yelped, the car jerked, and her pulse kicked into overdrive. Sucking in a hard breath, Daphne angled the vehicle toward the side of the road. Her tires kicked up gravel as they crunched onto the shoulder. She put the car in park and waited.

Her mouth was dry, and the ice cream had turned sour on her tongue. She gritted her teeth, reaching for the lid as she tried to fit it onto the now-crushed container. Her spoon clattered as she dropped it into a cup holder, and she set the deformed pint of ice cream on the passenger seat. Sticky hands reminded Daphne she hadn't had the foresight to steal a dish towel or even a napkin during her great escape.

Another glance in her rearview told her that whoever this deputy was, he was taking his sweet time. Meanwhile, her pulse sped and sweat beaded along her temple.

That's when she noticed her pants. More specifically, the gigantic, obvious wet patch centered around the crotch of her light-wash jeans.

Groaning, Daphne squeezed her thighs together, but all that did was make her feel wet and cold in places that had no business feeling that way at all.

She drummed her fingers on her steering wheel, trying to ignore the sweat gathering under her arms. The jump in Daphne's pulse made her scowl. It wasn't that she was afraid; it was just that she hated confrontation and couldn't bear the thought of doing something wrong, even when she'd been high on ice cream–flavored rebellion. Old habits and all that.

Any hint of strife, and Daphne's muscles tensed. After all, when she messed up, everyone treated it like some sort of calamity. A ticket would be the talk of the town—especially considering where Daphne would be working come Monday.

In her side mirror, she watched the truck's door open. It was dark, and he was behind the bright headlights, so all she could make out was the vague form of a man as he stepped out, closed the door, and turned to face her vehicle.

The deputy approached with slow, measured steps. Silhouetted by his overbright headlights, he looked broad and tall and imposing. Despite her best efforts, Daphne's pulse gave a nervous rattle.

Nothing to be worried about. Right? It was just a traffic stop, and Daphne hadn't done anything wrong. Had she? There was no need to be this nervous.

She glanced at her crotch, then at the ice cream. Was it illegal to eat and drive? Did it count as distracted driving? Had she been breaking the law without even realizing it? Her breathing became jagged.

No. She was being ridiculous.

Then again, she'd been swerving all over the place! Had he seen? Would he arrest her? Would she lose her job before she'd even had the chance to start?

The officer paused, studying the back of her car. Daphne gulped and lowered her window. His footsteps crunched on the gravel. Daphne waited, listening to the thump of her heartbeat in her ears and the sound of his approach.

Maybe she could talk herself out of it. She could bat her eyelashes or pull out some of that charm her sister had in spades. Ellie could talk herself out of anything, and if she did get in trouble, she somehow always spun it to her advantage.

Daphne couldn't talk herself out of an open door.

"License and registration." The deep voice reverberated through her bones, and Daphne made a squeak of assent as she gathered the documents. She passed them through the window, tilting her head to get a look at the man.

In the gloom, she could barely make out the planes of his face below the brim of his cap. Rain spattered it, dripping off the edge like a veil. He wore a dark-blue uniform under a matching blue windbreaker, his hard male lips pinched into a thin line. It hadn't just been the headlights, Daphne realized. He was broad and tall, especially when he loomed outside her car door with the added height of his authority.

In the wake of all her recent failures, Daphne felt very small as she waited for him to speak. The seconds dragged. The pressure of it was too much. She felt like she'd explode if one of them didn't say something.

So she went first.

"Just so you're aware," she started, gesturing to the dark patch on her light jeans, "I was holding a pint of ice cream with my thighs. This is condensation."

There was a moment of silence before he said, "Okay."

"I wanted to clear that up." Daphne gave him a businesslike nod. Just two people having a chat about the state of her groin, such as it was.

He was still for a moment, and Daphne wished she could see his face. "Daphne Davis," he mused, tapping her license against his palm. "This is a surprise."

Oh. He knew her. Of course he knew her! Daphne racked her brain. She'd looked up the Fernley County Sheriff's Department website when she got the job offer, and she hadn't recognized any of the names, except for Shirley Newbury, who'd worked the phones at the station since the dawn of time, and Hank Packer, who'd been there almost as long. The rest of the department had recently undergone significant upheaval—hence Daphne's presence on the island. She'd been offered a job at the sheriff's department precisely because of that upheaval.

But this man knew her. A local. He had to be.

She tilted her head to try to get a look at him, but the darkness was too deep, and his hat cast shadows over his features. He kept his head tilted, his brim concealing everything but the strong line of his jaw and the small, almost imperceptible curl of his smirk.

Was he staring at her crotch? Did he believe her about the ice cream condensation thing? Why had she even mentioned it?

Wait. *Was* eating and driving a crime? Had she just incriminated herself?

She sucked in a deep breath.

What would Ellie do? She needed to channel her sister and brazen her way out of this.

"Look, uh, sir, I'm not . . . This isn't . . . Is everything okay?" Her voice broke on the last word.

That was most definitely *not* what Ellie would do. Ellie would already have this guy grinning and waving her on her way. Either that, or her sister would lead him on a merry chase through the forest, get arrested, and somehow garner sympathy from half the island for her misdeeds.

Daphne glanced at the trees on the other side of the ditch lining the road. Could she . . . ?

No. God, no. The fact that she'd even considered making a run for it was proof that she was spiraling out of control. She glanced sideways at the deformed container of ice cream like it was to blame for all of this.

"Do you know why I stopped you?" There was a hint of something in the deputy's voice. Something Daphne couldn't place. An edge. Who was he?

"Was I speeding?" she guessed, knowing she hadn't been.

"Have you been drinking tonight?"

"I had a glass of wine with dinner," she admitted, "but that was three hours ago." The party at her parents' house was probably still going, but Daphne had left early and decided not to drink any more. She tended to get weepy with alcohol. Crying when she was supposed to be celebrating her sister's engagement was not what she wanted to do to set tongues wagging so soon after she'd arrived on the island.

She knew her life was just one more disaster away from falling apart completely. That didn't mean she wanted to announce it to everyone else.

"Step out of the vehicle, ma'am."

Now he was calling her "ma'am." "Is this necessary?" she complained.

"Step out of the vehicle," he repeated, his voice hard.

Daphne sighed and unclipped her seat belt. She opened the door and slid out, scowling as a fat raindrop landed on her nose. A gust of wind reminded her that her crotch was wet and cold. She planted her hands on her hips and lifted her gaze to meet—

"Flint?" she blurted out. "Calvin Flint?"

"That's Sheriff Flint to you," he said, tilting his head up so the light from his truck illuminated his face.

Daphne's stomach sank. This was just wonderful. Of all the people on all the islands . . .

Yeah, he was local. A local pain in her ass.

But she couldn't help the pop of her brow or the words that slipped out of her lips next. "Shouldn't that be *Acting* Sheriff Flint?" She blinked at him, angelic. "Sir?"

The former sheriff, Bill Jackson, had been arrested and charged for taking bribes on the job. Most of the department had gotten the boot in an event that had fueled island gossip for a year and a half. The dust had settled and the election for the next sheriff had been scheduled for the fall, but the chaos in the ranks of Fernley law enforcement was one of the reasons Daphne was here in the first place.

Apparently, it was one of the reasons Calvin freaking Flint was here too.

Flint's jaw clenched. He was clean shaven, but the shadow of his beard told her it had been hours since a razor had touched his skin. His eyes were the same hard chips of hazel she remembered from nineteen years ago, watching her like she wasn't worth the dirt under his gleaming black boots.

"Maybe I should get you to call me 'boss' instead," he suggested, eyes narrowing slightly. "Unless I read the wrong name on the paperwork this morning."

Oh, that was rich. He thought that, just because he wore a shiny new badge, he could push her around? Calvin Flint, of all people?

She snorted. That wasn't surprising. The Calvin Flint she'd known was a vindictive, sniveling worm who enjoyed prodding people until they snapped.

The good girl inside Daphne stepped aside, replaced with a creature made of snark and backbone. A creature that had been tucked in a cage and starved for a long, long time. A creature that looked at her supposed rebellion with the ice cream and said, *That's cute.*

She smiled politely. "Technically, your department hired me as a consultant. So you're my client, not my boss. If that concept is confusing to you, I can try to explain it again. I know these things can sometimes be difficult to understand." Her smile turned vicious. "Sir."

She was making it worse. She could tell by the way Flint's shoulders stiffened and the corners of his lips turned down.

Good. Served him right. Not that she was bitter about old high school bygones, but still. She and Flint weren't going to be besties anytime soon, even if they would be working together.

The rain came down heavier around them. The sheriff—*acting* sheriff—arched a dark brow. "Still the same know-it-all as you were at seventeen, huh. You haven't changed a bit."

Daphne stiffened. "Why am I standing here in the rain instead of warm in my bed, Flint? Or do you enjoy accosting women on deserted stretches of road at night? Is that why you joined the force? Being a dropout wasn't working for you, so you decided to lord your authority over anyone unlucky enough to step onto your turf?"

The air between them turned electric. Daphne knew the man before her was furious; she could sense it in the snap of static against her skin, the tension that stole over his body, and the way his eyes went from cold to glacial.

"I would stop talking if I were you, Davis," he warned quietly.

Normally, Daphne would comply. She'd lived her life trying to be the sensible one. She always double- and triple-checked her work. She actually read the terms and conditions for all the apps and services she used, instead of just clicking "Agree" and moving on. Sassing an officer of the law a day and a bit before she started working for the sheriff's department was not the way Daphne operated.

Well. Not usually.

Because Daphne was *good*. She'd worked hard all her life. Got the scholarships. Got the degree. Got the boyfriend who turned into the fiancé. She'd had a steady job as an accountant at a large firm, and life had been chugging along exactly as it should for someone so dutiful and responsible as she.

But now, as the rain grew heavier and soaked through the shoulders of her sweater, Daphne felt like a pressure cooker about to blow its lid.

She was back on the island where she'd grown up, facing off against the man who'd gotten in her way and almost made her lose it all. And not only were they going to be working together, but he was actually the *sheriff*. He was in charge.

And he was handsome, damn him! He'd been this scrawny little teenage bad boy with a chip on his shoulder the size of Fernley Island, and now he was . . . he was *this*. This muscular, grown-up, large-and-in-charge *man*. Not that she was attracted to him, but it galled her that he hadn't turned into a sad, balding, leather-skinned wreck like he was supposed to. Wasn't that what happened to high school rivals? They didn't pop out of thin air looking like part-time calendar models for *Sheriffs Illustrated*. They peaked at seventeen. That was how these things worked.

But Calvin Flint seemed to have peaked about two decades later, and Daphne had the horrible sensation that she was the one who was past her prime.

He was standing in the pouring rain, and his uniform still looked neat. How? That's what Daphne wanted to know. How did the hair sticking out from under his cap not look like a sodden mess, when she knew her own locks were plastered to her head like a helmet? How did the crease down the front of his pants look sharp as ever? Why couldn't he look the least bit soggy, just this once?

She was in a foul mood. She was mad about being pulled over. Mad about being pulled over *by him*. Mad about being on the island at all, with her broken engagement and bout of unemployment and swirling belly full of shame. Mad that she hadn't actually enjoyed any of that ice cream, after all.

And, fine. Daphne could admit that even though she was happy for her sister, seeing Ellie so happy and in love had been like a very thin needle being inserted right into the center of her heart. Because Ellie was a tornado turned human. She was well-intentioned chaos. She was impulsive and brash, and somehow that made her likable.

Daphne couldn't measure up. Ever since they'd been kids, Ellie had always eclipsed her. Not in school, or grades, or responsibilities. No, Daphne ruled those areas. But Ellie had more charm in her pinkie finger on a bad day than Daphne could have cobbled together during her whole life.

Daphne tried *so hard* to be good. To be responsible. To do what she needed to do. But the one thing she could never be was good *enough*.

As she stood in front of the man she'd least expected to see, facing the reality that she'd be seeing a whole lot more of him unless she quit her job and landed herself in an even worse position than her current one, Daphne couldn't curl into herself and play the good, dutiful, responsible citizen. She couldn't take the submission of it. The smirk she knew would grace Flint's lips.

She couldn't let him win.

Her chin lifted. "Is this the part where you frisk me? Because if you touch me, I'll—"

"You'll what."

The static against her skin became sharper, and the sheriff took one single step closer to her. Daphne locked her knees and stood her ground.

"I'm going to pretend you didn't say that, Davis," he told her in a low voice. "I stopped you because your left taillight is out."

Daphne deflated like an old party balloon. She combed her fingers through her hair and winced when they snagged on wet knots. "Oh."

"I could write you a ticket," Flint noted, "but I won't. Get it fixed before you come to the station on Monday. Now, go on," he said, dipping his head toward her car door. "I'll escort you home."

"How magnanimous of you," she said, sneering, because apparently she was petty and rude on top of it all.

"You're testing my patience, Cupcake."

Daphne stiffened at the old nickname delivered in such a dark tone. But two could play at that game. "It's what you deserve, Einstein."

His jaw worked, highlighting the hollows beneath his cheekbones and the sheer manly perfection of his bone structure. He was truly awful.

The only sound was the splatter of the rain. "Do you want a ticket, Davis? Because I'm more than happy to give you one."

She met his eyes and snorted. "Working together should be fun," she said; then she brushed past him and got in her car. Her hands shook as she put her seat belt on, and she wasn't sure if it was nerves or fury or the force of Calvin Flint's presence that was doing it. With a frustrated huff, she started her engine.

It wasn't until Daphne had her turn signal blinking to merge back onto the road that she realized she had, indeed, talked her way out of a ticket. Straightening, she glanced at the lights in her rearview mirror and squinted . . .

Then she let a small secret smile tug at the corners of her lips.

CHAPTER 2

"Did you know Calvin Flint is the acting sheriff now?" Daphne asked as she placed empty drink containers in the recycling bin in the corner of her parents' living room by the side door.

Ellie glanced up from where she was scrubbing a stain out of the rug. "Flint? Really? When did that happen?"

"Two days ago," their mother, Helen, said as she came in with a new trash bag, ready to pick up more of the remnants of last night's party. "It was just announced in Friday's paper. And don't think we've forgiven you about sneaking away last night, Daphne."

"If you can tell me what time I left, plus or minus one hour, I'll admit that I was wrong," Daphne replied.

When Helen just let out a dramatic sigh and bent over to pick up a crumpled napkin, Daphne shot a wry grin at her sister to hide her disappointment. She'd known no one would notice her leaving. Why did it still hurt to know it was true?

They'd all gathered to help their parents with the cleanup, since the revelry had gone on late into the night. Daphne had missed the part where Lionel, the old, grouchy, antisocial boat mechanic, had been coaxed into dancing with Faye, Hugh's mother, and had accidentally tripped and knocked over a lamp before crashing through a side table. The table was still there, flattened into kindling, evidence of all the merrymaking Daphne had thankfully avoided.

She really had to shake this mood. She was too young to be this bitter.

"Since when is Calvin Flint on the force?" Daphne asked, the bottles in the recycling clinking as she added another one to their number. "Last time I saw him, he was pleading his case to not get kicked out of Fernley High for the second time."

"He was serving over in San Juan County on one of the smaller islands and got the tap on the shoulder since he grew up local," Helen said. "They wanted to bring someone in from outside the force after everything that happened last year."

Daphne glanced at Ellie, who cringed. "Whoops," the younger woman said.

Daphne grinned. "Who knew you'd be exposing all that corruption when you just wanted to avenge a few sheep?"

Ellie laughed. "It all sort of snowballed."

"And now you're engaged."

Ellie's smile softened as she glanced down at her ring. "Yeah. Now I'm engaged."

Right on cue, the side door opened and Hugh stepped through. Tall, dark haired, and handsome, he filled the doorway and brought in a gust of fresh air while Ellie's dog, Louie, darted in around his legs. Gaze softening as he looked at Ellie, Hugh kicked off his shoes and crossed the space to wrap her in his arms.

Daphne busied herself with scratching Louie behind the ears while the two of them kissed and spoke in quiet, private voices. She heard Hugh murmur something about Valentine's Day and realized it was today. A wave of melancholy washed over Daphne as she stole another glance at the happy couple.

In the light of day, Daphne was even more ashamed of her feelings. She loved Ellie. She loved her parents and her grandmother. They were good, honest people who lived their lives with integrity. Sure, they expected a lot from her—more than they'd ever expected from Ellie. Wasn't that a good thing? She could rise to their expectations. She *had* risen to their expectations her whole life, barring a few notable recent exceptions.

So what if Daphne felt like a square peg in a family of round holes? She was still a Davis. She still belonged here in some capacity. Maybe she just had to figure out exactly how.

"Ladies," her father announced, sweeping into the living room. He spotted Hugh and added, "And gent. Breakfast is ready. The bread has cooled and is ready to slice." He presented them with a perfectly round boule of bread like he was a sommelier at a fancy restaurant displaying a thousand-dollar bottle of wine, complete with perfectly folded white towel over his forearm. "Would anyone like a taste?"

"You're such a dork, Dad," Ellie said, pulling away from Hugh's embrace.

"One slice for Ellie," he said, nodding. "Daphne? Hugh? Helen? And where's your mother, honey?"

"She'll be out in a minute," Helen said, planting a kiss on her husband's cheek before heading into the kitchen in front of him. "Who wants eggs?"

"I'll have some," Daphne said, joining the family at the oval dining table shoved into the cramped kitchen. She sat against the wall on one of the long sides while her mother put a cup of fresh coffee in front of her. "Thanks."

Her dad gave her the heel of the bread, generously buttered—the best part—with a wink and a smile. "For our favorite new arrival." He was looking a little worse for wear after the party, but Claude Davis was a man who smiled through his pain.

"Coffee," Grandma Mabel groaned from the hallway a moment before she appeared. She was made up and dressed, but she shuffled like her legs were made of lead. "I'm too old for parties like that."

"Didn't seem too old when you were tearing up the dance floor last night," Helen said, a smile tugging at her lips. "I did try to warn you, Mom."

"Quiet, you. Didn't I raise you not to talk back to me?"

Ellie snorted, and Grandma Mabel pinched her arm on the way by. She slid in next to Daphne at the table, resting her cheek against Daphne's shoulder for a moment. "You've always been the sensible one," Grandma Mabel lamented. "I should have followed your lead and gone to bed before things turned messy."

"Except Daphne's the one who got the police escort home," Ellie noted, eyes sparkling above her mug.

Shock shot down Daphne's spine like a jet of ice water. "How did you know that?"

Ellie laughed at Daphne's outraged expression. "You were spotted on the way home."

"By who?"

"I never reveal my sources."

"This island is a fishbowl."

"That it is," Grandma Mabel cut in. "What happened? Did you get a ticket?"

"Got away with a warning," Daphne replied. "Blown taillight. I bought one at the auto shop this morning. Was hoping Dad would help me fix it."

"Course I will," Claude said as he bustled to the table with toast, butter, and fresh fruit. "We can do it after we eat."

"And then you can drive me to the Winter Market," Grandma Mabel announced.

Daphne glanced at the gray drizzle outside. "In this weather?"

"What are you talking about? It's a gorgeous day out there. Everyone will be out."

And everyone was. Daphne parked on the street across from the elementary school, staring at the droves of raincoat-wearing people milling around the school's parking lot. The doors to the gymnasium were thrown open, and a few tents had been set up outside. The Fernley Island Winter Market ran from November through March and was well attended every week. Anyone could apply for a booth as long as they were selling handcrafted goods.

Mabel was out of the car in a shot, her umbrella spread open above her head as she beamed at Daphne. "There's a new coffee truck this year. Harry just texted me that their coffee is disgusting. I can't wait to try it."

Snorting, Daphne locked her car and followed, the hood of her jacket blocking the worst of the rain. It wasn't pelting down, but it was a steady kind of mist that soaked right through to the bone. They jaywalked across the street and entered the market's bustle.

Noise spilled from the open doors of the gymnasium, inside of which most of the booths were located. Outside were a few food stalls releasing steam into the rainy atmosphere, with people milling around holding warm drinks as they chatted, impervious to the bad weather. The coffee truck was near the entrance and the line wasn't too long, so Daphne and her grandmother joined it and shuffled forward.

"Why do you want to try the coffee if you know it's bad?"

"Harry could be wrong," Grandma Mabel pointed out.

"She could be right."

Grandma Mabel laughed. "Only one way to find out. Hello, dear," she called out to the teenage girl inside the truck. "One black coffee for me and—" She glanced at Daphne.

"Regular latte, please."

They paid and waited for their drinks, and Harry—full name Harriet—toddled up to them with a steaming paper cup in her hands. She was a few inches shorter than Grandma Mabel, with her gray hair wrapped in a plastic rain hood. She leaned on a butterfly-patterned cane and was accompanied by the third friend in Mabel's trio, Greta.

"Swill," Harry pronounced, lifting the drink. "They should get Vicky's back. She knew how to make coffee properly."

"You said Vicky's coffee tasted like dog's breath," Greta noted.

"It did, but it was still better than this."

Daphne heard her grandmother's name called out by the teenager in the truck and went and grabbed their drinks. She took a sip and coughed. "It's not the best," she conceded.

Harry grunted in the affirmative while Grandma Mabel took her own sip. Her face was blank for a moment, and then she said "Disgusting" before breaking into a broad smile. "The worst I've ever had."

The three ladies nodded and tasted their drinks again, grimacing to each other in the aftermath.

"Does the bakery still do those caramel sticky buns?" Daphne asked, glancing toward the gym doors. She could see two aisles of booths set up inside, with droves of people milling about.

"Usually sell out within an hour or two," Mabel answered, nodding. "Let's go see if we got here early enough."

The Winter Market was another one of those strange déjà vu experiences for Daphne. Everything was the same but slightly different. Every second vendor was a familiar face, except some of them had more gray hairs and kids running around their booths these days. The kindly old man who made the best rhubarb jam Daphne had ever tasted smiled as she stopped by for a sample. She pulled out her wallet to buy a jar. The hot sauce table was as popular as ever. The woman who wove her own wool rugs was busy chatting with the man who made unbelievable wood-turned vases, their wares displayed for all the passersby to admire.

People walked with their friends, children, and partners, stopping at booths, laughing, talking. The noise echoed all around, giving the whole market a pleasant hum. A busker strummed his guitar on a small stage in the front of the gym and tapped his microphone.

Daphne's shoulders relaxed. Fernley wasn't so bad. The sameness was comforting, and the changes she saw in people's faces and families made her realize that life had moved on here while she was gone, just as her own life had. Maybe she'd be able to find a place here, for however long she'd stay.

She slipped her jar of homemade rhubarb jam into her shoulder bag and hurried to catch up to her grandmother's group. They'd joined the line for the bakery booth, peering over people's shoulders to see what was left in the display cases. Daphne spied a fresh tray of sticky buns, so she was hopeful she'd get one by the time they got to the front.

"Long time no see!" the older woman behind the folding white table laden with baked goods exclaimed when she saw Daphne. "I heard you were back in town."

There was a short pause, and Daphne imagined the smiling baker was thinking about all the other things she'd heard about Daphne's less-than-triumphant return. Broken engagement, lost job, lost home, escort home from a certain scowling sheriff . . .

"Hi, Adelaide," Daphne replied, painting a smile on her face. "Business is booming as usual, I see."

"We've been so fortunate," she demurred. "What can I get for you?"

"Caramel sticky bun," she said, then perused the selection of bread. "Don't tell my dad, but I'll get one of your multigrain loaves as well."

"Claude still making bread, is he?"

"Nearly every day."

"Maybe one day I'll coax him to come work for me."

Daphne grinned, sincerely this time. "I don't think he'd want to give up his independence, even for the promise of unlimited baked goods."

"Your grandmother, then. Have you gone near an oven lately, Mabel?"

"You know I haven't," Mabel answered with a grimace. "Not since ninety-two."

"Shame," Adelaide replied, wrapping up Daphne's goods. "You had talent."

Daphne tapped her card on the reader and glanced at her grand-mother. "You used to bake? How did I not know this?"

"Sore subject," Harry grumbled. "I'd let it be if I were you, girl."

"She was my prime competition," Adelaide said, handing two brown paper bags over. "Her losing that pot was one of the only reasons I was able to get this little business started."

"It wasn't lost," Grandma Mabel said, getting heated. Her cheeks flushed red. "It was *stolen*."

Adelaide was already greeting the next customer, so Daphne shuffled out of the way. She glanced at her grandmother, searching the older woman's shuttered expression. "A stolen pot?"

Harry and Greta exchanged a long look. Greta was the one who patted Daphne's arm. "A cast-iron Dutch oven. Perfectly seasoned. You threw a handful of flour in there with a bit of water, bit of yeast, and poof! Perfect bread."

"There was a bit more to it than that," Mabel mumbled. "It was my mother's pot. She used it exclusively for bread. It was stolen at a potluck by a two-bit hussy who denied any wrongdoing, like the lying cheat she was."

"You know who took it?" Daphne asked, eyes wide.

"We all know who took it! Stole it right out of the cupboard while everyone was outside," Harry said, stamping her cane on the wooden floor. "But she denied it, and that was that. The police didn't bother with an old cooking pot."

Daphne glanced at Grandma Mabel. "Who stole it?"

The old woman's teeth gritted as she met Daphne's gaze. "Brenda Sallow." She snarled and stomped away from the baker's tent, the rest of the group following.

They wandered down the aisle as Daphne tore off a piece of cinnamon-swirled, caramel-drenched heaven. She chewed and frowned. "Brenda Sallow," she repeated. "Who's that?"

"An arrogant, self-serving hag who always thought she was better'n she was," Grandma Mabel shot back, venom lacing her words.

"May she rest in peace," Harry added solemnly.

"Apple didn't fall far from the tree," Greta said as the four of them stopped to admire some handmade jewelry. "Eileen wasn't much better than her mother. And look what she made of herself."

"Certainly moved up in the world," Grandma Mabel agreed.

"Eileen Sallow," Daphne repeated. "That rings a bell."

"She goes by Eileen Yarrow now," Mabel said, turning away from a tray of rings to keep marching down the farmers' market aisle. She glanced at Daphne, brows raised. "But you would've known her as Eileen Flint."

"Mrs. Flint," Daphne said through clenched teeth. "Calvin Flint's mother."

"The one and only," Mabel said, nodding to the man in question as he appeared silhouetted in the gymnasium doors. "Now, not only has little Eileen married up, but her son has landed on his feet too. And I still haven't gotten my mother's prized Dutch oven back."

Daphne's gaze flicked from the sheriff to her grandmother, then back to the sheriff. He walked inside, and most people swerved around him like a school of fish avoiding a shark.

Calvin Flint wore jeans and a black raincoat. He was off duty, Daphne deduced, but he still looked like a cop. He scanned the market with the look of someone who wouldn't tolerate trouble, his gaze snagging on Daphne.

One dark brow arched. Daphne tore off a piece of sticky bun and stuffed it in her mouth. She turned around and led the older ladies down the next aisle.

She didn't start her new job until tomorrow morning, which meant she didn't need to entertain annoying, self-important sheriffs who were petty enough to pull out old high school nicknames just to needle her.

"Who's Eileen married to now?" Daphne asked as she stopped to admire a stall full of hand-knitted baby clothes. Not that she wanted a kid anytime soon, but the tiny clothing was adorable.

"Archie Yarrow," Greta supplied. "The former mayor."

"The one whose house Mom burned down?" Daphne asked, glancing at her grandmother.

Grandma Mabel's lips tugged at the corners. "Allegedly burned down. That was Archie Sr.'s father, Edward; Eileen married Archie Sr., who was mayor after his father, and the current mayor is his eldest, Archie Jr."

"Not much creativity in the Yarrow family, in names or professions," Greta noted.

"Never been prouder of that girl of yours than when she set fire to that man's front porch," Harry said, nodding at Grandma Mabel, who beamed.

Daphne's mother had been as much of a wild child as Ellie, and judging by the stories that had filtered down from Grandma Mabel, the older woman hadn't been much tamer. It was Daphne that was the odd duck in the family.

"Huh," Daphne said, tearing into her bun once more. Her fingers were sticky with caramel, but it was too delicious to stop. "When I was in high school, people used to tease Flint about the fact that he was poor."

"After her first husband died, Eileen wasted no time," Grandma Mabel said, picking up tiny pink booties from the baby clothes stall. "Now she's married into Fernley political royalty, and her son is sheriff."

"Acting sheriff," Daphne corrected. "He hasn't won the election yet."

Grandma Mabel grinned, her earlier moodiness dissipated. "Right you are, honey. Looking forward to working with him?"

"About as much as you are to reuniting with Brenda Sallow on the other side."

The white-haired woman chortled and put the baby booties down, and they kept walking. Their shoes squeaked on the gym floors, and Daphne unzipped her jacket as she warmed up. She resisted the urge to glance over her shoulder to check where Flint had gone.

He probably wanted some jam. Or a sticky bun. Or maybe he was looking to arrest one of the peaceful Winter Market attendees, because he was a big bully who came from a family of lying troublemakers.

His maternal grandmother had allegedly stolen Mabel's precious Dutch oven back in the nineties. And his mother had married the former mayor. And now he was acting sheriff.

He'd terrorized Daphne in her senior year, almost causing her to lose out on her college scholarships. Grinding her teeth, she tried not to get fired up about it. She had to work with the man, after all, and it had happened nearly two decades ago.

But why was it that the people who seemed to deserve it least always came out on top? Why couldn't someone hardworking—Daphne, for example—see the fruits of their labors, for once?

Daphne sent out a quiet prayer that Adelaide had sold out of her buns before Flint could get any, because apparently she hadn't matured since her late-teen years.

A shout distracted her from her less-than-honorable thoughts. At the other end of the aisle, a commotion brewed. A man—midtwenties, maybe, average build, above-average height—was sprinting down the crowded aisle, a metal cashbox tucked under his arm.

"Stop! Thief!" The jam salesman came hobbling into view, red faced and panicked. Wiry gray hair stuck out from under his cap, his arm flung out toward the man with the cashbox.

The thief vaulted over a small child and didn't spare a glance backward. He dodged around a stroller and came pounding down the lane toward Daphne.

Normal, everyday, sensible Daphne would step out of the way and let someone else deal with the cashbox thief. There were dozens of people between him and the exit. Someone else could handle it. Hell, the sheriff could handle it. That was his job. She'd shake her head and watch, of course, but she'd stay far away from anything that might be trouble. Daphne didn't get in the way of trouble. She avoided it at all costs.

But normal, everyday, sensible Daphne seemed to have forgotten to get on the ferry a few days ago, leaving a bitter, angry, vengeful Daphne in her place.

And *that* Daphne was unpredictable.

Things happened quickly.

The thief's shoes slapped the gym floor as he sprinted toward the exit. His eyes were wild, his hair greasy and windblown, the gray cashbox tucked under his arm like a football.

Daphne had seconds to act, and no time at all to think. She dropped her baked goods on the ground and let her shoulder bag slide to her hand. The thief came sprinting closer. Five yards. Three. Daphne wound her arm back and swung.

The mason jar full of delicious rhubarb jam gave the shoulder bag decent heft. When it connected with the thief's face, he gave a startled yelp, his feet running on while his head snapped back.

But Daphne had underestimated him. He got his feet under him and dodged her second swing. She let out a garbled yell, winding back once more.

Then his fist came for her face.

CHAPTER 3

Calvin had just wanted to see if Adelaide Gable's caramel sticky buns were as good as he remembered. Besides, he figured being seen at the market would be good for his image. He could make small talk, have the residents see him in his civvies, and start ingratiating himself with the community. That way, they'd forget his past transgressions and see him as the upstanding public servant he'd become—against all odds.

The job was easier when people weren't afraid of him. He preferred forging bonds with the people he was meant to serve and protect. He'd grown up in the years since he'd left Fernley; he wanted to know if people could look beyond his past and see him for who he was now.

And if they didn't, well, he wasn't obligated to run in the election in the fall. He could go back to his old job and leave these shores for good.

So the Fernley Winter Market was meant to be an easy Sunday-morning stroll filled with polite small talk and maybe a delicious treat.

He hadn't expected to have to stop a thief.

And he certainly hadn't expected to watch Daphne Davis get slugged in the face either.

His heart gave a lurch as Daphne's head snapped back, blood spraying from her nose in a grisly crimson arc. The thief stumbled forward, his shoulder banging into hers, and he made to push her out of the way.

But the crook underestimated Davis. She let out a battle cry worthy of a Valkyrie and clung to him, tripping him over her outstretched foot as she went down. He landed on top of her, and Calvin lost sight of them in the crowd.

Feet pounding on the squeaky wooden floors, Calvin shouted for people to move out of the way as he sprinted toward the action.

"Get him!" an elderly lady screamed. "Kick him in the balls, Daphne!"

"Police!" Calvin shouted, which had precisely zero effect on the fight beyond.

The crowd parted as he approached, and he saw the thief clamber to his feet, but Daphne reached for him and grabbed his belt. The thief yelled as his jeans were dragged down, and he was forced to drop the cashbox to cling to the front of his pants, lest he flash the farmers' market crowd with a full-frontal assault.

Blood gushed from Daphne's face. Her eyes flashed as she hung on to the belt, and she was dragged three feet while the thief tried to stumble away. The front of her jacket was covered in slick red blood. It coated her lips and teeth.

She looked feral. Calvin had never seen that expression on her face before. Not studious, good-girl Daphne, who bristled and looked down her nose at him whenever he'd poked her. Not the girl whose eyes had narrowed when he'd dared speak to her directly. Not the girl who stuck her nose in her books and ignored the world around her like it had done her wrong, when in reality she should've been thankful for everything she had.

That Daphne was gone, and in her place was a snarling, screaming beast clinging on to the thief's belt like she'd die before letting go.

He hadn't known she'd had it in her. He would've expected her to shy away from a fight that had nothing to do with her. The Daphne Davis he knew was selfish. She only cared about herself and her future.

The thief turned and tried to break Daphne's hold. His foot wound back, and Calvin could tell he wanted to kick the woman currently preventing his escape.

Strength rushed through Calvin. In two strides he was on them, wrapping his arms around the thief's torso as he wrenched him away from Daphne. He took the thief down to the ground and held him there, then glanced at Daphne.

Panting, he took in her bloodied snarl. "You good?"

She flopped onto her back on the gym floor, tongue darting out to lick her lip. She grimaced. "What do you think, Einstein?"

"Not the time, Cupcake," he shot back through clenched teeth. "Are you injured?"

"My face hurts," she said.

"Not surprised," he answered. This couldn't happen when he was on duty and had all his gear, could it? No. That would be too easy. He had some plastic cuffs in his truck, but he wasn't walking away until he knew Daphne was all right.

It took a few minutes to get everything settled and the perp fully subdued, by which time Daphne was surrounded by old ladies trying to blot the blood from her face and clothes. As he dragged the thief to his feet, he glanced over at the woman who'd helped him take the man down.

Her face was still smeared with blood, but most of it had been wiped away. Her shirt was a disaster. What in the world had possessed her to get in the middle of this? Calvin had been *right there*. She could have been seriously injured because of her stupidity, which was something he never thought he'd ever think about a brainiac like her.

Anger burned away the last of his worry for her. "You're coming to the station," he told her.

Daphne lifted her gaze to his, her nose pinched between her fingers. "Is that an order?"

She had to be the most irritating woman on the planet. *You're goddamn right it's an order,* he wanted to bark. Instead, he took a breath and did his best to cool his temper. "I need you to make a statement, and we can get your nose looked at while you're there."

Her eyes were already swelling, and she'd have nasty bruises come morning. Calvin wished he'd run a bit faster to stop her from getting hit in the first place.

No.

On second thought, he wished Daphne had used that big brain of hers to rustle up some common sense and dodge the punch when she had the chance.

"Go ahead," one of the old ladies said, helping Daphne to her feet. "You did good, honey."

"Thanks, Grandma."

"I still think you should've kicked him in the balls."

"I'll try that next time."

"There won't be a next time," Calvin cut in, voice harsh. "I'll drive."

"Yes, sir."

His scowl didn't seem to cow her, but she followed as he walked the thief to his truck, tightened the plastic cuffs on his wrists, and loaded him into the back seat of the cab. Daphne got in the front, and he circled around to get behind the wheel. She held a tissue to her nose and struggled with the seat belt until he huffed and clipped it in for her.

"Thanks," she said, and sighed as her head hit the headrest.

Calvin ground his teeth and glanced at the man in the back seat. He was curled up against one of the doors, looking crumpled and unlikely to try anything stupid. At least one of them was reasonable. Calvin drove to the station.

When they got there, he let one of the deputies on duty handle the paperwork and walked Daphne to his office. She slumped into a chair and winced as her hand jarred against her nose.

"I've never gotten punched in the face before," she said, pulling the tissue away from her face to look at the blood soaking into it. Her blue eyes looked a bit wider than usual when she met Calvin's gaze. "How bad do I look?"

She looked awful. "I've seen worse."

She prodded at her face. "Everything hurts."

He batted her hands away and used his fingers to tilt up her chin. She blinked up at him with those clear blue eyes, but he kept his gaze on her injuries. He ran his fingers over the sides of her nose as gently as he could, his stomach clenching as she hissed. "Doesn't look broken, but you should get some ice on it for the swelling. You'll have nasty black eyes for a while."

Daphne grunted in response. For reasons Calvin couldn't quite explain, he kept his fingers on the edge of her jaw as he tilted Daphne's face to inspect her wounds. Her skin was softer than he'd expected, like silk. Her jawbone felt almost delicate as his finger pressed into it to get her to turn her head. There was a drop of dried blood below her earlobe.

He should have run faster, and she should have stayed out of the damn way.

"You should get checked out at the medical center," he told her. "You could have a concussion."

"I'm fine."

"Don't be stupid, Davis."

"I'm *fine*."

"Still stubborn as ever, huh."

She glared at him, and Calvin felt his lips twitch at the corners. She'd always been easy to rile up, even though she tried to hide it. Tried to pretend she was levelheaded and bookish. Now that his blood had stopped thrumming so hard and he could think a little more clearly, he figured it made sense that Daphne had gotten her face in the way of the cashbox thief's fist. Her temper was brittle and likely to snap, and those book smarts of hers didn't seem to extend to the real world.

He let go of her face and leaned against the edge of his desk as he folded his arms. "What possessed you to get involved?"

"I don't know," she said. "He was robbing the jam man. I like the jam man. The thief was coming right at me, so I hit him with my purse. I wasn't thinking."

"Clearly."

That earned him a glare. "I stopped him, didn't I?"

"Next time, you let me handle it."

"You weren't there, genius."

"I was on the way."

"What if he got away? I slowed him down long enough for you to catch up."

"Davis, I'm serious," Calvin said through gritted teeth. "You can't put yourself in the line of fire like that."

"That's a funny way of saying thank you."

Calvin grunted and stalked out the door. She drove him crazy. There was no way he'd be able to do his job with her working in the building. Just the sight of her would send his blood pressure skyrocketing, never mind if she opened her mouth. And she would. The good-girl act was total bullshit, as far as Calvin was concerned. How she'd convinced everyone that she was the responsible sister was a mystery. At least Ellie was predictable in her unpredictability.

But the department couldn't afford any wasted time finding someone else. Money was tight, and he needed to figure out if there were any snakes in the grass the feds had failed to sniff out. Daphne, for all her faults, *was* an intelligent woman and an accomplished accountant, of which there weren't many on the island. He needed her to stay here and tell him where all the sheriff's department's money had gone so he could do his job. It was seven months until the election, and Calvin had to know what was going on under the surface. He'd be damned if he left this place worse than he'd found it, even if he didn't end up as the island's permanent sheriff.

There was no way people would look at him, shake their heads, and say that they'd made a bad call in asking him to be acting sheriff. He wouldn't give them the satisfaction. He'd *changed*, damn it.

He needed Daphne, so he'd need to deal with her presence, as irritating as it would be.

By the time he got an ice pack and the first aid kit, his anger had dialed down a few notches. He cracked the ice pack to get it working and handed it over. "Put that on your face. You're already swelling."

"It's a good thing you didn't become a doctor, Flint, because your bedside manner sucks."

"When you hear my bedside manner, you'll know, Davis."

She snorted and put the ice on her face.

"Now. Start at the beginning and tell me what happened."

By the time Daphne was done, Calvin had paced the length of his office two dozen times. It was his day off. He shouldn't have had to deal with this on his day off.

And every time he looked at Daphne with all the blood and swelling, he got a funny pinch in his chest. He should've been faster, or at least followed her down the aisle of the farmers' market, like he'd wanted to in the first place.

"And the worst part is, I dropped my caramel sticky bun on the ground," Daphne finished, "*and* my multigrain loaf." She reached into her purse and pulled out a mason jar filled with pink jam. "But at least this survived."

"I'll have to confiscate that as evidence."

She clutched the jar to her chest. "Don't you dare."

A smile tried its best to curl at the corner of his lips, but he turned away so she wouldn't see it. "Keep the ice on your face as long as you can manage. You'll look like hell tomorrow."

"You sure know how to make a woman feel good about herself."

"Just telling you the truth so you're emotionally prepared for it."

She dragged herself to her feet with a snort. "Right."

"You need a ride home?"

"I'll manage. One police escort was enough for my first week back on the island."

"See you tomorrow, Davis."

"Unfortunately," she mumbled, and walked out of his office. He glanced out the window to see her shuffle outside, that jar of pink jam still clutched in her hand, the other busy holding the ice pack to her face.

Shaking his head, Calvin tore his gaze away and resigned himself to a few hours of work on his only day off.

CHAPTER 4

Daphne was not emotionally prepared for the state of her face in the morning, no matter what Flint had said to warn her. Her nose was still swollen, and she had two puffy black eyes that morphed to purple and green around the edges. Makeup wasn't even an option. Her face was too tender and swollen, and she doubted she had any products that could actually cover this level of damage.

Being a vigilante wasn't all it was cracked up to be. She'd be happy to be locked in a room with old financial records for the foreseeable future.

Her grandmother had updated the family about the goings-on at the farmers' market, so Daphne had had a visit from the whole gang for dinner. Her mother had fussed, her father had congratulated her, and Ellie had given her a high five. Grandma Mabel had gone to get her a new loaf of bread from Adelaide Gable, who had thrown in a half dozen cookies as well. Daphne was a hero, apparently.

Now, Daphne shuffled to the kitchen in her tiny one-bedroom apartment and made herself a slice of multigrain toast with a thick layer of rhubarb jam. She sipped her coffee and tried not to wince every time she moved her face. Getting punched in the nose was not in her top ten most favorite activities. Neither was getting chastised by an acting sheriff with an overinflated sense of importance.

Seriously—not a single thank-you. Not one! The man was unbelievable.

However, when she walked into the sheriff's department, she was greeted with a round of applause and a few hoots. Shirley Newbury hustled toward her and wrapped her in a big hug.

"Well done, you," Shirley said, squeezing Daphne's shoulders. "Way to make an entrance."

"Now we know not to mess with the accountant," one of the deputies called out, and laughter echoed around the room.

"And here I thought you were the quiet sister," an older deputy said, grinning at her. His name was Hank Packer, and he'd been with the Fernley force for three and a half decades. He'd survived the corruption storm with his staunch I'm-just-here-to-do-my-job attitude, which had served him well ever since he'd started working at the sheriff's department.

"I am the quiet sister," Daphne protested. "I just don't like to see good people get robbed."

"Hear, hear!" Shirley said, and hooked her arm through Daphne's elbow. "Now, let me show you around. We've set you up in one of the interview rooms. I wasn't sure what you'd need—" The phone rang, and Shirley glared at it. "Hold on." She walked over to it and answered. "Sheriff's department. Uh-huh. Okay. No problem. We'll send deputies out." She hung up and glanced at Hank. "Chuck Rutgers's alpacas have jumped the neighbor's fence again. Apparently, Iris is threatening to shoot them all if Chuck doesn't get them under control. She's got her shotgun out and is waving it around."

Hank grabbed his jacket with a sigh. "I'll handle it."

"Now," Shirley said, smiling at Daphne. "The interview room. We weren't sure what you'd need, but you just have to let us know, and—Sheriff Flint! Good morning."

Daphne turned to see the sheriff standing by the front door. Sunlight carved the shape of him against the glass door, limning those broad shoulders in gold.

"Shirley," Flint said with a nod; then his gaze slid to Daphne. "Davis," he greeted, gaze lingering on her bruises. His jaw seemed to tighten slightly before he looked at Shirley again. "What's this I hear about a shotgun?"

"Just Iris Whittaker getting carried away about Chuck Rutgers's alpacas again. Chances of any shots being fired are low, but Chuck and Iris do tend to get worked up when they butt heads. Hank's on it."

The sheriff met Hank's gaze as he ambled toward the door where he stood. "Mind if I ride along?"

"Suit yourself," Hank replied with a genial nod. "You might as well meet Iris and Chuck sooner rather than later."

"Regular callers," Shirley mumbled to Daphne in explanation, then ushered her toward one of the interview rooms at the back of the main room. "Here we are! It's not much, but we're a bit strapped for space. The extension the department was supposed to build is, well . . ." She glanced down the hall at a plastic-covered doorway. "Let's just say it hasn't been finished, and now with all the money being frittered away . . ."

Daphne nodded. "That's why I'm here."

"And aren't we lucky to have you! Kitchen's just down that hall. Wash your own dishes. If you finish the coffee, you put on a fresh pot. Fridge gets cleared out every Friday afternoon, so unless your things are labeled and dated, they're gettin' tossed. Other than that, holler if you need anything!"

"Will do. Thanks, Shirley." When she was alone in the tiny box of a room, fluorescent light flickering overhead, Daphne set her shoulder bag down on the table and planted her hands on her hips.

The job shouldn't be too difficult. She'd been hired to figure out what had happened to the department's money while Bill Jackson had been in charge. After the upheaval that had happened, no one had any idea what leaks needed to be plugged, and whether there were any other less-than-savory people who needed to be rooted out and exposed.

Daphne knew that it was probably plain old incompetence and mismanagement that had caused the department's coffers to run low. The former sheriff and his cronies had been taking bribes from people left and right, but the federal investigators hadn't found any evidence of embezzlement of public funds. They'd been focused on the drugs and the money laundering, though, so it was possible they'd missed something.

She'd have to untangle years of finances and figure out a path forward. Just her, her computer, and honest, logical numbers. No people who might punch her in the face for doing a good deed. No scowling ghosts from her high school days come back to haunt her. Just old financial records that needed to be made right.

Easy.

Or so she hoped.

She stripped her jacket off and set her computer up, then wandered to the far side of the room, where boxes had been stacked. She opened them one after another to find faded invoices and crumpled receipts. At least she had somewhere to start.

Needing coffee, Daphne wandered out and across the room to the area where Shirley had pointed. A small kitchen was tucked around the corner. She poured herself a mug of coffee and ambled back toward her office, letting her feet take her toward the unfinished extension at the back of the building. She took a sip of her coffee, pleasantly surprised as the taste hit her tongue. It was better than the coffee truck brew, that was for sure.

Before she pushed through the plastic-covered door, she saw another small hallway running the length of the rear of the building. She could see a few holding cells lined up along the back wall. Curiosity got the best of her, and she walked down to see if anyone was inside.

In the farthest cell was the farmers' market thief. He sat on a metal bench bolted to the wall, eating a sandwich. He looked up when Daphne appeared, and his eyes narrowed.

"Hi," she said.

He bit into the sandwich and chewed. Once he'd swallowed, he said, "Hi."

They stared at each other. Daphne took a sip of coffee. She wasn't sure why she was here. "You been here all night?"

The would-be thief nodded. "Sorry about your face."

She huffed out a laugh. "Thanks. Never been punched before. Wasn't expecting the black eyes."

"Your purse got me good," he replied, pointing to his own bruised temple. "You carry rocks around for fun, or something?"

"Jam jars," she explained.

He snorted and took another bite. Daphne sipped her coffee. She'd never spoken to someone through bars before. She was experiencing all kinds of firsts.

"What's your name?"

His eyes narrowed. "Ryan Lane. You?"

"Daphne Davis. Why'd you do it?"

"Do what?"

Daphne rolled her eyes. "You know what. Why'd you steal the cashbox?"

"Felt like it."

She tilted her head and studied the man in the holding cell. He was hunched over his sandwich eyeing her suspiciously, the bruise on his temple already turning green. He looked younger than she'd initially thought. Maybe still in his teens. A pang of sympathy went through her. "Why'd you feel like it?"

"Maybe I needed the money. Bills overdue. Mom's rent's behind, and she sure as hell isn't going to get any extra money by the end of the week."

Daphne held her warm mug and nodded. "You got a job?"

"I did, until I was fired last Monday."

"What for?"

He scowled and took another bite of his sandwich, tearing at the bread with his teeth. He chewed angrily and met her gaze. "Missed one too many shifts. But I can't help it that there's no gas in the car and no one to bring me to town." He seemed resentful that he'd opened up that much, and he spun around on the bench so his side was to Daphne.

The conversation was clearly over. Daphne turned and then started when she saw Calvin Flint leaning against the wall just out of sight of the holding cells. He watched her steadily, then tilted his head to indicate that she should follow. When they'd left the holding cell area and turned the corner, Daphne glanced up at him.

"How were the alpacas?"

"They survived, as did Chuck and Iris. Iris put the gun away and got a warning. Chuck was told to fix his fence. Hank told me to expect another call within three days."

Daphne bit back a smile. "Is being sheriff all you thought it would be and more?"

"I feel very qualified to be a kindergarten teacher."

Daphne laughed, then winced as pain shot through her face.

"Still sore?"

She grunted. "Likely will be for a while."

"What do you think of Lane?" He led her toward the kitchen, and Daphne realized the hallways connected to the main room in a big U shape, with interview rooms in the center and her new office on the opposite side to the kitchen. They stopped in front of the coffee machine, where the sheriff filled up her mug before pouring one for himself, draining the last of the carafe into his cup. Daphne was slightly surprised to see him follow Shirley's rules by immediately setting another pot to brew. Apparently the sheriff wasn't too self-important to keep the communal kitchen operating smoothly.

Maybe he'd grown up in the years they'd been apart.

She leaned against the counter and pursed her lips. "I think he probably felt desperate and acted impulsively yesterday. He's younger than I thought."

"Turns eighteen in three weeks," Flint said.

"Old enough to know better."

Flint grunted. "Worked at the tech repair shop on Seventh Ave up until he got fired for too many no-shows. His bike got stolen three months ago, and the family only has one car. Owner said he's a bit of a tech whiz kid, but he couldn't keep him on if he wasn't reliable."

"He said he wanted to help his mom pay rent with the money."

"The Lanes don't have much," Flint agreed. Daphne glanced over and noted the tightness around his eyes, the way his hand clutched the edge of the counter so hard his knuckles were striped white and red. She wondered if he was thinking of his own upbringing. The Flints hadn't had much either.

"What are you going to do about him?" she asked.

He turned to face her, hazel eyes steady as they met her gaze. He had thick lashes, she noticed. She'd always thought his eyes were too pretty for the rest of his face, but now that the rest of him had grown up, they seemed to fit. He had a few fine lines around his eyes, a bit of roughness from wind and weather on his skin. He arched a dark brow. "Depends how you feel."

Daphne frowned. "Me?"

"You're the one who got hit." Flint's arm moved, then stopped, like he'd caught himself reaching up to touch her bruises. He flexed his hand and turned to look at the progress of the coffee maker.

Daphne hummed. "I saw his temple. I think we can call it even."

Flint glanced over and watched her for a beat, then dipped his chin. "I'll let him sit in that holding cell for a while, then slap him with a warning and let him go. I spoke to Mr. Stringer, the jam man, and he doesn't want to press charges. He's just glad he got his cashbox back. Was only about two hundred bucks in there, anyway. Mostly, people are talking about what a hero you were."

Was that a smile twitching at the corners of his lips?

Daphne straightened her spine and gave him an arch look. "And you disagree?"

"I know you better than they do, Cupcake," he said.

"What the hell is that supposed to mean? And stop calling me that."

"You can pretend to be a nice, responsible, boring woman as much as you like, Davis, but I know the truth."

Daphne opened her mouth to retort but was interrupted by the ringing of his phone. Flint pulled it out of his pocket, his brows tugging together when he glanced at the screen. "Gotta take this. Don't let all the accolades get to your head."

"You're a prick, Flint."

He flashed her a smile on his way out, and all Daphne could do was seethe as he walked away. His butt looked good in the dark-blue uniform pants, which—wait, no. No, his butt didn't look good. Well, fine, one couldn't deny that it *did*, but the sheriff's ass was none of her business. Especially when it was attached to such an insufferable man. She was here to study the numbers. Nothing more. Nothing less.

Best get back to it.

CHAPTER 5

Calvin closed the door to his office behind him as he swiped to answer the call. "Mom," he clipped. "What's up?"

"Darling!" she exclaimed, which made Calvin frown harder. *Darling?* They didn't have that kind of relationship, though Eileen had been trying hard to pretend they did.

"I'm at work."

"Too busy to talk to your poor old mother, huh," she said, the pout evident in her voice.

Calvin ground his teeth. He kicked his chair back from the desk and dropped into it, then pinched the bridge of his nose. She was going in hard on the guilt trips within a few seconds. Pretty standard fare for Eileen Flint. Or no—it was Eileen Yarrow now. Had been for damn near a decade. That was a new record for Husband Number Four. Calvin forced himself to calm his tone as he asked, "What can I do for you?"

"I wanted you to hear it from me," she announced.

"Oh?"

"Archie and I have decided to renew our vows!"

"Congrats," Calvin said, keeping the sigh he wanted to release firmly behind his lips. "When's the big day?"

"On our ten-year anniversary! March thirteenth. About a month from today. We're sending out invitations this afternoon." She hesitated for a brief moment. "One of them is addressed to you."

He closed his eyes. He'd only just arrived on the island a week ago and had successfully avoided committing to anything involving his mother. He wasn't sure he wanted anything to do with her at all. He'd changed and grown up, sure, but that didn't mean he'd forgiven her. Playing the dutiful son at her vow renewal wasn't something he wanted to add to his to-do list.

"I'll check the schedule, but I'm not sure I can make time—"

"Of course you can make time. Look, I know you might not want to be there for me. I get that, okay? But you know that Archie was mayor for years, don't you? And now his son has taken up the mantle. This will be the perfect opportunity for you to meet all the movers and shakers on Fernley ahead of the election in the fall. Don't you think?" Her voice was hopeful, if a bit forced. She really wanted him to come.

Calvin leaned back and stared at the stained ceiling tiles above, grimacing. He didn't even know if he wanted to run in the election for Fernley sheriff, let alone schmooze his way to a victory using his mother's connections. The fact that his mother had any connections at all was almost unbelievable.

But—ten years. That was how long she'd stayed married to Husband Number Four. A new record. Maybe it was the real deal. Maybe she'd changed just as much as he had. Sometimes, it almost seemed like she was genuinely happy that he was back on the island.

Calvin had grown up and changed in the years since he'd scraped by with his high school diploma and gotten off this rock of an island. Was it so hard to believe his mother might have grown up too? Didn't he owe her a chance, at least?

"It broke my heart when you couldn't make it to our wedding, you know," Eileen added quietly. "I mean, I understand, but I wish . . ."

Calvin almost snorted. Broke her heart, did it? Did it break her heart when she left Calvin to fend for himself for the entirety of his childhood? Did it break her heart when there was no food in the fridge? When he had no one to rely on, no one to help him out of that hole because she was too busy trying to find the next man to sink her claws into?

But he was the acting sheriff, and he'd be expected to show his face. If he blew the event off, it would make his job that much harder for however long he stayed in it. And as much as Calvin hated to admit it, his mother was right. He needed to meet more of the island's residents, if only to get a sense of how things had changed in the years he'd been away—and how they hadn't.

Plus, there was someone else to think about, and his mother knew it. As if she could read the direction of his thoughts, Eileen said, "Ceecee will be crushed if you don't come, Calvin. She's already got her dress picked out, and she wants you to wear a matching tie. Hope you like hot pink."

Calvin's protests disintegrated as easily as wet cardboard. His half sister was one of the main reasons he'd taken the job on Fernley. She was a bright, adventurous kid who didn't deserve to grow up the way he had. It had been a shock when he heard his mom had fallen pregnant in her midforties, but Calvin hadn't been able to turn his back on his little sister the way he wanted to do with his mother. He remembered being nine, remembered the anger and devastation of realizing no one cared. He wasn't going to let that happen to someone else.

"All right. I'll put it in my calendar."

"Great!" Eileen exclaimed. "We're giving you a plus-one."

"Okay." Not that he'd need one.

"I've already told the Deacons that you'd be happy to take their daughter along—"

"What?"

Calvin sat up. Rubbing elbows with the who's who of Fernley political circles was one thing. Being set up on an excruciating date by his neglectful, self-absorbed mother was quite another. That's where he drew the line.

"I just thought with you being new here, you might want to meet someone your age," Eileen said, helpful as ever. When was she going to drop the act of the caring mother? They had too much history for him to believe a second of it.

He knew that tone. Eileen Yarrow was a woman who pretended to be flighty to hide the bulldog within. Once she latched on to an idea, it was near impossible to get her to let go. Ask any of her husbands. She'd latched on to them until she'd decided to toss them aside.

Calvin's thoughts sped up. He couldn't simply refuse the date, because it would be thrust upon him. He couldn't avoid the event. There was only one option left.

"I already have someone to bring," he blurted out.

There was a short pointed silence. "You do?"

"Yeah," he lied. "I'll bring a date. Tell the Deacons I'm sorry, but I won't be able to accompany their daughter."

"Are you sure? Jenna is very pretty, and their family owns a big—"

"I have a date, Mom," he repeated, heart thundering.

"Are you seeing someone?"

It was Calvin's turn to be quiet for a beat. "Sort of," he lied.

"'Sort of'? What does that mean?"

"It means we aren't exactly shouting it from the rooftops yet."

"Am I allowed to know her name?"

"You'll meet her at the event."

"'Meet her'? So I haven't met her yet? Is she from Fernley?"

"Oh, someone just knocked on my office door, *gottagobye.*" He hung up the call and tossed the phone aside like it would turn into a venomous snake and bite him. Then he combed both hands through his hair and groaned.

There he stayed, mind whirling, wondering how he'd get out of this one. He could make up an excuse and go on his own, then endure his mother's comments. That was probably the best option, because otherwise he'd have to actually find a date to bring to his mother's vow renewal.

He couldn't in good conscience submit someone to that kind of torture. And anyone who *wanted* to go wouldn't be someone he'd willingly spend time with in the first place. It would be an evening of gritting his teeth and pretending to be happy for a woman who had failed in her duty to him.

But coming to Fernley was supposed to be the turning over of a new leaf. Calvin had grown up. He'd made something of himself. Sure, he still nursed old wounds and he'd become strict with himself out of necessity, but he wasn't the angry, hurt kid he'd once been.

He could be happy for his mother. Or at the very least, he could acknowledge her happiness and wish her the best. And he'd be there for Ceecee, which was what mattered most.

A knock on the door made him glance up. Daphne poked her head through the opening. "Shirley's taking lunch orders. Any requests?"

He met her blue eyes, wishing those bruises would heal already. He hated looking at the evidence that he'd been too slow. In a month, they'd be all gone. Maybe . . .

No. Was he delusional? Did it take one simple conversation with his mother to make him lose all his common sense?

Daphne would sooner bite his head off than attend a family event with him. Besides, why would he want to spend any more time than necessary with her? Sure, it was fun to needle her into snapping back, but that was different. To bring her along on what could potentially be called a date . . .

Hell no.

Even if he decided he wanted to torture himself for an evening, and even if Davis agreed, his mother would kill him for bringing Daphne to the vow renewal. The Davis women had a reputation for trouble on the island, even though Daphne was supposedly the exception. But judging by what had happened at the Winter Market, who knew what kind of chaos Daphne could cause?

Which made him think: Maybe he should bring Daphne along, just for the entertainment value. He could pay her. Would she want money? There had to be a reason she'd accepted this job in the first place, a reason she'd come back to Fernley. Maybe she was like him—here to exorcise old demons. They could find common ground.

"Flint? Sandwich?"

He blinked. "Nah," he said. "I've got to go out. I'll grab something while I'm on the road."

"Suit yourself," she said, and let the door close again.

He waited a full five minutes before gathering his things and heading out to his truck. He had paperwork to do at the office, and no real reason to go for a drive, but judging by the direction his thoughts had taken, he needed to get away.

The day he told himself it was a good idea to take Daphne Davis out on a date was the day he'd know something had gone seriously wrong.

CHAPTER 6

The financial records were a complete disaster. It took Daphne two full days to sort the boxes of receipts chronologically; then came time to start reconciling the expenses with the digital records. To anyone else, it would be tedious, mind-numbing work. To Daphne, it was meditative. She could forget about her bruised face, the sheriff in the office across the building, and all the failures that had led her to be sitting in an interview room at the Fernley County Sheriff's Department.

All she had to do was take her time and tease out the mystery of where the department's money had gone. Line by line. Invoice by invoice. Year by year.

She'd always been good at this kind of work. Details, numbers, spreadsheets. Where the rest of her family couldn't sit still for longer than five minutes, Daphne could sink into a state of flow when presented with a thorny problem. It gave her an odd, quiet thrill to untangle all the threads of the past based on nothing more than a few faded records.

No wonder her family thought she was weird.

By Thursday, she had no insights about the department's money yet, other than the fact that the former sheriff had been liberal in his definition of work expenses. So far, nothing stood out in terms of blatant crime, though. Just a few too many lunches on the department's dime. She'd have to dig deeper.

Her stomach grumbled, and she realized she'd been hunched over her records for four hours straight. After stretching her back until it cracked, Daphne let out a sigh and stood. She shambled to the kitchen and warmed up her container of leftover lemon chicken and roast potatoes. After snagging her small side salad from the fridge, she ate while nodding to the deputies and staff who wandered in and out of the kitchen.

"How goes it?" Hank Packer asked, smelling of the outdoors as he crossed toward the coffee machine. "Haven't heard a peep from that office of yours all week."

Daphne speared a piece of potato and smiled at him. "It's slow going, but I'm getting there," she said, which was the kind of meaningless platitude that people accepted when faced with an accountant ready to speak about their work. "Anything exciting happening out there in the real world?"

Hank snorted. "The usual. You know how it is. Few kids spray-painted the side of the grocery store and bragged about it at school. You shoulda seen their faces when we pulled them out of class this morning."

Daphne chuckled. "My sister got pulled out of class by the cops one time. She'd gone joyriding with one of her friends the night before, and they flipped a car. My mother was horrified."

Hank smiled as he filled his travel mug with fresh coffee. "She was a wild one," he agreed, then turned to smile at Daphne. "Your parents were lucky they had you to balance things out."

The bite Daphne had just taken turned thick and gluey in her mouth. She tried to smile at the older man as he lifted his mug and said goodbye, but her expression dropped as soon as he'd walked out. People always said that kind of thing to her. Her parents were lucky. She was so well behaved. She'd been such a good girl.

Then they turned around and brightened when Ellie walked in, leaving Daphne to watch on, wondering why no one cared about anything she had to say. She became a preachy, holier-than-thou teenager who looked down on Ellie for all her troublemaking proclivities. She'd wanted nothing more than to be safe and successful.

And where had it gotten her?

The man she was supposed to marry had told her he'd fallen out of love with her. In that horrible, heart-wrenching conversation, he'd told her she was boring. He wanted more spontaneity. More passion. He hadn't ever imagined marrying an accountant, and he didn't think he could go through with it. He saw himself with someone who took more risks.

In other words, he thought he could do better. So no matter how hard Daphne had tried to craft a safe, stable life for herself, she'd still had the rug pulled out from under her and had landed on her ass.

What was the point? Why try to be good when life could decide to punch you in the face without provocation? Why try to control anything at all?

Maybe all these years, she'd had it wrong. She should've been out joyriding with her friends instead of working for the college scholarships she'd needed to get off this island. She should've taken risks, and maybe a few of them would have paid off by now.

Shaking her head, Daphne washed her lunch container, dried it, and tucked it under her arm. She was halfway across the main room when the station's front doors opened, and a beautiful woman walked in.

She was tall, her hips swaying with every step. Her heels clacked on the hard flooring, her black dress hugging her curves to perfection. Her hair was bouncy and golden, curled in sleek, even waves, which had to be some kind of black magic considering the humidity outside. She slid off oversize sunglasses to reveal expertly applied makeup, her gaze scanning the room.

Jenna Deacon had gone from a pretty teenager to a drop-dead-gorgeous woman. They'd had very few interactions in school. Jenna hadn't been mean to Daphne; the more popular girl had simply ignored her. Compared to the annoyance and torment Calvin Flint had inflicted upon her, Jenna's treatment had been a welcome relief. Daphne didn't mind being left alone.

"I'd like to report a crime," she announced. "Is Sheriff Flint here?"

"*Acting* Sheriff Flint," Daphne muttered under her breath a moment before the man himself filled the doorway to his office.

The sheriff blinked at the woman, then arched his brows. "What can I do for you?"

"I'd like to report a crime," she repeated, her voice slightly breathy.

Flint straightened and nodded, clearing his throat as he took in the gorgeous woman. "Sure thing," he said, and gestured to his office.

Daphne's gut gave an uncomfortable squeeze. It wasn't jealousy. No. It would be truly pathetic to be jealous of a woman who hadn't known Daphne existed in high school, especially when Daphne didn't even like Calvin Flint and didn't care who he shacked up with.

What made discomfort slither through Daphne was an old, familiar feeling of inadequacy.

She wasn't impulsive and charming like her sister. She wasn't beautiful like Jenna. She wasn't spontaneous like her ex-fiancé Pete had wanted. She was only good enough to be the safe option that could be tossed aside when something better came along.

Jenna flicked her hair over her shoulder and planted a hand on her hip. "It's a crime that you already have a date to your mother's vow renewal, Sheriff," she said, facing off with Flint. "I think someone should arrest you."

Daphne's eyes widened. She met Shirley's stunned gaze across the office, and a few heads popped up over the tops of cubicles to watch the unfolding train wreck like groundhogs checking for the first sign of spring.

Flint blinked, his head rearing back an inch. "Excuse me?"

"You heard me," she said, stepping closer, a coy smile on her lips. "Who is she?"

Daphne didn't know whether to be horrified or amused. A full-body cringe went through her at the other woman's attempt at flirting—

Until a slight flush reddened the sheriff's cheeks. Daphne couldn't help but stare at him in horror. Was he . . . Was he *enjoying* this? He was actually affected by this woman speaking to him like that in front of all his coworkers?

Of course he was. She was gorgeous. If Daphne did something like that, she'd be laughed out of the station. Not that she would, because it would be risky. It would be putting herself out on a limb with no guarantees of success. It would be antithetical to everything that made Daphne who she was.

Daphne realized her mouth had dropped open, so she clamped it shut.

"Uh . . . ," Flint started, blinking. "She's, um . . . my date . . . Listen, I know that my mother probably promised you that I would take you, but surely there's someone else who would be better company . . ."

"Maybe I like a man in uniform," Jenna said in a husky voice.

Shirley let out a squeak as she furiously typed something on her phone. Daphne just watched on as the wallflower that she was, glued to her spot on the floor with her Tupperware container tucked under her arm. She felt unbearably plain, even though the secondhand embarrassment made her want to puke.

Then Sheriff Flint turned his head and met her gaze across the room. When he saw the look on Daphne's face, which was probably some mix of glee, self-loathing, and horror, his eyes narrowed. He turned back to Jenna. "Actually, my date—"

A loud screech rent the air, followed by a thunderous crash. Outside the station, glass shattered, metal clanged, and the most horrifyingly entertaining interaction Daphne had ever witnessed was eclipsed by shouts of panic on the street.

CHAPTER 7

Smoke curled from the hood of the pickup that was embedded in the front of the corner store down the street. On the opposite corner, an old beige Honda had jumped the curb and nudged a lamppost just enough to scratch the front bumper. Three doors swung open, and three old ladies jumped out.

Calvin scanned them; they seemed unhurt but shocked. "Stay back, ladies," he instructed them, and sprinted over to the driver's side of the pickup truck. Behind the wheel, he could see a middle-aged man blinking at the destruction before him.

"He's a maniac!" one of the ladies called out. She had white hair curling around her head and blue eyes flashing with indignation. He recognized her from the market; she was one of the women who had been with Daphne. Her grandmother?

"Ran a red light and swerved onto our side of the street!" The grumpiest of the three crossed her arms and snarled at them, her cane clacking against the side of the car.

Two deputies went to talk to the ladies while Calvin turned back to the alleged culprit. He opened the driver's door. "Are you hurt?"

"Those old ladies ought to have their licenses revoked," the man shouted. He had a beer belly and scraggly brown hair. "They're blind if they think that was my fault!"

"You're the one who should have your license taken!" Daphne's grandmother yelled.

"You're too old to be on the streets!" Spittle flew out of the man's mouth and landed on Calvin's cheek.

He wiped it off, then put his hands up and stepped into the man's line of sight. "I'm going to have to ask you to calm down," he said in his best Sheriff Voice. "We'll figure out exactly what happened."

"What happened is those old hags need to take their driving tests again. I could have been killed!"

"You!" The angry old lady stomped over, leaning on her cane. "*You* could have been killed? If it weren't for Greta, you would've run us down!"

Calvin made eye contact with Hank and Teri, one of the female deputies on the force, and nodded for them to usher the trio of old ladies out of the man's line of sight. He turned back to the pickup driver. "What's your name?"

"I think I have whiplash," he said, rubbing his neck.

"Your name," Calvin repeated.

"Bobby Troy," the man grumbled, peering around Calvin's shoulders to glare at the women.

Before he could react, Calvin heard Daphne's panicked voice. "Grandma?" Glancing over to see Daphne sprinting toward the other car, he watched her hug one of the ladies and check her for injuries before moving to the two others.

"I'm all right, honey, thank goodness. Crazy people on the roads these days. Look at that thing. It can't be roadworthy."

Calvin must have gotten distracted by the worry in Daphne's voice, because he hadn't noticed the pickup driver move until the man was sprinting across the pavement toward the old ladies.

"That's my truck you're talking about!" he yelled, arms pumping as he sprinted across the road.

Calvin was just a few feet behind Bob, but as he lunged to grab on to the running man, all he got was a handful of cotton shirt. Horror slid through his veins as he saw panic and shock flash across Daphne's face, followed by grim determination.

"Daphne, get out of the way!"

She did no such thing. She sidestepped in front of her grandmother and braced herself. A second later, the man barreled into her and sent her tumbling. She let out a grunt and rolled on the pavement as Calvin threw himself at the pickup truck driver, tackling him to the ground and then holding him there. His cuffs were in his hand a second later. The man squirmed, then went still, a shout stuck halfway up his throat.

Panting hard as he hauled the man up to his feet, Calvin glared at Daphne, who was sitting on the asphalt, looking dazed.

"Are you hurt?" he barked.

She met his gaze. "No."

"Will you stop being a damn hero, Davis? I can't spend all my time worrying about what injuries you're suffering when you're getting in the way of me doing my job." His voice was harsh, and he wasn't sure if he was angry or just spooked by the way Daphne had gone flying over the asphalt. Her face was still a mess, and if she'd hit the curb wrong . . .

"I was getting in the way of my grandmother being attacked by a maniac, Flint," she shot back.

Said maniac bared his teeth. "She deserved it for insulting my truck."

"Oh, shut up," Calvin muttered, then guided the man to the sheriff's department.

An ambulance parked nearby, and he paused long enough to see the paramedics jump out. He nodded to Daphne and her grandmother. "Davis just got knocked to the ground. Check her for a head injury. She doesn't seem to be thinking straight. This one will be in a holding cell."

"I'll take him and check him for damage," Teri said. She was a volunteer EMT as well as a sheriff's deputy, so Calvin handed the man off.

Daphne was hauled up to her feet as she insisted the paramedics check the old ladies ahead of her. Calvin watched on, his anger mounting. Couldn't she just listen to him *one* time? As if she sensed his thoughts, her gaze slid over to meet his. She scowled at him, blue eyes flashing. God, but the woman was infuriating.

Not wanting to bark at Daphne any longer, he turned to the destroyed corner store and headed inside. The shopkeeper had his phone in his hand, probably already calling up his insurance. He looked up and nodded. "Sheriff Flint."

"Did you see what happened?"

"Heard the screech of tires and then looked up just in time to see him coming through the window. I've got cameras pointed at the front door that might have recorded something useful."

"I'll take a copy," Calvin said, his gaze shifting to make sure everything was under control outside. The paramedics were working on the old ladies while Daphne watched on.

The woman made no sense. She was happy to stay locked up in her little office for hours on end, and then she went and got in the way of dangerous people who obviously didn't mind doing her harm. He didn't know whether to be angry or appreciative. How everyone saw her as the less impulsive sister was a mystery. She was a menace.

Unable to help himself, he walked across the street and stopped in front of where she sat on the curb. "You're a menace," he informed her.

She had her arms crossed on top of her knees and looked up at him through two bruised eyes. The swelling had gone down, but her skin was still mottled a thousand shades of purple, green, and yellow. She arched a brow. "Does the sheriff's department offer sensitivity classes about how to say thank you? Because I think you could use some."

"Do you enjoy getting hurt? Is this some sort of fetish?" His jaw was tight, and he couldn't decide if he wanted to shake her until her teeth rattled or wrap her in his arms and never let go. She could have been hurt—seriously hurt.

"If this is some twisted attempt at finding out my fetishes, it isn't working, Einstein."

"How about this, Davis. Next time some deranged maniac comes running at you, you *get out of the way*."

Daphne stood up and glared at him. She leaned forward so her chest nearly brushed his. The scent of her went straight to Calvin's head. When she spoke, her voice was low. "Don't pretend like you care, Flint."

"What's that supposed to mean?"

"You can play good guy now, but we both know you've hated me for almost twenty years. A fancy uniform and a shiny new badge doesn't change that."

He blinked, staring into those startlingly blue eyes. Even with the bruises, she was a beautiful woman. Fierce in a quiet sort of way that no one seemed to notice except for him. He wondered if she hid that steel on purpose, if she liked being treated like Little Miss Goody Two-Shoes because it made people underestimate her. Then her words sank in. "You think I hate you?"

"Oh, please."

She smelled floral and feminine, and the urge to shake her gave way completely to the urge to wrap her up and make sure she was okay. Calvin resisted. How he could be at war with himself around this woman was a mystery. It'd been the same all those years ago. She'd been so smart, so determined to make her way in the world, and he'd been the loser who had to repeat his senior year. He was nothing compared to her—and she reminded him of it at every chance. Her nickname for him, Einstein, wasn't a compliment.

But she'd taken a punch and a tackle that should've been aimed at him. She hid behind her books and her spreadsheets, then went and acted like a reckless lunatic, and Calvin couldn't help his desire to find out which version of her was the real one.

He took a deep breath, and in a softer voice, he asked, "Are you hurt, Daphne?"

She blinked, as if startled by his tone. "No. No, I'm fine. I hit the ground and rolled. I've ruined another shirt, but I'm okay." She nodded to the gash in the side of her shirt, where a sliver of skin was exposed.

Calvin stared at the curve of her waist through the rip while his mouth went dry; then he nodded. "Good," he said, and stalked away.

Scanning the gathered crowd, Calvin noted that Jenna Deacon seemed to have left at some point during the ruckus. He hoped that was the last he'd see of her. One nightmare of a woman was more than enough, and if he had to choose between Jenna's flirting and Daphne's animosity, he'd choose Daphne every time. Whatever that said about him, he didn't want to look at it too closely.

It took a few hours to get everything sorted out. By the time a tow truck had removed the pickup and the shopkeeper had begun boarding up the corner store window, statements had been taken and security footage had been acquired from every camera in the area. The mystery of who was at fault had been solved. The truck had run a red light and swerved into the old ladies' lane when he turned. Bobby Troy was lucky that Greta, the driver, had reflexes that belied her age.

The culprit had been checked over and cleared by the paramedics, and he was cooling his temper in one of the holding cells.

Calvin headed back to the station to start on the paperwork.

He paused at his office door and swerved to keep walking toward the back of the main room. Through the narrow window in the interview room door, he saw that Daphne was back at work, squinting at her computer with papers stacked in neat piles all around her.

The other side of her. Studious, intelligent Daphne Davis, who fooled everyone into thinking she was boring.

He knocked and opened the door when she glanced up.

"How's your grandmother?"

Daphne gave him a flat look. "Over the moon. She hasn't had anything this exciting happen to her for years, she says. She's fielding phone calls from half the island. Apparently someone convinced the shopkeeper to share his video footage, and it's all over social media."

Of course it was. "I'm glad no one was hurt."

"Me too."

He leaned against the doorjamb and nodded to her paperwork. "How's it going?"

Eyes narrowing slightly, Daphne studied him for a beat. He wondered what it would take to get that suspicion out of her gaze. "Do you actually care, or are your eyes going to glaze over as soon as I start talking?"

He came around her desk to peek at her computer screen. It was covered in the tiny boxes of a spreadsheet, many of them filled in with colors and numbers that immediately made his head hurt. "My eyes'll glaze over," he admitted, and was rewarded with a sparkle in Daphne's gaze as she tried to hide her smile.

It was a rush to glimpse that hidden expression on her face, a shot of adrenaline to his veins. Did she really think he hated her? Sure, they hadn't gotten along in high school, but that was because Calvin was an angry kid who blamed everyone for his pain. She had everything he'd craved. Daphne had come from a loving family. She was smart and pretty and calm. She had college dreams and scholarships and a *future*. In his teenage urges to destroy everything around him, he'd wanted to knock her off her high horse. It had been petty and wrong of him, he knew.

But he hadn't *hated* her. He'd never hated her.

"Looks like you're making progress," he said, just to break the silence.

"It's slow, but it's going well," she finally told him. "Nothing's jumping out at me so far, other than your usual mismanagement of funds. I'm about to go through all the invoices for that extension that only got half-built out back. I walked through it this afternoon, and it looks like the contractor just picked up his tools in the middle of the job and walked off."

"From what I hear, that's exactly what happened, but you know how it is around here. Hard to get a straight answer through all the gossip."

She put her hand on a stack of invoices and drummed her fingers, then narrowed her gaze at him. "Speaking of gossip. What was that about earlier?"

Calvin leaned on the edge of her desk, one foot on the ground, the other hiked up so his knee angled toward her. He crossed his arms. "What was what about?"

Daphne's voice dropped to a breathy, seductive register as she fluttered her eyelashes at him. "'Maybe I like a man in uniform'?"

The shot of lust that ran through Calvin's body made him jerk back and drop his dangling foot to the floor. He cleared his throat and tried to hide his reaction with a glare. "Don't, Cupcake."

She laughed, and it was such a bright, pure sound that it did nothing to quell the heat in his blood. She leaned back in her chair and arched a brow at him. "I didn't know you and Jenna Deacon had a thing."

"We don't. You know her?"

"Don't you? We were all in senior year together. She was in half our classes."

Calvin frowned. Most of what he remembered about his senior year was his annoyance at having to repeat it, drinking himself into a stupor at every opportunity, and perfect little Daphne Davis. "Was she?"

Daphne rolled her eyes. "You're telling me she just came down here and gave us all that little show, having never dated you at all?"

"A little show you seemed to be enjoying, by the way."

Her smile was sharp, and it sliced right across Calvin's chest. "It was awful. I loved it."

Scrubbing his palms over his face, Calvin let out a sharp breath. "My mom's trying to set me up with her. She might have suggested that I take Jenna as my date to her vow renewal next month."

"I see."

Calvin dropped his hands and curled them around the edge of Daphne's desk. Meeting her gaze, he shook his head. "I'm not going to take her."

"Why not?"

"I'm not in the habit of letting my mother set me up on dates."

"Jenna seemed more than willing."

"She's not my type. I told my mom I already had someone lined up."

Daphne nodded. "Right. So who's the lucky lady?"

"Why do you want to know?"

"I want to give her a heads-up that she might have to fight Jenna Deacon for you." Her blue eyes were piercing as she held his gaze, mirth buried somewhere deep. "Give her the chance to think about whether dating you is worth the hassle."

"I thought maybe you wanted to get in line behind the other two."

"In your dreams, Flint."

"I'll put you down as a maybe," he told her, if only to hear the outraged squeak that came out of her mouth. Calvin headed for the door. When he was back in his office, he finally let his lips curl into the smile he'd been biting back.

He might have been in his thirties, but apparently, Calvin still enjoyed poking at Daphne until she snapped.

CHAPTER 8

The small windowless interview room was a time warp. It took a while to shake off Flint's visit, but once Daphne started losing herself in numbers again, the hours passed without her noticing. By the time she came up for air that evening, there'd been a shift change and the sky was dark outside. Considering it got dark around four thirty in the afternoon, that in itself didn't mean as much as the new faces milling around the building. With her jacket unzipped and her purse slung over her shoulder, she shuffled to the front doors on stiff legs.

Lights were on in the sheriff's office. Through the open door, Daphne could see him at his desk. Flint frowned at his computer screen, pecking at the keyboard with his index fingers like he'd never used a keyboard in his life. He looked up when she poked her head in.

"I hadn't realized you were still here," he said.

"I was just about to say the same thing."

"Paperwork from this morning," he grumbled, shoving the keyboard away. "You make any discoveries this afternoon?"

"Well, actually . . ." Daphne hesitated. She hadn't made a discovery, exactly, but some of the invoices from the renovation were weird.

He arched his brows. "Is that a yes?"

"It's just strange, is all. Some of the invoices for the work on the extension out back were fully paid in advance. I walked through the area, and it still looks like a building site. I don't understand why the contractor would have been paid when the work was never completed.

It's possible the funds were recovered later, but I haven't been able to find any evidence of it if so."

"Hmm." Flint frowned and rubbed his jaw. "I haven't heard of any lawsuits or attempts to recover any money. Shirley just said the whole thing fell apart because of personal disputes between the contractor and the former sheriff, and it was never finished. It *is* weird that they would've been paid in full."

"Right?"

"You got the contractor's name?"

"Jerry Barela of Barela Contracting."

Flint nodded. "He's got an office here in town. We'll go talk to him tomorrow."

Daphne blinked. "'We'? As in, you and me?"

"You're the one with the information. You might as well be there to ask the questions."

"Oh. Okay."

A slow smile spread on the sheriff's lips. It looked wicked and teasing, and it made a strange sensation tighten in Daphne's gut. "You nervous, Cupcake?"

Straightening her shoulders, she glared. "Of course not. I'll see you tomorrow. Good night." Whirling on her heels, she strode out of the station without looking back. It was a short walk to her apartment, where she didn't even bother heading upstairs before jumping in her car and heading to the north of the island, where her parents lived. She'd be late for dinner, but she wanted to check on her grandmother. If that took her far away from a certain sheriff, well, that was just an added bonus.

Grandma Mabel was completely fine, basking in the fame generated by her accident. She sat in an armchair in the living room with a drink in one hand and her phone in the other, regaling whoever was on the line with a play-by-play of the events.

Daphne waved at her and wandered into the kitchen, where she found her father cleaning up the dishes from dinner. "Hey, Dad."

"Daphne! I left your plate in the oven."

"Ooh! Shepherd's pie. Yum."

"Seemed like a day for comfort food," Claude replied, scrubbing a saucepan. "Heard you took a beating today. Another beating." He gave her a significant look.

"I wouldn't say it was a beating. I got tackled. I'm fine."

"Your grandmother's been fabricating details in every retelling, then. To hear her talk about it, you went toe to toe with a pro boxer."

Daphne groaned as she pulled her plate from the oven. "I'll never hear the end of it." She tucked in to the dinner and let out a long sigh. Even though she'd never exactly felt like she fit in with her own family, it still felt good to be able to sit in the kitchen at their old wooden table and eat a home-cooked meal. Her dad was a great cook.

"Did you know Grandma used to bake bread?" she asked.

Her father leaned against the edge of the sink as he dried the saucepan. "Mabel? Of course. She's the one who got me hooked."

"She told me she stopped when her favorite pot got stolen."

A rough grunt escaped her father's lips as he nodded. He put the saucepan away and grabbed a handful of utensils to dry. "That was a whole drama. Brenda Sallow. They used to play nice, but they hated each other. Brenda denied ever taking the pot, but everyone knew."

"And Grandma never tried to get it back?"

"Oh, she tried! Of course she tried. But Brenda must have hidden it anytime they went over, and when she found your grandmother snooping through her cupboards, Brenda kicked her out, and that was the end of that."

"What was so special about the pot?"

Claude let out a little puff of breath and shrugged. "It was Mabel's mother's. A family heirloom, I guess you could say. And it did make good bread. Perfect crust every time. I bought her a new one a year or so later, but she told me to keep it. Had no interest in bread."

"That was it. No more baking for Grandma."

Claude nodded and put the silverware away while Daphne ate her dinner. It was petty and absurd to give up a hobby because of one stolen pot, but Daphne could understand it. Her family was full of stubborn, righteous people.

Daphne was the one who'd always been willing to bend. She compromised for the sake of peace and stability. If her precious heirloom pot had been stolen, she probably would have tried to reason her way into getting it back, then just let it drop and bought a new one. She would've folded.

When her father sat across from her, Daphne looked up.

"How are you doing?" he asked quietly.

"I'm good. Work's good. I like my apartment."

He gave her a look like he knew she was full of shit. "I mean how are *you*, Daphne. You haven't talked about Pete at all. Or how it feels to be back here."

Even now, after all these months, her ex-fiancé's name still made her shoulders stiffen.

"It's been nearly two years, Dad. What's there to talk about?"

"You didn't even mention it when it happened. We wouldn't have found out if Ellie hadn't gone to stay with you."

"It" being Pete deciding that he didn't love her anymore. That she wasn't exciting enough. That he'd never seen himself with a boring accountant like her for a wife.

"It was a breakup," she said, pushing the last of her food around her plate. "It sucked, and I got over it. He's seeing someone new now."

She'd blocked him on social media after they'd parted ways, of course, but there had been moments of weakness in the months that had passed. She knew he had a girlfriend, and they'd moved in together recently. The girlfriend was beautiful. They'd been skydiving together.

"Hmm," her dad replied.

"It's like Grandma with the pot," Daphne explained. "The pot's gone now. It's done. Like that relationship."

"So you're never going to date again?" He arched his brows. "Like your grandmother and her favorite hobby?"

"Of course I'll date again. Just . . . not right now. I need to focus on work."

Besides, who would she date? Who would be interested in a dull woman with a dull job who never took any risks? Even the thought of going to talk to a contractor about her very reasonable questions made her nervous. What kind of man would stick around when she was utterly devoid of any kind of bravery?

"Your face is looking better," her dad said, nodding to the black eyes.

"Yeah, putrid green and yellow are my colors. The touch of dark purple really brings out my eyes."

He laughed and shook his head, then turned when Grandma Mabel ambled through the doorway. She slid into the seat next to Daphne's and bumped her shoulder against her granddaughter's.

"We're famous, Daphne. Between your run-in with that Lane boy at the Winter Market, your sister's heroics a year and a half ago, and my near miss with that maniac in the truck, we'll never have to buy our own drinks again."

The older woman's words made Daphne's throat tighten. She'd never been lumped in the same category as the rest of her family before.

Maybe there was a drop of bravery in her, after all.

The next morning, Daphne sat behind her desk and gathered all the relevant invoices she needed to talk to Jerry Barela about the work he'd done on the station's unfinished construction work. She was reviewing her list of questions when her doorway darkened.

"Ready?" Flint asked. He wore his perfectly pressed uniform and a pair of very shiny black shoes. His dark hair was combed back from his forehead. He always looked immaculate, she noticed. She wondered why he kept himself buttoned up so tightly.

Today, there was a wicked sparkle in his eyes.

It was a challenge. And for once, Daphne didn't feel the need to back down. She closed the manila folder over her gathered invoices and notes and slid it into her bag. "Lead the way, Sheriff."

When they got to his truck, Daphne slid into the passenger seat and buckled herself in. She took a deep breath. "How are we going to approach this?" she asked as Flint turned the key in the ignition.

He glanced over. "We'll just ask him some questions and see what he says."

That was vague and utterly unhelpful. Daphne rolled her eyes. "You want to take the lead? I can go over the invoices with you now."

The sheriff leaned a forearm on the steering wheel as he turned to look at her, his eyes narrowed. Firm lips pressed into a line, he tilted his head. "You're more than capable, Cupcake."

"Will you stop calling me that? I hated it in high school, and I hate it now."

"That's what makes it fun." His lips curled as he put the truck in gear, and they headed toward the other side of town.

The truth was, Daphne didn't hate the nickname as much as she had the first time he'd said it. Besides, he was giving her a vote of confidence. Most people would expect her to crumple and scurry back to her books. Flint didn't seem to consider that an option.

It felt . . . good, Daphne decided. It made her heart beat a little bit harder and her palms grow damp, but she liked that he believed in her. Not many people did, except with things like accounting and to-do lists. She took a deep breath and watched the buildings go by while she got used to the feeling of Flint's confidence in her.

Carlisle was the only town on Fernley Island, and the location of the island's ferry terminal. The town was built on a gentle slope, so most of the residences had a view of the water. The sheriff's department was near the top of the slope, just down the street from the medical center, so they turned onto one of the main arteries leading down toward the water, then turned right to head toward the industrial side of town.

They left quaint shops and artisanal bakeries behind as they drove toward their destination. They passed workshops and warehouses, along with equipment-rental yards and a few smaller businesses. Barela Contracting was located beside a glassblowers' workshop, with a big yard full of stacked lumber and machinery behind the construction office's main building.

Flint parked the car in the front lot, and they got out. Daphne took a deep breath, reached into her bag to make sure the manila folder was where she'd put it, and followed the sheriff inside.

He believed she could do this. Now she just had to convince herself of the same thing.

CHAPTER 9

Jerry Barela was in his midfifties and possessed a wealth of curly salt-and-pepper hair. He was sitting behind a messy desk squinting at a computer screen when Calvin walked into the office just ahead of Daphne. Calvin had seen her square her shoulders before entering, had seen that stubborn clench of her jaw as she stepped over the threshold.

"Mr. Barela?" Calvin asked, coming to a stop in front of the desk.

The older man leaned back in his ancient rolling office chair and arched his brows. "Morning. Is there a problem?"

"No problem. I'm Sheriff Flint and this is Ms. Davis. We were hoping to ask you a few questions about the work you did over at the sheriff's department a few years ago."

Jerry snorted as he combed thick fingers through his hair. He wore a gold wedding band and no other jewelry. "What do you want to know?"

Calvin glanced at Daphne, who took a deep breath as if to center herself. Calvin wondered why she'd be nervous when she was the one who'd tried to stop not one but two criminals by putting her body on the line. How was this any more nerve racking?

She straightened her spine and gave the other man a nod. "Hi, Mr. Barela. Could you tell me why the work on the extension was never completed?"

The man spread his arms. "I never got paid, that's why. Do you work for free?"

Daphne frowned. "You weren't paid?"

"Got the deposit and started working, bought all the supplies, and then zilch."

"I have invoices here that are marked as paid." She dug through her bag and brought out a folder filled with old paperwork. After flipping it open, she found an invoice stamped with "PAID" with a bank confirmation stapled to the back, and handed it over to the contractor.

"This is an invoice for insulation and drywall as well as the electrical rough-in. It's dated four years ago and is marked as complete. I walked through the extension yesterday, and it doesn't seem to have more than a frame and a bare concrete floor."

Barela pawed at his desk, then seemed to remember his glasses were hanging off a string on his neck and put them on. Furrowing his brow, he read the invoice. After a few moments, he handed it back. "Don't know what to tell you, Ms. Davis. I never got the money."

"And is this your bank account information?" Daphne pointed to the bank confirmation on the second page.

Barela looked at the string of numbers, then turned to his computer and tapped it a few times. A printer whirred, and he grabbed the fresh sheet from the tray. He handed it over to Daphne. "Payment information is at the bottom of every quote. Hasn't changed in thirty years."

Daphne frowned as she compared the two account numbers, then nodded. "May I keep this?"

"Be my guest," he said, waving a hand. "I can even show you all the materials that we bought for the job and haven't been able to repurpose."

Calvin met Daphne's gaze, then turned back to Barela and nodded. "Sure."

The man groaned as he stood, then ushered them through the back door. He paused, grabbed a couple of fluorescent vests and hard hats, and handed them over before donning a hat of his own. The hard-packed gravel of the lot crunched as they stepped onto it, neat rows of stacked materials spreading before them. A forklift moved a pallet of PVC pipes at the far end of the yard, while Barela led them in the opposite direction.

They entered a small warehouse cluttered with materials. A saw whined as carpenters assembled a frame to the right. Barela nodded to the men as they glanced up and watched their troupe walk by, then led them down to the far end of the warehouse.

"We repurposed most of the timber and drywall, but the flooring and electrical fittings were a loss. I had half a dozen guys working on that place for three months before I called it quits," he said. "That bastard Bill Jackson gave me the runaround, and I finally told him I wouldn't be back until the money was in my account." Barela snorted as he shook his head. "That was it. Never saw a dime, so I never went back."

Calvin glanced over to see Daphne peeking at the flooring and taking notes. She looked good in her hard hat and vest, staring at everything like she could figure out the mysteries of the world just by digging into the financials. She had a little wrinkle between her brows, her lips pursed as she turned to the light fittings stacked on nearby wire shelves.

Jerry Barela had no idea who he was up against.

Calvin turned to the contractor. "Was Bill Jackson your main point of contact for the work?"

"Yeah, him and—"

A yelp made them both turn toward Daphne, who was stumbling back from the shelving while a cat yowled at her feet before darting across the concrete floor.

In two long strides, Calvin had his hands on her arms to steady her. "You okay?"

"Fine," she said, breathless as she hunched over, folder hugged tight to her chest. "Did you see that cat?" She pointed to where the animal had run. By the time Calvin had turned back around, Daphne was already hurrying toward the exit.

"Davis?"

"That's just Dumpling," Barela called out. "She won't hurt you."

"I'm allergic!" Daphne said, almost sprinting away.

What the hell was she doing? Had she seen something? Were they in danger?

One hand on his holster, Calvin scanned the area as he followed her. He kept one eye on Barela as his blood thrummed. They passed the two carpenters and were back out in the main yard within moments.

"Daphne! Slow down!" Calvin called out, jogging behind her. He watched her toss her hat and vest on Barela's desk as she booked it out of the contractor's office. Calvin did the same and turned to the contractor, who was staring at them both like they'd lost their minds. "Thanks, Mr. Barela. We'll be in touch if we have any more questions."

"Is she okay?"

"It's a bad allergy," Calvin lied.

"Gosh."

"Thanks again," he said, and rushed out the door to find Daphne huddled next to his truck. She was doing something, but she had her back to him.

"What's going on? What was that about?"

Daphne glanced over her shoulder, and . . .

Was she *blushing*?

"I panicked," she admitted.

"About what?"

After scanning their surroundings and finding them devoid of other people, Daphne turned. Calvin's eyes bugged as he saw the state of her shirt. She was wearing a dark-blue button-down tucked into gray pants, which was pretty similar to what she wore every day. Office-appropriate, staid, conservative clothing. Except her button-down had lost a few buttons at some point and had a big horizontal rip across the chest area. It was being held closed by Daphne's clenched fists.

And she wasn't doing a great job.

The rip in the fabric cut across her breast, so Calvin got a clear view of an expanse of skin he had no business viewing. Her breast was lovingly cradled by red lace.

Red lace.

The woman dressed like the accountant she was, except she wore undergarments like *that*.

As Daphne tried to paw at the fabric to cover herself, the middle of the shirt gaped open and gave him a view of the little red bow and sparkly charm dangling right at the base of her cleavage.

Tearing his gaze away, Calvin turned, cleared his throat, and stared at the overcast sky. "I, uh. Your shirt's ripped."

"How perceptive of you. That's why you get the big bucks, Einstein."

He glared over his shoulder, but while his back was turned, Daphne had dropped her hands to fiddle with the working buttons of her shirt, and now he could see even more red lace cupping perfect breasts. Had she always had those things hiding under there? Full and lush and . . .

His mouth watered, and he forced himself to turn around again.

"My shirt snagged on that shelf, and when that cat ran out, I jerked back." She clicked her tongue. "Another shirt ruined."

Calvin's cock was hard. Why was his cock hard? Apart from the lingerie and the tits, of course. Those tits belonged to Daphne Davis, though. They had no business making him feel like this. Sure, he liked driving her crazy, and she'd used that hot breathy voice the day before, and okay, yes, she was an attractive woman in an abstract sort of sense, but he hadn't realized . . .

"You always wear that kind of underwear, Davis?" Why was his voice suddenly full of gravel?

"What kind of underwear?"

"The red, lacy kind of underwear."

"Wouldn't you like to know?"

Yes. Yes, he would.

"It's none of your business, Flint."

That was true. "It's just a surprise, is all," he said, finally managing to think of something other than full breasts cupped in red lace so that he could actually unlock his truck. He moved to the driver's side and reached over his seat to grab the small duffel he kept in the back. Daphne opened the passenger door.

"It's a surprise that I wear nice underwear?" She glared at him across the cab of the truck.

Calvin impressed himself by not letting his gaze drop to the fantastic view he could glimpse in his peripheral vision. "Well . . ." He rifled through his bag to find his spare uniform shirt. "Yeah, Davis. It is. I didn't peg you for a red lace lingerie kind of woman."

"That'll teach you to make assumptions. Now can we get out of here so I can go home and change?"

"Put this on," he said, tossing her the shirt. "I'll drive you home."

She grumbled something that might have been gratitude, and Calvin got behind the wheel and kept his gaze firmly fastened out the windshield until Daphne had slid in beside him and buckled herself in. Then he glanced over and felt an odd sort of satisfaction at the sight of her wearing his clothes. In his defense, a good portion of his blood was currently occupied in places other than his brain.

He put the truck in gear and drove to Daphne's house.

CHAPTER 10

The shirt smelled like him. Daphne tried to ignore it, but it was a soothing, masculine kind of scent that made her dizzy. She needed to get it off before she actually started thinking Calvin Flint was attractive. Between her checking out his butt and now wearing his clothes, they were getting far too intimate with each other. Next thing she knew, she'd be getting along with the man, which would be some kind of betrayal of teenage Daphne's memory.

This was the guy who'd almost made her lose her scholarships. The guy who wouldn't leave her alone, who made fun of her for caring about school. He'd made it his mission to annoy her for her entire senior year. So what if he smelled good? That didn't make up for him being an irritating jerk.

Calvin parked outside Daphne's apartment building and cut the engine. When he slid out of the truck at the same time she did, Daphne narrowed her eyes.

"What are you doing?"

"Making sure you don't abscond with my spare shirt."

"I can promise you, I won't abscond with anything of yours, Flint."

"I've only got the two, and I've had enough women 'borrow' hoodies to be suspicious."

Deep offense struck in the middle of Daphne's gut. "You're putting me on the same level as women who try to be cute and steal your clothes?"

"There's nothing cute about it, Davis. Now you can either let me in so I can get my shirt, or we can stand here and argue about it."

"You know what?" She huffed and started unbuttoning the top. "Here."

"Wait. Hold on—"

"Abscond with this, Flint." She pushed the top into his chest, not even caring that her breasts and stomach were being kissed by fresh, cool air. His hands came up to catch the shirt, brushing her fingers in the process. Little shivers danced across her skin at the contact, which was probably a sign that she needed to get out of the cold and warm herself up. The sides of her own shirt, which she'd left on unbuttoned underneath his, were fluttering in the cold February breeze. "I'll see you back at the station. And stop staring at my chest, you perv."

His eyes snapped up to her face. "I wasn't staring at anything."

Scoffing, Daphne spun toward her door and fumbled with her keys for a few moments. Why were her hands trembling? Why did she feel flushed and strange? It wasn't because of the expression on Flint's face when he was looking at her breasts. She was cold—that was all. It was chilly out, and she was hardly wearing anything.

The key finally slid home, and she unlocked the lobby door. Once she was safely inside, she heard Flint's truck rumble to life, and Daphne let out a sigh of relief.

What a disaster.

The disaster continued late into the evening. Following an afternoon spent at the sheriff's department sorting through old financial records to figure out whether Jerry Barela had been telling the truth—and doing her best to avoid the sheriff—Daphne said her goodbyes, made herself dinner, then headed out to Mickey's Bar.

It was Friday night, and her dad's band, Old Dog New Trick, or ODNT for short, would be playing for their regular packed crowd of local fans and friends. Daphne walked into the dim, not-quite-a-dive bar and scanned the room for familiar faces. Her dad and his band were setting up onstage while music played on the speakers. She spotted her sister sitting at the bar with her best friend, Wynn, and cut across the old floorboards to join them.

When Daphne was a few feet away, Wynn saw her and smacked Ellie's shoulder.

Spinning on her barstool, Ellie looked at Daphne with an expression of such pure glee that Daphne froze.

"What?" Daphne demanded.

"You," said Ellie with a devilish smile on her lips, "are very naughty."

"What are you talking about?" She slid onto the stool next to Ellie's and hung her jacket and purse on the hook between her knees. She made eye contact with the bartender, who was busy pouring someone else's drinks but nodded as if to say he'd come by in a moment.

"I'm talking about you and Calvin Flint."

Daphne's neck cracked as she whipped around to meet her sister's gaze. "What?"

Wynn laughed. "Everyone's talking about it."

"Talking about *what?*"

Ellie cackled. "I think a better question is, 'What were you doing with him during work hours this morning?' Naughty, naughty Daphne."

The bartender ambled over and leaned his palms on the bar. "Daphne," he greeted. "What can I get for you?"

"Gin and tonic, please."

"And will the sheriff be joining you tonight?"

Daphne jerked back. "What? Okay. Someone needs to tell me what the hell is going on here."

The bartender laughed and made her drink while Ellie sipped her beer, then smacked her lips in a distinctly self-satisfied way. "You were spotted, Daphne."

"Talking to Jerry Barela? That was work related."

Wynn arched her brows as her eyes sparkled. "Not from what we heard."

A drink glass thunked against the wooden bar top, and Daphne glared at it, then at the bartender, then at the two women beside her. "Enough. What have you heard?"

"Oh, only that you showed up at your house around eleven o'clock this morning wearing the sheriff's shirt, which you then stripped off in the middle of the street to flash him your boobs."

"*What?*"

Ellie threw her head back to laugh so hard she nearly fell off her stool. "Your face, Daphne!"

"That's not what happened!"

"So you weren't wearing Calvin Flint's uniform?"

Daphne blinked. "Well. Yes. I was, but—"

Wynn wheezed, and Ellie leaned her head on her best friend's shoulder as she laughed.

"Stop that," Daphne hissed. "My shirt ripped, and he gave me his spare uniform. Nothing happened."

"You didn't strip down to your bra in the middle of the street?"

Heat prickled on Daphne's cheeks. She took a gulp of her drink and glared at the ice clinking in her glass. "He was being a jerk, so I gave him his shirt back to stop him coming up to my apartment."

"Uh-huh," Ellie said, wiping the tears from her eyes.

"So," Wynn started, leaning in, "is he any good?"

"Good at what?" Daphne screeched.

The two other women wiggled their brows. It was Ellie who said, "You know."

"Good at police work?" Daphne filled in, baring her teeth at them. "Debatable. Good at being a pain in my ass? Absolutely."

Ellie clicked her tongue and shook her head. "You better get your story straight, Daphne, because this has already spread all over the island."

The bar door slammed open, and Grandma Mabel and the rest of her gang strode in. Without a moment's hesitation, they made their way to Daphne at the bar.

Grandma Mabel crowed, squeezing Daphne's upper arms. "Good girl," she said. "I knew you had a little fire hidden in there."

"Grandma, you've got the wrong idea. This is all getting blown out of proportion. Nothing happened between me and Flint."

"So you weren't wearing his clothes this morning?"

"Well, yes, but—"

"How do you feel about a joint wedding? You and your sister, together?"

"What? No!"

Grandma Mabel nodded. "You're right. You should each get your own time to shine."

"Shame about his family," Harry cut in. "You think Calvin would want to invite them? Maybe you can elope."

"We aren't getting married!" Daphne shouted, then sank her head between her shoulders as half the bar glanced over.

"Good for you," Greta said, patting Daphne's hand. "Better to have fun while you're young. Why should men be the only ones allowed to sow their wild oats?"

"Exactly," Grandma Mabel said with a decisive nod. "Now. How was it?"

"It was nothing," Daphne hissed. Her face was so hot she was sure it was beet red. Her hands were clammy, and the speed of her pulse couldn't be healthy. "Nothing happened."

"Well, that's too bad," Greta said with a frown. "He didn't get you off? Even after you flashed the whole street for him?"

"That's not what happened!"

"That's not what I heard," Grandma Mabel said, blue eyes gleaming.

Meanwhile, Ellie and Wynn were choking on their laughter, doubled over as each clung to the other's shoulders for support.

Daphne buried her face in her hands and groaned, then straightened her spine. "We were talking to Jerry Barela. My shirt ripped. The sheriff offered me his spare uniform. I gave it back before heading inside."

"Rhonda told me you were wearing some *very* risqué undergarments, honey," Grandma said, then slung her arm around Daphne's shoulders. "That makes me happy. Every woman ought to have beautiful underthings. The fact that Calvin Flint is the lucky guy who gets to see them is beside the point."

"He doesn't 'get to see them,'" Daphne protested. "He saw them due to unforeseen circumstances. And wait. Rhonda? Is she the one who's been spreading lies about me?"

Rhonda Roberts owned the most popular ice cream shop on the island. She was a lovely woman, but Daphne wouldn't hesitate to give her a piece of her mind for spreading malicious lies.

"She saw your bra from her living room window," Grandma Mabel said. "Can you blame her? She said the sheriff looked thunderstruck. Red lace will do that to a man, though."

"I'm going to kill her," Daphne said through clenched teeth.

"Shame he's so bad at making love," Greta added. "I wouldn't expect that from such a strapping young man."

"No?" Harry asked, brows arched high on her wrinkled forehead. "The pretty ones are always the laziest."

"We didn't have sex," Daphne hissed, then pushed her stool back and stood. "I need some air."

She stomped across the bar, feeling the patrons' eyes on her back, ready to march across the island, find Flint wherever he was, and demand that he *fix this, and fix it right now.*

But she didn't have to march far. Halfway to the door, Daphne watched it swing open to reveal the sheriff himself standing in the opening, a thunderous expression on his brow. And when his eyes landed on Daphne, his lips pinched into a thin line.

The bar was utterly silent. Someone had even turned down the music, which put one more person on Daphne's shit list. Everyone in this bar would hear every word between her and the sheriff, and their gossip-addled brains would twist it to suit their purposes.

She would kill him. She'd kill him for being such a jerk about the uniform, for making her act out to the point that she'd stripped it off in the street. She'd kill him for making her feel off balance all the time, for pushing her off the foundation of safety and stability that was her happy place.

He was the cause of all this. With all his dark-haired, hazel-eyed good looks. With his stupid, glorious return to the island that had absolved him of all his teenage sins. With his authority and his uniform. He was the reason everyone on the island was talking about her.

And all he said as he stood in the doorway was "We need to talk, Cupcake."

CHAPTER 11

Calvin watched as steam came out of Daphne's ears. She ground her teeth as the two of them faced off, the only sound in Mickey's Bar the wolf whistle of a patron hidden in the corner. After tearing his gaze away from Daphne, he glared in the direction the sound had come from and heard a smattering of laughter ripple through the crowd.

He stepped out of the doorway and held the door open for Daphne to stomp through.

"Talk," she said, stopping just beside the door to cross her arms. She'd left her jacket inside, and Calvin could see goose bumps already rising on her arms.

"Let's talk in the truck," he said, gesturing to his vehicle. He ignored her impatient huff and got behind the wheel, turning on the heat while he gathered his thoughts.

The call he'd received from his mother an hour earlier had been unexpected. The fact that she thought he was sleeping with Daphne Davis even more so. But that wasn't the worst of it.

"There's some chatter," he started, "about you and me."

Daphne let out a bitter snort. "So I've heard."

Good. That made things simpler. "My mother just called me."

"Before you say anything else, can I just say that this is all your fault?"

Calvin jerked back. "My fault?"

"Yes!"

"Am I the one who ripped your shirt and then stripped down in the street?"

"No, but you're the one who gets pleasure from driving me crazy! I'm normal around other people. I'm quiet, I do my work, and I go home. I don't get why you make me so insane."

"Well," Calvin said, leaning back. "I tend to have that effect on women."

"Give me a break."

He laughed. "Listen, this is as inconvenient for me as it is for you."

"Maybe if we ignore it, it'll blow over."

Cringing, he turned to look at her. The streetlights illuminated her profile, and in this light, he could hardly see her fading bruises. She wore a low-cut shirt with short sleeves and a few little white buttons that drew his eye to her cleavage. Earrings dangled in her lobes, and she'd brushed a bit of sparkly makeup on her lids at some point. Her lips looked pink and glossy. She was pretty and feminine and delectable, and he wanted to haul her over to his lap so he could taste her. He wondered what color her bra was, then tore his gaze away and chastised himself for letting his thoughts wander in that direction.

They had a problem. *He* had a problem. He couldn't afford to mess this conversation up.

"My mom thought I was cheating on my date to her vow renewal with you."

Daphne met his gaze, then hummed. "I see. And did your date get wind of it?"

A long sigh slipped through Calvin's lips, and he kneaded the bottom of the steering wheel to try to let out some nervous energy. "See, that's the thing. There is no date."

"What do you mean? You told me you had a long line of women waiting for the chance to go to your mom's event with you."

He cringed. "That . . . might not have been strictly true."

"So take Jenna."

"We've covered this. She's not my type."

"I don't get why you're telling me all this."

"Well, when my mom accused me of cheating on my nonexistent date, I might have suggested that there was no cheating involved, because my date was actually . . ." He trailed off and glanced over at her, waiting for her to meet his gaze. Gravel rattled in his throat as he tried to clear the blockage.

"Your date was actually . . . ?"

Might as well come out with it. "You," Calvin said. "I told her my date was actually you."

Daphne blinked. Blinked again. Calvin could practically hear the gears grinding in her brain as the reality of his words was processed. Then her face was a rictus of horror, and she reared back so far her head hit the passenger window.

"Careful," he hissed, reaching for her.

She batted his hand away. "You said *what?*"

"It's just one event, and I would owe you," he rushed to say. "It's really low key; she's hosting it at her house. Just a little casual gathering, really. And look, I know it's not ideal, but—"

"Absolutely freaking *not*, Flint. How could you possibly tell her that? Call her right now and tell her you lied and you'll take Jenna. Get your phone."

"I'm not taking Jenna."

"Why not?"

"If I take her to the vow renewal, my mother will push her on me even more aggressively, and it'll be a nightmare to get her to back off. You saw how she was when she came to the station. Besides, I'm not into her!"

"You're not into *me!*"

Calvin paused. "Regardless," he started, and Daphne held up her hand.

"No."

"It's one evening, Davis. You want money? I'll pay you."

"There isn't enough money in the world for me to attend your mother's vow renewal on your arm, Flint." Daphne crossed her own arms and stared out the windshield. Her pose drew his attention to her breasts again, and he really needed to stop looking at her like that, but had she put something sparkly on her cleavage too? Why did her skin look so damn kissable?

What was *wrong* with him?

Calvin tore his gaze away. "What did you think of Jerry Barela?" he asked when the tension in the truck got too much.

Daphne glared at him. "You're asking me that now?"

"Well, every time I went to your office to debrief, the door was locked or you were out."

"That was by design, numbnuts."

"So you're avoiding me?"

"Of course I'm avoiding you."

"Because you ripped your own shirt?"

"I'm not doing this," she said, reaching for the door handle, "and I'm not going to the vow renewal. Find someone else. All I want is to do my job and have a nice, quiet life. I'm not going on fake dates with acting sheriffs. That's not who I am. I'm sitting in my office and sorting through financial records, and that's it."

She had one foot on the pavement when Calvin said, "Liar."

Daphne stood just outside the car, holding the passenger door open. "Excuse me?"

"You did this when we were kids too. Pretended to be some quiet mouse of a girl who just wanted to stick her nose in books. That's not who you are."

"Oh, now you know who I am?"

"I know you want more than to just sit at a computer looking at old records."

"And how could you possibly know that?"

"Because of the way your eyes lit up when you were talking to Barela! Because you love giving as good as you get."

"I do not."

"You do with me."

Her chest heaved with every inhale as she glowered from just outside the car. "I want a quiet, stable, safe life. I thought I had it, and I lost it. I'm not going to jump off the deep end just because you think you know me better than I know myself."

"Maybe you should, Davis. Maybe you should try jumping."

"Maybe you should mind your own business." She slammed the passenger door and didn't look back as she headed inside.

Calvin's heart thumped. She drove him up the fucking wall. How could she pretend that all she wanted was a quiet life? How could she intentionally make herself so much smaller than she was?

She thought she could just fling vitriol at him and stomp away, but she was wrong. Calvin had been through a lot in his life. He'd endured his father's death and his mother's neglect. He'd made it through the chaos and anger of his teen years, the alcohol and the fury and the self-destruction. He'd cleaned himself up. He'd made something of himself. He'd learned that being honest with himself was the only thing that mattered in the end, the only thing that could keep him sane.

He'd had to be honest with himself that he couldn't touch alcohol after abusing it as a teen. Honest that his mother had hurt him. Honest that he was confused about his place on Fernley, his place in his family, but he was willing to try to figure it out, if only for his little sister's sake.

So he might as well be honest about something that was right in front of his face.

He wanted Daphne Davis. Wanted her to stop fighting herself. Wanted her to stop hiding herself away because she was afraid to face what was inside her.

And he wanted her for himself. In his arms. In his bed.

The truck's door slammed behind him, and he followed her inside.

CHAPTER 12

Daphne had just slid onto the stool she'd vacated earlier, then waved to the bartender for another drink. Three seconds later, someone sat down to her left.

She didn't even have to glance over to know who it was. "Go away."

"No," Flint replied.

"You'll make the gossip worse."

"Good. Maybe you'll agree to be my date."

"Look at you two lovebirds!" Grandma Mabel crooned as she came over, slinging one arm around Flint's shoulders and one around Daphne's.

"The sheriff is harassing me," Daphne corrected her.

Her grandmother just laughed. "Glad to see someone's finally able to get Daphne out of her shell."

"My shell is wonderful," she protested. "It's safe. I like it. I don't need to get out of it."

"Cupcake is just embarrassed about the gossip. You know how shy she is," he added with a broad smile, but Daphne heard the hidden dagger in his words. The jerk didn't think she was shy at all.

"If you call me Cupcake one more time, I will stab you in the neck, Flint."

He met her gaze, hazel eyes flashing. "Do your worst, Davis."

"Young love," Grandma Mabel said with a sigh; then she patted Daphne's shoulder and walked away.

Daphne watched her, then swung her gaze across the room to see a few people ducking away from her glare. She looked at the sheriff. "This is your fault."

"I don't know what you're talking about."

"Do you get off on driving me insane?"

Flint turned to face her, something like interest sparkling in his gaze. "Should I answer that honestly?"

"I hate you," she spat, cheeks burning.

"Wow," Ellie said, leaning over. "I've never seen Daphne so fired up. When did this all start? Have you guys been seeing each other in secret? Is that why you both moved back at the same time?"

"No," Daphne exclaimed as Flint leaned an arm on the bar in front of her and said, "Maybe."

Ellie's eyes widened as she exchanged a glance with Wynn. She turned back to Daphne. "I didn't know you had it in you."

"Oh, she does," Flint said, then grunted when Daphne elbowed him in the gut. Wheezing slightly, he smiled at Ellie. "She's a firecracker behind closed doors."

Daphne leaned forward and grabbed one of the little plastic drink stirrers the bartender kept next to the sliced limes. She held it in a clenched fist and angled her body toward Flint. "Carotid or jugular? Your choice, Flint."

In the dim light of the bar, his eyes were the color of whiskey. He gave her a dark smile. "Try me, sweetheart."

Her heart thumped wildly as her lungs constricted. She was hot all over. Anger had burned a path through her, and now all she could do was glare at the sheriff as he leaned toward her, the clean, dizzying scent of him teasing her nose. She inhaled through her teeth and said, "I thought you'd changed, but I was wrong."

His lids dropped to half-mast, gaze landing on her mouth. Daphne fought the urge to lick her lips, focusing instead on the feel of the hard plastic pick clenched in her fist. Her pulse pounded in her throat and wrists. Between her legs.

"Maybe you're right," he finally replied, and leaned back while he turned toward the bar to order a soda water.

The background music died down, and everyone turned to see the band take the stage. Daphne's father hooked his saxophone to his neck strap and adjusted the flat cap on his head, then nodded to the big man who sang and played lead guitar. A moment later, ODNT was playing one of the originals on their brand-new album, and the focus of everyone at Mickey's Bar was finally off Daphne and the sheriff.

She felt him shift closer. Felt the press of his thigh against hers. Felt the heat of his breath on her neck a moment before he asked, "Want to dance?"

When she turned her head, their faces were inches apart. She could see the little flecks of green and gold in his irises, the length of each individual lash framing eyes that were too beautiful to belong to such a vile man. Not wanting to give him an inch, she held her ground, her heart thundering when his gaze dropped to her lips once more.

It wasn't anger blazing a path down the middle of her anymore. It was something much, much worse.

"So?" he prompted, voice low.

"Flint," she said softly, and watched him lean a fraction of an inch closer. When she couldn't take it anymore, she said, "I'd rather die than dance with you right now."

She slid off her stool and grabbed her jacket and purse to walk toward the table her grandmother and mother had commandeered near the stage. The sound of Flint's low laughter chased her all the way there.

It was a few hours later when Daphne finally left Mickey's Bar. Her grandmother hooked her arm in Daphne's so they could walk out together. Taxis were scarce on Fernley, and the wait for one that would be willing to drive all the way to the north end of the island to drop Grandma Mabel home would be upward of an hour. Daphne had had more than a few drinks to drown her sorrows while Flint watched her as he sipped soda water at the bar, so she wasn't fit to drive either.

"Want to walk over to my place and have a coffee while we wait for Dad to finish up?"

"That sounds wonderful, honey," Grandma Mabel replied, patting Daphne's arm.

It was a cool night. The sky had cleared to reveal a carpet of glittering stars. The air was damp and fresh, and the two of them made the walk to Daphne's apartment in companionable silence while their breaths puffed in front of them in white clouds. They were almost at the door when Grandma Mabel spoke.

"What's really going on between you and the sheriff, Daphne?"

"I don't want to talk about this right now, Grandma."

"I'm sorry if I teased you too much," the older woman said. "It's just so rare to see you get fired up about anything. You're usually so stoic. I got carried away."

Daphne unlocked the lobby door and held it open for her grandmother. The apology had softened her, and she found herself sighing. "It's okay. It's just gossip. It'll pass."

"I think he likes you."

"Grandma," Daphne said with a groan.

"I do!"

"He hates me. He has for years."

"Maybe." Grandma Mabel took her time on the stairs to the second story, and Daphne kept her arm free so she could support her grandmother's elbow on the way up. When they reached the top landing, Mabel glanced at Daphne and smiled sadly. "Maybe I was just excited about seeing a little spark between you and someone else after everything that happened with the dog."

"The dog" was Grandma Mabel's name for Pete, Daphne's ex-fiancé, which was pretty rude to dogs, all things considered. But only a cowardly mutt of a man would turn around and break things off in the way Pete had, Grandma Mabel said.

"That's old news, Grandma."

"Is that why you still get that sad look in your eyes whenever anyone brings him up?"

Daphne busied herself unlocking her apartment door, then kept her eyes averted from her grandmother's while she went to the kitchen and brewed a pot of decaf. "I'm not sad about it anymore," she finally replied. "It's done."

"He hurt you."

"He did. I survived."

"I want more for you than just survival." Grandma Mabel let out a tired groan as she sat on one of the chairs at Daphne's tiny kitchen table. "My legs are too old for dancing," she complained.

"You looked pretty good to me," Daphne said with a smile as she prepped the cups. She didn't have any treats, except for a packet of half-stale cookies in the pantry, so she set a few of them on a plate and sat down across from her grandmother.

"You really have no interest in the Flint boy?" her grandmother asked, eyes sharp as she looked at Daphne.

"I really don't," Daphne replied, but the response felt hollow. He was handsome, and she didn't *hate* the way her heart sped up when they bickered. On a few occasions, she'd thought maybe he was looking at her with the eyes of a man who was appreciating a woman. But he was also Calvin Flint, who took pleasure in tormenting her. He'd probably love it if she made a fool of herself with him.

"You deserve a second chance, honey," Grandma Mabel said quietly.

The coffee machine sounded like it was about done brewing, so Daphne got up and poured a couple of cups. When she sat down, she took a sip and tried to put her feelings into words. "Maybe I deserve one," she finally replied. "I'm just not sure I want it. When Pete told me he wanted more passion, it . . . I don't know, Grandma. It's like it broke something in me. I'm not passionate or spontaneous or fiery the way you and Mom and Ellie are. I can't change who I am."

"You sure about that? You seemed passionate enough, the way you and the sheriff were glaring at each other."

"That's different."

Grandma Mabel narrowed her eyes as she sipped her coffee, then bit into a cookie and chewed. "What would you call it when you got in the way of that man trying to steal the cashbox at the farmers' market? Or stepping in front of me when that maniac came barreling toward us for the accident that he caused?"

"Temporary insanity, probably."

Grandma Mabel snorted, derision dripping from the sound. "Daphne, be serious. You have a spine. Yes, you like numbers, and you cared about your grades, and you wanted more than this island could provide for you. But you are my granddaughter, just as much as Ellie is. I love you both. Just because you enjoy sinking your teeth into problems that make most people want to fall asleep doesn't mean there's anything wrong with you."

Tears stung Daphne's eyes, and her throat was too tight to speak.

"Maybe the dog just wasn't the right man for you." Grandma Mabel continued: "I don't believe for a second that you're not a passionate person, Daphne. He just said those things to excuse his terrible, cowardly behavior and make it feel like it was your fault. His words shouldn't define you."

"They don't. It's just that at least for now, I'm done with men. The way you were done with baking when you lost the pot."

"It was stolen, not lost," Grandma Mabel shot back.

Daphne put up her palms. "Right. Sorry. But my point stands. The pot got taken, and it changed you. You could have bought a new one or baked bread without one. But you didn't. You stopped. I have a right to stop trying to date when my vision for my future was taken from me."

There was a long silence as they ate stale cookies and drank their coffee.

"That old cast-iron pot wasn't really about baking bread," her grandmother finally said. "It reminded me of my mother. She taught me how to cook. We'd make all kinds of breads together, and she swore that the pot was the reason they turned out good. She said the new ones just weren't the same, and that specific Dutch oven had some kind of magic in it. I didn't really care about baking; I just cared about those precious memories with my mother. After she died, it was one of the only things I had left of her. I thought I'd have it forever; the thing was near indestructible. So yes, I stopped baking bread. Baking just didn't mean anything to me anymore." She leaned forward and put her hand on Daphne's, her skin thin and soft and wrinkled. "But I still have a lifetime of memories. I want you to have a life full of memories, Daphne. Beautiful, rich memories that aren't clouded by the actions of someone who didn't recognize your worth."

Daphne brushed her hand across her face to wipe the tear that had escaped down her cheek.

They both jumped when Grandma Mabel's phone rang. The older woman glanced at the screen. "Your mother and father are downstairs. I'd better not keep them waiting."

Standing, Daphne wrapped her arms around her grandmother and squeezed. "I love you, Grandma."

"Not as much as I love you, honey."

She walked Grandma Mabel to the front door and waved at her parents before trudging back up the stairs and locking herself inside her apartment. The walls were bare and the furniture was generic. It wasn't a home.

Was she living a smaller life than she should? Was she letting her broken engagement cloud her decisions?

But what was the alternative? Go to some vow renewal with Flint and pretend to be his date? Why? What possible reason could she have to—

Daphne froze in the process of clearing the table. She stared down at the half-empty mugs of coffee, the crumbs on the cookie plate, the stamp of lipstick her grandmother had left on the rim of her mug.

The family heirloom that meant so much to her grandmother had been taken by Flint's grandmother. If anyone had it, it would be his mother. The vow renewal would happen at his mother's home.

The chances of that old pot still existing were slim. It was almost inconceivable that anyone would keep the thing, especially when it meant so little to anyone other than her grandmother. But *if.* If it still existed, it would be in Eileen Yarrow's kitchen. A place that normally would be completely beyond Daphne's ability to access.

Unless she went to the vow renewal as Calvin Flint's date.

STEP TWO: CONCOCT A COVER STORY

CHAPTER 13

The last thing Calvin expected, an hour after getting home from Mickey's Bar, was his phone to light up with a call from Daphne. He'd already lifted her number from her employment file and saved it in his phone, seeing as she seemed to be hell bent on getting herself seriously injured as quickly as possible. He'd figured he might as well have a way of reaching her in case things went wrong, which they seemed to do often when she was involved.

Staring at the screen for a moment, he kicked his feet up onto the coffee table and swiped to answer. "How bad is it?"

There was a pause. "Excuse me?"

"You're calling me after midnight, and I left you with all your limbs attached a little over an hour ago. Something must have gone horribly wrong."

"This was a terrible idea."

The phone went dead. Calvin stared at the screen, blinking. The woman had hung up on him. After *she'd* called *him*. Three seconds later, she answered his call.

"Forget it," she said without preamble.

"Talk to me, Cupcake."

"You're making this exceedingly difficult."

"If I knew what was going on, maybe I could make it easier."

"I very much doubt that."

Calvin leaned his head back on his sofa and stared at the ceiling, smiling. "Let me guess. You've reconsidered the vow renewal invite." The pause that followed made him sit up. He frowned, propping his elbows on his knees. "Davis? You're not . . . *Have* you reconsidered the vow renewal invite?"

Her sigh ruffled through the earpiece. "I think we may be able to come to an understanding."

"'An understanding,'" he repeated, not sure how the word tasted on his tongue. She wasn't exactly volunteering to jump into his bed. Then again, an understanding wasn't a no.

"I might be persuaded to go to the event with you," she started, "as a way to temporarily fight fire with fire."

"I'm not following."

"You saw our audience at Mickey's. They were loving the tension. The more I denied things between us—and, by the way, the more you played into it, which I did *not* appreciate—the more everyone in town wanted to talk about it. I think if we pretend to be lovey-dovey with each other"—she paused for emphasis, and Calvin could very clearly picture the narrow-eyed look she'd be giving him if they were facing off with each other—"*temporarily*, then we can stem the worst of the gossip."

"An interesting hypothesis, Ms. Davis. How very academic of you."

"I truly despise you, you know that?" Daphne asked, but there was no heat to her words.

Calvin bit back a grin. "So, what? We reconnected last week, and now things are moving quickly? We're infatuated? The honeymoon stage?"

"Too juicy. We need to make this boring. It's anti-gossip. Maybe we've been chatting for months. The job openings were the perfect opportunity to reconnect in person."

"I don't see how that's any less juicy. The new sheriff hiring a consultant he's been banging?"

"We have *not* been banging."

"Cupcake. Come on."

He could hear her footsteps, rhythmic and echoing. She was pacing. "Okay. Did you have anything to do with me getting hired for the consultant job?"

"The decision was made before they brought me on board."

"Hmm. All right. That helps, but it still doesn't look good. We wouldn't have cleared the relationship with anyone, and it's got just enough spice to keep people talking. We might have to go back to your original idea, as terrible as it was."

"That we met on a desert stretch of highway, I pulled you over, and we've been tangled up in each other's bedsheets ever since?" Calvin let his voice drop, but he didn't expect his pants to get tighter at the images his words conjured up.

"Do you want me to go to this event with you or not?" Daphne snapped.

That tone of hers wasn't helping the pants-tightness situation. He was discovering just how much he loved it when she got snippy with him. But there was only one answer he could give to that question. "Yeah, I want you to go."

"Fine. So stop saying ridiculous things."

"What was ridiculous about what I just said?"

"It was—the bedsheets—I'm not—" She stopped talking abruptly, and Calvin wondered whether she was blushing. Her pacing had stopped. She took a deep breath. "We're taking things slow. Okay? We can go with the 'reconnecting after you pulled me over' thing, since everyone knows about the traffic stop already."

"Can I ask why you're doing this? Wouldn't it be easier to just let this gossip die on its own? People will stop talking eventually."

"Maybe I'm trying to be nice and do you a favor."

"Hmm," Calvin mused. "Nope. That's not it. Try again."

He could've sworn Daphne's answering huff was almost a laugh. "I think we can make the gossip peter out quicker this way. I'm not a very exciting person. And besides . . ."

"'Besides'?"

"When we break up, it'll give me an excuse to leave the island."

Calvin blinked. Frowned. Stared at his coffee table until her words made sense. "You're leaving? You just got here."

"I don't know what I'm doing, but I do know that getting my family to understand my desire to go will be hard enough without having a valid excuse. They're . . . worried about me."

"Why are they worried about you?"

"They think I'm still hung up on my ex."

"Are you?"

"Am I what?"

"Hung up on your ex?"

"No! Anyway, it's not relevant. If everyone thinks we're going steady—"

"'Going steady?' Who says that?"

Daphne let out a cute little growl. "Having a conversation with you has got to be the most frustrating experience of my life."

Calvin relented. "Fine. So, we convince everyone we're a very boring couple with boring lives, you go to the event with me, and in exchange, I help you leave the island when the time comes?"

"All I ask is that you don't trash my reputation. I'll do the same for you, of course. We can say we discovered we were very different people and a relationship was never going to work, which everyone will understand because we are."

A hum left Calvin's throat. They were different, but Calvin wasn't quite so sure he concurred with Daphne's analysis. Agreeing with her scheme meant that he could take her to his mother's vow renewal, which would save him from having to come up with some excuse as to why he'd lied to his mother in the first place. It would mean he'd get to keep an eye on Daphne and make sure she didn't put herself in the way of an angry man with a mean left hook again. But it also meant there was a predictable end to the agreement, and that she'd use him to make her next escape off the island.

He'd only just admitted to himself that he wanted her. Now he had to give her up?

"Flint?"

"I'm here," he said, frowning. The alternative was not getting to be with her at all, so in the end he had no choice. All he could say was "I agree to your terms" and then listen to the sound of Daphne's sigh.

"Okay," she replied. "Okay. Good."

"We're officially dating."

"We're taking things slow."

"We're banging each other's brains out."

"Flint!"

He laughed, wishing he could see her face. He'd bet her flush went all the way from her cheeks down to her neck. "We're taking things slow," he said, conceding.

"This is a terrible idea."

"It's only a few weeks."

"A lot can happen in a few weeks," she replied, sounding glum.

"That's true," Calvin replied, hoping she didn't hear the eager note in his voice.

"Well. I'm going to bed. Nice doing business with you."

"Same—"

Calvin pulled the phone away from his ear, clicking his tongue when he confirmed that she'd already hung up the call. He tossed his phone aside and exhaled, scrubbing his palms over his face until the image of Daphne's blush had dissolved from his mind.

He was officially fake dating the woman he was already half in love with. And she was right about one thing.

It was a terrible idea.

CHAPTER 14

Concealed on three sides by a vinyl booth, Daphne leaned over her coffee at the Sunrise Diner and met her grandmother's gaze. Greta sat to Daphne's left, and Harry was beside Grandma Mabel. The three older ladies considered Daphne's announcement, but they said nothing.

"So when you said nothing was going on between you and the sheriff . . ." Grandma Mabel's brows lifted.

"I may have overstated the case," Daphne admitted.

She'd thought about this long and hard last night, and decided that she'd tell her grandmother her plan to get the pot back. She'd hemmed and hawed with herself about how to explain the chain reaction that had led to Flint inviting her to his mother's event, and she decided that partial truths were the way forward.

The three dragons sitting with her would gobble up any hint of gossip about the arrangement with Flint being fake. If they were going to survive the next month without anyone finding out—and keeping Daphne's plan alive to retrieve the Dutch oven—she'd have to lie at least a little.

If she told her family the whole truth, there was no telling how they'd spin the story when they inevitably let it spill. She'd been telling Flint the truth on the phone; the simplest solution was for Daphne to admit that the rumors were true. Denial would only fuel them further. Besides, she really did want an easy out. Being back on the island made her feel twitchy.

"He asked me to go with him to his mother's vow renewal," she explained, "but nothing serious is going on between us. We're, um . . . you know. Taking things slow."

Flint's words played on a loop in her mind. *Banging each other's brains out. Banging each other's brains out. Banging each other's brains out.*

Judging by the interested gleam in the three old ladies' gazes, that same loop was playing in their minds too.

Keeping her cringe contained, Daphne dipped her chin. No going back now.

"So you've secretly been dating for weeks?" Greta asked, frowning. Across from her, Harry leaned forward to listen.

Daphne shook her head. "No. When he stopped me on my way back from the party at my parents' place, we reconnected."

"I bet you did," Grandma Mabel cut in, and Daphne shot her a glare.

"Nothing exciting is going on," Daphne clarified.

"Did you see the way they were looking at each other?" Harry scoffed, looking at Mabel. "There's a lot of something going on."

"Amen," Greta put in.

It was time to get this conversation back on track. "Anyway. I think this vow renewal might give me a chance to get your pot back, Grandma. I haven't told Flint about it, obviously. But if the pot still exists, it'll probably be at his mother's house."

The words hung between them. Grandma Mabel's brows furrowed deeply as she studied Daphne.

Certainty settled over Daphne. Her grandmother was going to tell her that she shouldn't do something so stupid. She would remind Daphne that she was the good, responsible daughter, and she ought to know better than to come up with some harebrained scheme about getting an old cast-iron pot back. It was a silly idea that would almost certainly end in her humiliation.

She wasn't brash the way Ellie was. She wasn't the type of person who could pull this off.

A heavy weight sat in the pit of Daphne's stomach as she waited for her grandmother to speak.

Of course it was a stupid idea. Of course she should know better. She needed to keep her head down, focus on work, and get her life back on track. So what if her engagement had ended in the most mortifying way possible? It didn't mean she had to change her entire personality. She'd already been punched in the face and tackled, and she'd only just moved back to Fernley. Daphne needed to return to herself. The safe, responsible woman who went to work, meal prepped, and checked her retirement projections on a weekly basis.

That Daphne hadn't needed to prove herself to anyone.

Then again, that Daphne had been told she was boring and worthless and not wife material. She'd been laid off and kicked out of her home. What did that Daphne *actually* know, other than the wonders of compound interest?

Something had changed. She'd felt it the moment Calvin Flint had pulled her over the night of her parents' party. Daphne was so *sick* of making herself small, of living her life between the lines.

She wanted more.

Was this a silly way of achieving it? Probably. But it felt right. She could do something for her family, prove to them—and herself—that she wasn't just a boring, studious accountant. She wasn't just Good Girl Daphne. She was a Davis.

As if Grandma Mabel could hear her thoughts, the older woman gave Daphne a decisive nod. "If we've learned one thing from your sister's escapades," she proclaimed, "it's that you need a getaway driver. Greta?"

"I'm in," the other woman said, lifting her white ceramic mug.

"I guess that means I need to RSVP yes to this vow renewal," Harry grumbled, then raised her own mug to meet Daphne's gaze. "You'll need an inside woman."

"You're invited?"

"Archie Yarrow—the happy husband celebrating a decade of married bliss, that is, not the twerp calling himself our mayor—was my late husband's son-in-law," Harry explained. "We send each other invitations to events, knowing the other will refuse."

"Until today," Grandma Mabel cut in, cackling. "I'll be your second-in-command." She nodded to Daphne's cup; then the four of them clinked their mugs to seal their pact.

"This is going to be fun," Greta announced. "The accident the other day gave me such a buzz. Wrenching the wheel. The crash of the corner store windows behind us. That turkey running at Daphne and tackling her to the ground." The old woman shivered, a dreamy smile on her lips. "I haven't felt that good since my wedding night."

"Thrilling," Mabel agreed.

"Makes me feel like I'm sixty again," Greta added.

Daphne had no idea what she'd just unleashed. This might have been her worst idea yet. Actually, she could almost guarantee it.

And for the first time in her life, the fact that it was impulsive and silly and likely to end in disaster actually made her want to do it more.

"We need a plan," Mabel said, digging through her purse for a pen as Greta pushed a napkin toward her. "Does anyone know the layout of the house?"

"No. But we could break in under the cover of darkness and case the joint," Harry suggested.

Daphne jerked, gaze snapping to the silver-haired ball of fury across from her. This was getting out of hand, and it'd only been a few minutes. Daphne cleared her throat. "Grandma, we don't even know if that old pot still exists. Eileen would have moved houses at least a few times in the past thirty-odd years, and who's to say she kept it when her mother passed? Maybe we should confirm the pot's there in the first place."

"Brenda used to gloat about that pot every time we got together," Harry said, lips curling into a snarl. "Eileen would join in. I bet she kept it as a trophy."

This was sounding less and less like a good idea the longer Daphne sat there. Her big self-affirming plan to Do Something Stupid might *actually* be really, really stupid. Maybe she was still buzzed from last night. "A trophy? Like a serial killer?"

"It really did make the best, crustiest bread," Greta added. "I think it's worth the risk. Besides, Mabel, it's your mother's pot. It should be in your family."

"It's an heirloom," Harry agreed, putting her mug of coffee down with a decisive clink.

Most families had valuable jewels and precious wedding dresses as heirlooms. Daphne's family had a pot. She rubbed her temples.

"We'll work on the assumption that the pot still exists, and that it's in the Yarrows' kitchen," Grandma Mabel said, and the other ladies nodded.

"Let's drive over there now," Greta suggested. "Maybe we can get the lay of the land and come up with a preliminary plan."

"Wait—"

Daphne's protest was lost in the shuffle of the three women gathering their things, leaving cash on the table, and then shuffling out of the booth. She had no choice but to follow. The alternative was letting three insane women loose on Eileen Yarrow's house without supervision.

Despite her hesitations, as she slid into the back seat behind Greta in the driver's seat, a little bud of excitement was blooming in the pit of her stomach. She felt the same way she had when she'd gathered the documents to go talk to Jerry Barela. As if finally, for the first time in her life, Daphne was making a decision that hadn't been set out before her based on what she should do. She was doing something because she wanted to, because she was capable. Because she was brave, or stupid, or both.

And that felt good.

Greta drove them out to the southeastern point of the island. Fernley National Park took up most of the eastern shore, and abutting it was one of the wealthier neighborhoods on the island. Ellie's ex-fiancé had lived there before he went to jail. Lionel did as well, but not because he was wealthy. He'd refused every offer to sell his place by developers and wealthy buyers, no matter how much the elite grumbled about his rickety marina and tiny overgrown property.

The houses got bigger and farther apart from each other as they drove through the area, with stone fences and wrought iron gates encircling manicured yards. Tall, mature trees lined the roads, with patches of forest still surviving between the streets and developments.

"Archie bought the old brick place on Seaview," Harry said, pointing right when they came to a four-way stop. Greta nodded and took the turn. "He tore it down and built a monstrous home. I'm sure that vow renewal is a way for him to show off his new mansion."

They drove down a road that curved along the coastline, with long drives leading to big houses on either side. The hillside was steep here, with the big homes nestled in the trees to overlook the Salish Sea and the mainland coastline in the distance.

Harry pointed to a house on the high side of the street that had an A-frame front with massive windows. The roof was clad in cedar shingles, the front siding a beautiful dark green. It didn't look monstrous to Daphne. It looked beautiful.

"That's it," Harry said. "Park here."

Greta wrenched the steering wheel, jumping the curb as she parked. Daphne pinched her lips and decided it wasn't the right time to make comments about her suitability as a getaway driver.

They sat in the car and looked at the big house.

"Now what?" Daphne asked.

"Now we wait," Harry said.

"Wait for what?"

Grandma Mabel, who was in the back seat with Daphne, glanced over. "We're casing the place, honey. We wait to see whatever we can see. Who goes in and out. How many staff members they have. What cars they drive. Who's visiting. That kind of thing."

Daphne blinked. "Do you . . . do this often?"

"Not *often*," Greta said, wiping her glasses on her shirt before sliding them back on, which answered precisely nothing.

Daphne had just opened her mouth to prod the ladies once more about their extracurricular activities when the gates to the Yarrow mansion swung open, and a familiar truck drove out and turned onto the street.

A breath gasped out of Daphne's lips. She tried to slouch down in her seat and choked herself on her seat belt. The three older ladies, oblivious to her panic, stared at Flint's truck while making no attempt to conceal themselves.

"Go!" Daphne choked out. "Go!"

"Go where, honey?" Mabel asked, leaning over to get a better look at the truck.

"Go somewhere! Away! Not here!"

The truck approached their position. Was it Daphne's imagination, or did it slow down?

No. Not her imagination.

The truck stopped.

"Uh-oh," said Harry.

The driver's door opened, and a booted foot landed on the pavement.

"Might be time to skedaddle," Mabel pointed out.

"You know, I think I agree with you," Greta said, and reached for the ignition.

Calvin Flint took a step toward them, his gaze flicking from the damaged front bumper of Greta's car to the windows, where he could definitely see the four of them staring at him with wide eyes.

"Hang on, ladies," Greta said, and she slammed on the accelerator. The smell of burnt rubber filled the air as their wheels spun on the pavement; then Greta's old beige Honda was off like a shot down the quiet residential street.

CHAPTER 15

"Who's that?" Ceecee asked, her face stuck between the two front seats as she looked through the rear window.

"I'm not sure," Calvin replied, but he had a fair idea. He buckled himself in and checked on his sister. "Face the front, Ceecee. We'll go see what they wanted."

"A car chase?" Her face lit up as she bounced on the seat.

"Something like that," he said, and swung the truck around to follow Greta's Honda. He could have sworn Daphne had been sitting in the back seat. But what would she be doing outside his mother's house?

"They went that way," his little sister said, pointing. "I saw them turn."

"Good work, kiddo," Calvin said, taking the turn. The Honda's taillights turned in the distance. They were heading toward town.

"Catch them!" his little sister urged, one hand gripping the door, the other curled around the edge of her seat. "This is way better than the movies."

Calvin hummed and followed the road, though he'd lost sight of the other car. "You don't mind doing this? We can still go to the movies."

"No way," his sister said. "I want to see why they were spying on us."

"We don't know that they were spying," he said, but his eyes narrowed. He was pretty sure Daphne *had* been spying on him, along with her grandmother and company. Had they followed him to the house? Why?

Heart thumping, Calvin turned toward Carlisle. He grimaced when there was no sight of Greta's car. Ceecee looked around, peering down every cross street, her feet kicking as she did.

"You see them?" he asked.

"No. They got away." Her eyes were wide as she glanced over at him, disappointment clearly written on her face. "What are we going to do?"

Calvin pulled in to the side of the road and turned to his sister. "Well, that's up to you," he said. "Today's our hangout day, so you get to decide. We can still make the movie, then have dinner and ice cream like we planned. Or we can drive around and try to find them."

"Drive around and try to find them!"

He bit back a smile. "Okay, but Ceecee, you have to do as I say. If you're riding along with me, it means you listen when I tell you to do something."

"I will. I promise." She gave him a huge smile. Her two front teeth had a gap between them, and her cheeks were full and rosy. She was a cute kid, and she lit up when he made time for her.

This was why he was on Fernley Island. That smile. That little girl, who deserved so much better than what he'd had.

Calvin's heart gave a thud. When he'd rung the doorbell at his mother's house, he'd shifted his weight from foot to foot and tried to ignore his discomfort. His mother had answered the door, and her face lit up with hope that she'd quickly tried to hide. She'd led him to Ceecee's room, which was clean and full of toys. Nothing like his room had been at nine years old.

Ceecee had run over to give him a hug, then wrapped her arms around her mother's middle while Eileen bent down to press a kiss to Ceecee's head. They'd seemed like a perfect mother-daughter pair. Calvin's heart gave a lurch, and a strange mix of longing and jealousy had moved through him.

But what if it was a lie? An act? What if, under the surface, Ceecee was going through what Calvin had endured?

If so, Calvin knew that even though she lived in a bigger house, with nicer clothes and new shoes anytime she needed them, his little sister would be alone. She'd be learning that the adults in her life didn't care enough to get to know her. Didn't care enough to listen to her, to spend time with her. Soon she'd be a teenager, and the hurt growing under the surface would turn to anger. Anger would turn to self-destruction.

He knew, because he'd been through it.

He couldn't let that happen.

If he'd had one person—just *one* person—show him the kind of attention he'd needed, Calvin wondered if he would've struggled the way he had. He had his first drop of alcohol at fourteen years old. By eighteen, he was a drunk. It took three more years to clean himself up, and those were the hardest three years of his life. He had to feel all the pain he'd numbed for his entire existence. Had to take stock and decide to be better.

Ceecee wouldn't go through what he'd gone through. He couldn't let it happen.

So, as he met his little sister's glittering gaze, he knew that he'd give her anything she wanted as long as it put a smile on her face and saved her from the kind of pain he'd experienced. Even going after a bunch of old women and Daphne to question them about their loitering outside his mother's house.

"Pinkie swear," he said, sticking out his finger. Ceecee grinned at him and hooked her pinkie around his. They shook, and Calvin repeated: "You do what I say. No complaining."

"No complaining," she vowed, and Calvin's eyes narrowed when she didn't repeat the first part of the promise.

"If I tell you to stay in the car, you stay in the car."

"I promise."

They kept their pinkies hooked around each other, and Calvin met her eyes. "Let's go find them."

Ceecee let out a squeal and clapped her hands, then slapped them against her mouth, then let out another squeak. He laughed, easing back out onto the road as he made his way to Daphne's street.

If it had been anyone but Daphne and her insane grandmother's group of friends, he would've called it in and gotten someone on duty to check it out. But after what had happened the night before at Mickey's, Calvin wasn't going to let anyone else question the woman he had in his sights.

Daphne was his, whether she knew it or not.

As he parked outside Daphne's apartment, he glanced up at the building. He wasn't sure which window belonged to her, so he got out, gave Ceecee a stern look, and told her to stay in the car, and then went to ring Daphne's buzzer.

No one answered the intercom, but he did hear the whir of a car window going down. Turning, he watched Ceecee's face take on angelic innocence through the opening as she said, "I'm still in the car."

He gave her a flat look and turned around before his smile gave him away. Little rascal. After buzzing again, he waited, then pulled his phone out and called her. He wandered over to the passenger side of his truck and tweaked Ceecee's nose as the phone rang. His sister squeaked and jerked back, then let out a laugh.

Then Daphne answered. "Hello?"

Calvin straightened. "You home?" He turned to study the building again.

"I—what?"

"Are you at home?"

"No. Why?"

"I wanted to talk to you about something."

"What's that?"

"Just a question I had," he said. "I'm at your place."

"I'm not home," she answered. "I'm busy."

Frowning when he heard a voice in the background that sounded older and female, Calvin grunted and headed for the driver's door of his truck. "Busy sitting outside my mother's house in a car with your grandmother and her friends?"

"What?" Daphne's voice went up two octaves. "I have no idea what you're talking about."

She was a terrible liar. "You're a terrible liar."

"Oh, you're breaking up. I gotta go!" And the line went dead.

Ceecee was staring at him, eyes wide. "Who was that?"

"She was sitting in the back seat of that car."

"Who is it?"

"Daphne Davis," Calvin replied through clenched teeth.

"Oh, your girlfriend!"

Turning to meet his sister's gaze, Calvin frowned. "What?"

"Mom was soooooo shocked when she heard. But then she got all happy because she said you were settling down. And then she tried to play it cool, but I could tell she was all over the place."

"What does 'all over the place' mean?"

"She asked me if I wanted a snack like seventeen million times."

Calvin huffed. It didn't sound like the mother he'd grown up with, but what did he know?

"Is she really your girlfriend?"

"Who?"

"Daphne. Is that why she was spying on you? She wanted to see what you were up to."

"No," Calvin replied, then paused. He didn't know what Daphne had been doing. "It's complicated."

"Are you in love with her?"

"What? Why are you asking me this?" He drove down the street and turned toward one of the main arteries through town. Where would they have gone? Mabel's house, or one of the other two?

"It's just that usually, people date people they love."

"Not always."

"So you don't love her?"

"I—Ceecee, drop it, okay?"

"Mom said Jenna Deacon had been asking about you, but she was happy you'd been telling the truth about having a date."

"Of course I was telling the truth," Calvin grumbled, even though he hadn't been. "Did she not think I could find a date on my own? And what do you mean, Jenna Deacon was asking about me?"

Ceecee shrugged. "I dunno. That's just what she said." She kept her eyes peeled, scanning the road around them. "Where do you think they went?"

"They're not criminal masterminds, and the island isn't that big, so I think we can find out." He pressed a few buttons on the console until his phone rang through the system to connect to the station.

Teri answered on the second ring. "Sheriff?"

"You know Daphne's grandmother and her two friends?"

"Sure," Teri answered.

"Where do they live?"

"Mabel lives up on the north end with Claude and Helen Davis. Harry and Greta are neighbors. They share a duplex on Fourteenth Street."

"You know the addresses?"

"I'll find 'em," she said. "Something wrong?"

"No, just checking up on them."

"Roger," the woman said. "I'll send the addresses through shortly."

Calvin waited for Teri's message as he headed toward Fourteenth Street. Once the address came through, he parked in the duplex's leftmost drive, gave Ceecee a stern look as she lowered the window with an impish look on her face, then headed up the path to knock on the door.

There was no answer on either side of the duplex. A neighbor poked her head out.

"Something wrong, Sheriff?"

"I'm looking for Greta and Harry," he called over the hedge.

"Haven't seen either of them since this morning. They were heading to the Sunrise Diner for breakfast."

And after breakfast, they'd hung around his mother's house. Which meant there was only one more place they could be.

"Thanks," he said, and got back in his truck.

"We're heading to the north end?" Ceecee asked, following the direction of Calvin's thoughts.

He reversed out of the driveway. "We're heading to the north end," he confirmed.

"This is so much fun," Ceecee proclaimed. "But what if they're not at Mabel's house? Where will we go?"

"We'll do exactly what they were trying to do to us, kid," he said, grinning. "Stake 'em out and wait until we get some answers."

CHAPTER 16

Daphne's head ached. As they pulled up outside her parents' house, she barely heard the chatter from the three older ladies as she unclipped her seat belt and slid out of the car.

What a pointless exercise that stakeout had been. All she'd accomplished was being found out by the one man who couldn't know anything about this stupid scheme.

She'd be better off sticking to accounting. Clearly Daphne wasn't cut out for the high-risk lifestyle of stealing back decades-old cast-iron pots with the help of three geriatrics of dubious sanity.

"We'll have to go again and get a look at the backyard. I wonder if they have cameras," Mabel mused as she made her way to the door. "Do we know any hackers?"

"They definitely have cameras," Harry said, thumping after Mabel onto the porch. "Rich people love cameras."

"Maybe we can find a hacker on the dark web," Greta suggested. "My granddaughter said that's where all the criminals hang out."

Daphne rolled her eyes up to the sky and prayed for patience. "We don't need to hack any cameras," she said. "I just need to get in there, find an excuse to wander away from the party, and then look through the cupboards until I find the pot."

"That's a terrible plan, honey," Mabel said. "What if they have caterers? You'll never get access to the kitchen cupboards."

"But a hacker will?"

"What will you do with the pot once you find it?" Grandma Mabel asked, pushing the door open with her hip. She stood in the doorway and met Daphne's gaze. "Huh?"

Daphne put her hands on her hips. "I'll throw it over the fence and retrieve it after everyone leaves. You said it yourself: the thing was indestructible."

"The event will probably be at least partially held in the backyard, depending on the weather," Greta pointed out. "You don't think people will find it weird that you're tossing cookware around?"

"I'm starting to think this is a bad idea altogether," Daphne said. "We still haven't established whether or not the thing exists."

"What we need," Harry proclaimed, "is a distraction. Can your granddaughter get us any explosives on the dark web?"

Greta pursed her lips as she set her bag down on the coffee table as they all made it into the living room. "I can ask—"

"No explosives," Daphne said, slicing her hand through the air. "No more stakeouts. No hackers. This whole thing has gotten out of control, and we haven't even done anything."

"Don't lose your nerve because of one little car chase," Grandma Mabel chided, coming back into the living room from the kitchen with a tray laden with mugs and fixings for coffee. In the kitchen, the coffee machine gurgled.

"Wasn't much of a car chase," Greta added. "I lost him within two minutes."

"Doesn't say much about the Fernley County Sheriff's Department, does it?" Harry said, getting her mug ready.

Daphne dropped into the ancient couch that had been a fixture of her parents' living room since before she was born. She rubbed her temples and wondered where it had all gone wrong.

"Were you in a car chase, Mom?" Helen wandered into the living room on her way to the kitchen. She reappeared a couple of minutes later with a glass of water and the coffeepot, her brows drawn. "And you had Daphne with you?"

Coffee sloshed into waiting mugs while Helen shot her mother a long look.

"Daphne is more than capable of handling herself," Mabel said, which, oddly, made Daphne's chest warm. She didn't exactly agree that she was cut out for car chases and covert operations, but it was nice to get a vote of confidence from her grandmother anyway.

"Who was chasing you?"

"Sheriff Flint," Harry replied with a click of her tongue. "Big ole truck and no clue how to handle it."

"Typical," Greta supplied, shaking her head.

"You can say that again," Mabel agreed, lifting her mug. "If I had a nickel . . ."

The three ladies chortled, and Daphne exchanged a glance with her mother. Helen gave her a sympathetic look. Daphne took a deep breath and went through her mental filing cabinet full of excuses she used to get out of social engagements. Today, she'd use Old Faithful, because no one ever seemed to question an accountant who wanted to get back to her precious numbers: "Well, I've got a bunch of work to catch up on, so—"

Outside, the sound of an engine drew closer before cutting off. All eyes turned toward the noise. Her mom's car had been parked in front of the house when they'd come up, and Daphne didn't immediately recognize the noise of this particular engine. Too loud for Ellie's. Didn't have that rattle her dad's car had.

There was something familiar about it, though . . .

She clutched the arm of the couch as her eyes went wide. "Oh, crap."

CHAPTER 17

Ceecee unclipped her seat belt and gave Calvin a determined scowl. "I don't want to stay in the car. I want to question the suspects."

He sighed as he looked at her, then at the house in front of which they'd parked. The little beige Honda was parked next to two other old cars, its dented front bumper confirming it was Greta's. Beyond the house, a few sheep grazed in a pasture ringed with trees. It was quiet here, with few cars driving past and neighbors far enough away that the house seemed to stand alone.

The Davises were good people. But he needed to keep his sister safe.

"Stay in the car," he said, "until I tell you it's okay to come out."

Her eyes narrowed. "Fine."

After getting out of the truck, he squared his shoulders and faced the front door. His shoes echoed on the wooden porch steps as he approached, keeping his ears open for any strange noises. All he heard was the distant calls of seabirds and the rustle of the wind in the trees. He rang the doorbell.

Footsteps approached. A lock scraped. The door opened, and Helen Davis stood on the other side. "Sheriff!" she exclaimed. "What a pleasant surprise." Her eyes slid past him, and she smiled wider. "And who's this?"

"I'm Cecilia, but you can call me Ceecee," the girl said, coming up beside Calvin as she stuck her hand out to shake Helen's. "Pleased to meet you."

"Pleased to meet you too, Ceecee," Helen replied, eyes sliding back to Calvin, who tried to hide his frustration.

He looked down at his sister. "I told you to stay in the car."

She just shrugged and stayed right where she stood. "I think I'll be more useful if I can be there for the interrogation."

Helen tilted her head and met Calvin's gaze.

Calvin rolled his lips inward and released a breath through his nose. Glancing at his sister, he considered ordering her back. But her eyes were bright, and he was a sucker for that little smile at the corner of her lips. Besides, he trusted Daphne. He just wanted to know why she'd been parked outside his mother's house.

He turned back to Helen. "I'm looking for the owner of that vehicle," he said, pointing to the getaway car. "May I come in?"

Helen pursed her lips and stepped aside. "They're in the living room," she said in a tone of voice that said she wasn't surprised, and closed the door behind him.

The house was worn but tidy, with evidence of many years of happy memories. Family pictures hung on the walls, threadbare rugs covered the floors, and a sense of calm permeated every room. Calvin slowed at the sight of Daphne's high school graduation picture hanging in the hallway, right next to Ellie's. He'd never sat for his photos; there hadn't been any point, when no one cared about his graduation, least of all him. Daphne beamed at him from the nineteen-year-old photo, as straight backed and determined as she was now.

Ceecee's head was on a swivel as her hand found her way into his. When they got to the end of the hall and turned into the living room, she shimmied closer to him so her body was pressed to his side.

"Greta," Helen said, "Sheriff Flint wants to talk to you about your car."

Three elderly ladies were sitting around the coffee table along with Daphne. A board game was set up before them, with coffee mugs on coasters in front of every player. All the mugs looked nearly full; the women hadn't been here for long. But Calvin already knew that.

Daphne glanced up and met his gaze, blinking innocently. "Flint?"

One of the ladies shifted to look at him, adjusting her bifocal glasses on her nose. "My car? What about my car? The tags are all up to date, and it's definitely roadworthy."

Calvin pursed his lips. "I want to know why it was parked outside my mother's house half an hour ago."

"Well, I never!" Daphne's grandmother said. "Outside your mother's house? Greta's car?"

"You're mistaken, Sheriff Flint," the third old lady said. "We've been playing Monopoly all day."

His gaze shifted to the property cards in front of her, half of which were upside down. When he looked at Daphne, her cheeks were bright red. He held her gaze as he asked, "Are you aware it's a crime to lie to an officer of the law?"

"Lying?" Greta exclaimed, grabbing the dice and rolling them. "Don't be ridiculous! Monopoly is a classic, and it's right here in front of us. And Saturday is for board games."

"You're going around the board the wrong way," Ceecee piped up to say, pointing at the way Greta's silver top hat was moving along the squares.

Greta made a big show of adjusting her glasses, then laughed and started moving the other direction. Calvin arched a brow at Daphne.

It took her about three seconds to crack. "I told them about the vow renewal," she said. "It was my grandmother's idea to go check out the house."

"We were curious," Mabel said, picking up her coffee.

"Wait," Ceecee said, dropping his palm to put her hands on her hips. "*This* is your girlfriend?"

"No," he and Daphne replied in unison.

Daphne forced a smile. "We're taking things slow."

Ceecee ignored them as she took a step forward and squinted at Daphne. She tilted her head. "She's pretty."

Daphne blinked. "Who are you?"

"This is my little sister," Calvin cut in. "Ceecee, this is Daphne."

"Are you in love with my brother?" Ceecee asked.

"No," Daphne replied, a little more vehemently than seemed strictly necessary.

"Then why are you dating him?"

"We're not—" She exhaled sharply. "Look. We work together. We're taking things slow." She repeated the last sentence like it was her lifeline. Calvin arched a brow, and Daphne scowled at him.

Ceecee hummed. "But you're going to my mom's vow renewal together. That's a date. So you're dating. That means you're girlfriend/boyfriend. That's how it works."

There was a silence. Daphne's jaw worked as she frowned at Ceecee, then flicked her inscrutable gaze to Calvin. "Right," she said.

Despite himself, Calvin's heart gave a heavy thump. "Can't argue with that logic."

Daphne's brows nudged ever so slightly toward each other. Then she smiled at Ceecee. "Your brother seemed a little desperate for a date. I was trying to be nice."

Calvin snorted.

"I'm glad you're coming," Ceecee announced. "Otherwise, Calvin will be alone, and that's embarrassing."

"That's true," Mabel agreed. "That would be embarrassing."

Calvin needed to get this interrogation back on track. His eyes narrowed on Daphne's. "Why did you speed off when I spotted you, if all you were doing was satisfying your curiosity?"

"We panicked," Greta said.

"*You* panicked," the third old lady said. "I was fine."

"Why did you panic?" Calvin asked.

Greta blinked at him until Mabel said, "You're a cop. Panicking when you're doing nothing wrong in front of a cop is normal, no?"

Calvin tilted his head. "Well . . ."

"Here we go!" Helen came gliding into the living room with a tray laden with snacks. "Daphne, scoot over so the sheriff can have a seat beside you. Ceecee, darling, do you want a drink? We have orange juice or water. I have sparkling water too, so we could do a fizzy orange juice drink with a funky straw, if you want."

Ceecee brightened. "Really?"

"Come pick your straw," Helen said, and Ceecee was off like a shot. Calvin almost called her back, but he heard her excited chatter through the kitchen doorway along with Helen's kind responses, and he didn't have the heart to drag her away.

That kind of motherly attention was exactly what Ceecee deserved. It was what had made him so horribly jealous of Daphne when they'd been in school together, and he could now sit back and let his sister enjoy the attention, at least. Helen had been the school nurse, so she was used to dealing with kids. Ceecee would be fine with her for a few minutes.

It would give him time to figure out what the hell kind of game Daphne was playing. Suddenly her reasoning during their phone call last night seemed a little suspect. Why *had* she agreed to attend the vow renewal with him?

Calvin took a deep breath and shuffled between the coffee table and the couch to take a seat next to Daphne. The three ladies before them looked at the two of them, big smiles on their wrinkled faces.

"Daphne's father loves to bake," Mabel said all of a sudden, picking up a slice of bread from the platter Helen had put down. She smeared a healthy layer of herbed cream cheese over it, then met Calvin's gaze. "Does your mother like to bake, Sheriff?"

"Huh?" He frowned. "Um. No, not really. Not that I know of, anyway. We haven't been that close since I moved off-island."

"Hmm," Greta said. "That's interesting."

"What about your grandmother?" the third woman asked, fingers drumming on the top of her butterfly-patterned cane. "Did your grandmother like to bake?"

There was a pointed pause. Beside him, Daphne put her elbows on her knees and massaged her forehead. A long sigh slipped through her lips.

Calvin cleared his throat. "Yeah, she did. She used to have fresh homemade bread whenever we'd go over to visit on the weekends." She'd passed when he was young, just a year after his father had passed, and most of the good memories of his childhood had died with the two of them. After his grandmother's death, there hadn't been anyone around who seemed to care about him. His mother did her best to move on, and Calvin was left to deal with his grief on his own.

The three older ladies let out interested hums and leaned back in their seats, watching him with piercing eyes.

"Why do you ask?" He nodded his thanks as Greta pushed the platter of snacks closer so he could grab a cracker and a slice of aged cheddar.

"I knew your grandmother, you know," Mabel said, voice casual. "I remember she had a beautiful cast-iron Dutch oven that was her pride and joy. She used it to make the crustiest, most wonderful bread I'd ever tasted."

"Perfect crumb," Greta added with a solemn nod.

"It was okay," the third lady grumbled.

"Harry," Mabel chided. "Please. The bread was perfect."

"Oh, all right. It was delicious," Harry replied, scowling at Calvin like he'd personally offended her.

"We all wished we had a pot like Brenda's," Mabel said, folding her hands on her knee as she smiled beatifically.

Daphne was very still beside him. When he glanced over, she was giving her grandmother a strangely intense look. What kind of madness had he stepped into? Were all Daphne's family members this weird? And he still didn't quite buy their explanation for why they'd been staked out in front of his mother's house. At a stretch, he could buy that they were curious about the event venue. But that wouldn't justify them speeding off as soon as they'd spotted him. They'd panicked, according to Greta and Mabel. But these were women who had egged Daphne on when she'd attacked a thief at the farmers' market. Women who hadn't been shy about taunting Bobby Troy about his precious truck in front of the entire sheriff's department. They didn't get nervous in front of law enforcement. They certainly didn't panic.

"So?" Mabel asked, smiling encouragingly. "Do you remember the pot?"

"Uh, maybe," he said, frowning. "Actually, yes. A sort of ugly thing, right? And horribly heavy."

Mabel let out a noise that might have been one of outrage. Calvin frowned as Harry reached over and put a hand on her arm, as if to hold the other woman back. There was something going on here, but Calvin couldn't quite figure out what it was. His instincts were screaming at him. These women were digging for something. They'd been watching his mother's house, and now they were trying to get information from him.

But what? It couldn't be about an old pot. Had they been wanting to rob the house? But Daphne would never do that, and these ladies didn't look like they could move fast enough to commit a burglary. Stranger things had happened, though . . .

His mind whirled. Daphne understood what the ladies were asking about, and she wanted them to stop. That was evident by the tightness of her shoulders and the way her lips were pinched into a bloodless line. That only happened when she was trying to hold herself back from saying something she'd regret. He knew, because that was the expression she had on her face whenever Calvin was doing his best to needle her into a reaction.

So she felt strongly about this—whatever "this" was. And Calvin was on the outside, scrambling to figure it out.

He decided to play along and give them a little crumb of information to see how they'd react. "I think my mother brought that pot home when we cleared out my grandmother's house," he said, "but I'm not sure what became of it. She's a bit of a pack rat, so I wouldn't be surprised if she still has it stashed somewhere."

The older ladies—and Daphne, strangely—inhaled so sharply they sucked nearly all the air out of the room.

Calvin frowned.

It was Mabel who recovered first. She smiled at him and said, "Well, isn't that wonderful? I love a good pack rat. Say hi to your mother for me, won't you? And Daphne was just telling us how excited she was to be able to go to her vow renewal. I heard it's going to be a beautiful ceremony."

"Was she?" Calvin mused, turning to meet Daphne's gaze. "How excited are you really, Cupcake?"

She leaned back against the couch, closed her eyes, and pinched the bridge of her nose like she was one second away from giving up on life, finding an uninhabited island away from everyone she knew, and becoming a hermit. She opened her eyes and met his gaze unblinkingly. "I'm thrilled," she told him. "Can't wait."

His smile was sharp. "That makes two of us."

"You'll need a dress," Mabel said. "What's the dress code?"

"Cocktail," Calvin answered, eyes still on Daphne. Her cheeks were flushed. He wondered what color her bra was today.

"I have a dress," Daphne said, tearing her gaze away from his to look at her grandmother.

"Good. That's settled," Mabel said, and there was something in her demeanor that made Calvin's instincts sit up and take notice. A note of triumph in her tone, or maybe a gleam in her eyes.

Something was definitely going on here. Daphne hadn't agreed to go with him out of the goodness of her heart, and he wasn't sure it had anything to do with quieting down the island gossips. She might be looking to lay some groundwork for her future exit plan, but that didn't ring entirely true. There was something more.

Still, he couldn't help the feeling of satisfaction that was coursing through him. She'd agreed to come with him. Out of everyone on the island, he couldn't think of a better date. Even if she was hiding something from him.

To his left, the side door opened. All eyes turned to the woman who strode in. Ellie, Daphne's sister, dropped her purse and blew a raspberry, pushing her disheveled brown hair off her forehead. "You will *not* believe what just happened!" She crashed into a chair and regaled them with a story involving a run through the forest and a supposed cougar that turned out to be the neighbor's dog, and all the old ladies in the room hooted with laughter.

Beside Calvin, Daphne seemed to shrink into the couch. All the attention in the room had been sucked up by Ellie's entrance, but his eyes were drawn to the wrinkle in her brow and the way the sparkle had faded from her eyes. She listened to her sister's story, and something like sadness entered her expression.

She met Calvin's gaze when he nudged her with his shoulder.

"You still want to do this?" Calvin asked quietly.

"Do what?"

"You know what."

Her lips curled ever so slightly, but the sadness he'd caught hadn't quite left her eyes. "I don't know what I want anymore."

Calvin wondered what was making her look so down. He wondered why, exactly, she'd agreed to be his date. He wondered why her grandmother had questioned him so strangely. But mostly he wondered about whether Daphne was looking forward to their date, even the tiniest bit.

Before he could probe her for answers, Ceecee came back in the room with Helen. His little sister's voice was bright as she said, "At least my aunt Kathy will be happy that there's enough time for Daphne to learn the choreography. She started teaching it to Jenna Deacon, but Jenna was *really* bad, and Kathy was getting *super* frustrated. I had to go hide in my room for a while because I knew she was soooooo mad. And really, it's not that hard. Even a baby could learn the steps. I can help Daphne, but only if she's better than Jenna Deacon. I don't think anyone can help Jenna Deacon. She dances like a malfunctioning robot."

Calvin felt Daphne go still beside him, and his own muscles seized up. Brows tugging low over his eyes as he caught his little sister's gaze, he couldn't help the tightness of his voice as he asked, "What's this about choreography?"

STEP THREE: FAKE IT TILL YOU DATE IT

CHAPTER 18

Daphne sat in Flint's truck and glared at the wrought iron fence outside his mother's house. It was midmorning on a gorgeous sunny Sunday, and there were a million places she'd rather be than outside Eileen Yarrow's house with Calvin Flint at her side.

"We don't have to do this," the man beside her said.

She tore her gaze away from the fence and traced the line of his clean-shaven jaw, the little divot in his chin, the shape of his lips. When she met his eyes, she was surprised to find them soft and sincere. Sunlight lit half his face, highlighting the color of his irises.

It should've been illegal for a man to have such nice eyes.

"Look, coming with me is one thing," he continued, "but learning some ridiculous dance is another. I understand that. I'll get it if you want to back out."

"Stop being so nice to me," she said. "It's weird."

"You know what's weird?" he asked, leaning his head against the headrest.

"What?"

"Your grandmother, Cupcake. She's weird. What was all that about yesterday? Grilling me about some old pot?"

Daphne shifted uncomfortably in her seat and tried to affect a careless wave. "She was just reminiscing. She does that sometimes. And she's not weird, okay. She's wonderful."

"The two aren't mutually exclusive. Just look at you."

Her gaze cut to his, and he let out a laugh at whatever he saw written in her glare. Then his words sank in, and Daphne realized he'd called her wonderful. Pausing, Daphne tried to make sense of that strange new piece of information. What had he been thinking when that wave of self-pity washed over her as Ellie walked in and overshadowed her for the millionth time with a silly story about a dog? And why had it made her feel so unbearably special when he'd noticed her?

Flushing, Daphne reached for her door handle.

"Wait," Flint said, his hand dropping to her forearm. The heat of it sank through her jacket into her skin, and Daphne held back the shiver his touch caused.

"What?"

"Should we go over our story? Your family didn't exactly seem satisfied with your 'We're taking it slow' spiel."

"Don't worry about them. They think I'm moving on from my ex, and they're excited," Daphne said, rolling her eyes.

"You keep mentioning him," Flint noted, the corners of his eyes tightening slightly.

"Feeling threatened, Sheriff?" Daphne snorted. "Don't bother. We broke up nearly two years ago."

"Mm." He moved his hand from her forearm and rubbed his chin. "So what's our story?"

"'Story'?"

"We covered the traffic stop. But we should add some details for color. Our first date. What we like about each other. That kind of thing."

"We . . ." Daphne drifted off, frowning. "I can't think of anything I like about you."

Flint laughed, deep and sincere. He shook his head. "You never let up, do you?"

A little flame burst to life in Daphne's chest. She discovered she liked making him laugh. Licking her lips, she shrugged and said, "The closer we stick to the truth, the better."

His eyes were oddly intense. "Yeah," he said. "All right. I pulled you over for a traffic stop, and we reconnected after nineteen long, lonely years apart. There was a spark, and now we're here. We'll make up the rest as we go."

His words made Daphne strangely uncomfortable. They were a little too close to the truth. He was rewriting history in a way that made it sound like there was something real between them. But wasn't it better that way? They needed to convince people they were seeing each other for at least the next three weeks, since that's when the vow renewal would happen. And it wasn't like they could pretend nothing was going on after she'd flashed her bra at Rhonda Roberts the other day. They either had to commit to this, or Daphne had to forget about ever getting her grandmother's heirloom back.

"Right," she finally said, and reached for the door again. "Let's get this over with. Your sister better have been serious about helping me with the choreography. I'm an accountant, not a dancer."

"I'm banking on her helping both of us," he replied as they walked toward the gate, his shoulder brushing hers. There was a human-size gate beside the driveway, so they stepped through. Daphne followed Flint up the steps on the steeply graded front lawn to the entrance.

It was a gorgeous home, nestled in mature gardens that would soon begin to bud. Moss grew between the paving stone steps. The A-frame house had cedar shingles and huge windows, and Daphne could spy chunky timber furniture and tasteful artwork inside.

Then she banged into Flint's shoulder as he abruptly turned around to speak to her. The contact startled her, and she discovered she had cat-like reflexes, not because they were quick, but because the slight nudge of his shoulder against her chest had made her spring and stumble away from him like she'd been zapped by a high-voltage electrical cable.

Her heel sank into one of those mossy gaps in the pavers before catching on the edge of the stone. Daphne's arms windmilled as she yelped, the steep incline doing nothing to prevent her fall. And wasn't this just typical? She was going out on a limb to come here and be uncomfortable while she learned some ridiculous choreography for some woman she didn't even know, accompanied by a man she couldn't stand, all because she'd promised her grandmother to recover some heirloom that had probably been destroyed years ago.

Now she'd crack her head on stepping stones and roll down the hill like the uncoordinated clown she was.

Except that's not what happened.

A strong arm banded across her back and tugged her forward until she crashed against a broad, warm chest. Flint wrapped his other arm around her upper back while her own hands came to curl in his shirt, her breasts pressed against his pecs, her breaths sawing in and out of her lungs.

He held her close, his cheek at her temple. Warm breath coasted over the shell of her ear as he exhaled. "You okay?"

His scent was everywhere, and Daphne realized she was trembling. It wasn't right that someone so annoying should feel this good with his arms wrapped around her. His shirt was soft against her cheek, and the tip of her nose nudged against his neck.

Flint's hands spread out over her back so she could feel the heat of his palms through her jacket.

Her heart rattled. Some kind of temporary madness overtook her, because Daphne made no move to extricate herself from his hold. And it was a *hold*. He kept her pressed against the length of him, both arms keeping her right where she was. The whole world narrowed to just him. The scent of his skin. The stubble already roughening his jaw as his head dipped slightly. The heat of him. The strength of his arms around her.

It felt so good that Daphne lost herself for a moment, clinging to his shirt, little micro movements bringing them impossibly closer together. Her fingers unclenched and spread out over his shoulders. His head dipped so his lips were near her cheek. Tight bands encased Daphne's chest, making it hard to breathe as she shifted, her own lips brushing his jaw.

Kissing him would be ridiculous. They worked together. They were pretending. She hated him, mostly. She wasn't even attracted to him, other than those weird moments when she was. Like right now, for example.

The arm he held tight to her lower back shifted, and the tips of his fingers dipped beneath the hemline of her jacket and shirt at her side. The contact of his skin against hers made an exhale rush out of her, and she shifted her head to meet his gaze. Their lips were an inch apart.

"Daphne," he rasped, and his hand slipped fully under her top so his whole palm was pressed to her side. Heat blazed through her core, which was ridiculous. She shouldn't have been this turned on by the feel of his hand against her waist, but she was.

"I tripped," she said, which was the only thing she could come up with when her brain was struggling to process all the stimuli it was experiencing.

"I know," he replied, and nudged her nose with his before dipping his head—

"Calvin! You're here!" a woman's voice called out.

They sprang apart, but one of Flint's arms remained wrapped around Daphne's waist. His hand was still against her bare skin as he swung them both around to greet the woman beaming at them from the front door. When his thumb stroked her waist, Daphne stopped trying to resist him and just stood there, reeling.

Did she . . . Did she want to sleep with Calvin Flint? And did *he* want to sleep with *her*? What was happening?

"Hey, Mom," he said, his thumb making another stroke over the skin of her waist. "You know Daphne Davis, right?"

Eileen Yarrow folded her hands in front of her stomach and seemed to force herself to stop smiling. "So glad to have you, Daphne. Come in! We have a lot of work to do."

Daphne forced her lips into a curve, then darted a glance at the man still stroking the bare skin at her side. The softness had fled from his features, and he stared at his mother through narrowed eyes. Was he

137

mad because she'd interrupted them? Daphne watched him take a deep breath and relax his shoulders. It didn't look like he was upset about their little moment being stopped. It looked like he was fighting against something much deeper.

"Ready?" he asked in a quiet, rough voice.

Maybe being wrapped in his arms had addled her brain, because Daphne found herself softening toward him. She wanted to ask him what had put those shadows in his eyes. She wanted to make him laugh again. "Yeah," she finally responded. "Lead the way."

"Five, six, seven, eight! And step right. And step left. Shimmy, shimmy, touch, tap! Turn, dip, turn, RAWR! Good, Ceecee. Mom, you're slow. You gotta keep up. Again! Five, six . . ."

Daphne blew out a breath and pushed a strand of hair off her sweat-slicked forehead. She glanced to her left, where Flint was scowling at his feet like he could intimidate them into doing what they were supposed to. They were in a vast living room that had been cleared of furniture, along with ten other amateur dancers. At the front of the room, near the French doors that led to a big backyard, was Eileen's sister-in-law, Kathy Yarrow.

Kathy was large and in charge. In her sparkly blue kitten heels, she topped six feet in height. Her shirt was a flowy blue-and-white number with swirls of sequins, paired with tight white jeans. Her hair was bleached to within an inch of its life, and her fingers were long and tipped in daggerlike nails. Her eyes were rimmed in thick black liner, with lashes clumped together with an unknown number of coats of mascara.

Archie Sr.'s sister was terrifying.

When Kathy clapped her hands, her multitude of rings let out ominous clanks. "Turn, dip, turn, RAWR—*no*. Stop! Cut the music!"

Archie Jr., the current mayor of Fernley Island, pressed a button on the sound system from his perch on a chair at the side of the room.

Daphne couldn't help the sideways glance she gave him. Why did he get to sit this torture out? He reclined in the chair next to the speaker, a bored expression on his face. He had beady eyes and thin, wet lips. Daphne disliked him immensely, mostly because he'd been nearly as annoying as Flint in high school, but he'd gotten away with it because his last name was Yarrow. From what she could tell, the arrogance and entitlement had endured to adulthood.

Kathy glared at the assembled dancers. She walked the length of the living area, turned on her kitten heels, and walked back. Ceecee peeked over her shoulder from her spot in the front-middle position of the dance troupe, giving Daphne big eyes.

Daphne stuck out her tongue, and Ceecee copied her. Daphne snickered.

"Is this funny to you, Ms. Davis?" Kathy asked in a quiet, dark voice.

Daphne's attention snapped back to the older woman. A few of the dancers turned to look at her, and suddenly she felt like a child who'd been caught doing something she wasn't supposed to. She resisted the urge to squirm. "No," she answered. "I think the dance is great."

It was a complete lie. Flint must have been able to tell, because he shot her a glance with a single raised eyebrow that said *You're still a suck-up, Davis.* Daphne resisted the urge to stick her tongue out at him too. In fact, it seemed important to keep her tongue far, far away from him right now.

"Of course the dance is great," Kathy snapped. "I choreographed it, didn't I? Those bruises of yours going to be healed up by the time we have to perform?"

Daphne touched the sides of her nose. It no longer hurt, so she nodded. "Probably."

"Good," Kathy answered. "Now—"

"Honey," Kathy's elderly mother, Dorothea, cut in, "do you think you could modify this? My legs . . ."

"Your legs are fine, Mom."

"I'm eighty-nine years old."

"Age is just a number," Kathy replied, squaring her shoulders. "Okay, people! We're going to go through this one more time. I want all of you to *focus*."

Flint sidled up to Daphne, the heat of his body soaking into her side. Daphne kept her eyes forward and her tongue firmly enclosed behind her teeth. "There's still time to back out, you know," he told her, voice warm.

"I said I'd do it, so I will." She could handle a little inconvenient lust. Maybe if they spent more time together, it would fade. She'd remember all the reasons he infuriated her, and she wouldn't wonder whether or not he was a good kisser.

This was about her family heirloom. About proving to everyone, including herself, that she wasn't boring and predictable. It wasn't about the man whose gaze made her burn up.

Flint huffed a laugh, the back of his hand brushing hers as he moved into position. Daphne ignored the thrill of it, ignored the way she seemed to sense every movement he made. She focused on Kathy's direction, using every ounce of brainpower to make sure she didn't step on anyone's toes. They made it through the bulk of the choreography, and Daphne's heart raced. They'd never made it this far without having to stop and reset. She grabbed one of the gigantic pink feathers from where they'd been placed at the sides of the room. Along with the rest of the dancers, she tented her feather over the middle of the circle, shaking it slightly as Kathy called out directions.

The intent was to have Eileen and Archie Sr. sneak in to the center of the group, then pop up through the feathers like a couple of cabaret singers exploding out of a giant cake. Daphne shook her feather as she held it in position. Kathy called out, "Hold! Hold! Hold!" Ceecee stared at the feathers with grim determination on the other side of the circle, little arms working hard to make that feather dance.

It was happening. They were going to make it through the entire choreography. Nearly four hours after they'd begun, they'd finally get a clean run-through.

"REVEAL!" Kathy screamed.

The feathers came up as their troupe fanned out to show the lovebirds in the center. The dancers were supposed to spin out as they stepped aside, so the feathers would float away from Eileen and Archie just in time for them to start their first dance.

And that's where things went wrong.

Dorothea spun in the wrong direction a beat too late, and her face connected with Flint's outrageously violent flinging of his feather. The man was a danger to society. The back of the sheriff's palm smacked the old woman across the jaw. Shouts echoed in the room.

And Daphne watched the poor old woman's dentures leave her mouth like they were a sentient monster in a horror flick. They flew in a perfect arc, grinning maniacally as they came at her, and she didn't even have time to lift her feather to block the impact.

The dentures hit her square in her left black eye. They were wet and warm and disgusting. Daphne screamed and flailed as she fell backward. Her foot caught on the edge of the rug, and she twisted in midair to try to break her fall. The giant pink feather went flying toward Archie Jr., who sat on his chair, staring at his grandmother with a look of abject horror painted on his features.

Daphne stumbled and crashed headfirst into his chest. Archie Jr. stomped on the arch of her foot as he tried to save himself, pushing Daphne away as he did. Pain lanced through her ankle as she tumbled to the ground, jarring her shoulder on the hardwood floors.

The dentures clattered and rolled under the sideboard, upon which the sound system blasted the music that was meant to be Eileen and Archie Sr.'s moment of glory.

Instead, chaos reigned.

Kathy wailed, using those impressive pipes of hers to destroy everyone's eardrums. People clustered around Dorothea, who insisted she'd be all right as soon as someone got her teeth back. Flint looked like a guilt-ridden mess, his big hands holding the old woman in place as he inspected her face. Archie Jr. sat up and shot Daphne a venomous look.

"I should have known inviting a Davis into our home was a bad idea," he hissed.

Daphne, clutching her sore ankle, glowered at him. "What's that supposed to mean?"

Archie Yarrow the Younger was a man of average height with a growing bald patch on the crown of his head. He was the same age as Daphne, and clearly her prejudices had been correct. He'd been as full of himself in his youth as he was now. Sneering, he said, "Your mother burned my grandfather's house down. Now look what *you've* done."

"I'm not the one who smacked your grandmother in the face, genius."

"Might as well have been. What Flint sees in you is a damn mystery. But I guess that's what happens when you run topless through the streets just to get a date."

Apparently the rumor had progressed. Wonderful. She glared. "Archie, I haven't spoken to you in almost two decades. What the hell is your problem?"

Flint appeared above her, his gaze flicking between Daphne and the mayor, who shut his mouth as soon as the sheriff appeared. Flint dropped to a crouch. "You okay? Saw you go down hard."

"It's fine. Archie broke my fall."

Archie blustered as he got to his feet, glaring at the two of them.

"I think I might have to keep you wrapped in bubble roll, Cupcake. You don't seem equipped to navigate the world on your own."

"Did you know I ran through the streets topless just to get a date with you?"

"When?"

"After we went to see Jerry Barela."

Archie's hands fisted where he stood, his gaze boring into the side of Daphne's head. She discovered she enjoyed standing up for herself. This new, nonboring version of Daphne had its benefits.

Flint's eyes glimmered as he ignored the man vibrating with fury above them. "I'm sorry I missed that."

Archie let out a snarl and stomped out of the room without even checking whether his grandmother was okay. Flint watched him leave, then turned back to Daphne. The lightness had gone from his expression. His brows were drawn, his eyes full of concern.

"Why are you looking at me like that?" Daphne asked, massaging her ankle.

The sheriff didn't answer. He watched the movement of her hands, and his frown deepened. "You're hurt."

"I'm fine."

"Can you stand?"

"I'm *fine*."

"Last time you told me that, you walked away with two black eyes without getting checked for a concussion. Your behavior since then indicates that was a mistake."

"You're an unbelievably huge asshole, Flint. Did you know that?"

He once again failed to respond, choosing instead to bat her arms away so he could wrap his hands around her ankle. The heat of his skin on hers was a shock. Daphne's teeth clicked as she clamped her lips shut, the whole of her attention focused on the feel of Flint's rough, calloused hands gently stroking every inch of her ankle, foot, and calf.

"Is Dorothea okay?" Daphne asked to distract herself from the onslaught, watching the older woman lower herself into an armchair.

Flint glanced over his shoulder, his hands still on Daphne's skin. "She says she's fine. I want to get some ice on her jaw. I should've been more careful."

Ceecee slithered under the sideboard and came out holding dust bunny–covered dentures. She glanced at the two of them. "Grandma said she's perfectly fine, but she wants a stiff drink and she's not doing the stupid dance, and if Mom doesn't like it, she can stick these dentures where the sun don't shine." Ceecee leaned toward them and lowered her voice. "She means her butt."

"She sounds like a wise woman," Daphne replied. "I might have to bow out myself."

Ceecee shot her a grin, then sprinted across the room to present her grandmother with the soiled dentures. Daphne's attention returned to the sheriff, who seemed wholly consumed with the state of her ankle.

"Can you move your foot?" A strand of hair fell over his forehead as he bent over her limb.

A spark lit between Daphne's legs as the sheriff's thumbs stroked down the front of her ankle, his other fingers curving around the arch of her foot. This was too much. Too intimate. Not intimate enough.

Whatever was happening between them was getting out of hand. Daphne needed to get away from him as soon as humanly possible. She tried to move her foot out of his hold and hissed as pain shot up the outside of her ankle. "It's sore."

"Let's get some ice on it," Flint said. He helped her to her feet, then slung one of Daphne's arms around his broad shoulders and held her waist like he'd never let go. "Hop if you can. It might hurt to put some weight on it." He guided her out of the chaotic living room and into the kitchen around the corner.

After sitting down at the built-in banquette seat in the breakfast nook, Daphne watched him open the freezer and hunt through the cupboards and drawers until he found a plastic bag. When he opened the corner cabinet, she spied pots and pans. One of them was the rough black of cast iron.

Her pulse quickened. Was it *the* pot?

"I'll run this out to Dorothea and then come back for your ankle," he said, lifting the bag of ice.

"Sure," Daphne said, eyes tracking him as he left the room. The kitchen door swung closed behind him, and Daphne was up in a flash.

She leaned on the counters and hobbled to the corner cabinet. She wrenched it open and fumbled with her phone. She snapped a couple of pictures, then closed the cabinet and hurried back to her seat just in time for Flint to push the kitchen door open again.

He glanced at where she was sitting as if to make sure she hadn't moved, then made her a bag of ice.

Daphne glanced at the pictures and grimaced when she noticed the camera had focused on a stainless steel pot in the foreground instead of the black cast-iron Dutch oven in the back. The pot in question was out of focus, the details of its lid blurry. Too late to get another photo, so she sent that one to her grandmother, gaze flicking to Flint's broad back as she waited for a response. When he turned around, a fresh bag of ice clasped in his upturned hand, Daphne's phone vibrated.

Could be, but it's blurry, Grandma Mabel texted. Three dots appeared below her message, and Daphne knew a slew of messages was incoming.

Heart thundering, Daphne flicked her phone to silent and turned it face down on the table. A chair screeched across the floor as Flint dragged it closer. He sat down as he wrapped a dish towel around the bag of ice, then scowled at her ankle for a minute.

It was kind of cute that he cared. Although Daphne wasn't sure he cared about *her* specifically. He probably just felt guilty that it was his fault that Dorothea had gotten smacked and, by extension, his fault that Daphne had been hurt. He blamed himself for her getting punched too, which was ridiculous.

She realized with a start that he wasn't the same person she'd known in high school. The man picking her foot up and gently placing a bag of ice over her injury wasn't bitter and rebellious. He wasn't intent on destroying himself and everyone around him. He might actually be a good man. The type of person who cared about other people's well-being, who cared about doing the right thing.

Why else would he have accepted the job as acting sheriff? From what Daphne had seen, it wasn't because he loved being back on Fernley.

"Why'd you come back to the island?" she heard herself ask.

The man currently tending to her injuries with surprising gentleness looked up and shrugged. "Wanted to make sure Ceecee wasn't having the same childhood I had."

Daphne sat back and let the words sink in.

No, he wasn't the same boy she'd known nearly twenty years ago. He was much, much better.

Suddenly, guilt churned in the pit of Daphne's stomach. She'd been lying to him about the reason she'd agreed to be his date. He didn't deserve that—but what choice did she have? It was either get her grandmother's pot back, or admit that Pete had been right about her all along. She was a boring, predictable woman who lacked passion and spontaneity. The best thing for her to do was find another steady job and crawl back into the shell that had been her safe haven her whole life.

But the thought of doing that made her want to cry.

"Painful?" Flint asked, gaze flicking between her eyes.

Daphne shook her head. "Just feeling sorry for myself."

His hand slid over her foot, thumb stroking her arch. "This is my fault," he said. "We should just forget about this whole thing. I'll tell my mother you can't make it to the vow renewal."

"No," Daphne blurted out. "No, I'll go. I said I'd go, so I will."

His hand was still on her foot, warm and strong and comforting. Hazel eyes met hers, hope sparking in them. "Yeah?"

"Yeah," she said, and it wasn't just because she wanted to get her grandmother's heirloom back. She still wasn't sure if that pot in the corner cabinet was the right one. As she sat there, basking in the warmth of Flint's care, she realized that she didn't want to let him down. And worse—she wanted to spend more time with him.

That was bad. That meant the lust she occasionally felt for him might not go away so easily. She needed to get away from him, but the fastest way to do that was for someone here to help her home. And there was only one person she could ask.

"You mind helping me up the steps to get to my apartment?" Daphne asked after the silence between them stretched too long.

Flint leaned back in his chair and crossed his arms. His spread knees framed her injured foot. "I do mind, Cupcake."

Daphne popped a brow. "You only like playing doctor when other people might be watching?"

A dark, wicked smile curled his lips. "Not quite. I mind because I'm not taking you home."

"Excuse me?" she scoffed and mirrored his position, crossing her arms to glare at him. "You want me to call a cab?"

"Wrong again, Davis. I'm taking you to the medical center. You're getting an x-ray for this ankle, and *then* I'm taking you home."

Daphne let out a grunt, slightly mollified.

Until Flint gave her a wicked grin and added, "*My* home."

CHAPTER 19

She fought him all the way to the medical center, but Calvin wouldn't budge. The woman was a danger to herself. She'd been on the island a little more than a week and already had had three incidents that had led to bodily injury. She needed full-time supervision, and there was no way in hell Calvin was leaving that to anyone else.

By the time she got her x-rays done and was wheeled out to the waiting room where he sat, she seemed completely worn out. The nurse who'd pushed her chair told them it wouldn't be long until the doctor would speak to them. Daphne thanked her, then turned to Calvin.

They watched each other for a long moment.

"Have you come to your senses yet?" Daphne finally asked.

"I was just about to ask you the same thing."

She rolled her eyes. "I'm going home tonight, Flint."

"Agreed. My home. I have a nice second bedroom and everything you need."

She took a deep breath, her hands gripping the arms of her wheelchair as if to stop her from launching herself at him. "Why?"

"Because if I drop you off at your apartment, you'll probably fall down the stairs and break your neck. I'd rather that not happen. I live in a single-story house. No steps to navigate. Less chance of catastrophic injury."

"I didn't know you cared so much."

Neither did he. But it seemed imperative that Daphne stayed somewhere close where he could keep an eye on her. He needed to protect her from herself. Somehow, he didn't think Daphne would respond well to him saying that out loud.

"I need you to finish the work you've started with the department's finances," he finally replied. "It would be inconvenient to have to find someone new."

Daphne hummed, then turned when a woman in scrubs and a white lab coat came walking toward them.

Fifteen minutes later, Calvin wheeled Daphne out of the medical center after confirmation that her ankle was only lightly sprained and should be fine within a week or two. All she had to do was keep it iced until the swelling went down and keep her weight off it.

Calvin let out a relieved breath. At least there was a bit of good news.

Once Daphne was in the passenger seat of his truck, Calvin got behind the wheel and turned on the engine. He paused, glancing at her. "So?"

Her skin was burnished gold under the glow of the streetlights. It was only dinnertime, but darkness had already blanketed the island. Rain drenched the outside world as the truck's heat blew over them inside the vehicle.

Daphne sighed, rolling her head on the headrest so she could look at him. "I'll come to yours," she conceded, and Calvin had to fight to hide the satisfaction that washed over him. "But only because I'm exhausted, and you're right about the stairs. As soon as I get some crutches and get more mobile, I'm going home."

"Deal," he said, and started driving.

Real estate agents would describe Calvin's home as the worst house on the best street. He'd inherited the three-bed, one-bath bungalow from his father's estate, and the neighborhood had grown and improved around it in the years he'd been gone. As he pulled up to the small worn-down home, a familiar tug pulled at his chest.

The house was familiar and unfamiliar all at once. It was layered with memories of his early youth, when things had been good, and the later years, when they hadn't. Stepping through the door the first time a few weeks ago had been surreal.

Now, it felt almost normal.

He helped Daphne up the path and through the front door. She leaned on his arm as she glanced around the foyer. His shoes were lined up as they always were. When he opened the closet, she peered inside at the jackets hanging within. He added his own, then hers, making sure to evenly space the hangers before closing the closet door.

Daphne watched him; then she swung her gaze to the living room. "You're very tidy," she noted.

He followed her gaze. He'd gotten rid of all his mother's knick-knacks, given the place a thorough cleaning, and set himself up as comfortably as he could. Couch, coffee table, TV, and fireplace in the corner. The remotes were lined up at the edge of the coffee table. His throw blanket was folded over the arm of the sofa.

"I like things to be neat," he said, which wasn't much of an explanation. The truth was his teenage years had been marked with such chaos that he now felt the need to keep his life as orderly as possible. Messes set him on edge. Clutter raised his blood pressure.

Things had designated places, and Calvin made sure that's where they stayed. He had routines and habits that kept him on the straight and narrow. Deviating from them felt too close to that out-of-control tailspin that had led him down the path of self-destruction all those years ago.

Daphne smiled at him, and it wasn't the razor-sharp smirk or the reluctant grin she'd sometimes try to bite back. It was a genuine look of appreciation. "I like things to be neat too," she said, and allowed him to help her to the couch. His hands lingered on her shoulders as he helped her settle. For a woman who was so strong, who had such a massive presence in his life these days, she seemed too fragile right now.

"Hungry?" he asked.

"Starving."

He nodded. A strange kind of satisfaction spread through him at the thought of having her in his home. Taking care of her. Making sure she was fed and rested.

There were half a dozen pizza places on the island, but only one of them was worth buying from. Calvin left Daphne on the couch with ice on her ankle, a blanket, and a glass of ice water, then ducked back out into the rain to pick up their pies.

Thirty minutes later, after a drive to the little hole-in-the-wall restaurant housed down a side road on the outskirts of Carlisle, Calvin was in possession of two Neapolitan-style pizzas. He nudged his front door open and found Daphne asleep on the couch, the TV playing an old rerun of *Friends* while her ice pack dribbled onto the rug below.

She blinked her eyes open when he walked in, looking like a sleepy little owl staring at him from behind her blanket. "I fell asleep," she said in a drowsy voice, as if he hadn't noticed.

Calvin's heart gave a squeeze. There was a kind of intimacy to the moment, a stillness that felt precious and breakable. "You want to go to bed?"

She sat up and rubbed her eyes. "No. I want food."

He hummed and set the boxes down on the coffee table before grabbing a new dish towel with which to wrap her ice pack. Daphne shifted on the sofa to give him room to sit down, but as soon as he did, the old, broken-down cushions dipped, and she fell into his side.

He froze for a second, but Daphne didn't jump back from him. She just leaned forward to grab a slice of pizza, then settled back against the sofa, her side pressed firmly against his. Twitching the blanket so it covered his legs, Calvin grabbed a slice for himself. Daphne turned up the volume, and they chuckled as Ross made a disaster out of leather pants, baby powder, and lotion.

When the next episode came on, Daphne shifted, and her head dropped onto his shoulder. The weight of it was comforting, the scent of her hair a delicate perfume. Not wanting to move, Calvin stayed that way until his arm went numb, then slowly lifted his arm to put it around her shoulders. Daphne's hand came up to rest against his stomach, and he was almost certain she was asleep as she nuzzled against his chest.

The right thing to do would be to wake her up and help her into the guest bedroom. But the couch was comfortable, she needed her rest, and Calvin told himself he'd finish watching the episode before disturbing her. If, in the process, he enjoyed the weight of her against his chest, and his own eyelids began to droop, well . . . that was just a natural consequence of warmth and comfort. Nothing more. It had been so long since he'd cuddled with someone. So long since he'd felt the kind of peace that swept through him.

In the recesses of his mind, as his eyelids became heavier, Calvin knew he shouldn't get used to this. Daphne was planning on leaving the island—planning on using him as an excuse to do it—and what was going on between them wasn't real. But the weight and warmth of her on his chest were real. The soft breaths ruffling his neck were real. The drugging comfort of her presence was real.

Eyes closing, he let himself enjoy it. Just this once.

He jerked awake at the sound of his phone screaming in the silent room. Daphne sucked in a hard breath, pushing herself off his body. Digging into his pants, Calvin grabbed his phone and swiped to answer.

"Yeah?"

"Two simultaneous break-ins," one of the deputies working the night shift informed him. "Figured you'd want to know right away. One at Barela Contracting, the other at Romano's."

Romano's was an Italian restaurant only a few blocks away, in the heart of Carlisle. It was one of many eateries owned by the Deacons and had been closed for renovations during the slow winter months. He drove by it every morning on his way to the station.

"On my way," he said. "I'll stop at Romano's first."

"Copy."

Daphne rubbed her eyes and stared as he heaved himself off the couch. "Is everything all right?" she asked.

"Couple of break-ins," he said, heading for his boots. "Jerry Barela got hit, along with Romano's."

"Jerry Barela?"

"Mm."

"That's odd. You think it has anything to do with us?"

"No idea," he said, but it was a valid question. Just a few days after they'd gone asking questions, the man got broken into?

Daphne's brows were drawn. "What's Romano's?"

"One of the Deacons' restaurants, over on Main. You need help getting to the bedroom? I might be gone a while."

"I'll be fine," she answered, shifting her leg so her foot rested on the ground. "I can hobble. I'll put all this away," she said, motioning to the pizza boxes. "Any special rules about where things go in the kitchen, or do you trust me to use my judgment?"

Smart-ass. Calvin bit back a grin. "I trust you. Call me if you need anything. Your room is the first door on the left. There's a spare toothbrush in the vanity. Help yourself to anything you need." He gave her a nod, threw on his belt and badge, and grabbed his jacket. He was at Romano's within seven minutes. A cruiser was parked out front, and the lights inside the restaurant were on. After parking behind the vehicle, Calvin went inside.

"Oh, Calvin!" Jenna Deacon threw herself at him, causing him to stagger into the windows at his back. "It's *awful*," she said. "Just awful. Imagine if someone had been here!"

Using his hands to unclamp Jenna's arms from his neck, Calvin pried himself free of her grip. "We'll figure it out," he said. "I take it you're managing this place?"

She sniffled and nodded. "My parents gave it to me to run. Once the renovations are done, I'll be in charge of the restaurant."

"Were you here when the break-in happened?"

"No. The alarm went off, and I was notified by the security company. They broke a window and came in through the back."

Calvin nodded and crossed the room to get a report from the deputies on the scene. The front of the restaurant was unfinished, with bare drywall covering the walls and ceilings and drop cloths on the floor. The kitchen looked to be mostly finished, although it still needed to be stocked with food and cookware. It gleamed silver with stainless steel countertops and expensive-looking equipment.

He made his way to the staff bathroom, which was where the break-in had happened. The window at the back of the building, above the sink, was shattered.

"See? That's where they came in," Jenna said, pointing at the broken glass.

Calvin frowned as he inspected the scene. Shards of glass littered the sink and floor, but if someone had come in through the opening, they were either very small or they'd abandoned the endeavor as soon as they'd broken the window. No one could squeeze through that opening—the window didn't open far enough to fit a human—and there was no evidence that someone had tried to squeeze their way inside.

He headed outside and inspected the alleyway at the back of the building. The doorway looked intact. No signs of forced entry. It was a thick steel door, so coming in through the window probably made sense. Picking the front lock would probably be a better bet, especially on a rainy night when everyone was indoors. But criminals weren't always the brightest bulbs.

A dumpster had been pushed up next to the wall, just below the broken window. It was half-full of building supplies and the scraps of the workers' lunches. An old, crusty mop was on the ground next to the dumpster, along with old food wrappers.

It was still raining, which meant any footsteps in the dirt and gravel were long gone. Calvin shone his flashlight all along the alleyway, then swung it up the wall and over the window.

He frowned.

A smudged, dirty handprint was visible on the wall just above the dumpster. It wasn't a full handprint, just a few streaks that looked like four fingers and a thumb.

He returned to the restaurant.

"Was anything taken?" he asked Jenna.

Arms wrapped around her middle, she blinked at him with big brown eyes. "No," she said. "We don't even have any cash here, with the renovations ongoing."

Nodding, Calvin did another walk-through. There were some tools stacked neatly in the corner. One of the tool bags was embroidered with Barela Contracting's logo.

He jerked his chin at the bag. "Jerry Barela doing this renovation for you?"

"Yes," Jenna answered. "He said he had another month of work to do, but he's on schedule. Why? You think he did this?"

"I never said that. Would he have a reason to break in?"

She shrugged. "I don't know. He's done a good job so far."

But why would Barela have a break-in on the very same night?

After leaving the rest of the deputies to finish up, Calvin made his way to the Barela Contracting yard. The parking lot was illuminated with floodlights, with another cruiser parked near the front door. He parked his truck next to it and paused when his phone buzzed.

Everything okay? Daphne wrote.

He stared at the words for a few long seconds. It was the first time anyone had checked up on him when he was on the job. It made a weight press down on his chest, and it was hard to breathe for a minute. She cared. No one had cared about him in a long, long time.

He shook his head. She was probably being polite. He was the one who was infatuated with her. The worst thing he could do was get carried away thinking she felt the same.

All good, he replied. How's the ankle?

A photo message came through a second later, showing Daphne's bare legs from the knee down, a fresh bag of ice on her ankle. She was in the spare bedroom.

His heart gave a hard thump. She'd taken her pants off? He sent her a picture of the Barela Contracting offices, but the camera focused on the rain dripping down his windshield, and the building beyond was blurry.

I'd rather be where I am, she wrote back, and sent him a photo of her face snuggled in a mountain of pillows.

He stared at the image until another message came through. Be safe, Flint.

Careful, Cupcake, he wrote back. It almost sounds like you care.

I just want to make sure I have a ride to work tomorrow morning, she answered.

He'd just snorted, thumbs poised over the keyboard, when a knock on his window made him jump. Teri stood outside his door, jerking her head toward the entrance to the contractor's office.

"Hey," he said, following her as they jogged to get out of the rain. "What's the situation?"

"Come inside. The place was ransacked. Someone stole a bunch of files, along with Barela's laptop."

The man himself was standing in the middle of a mess of paperwork and office supplies, hands on his hips, thunderous expression on his brow. He turned when he saw Calvin and jerked his chin in acknowledgment.

"Sheriff," Barela said in greeting. "Two visits in less than a week. Must be my lucky month."

"Walk me through what happened."

"Alarm went off. I drove straight over, was here within fifteen minutes. Didn't see anyone coming or going, but I walked into this."

"What was taken?"

"Some files and my laptop."

"Tools? Equipment?"

"I'll have to inventory the yard in the morning, but I don't think so. They left the hard drive, so I still have all my documents. Looks like they only had time to ransack my files. We only keep current projects stored out here, and whoever did this didn't make it to the back storeroom." He bent over and picked up a quote written on his company's letterhead. "Would this help you? It ain't my shoe, and I don't think it's Teri's either."

Calvin took the sheet of paper from Barela. It had a dirty shoe print on it in the corner, and what looked like cat prints down the middle. Looked like Dumpling had either interrupted the burglar or come to investigate once he'd gone.

"It might," Calvin said, studying the shoe print. Then his eyes skimmed the paper itself, and he noticed it was a quote for the Romano job. Teri put the paper in an evidence sleeve, along with any others they found that had been stepped on.

"You got insurance?" Calvin asked.

Jerry grunted. "Be bad business not to."

"We'll get you a report so you can make a claim."

"Thanks," the older man said as he surveyed the mess. His wedding ring glinted as he ran his fingers through his thick hair, barrel chest rising and falling with a deep sigh.

Would this man have broken into Romano's and then staged this break-in to cover his tracks? Calvin didn't think so, but it was something to keep in mind. Jerry Barela seemed like a straight shooter. He had a reputation for getting jobs done on time and on budget. He wasn't cheap, but his business had lasted decades on the island through all kinds of economic cycles. Staging some kind of elaborate break-in at two locations didn't seem like something he'd do.

Unless he'd been spooked by Calvin and Daphne's first visit for some reason.

"You hear about the break-in at Romano's?" Calvin probed.

The man grunted as he moved to his desk and dropped into his chair. "I'm heading over there as soon as we're done here to check if all our tools are still there."

"You think someone might have been targeting you?"

"Unless they wanted to haul out one of those twenty-thousand-dollar ovens, I don't see what else there is to steal in that place, other than our gear. We've had tools and supplies go missing from jobsites many times over the years. And these days, with the cost of everything increasing, people get desperate."

"Thanks, Jerry." Calvin nodded, then went to see Teri. It would be a long night, and he wasn't any closer to answering any of his questions.

Most of all, though, he wanted to go home to Daphne. A ridiculous thought, since he wasn't going home to her at all. She just happened to be staying with him because he'd bullied her into it. Still, the thought of waking up in the morning and seeing that sleepy look on her face drove him on through the long, cold, rainy night.

CHAPTER 20

Daphne's ankle felt better when she woke up. And, as much as she hated to admit it, Flint's guest bed was much more comfortable than the one in her apartment. She'd slept like a dream. She hobbled out to the kitchen, where she found the sheriff sitting at the table, sipping coffee. A plate with a few crumbs was beside him.

The kitchen was as clean as the rest of his place. She hadn't been surprised, exactly, when she'd put their leftovers away the night before. His uniform was always pressed, his jaw clean shaven, and his hair cut short and neat. Why would his house be any different?

Still, being in his space had felt like a narrow glimpse inside the man. She appreciated that he was tidy. It felt like something they had in common—an appreciation for order, for organization.

He looked up when she entered, his gaze dropping to her foot. "Morning," he said. "How's the ankle?"

"Better. Any coffee left?"

He pulled out a chair for her and got her a mug. "Toast?"

"Sure," she said, and watched him drop a slice in the toaster.

Turned out Calvin Flint could be a gentleman when he really wanted to be, which also wasn't a huge surprise if she forgot everything that she knew about him from high school. Daphne thanked him and took a sip before asking him about his night.

He gave her the rundown of what he'd seen, including the fact that there might have been a connection between the two incidents.

"So do you think the break-ins have something to do with us asking him questions?" Daphne frowned at the photos Flint showed her on his phone.

"I don't know," he answered. "But it's strange."

He checked his watch and got up to get ready for the day. Daphne watched him put his mug and plate in the dishwasher before putting the toaster in the cupboard below and spraying the countertops with cleaner. He moved efficiently, like he'd done the same tasks a thousand times. He walked out of the kitchen a moment later. She looked at the gleaming countertops and wondered why the sight of him taking care of his home seemed so significant.

Was it because Pete had been a bit of a slob, and the thousands of little tasks required to take care of a home had fallen to her? Her ex-fiancé wouldn't have even noticed crumbs on the counter. If he did, he might have brushed them onto the floor. A spray bottle would never have touched his hand. And he would have scoffed at the idea of putting a toaster away and out of sight. After all, he rolled his eyes whenever she insisted on making the bed. "You're just going to mess it up again tonight," he'd complain, which was true but also completely beside the point.

Watching a man clean his space without a second thought was something Daphne enjoyed, she realized. She enjoyed it a lot.

The doorbell rang, and Daphne hopped her way down the hall to open the door. Ellie stood on the other side with a small duffel bag full of Daphne's things. Daphne had texted her sister the night before to ask her to run some clothes down to Flint's place.

Daphne smiled. "Hey," she said. "Thanks for bringing my things."

"Course," Ellie said. "Your apartment is super depressing, though."

Daphne rolled her eyes and led Ellie to the kitchen. Ellie looked around, her eyes filled with delight as she handed the bag off to Daphne, who scowled at her.

"This is nice and cozy," Ellie noted quietly, peeking around the corner as if to catch a glimpse of Flint down the hall.

"It's temporary."

"Uh-huh."

"Shut up, Ellie."

"Hey, I'm happy for you!" Ellie laughed at the look on Daphne's face. "I have to get to work. And I can see you and the sheriff are busy here." At Daphne's glare, Ellie cackled, then said her goodbyes and left.

Daphne was starting to regret the fib she'd told about being involved with Flint. Three weeks was a long time to pretend to date someone, and her family was far, far too enthusiastic about the prospect.

But—was it a fib?

She frowned at the duffel bag on the chair beside her and decided that yes, it was. Flint wasn't as awful as she remembered. There were things about him she actually liked, such as the fact that he was a tidy person who knew how to keep his space clean. He could be funny once in a while, when he wasn't being insufferable. And fine, in an academic sense, Daphne could appreciate that he was an attractive man.

But this thing between them—it wasn't *real*. It was just until the vow renewal. Just until she could get her grandmother's pot back. They had to play nice until then, that was all.

Satisfied, she stood up and carried the duffel bag to her bedroom. Once Daphne was showered and changed, she came out of the bathroom to find a pair of crutches leaning on the wall outside the door. She hooked them under her arms, then made her way out to the living room, where Flint was waiting.

"Thanks for these," she said.

He glanced up from his phone, eyes doing a quick assessment of the crutches, then Daphne, as if to check that everything was as it should be. Daphne didn't know whether to be annoyed or appreciative of his care, so she turned to the front door instead.

Ten minutes later, they were at work, and Daphne lost herself in years-old financial records. She pored over any document she could find about the renovations, but nothing made sense. Barela said he hadn't been paid, but the accounts clearly showed funds being remitted, per the invoices. All to the same account—the one that apparently didn't belong to Barela Contracting.

When she cross-checked the account on the original invoices with the digital records, she was able to find the name of the company to which the funds had been transferred. Realist Trade Co. had received the deposits for the renovation. Not Jerry Barela.

By the time Daphne lifted her head, she had a crick in her neck and hours had passed. She needed food. After lunch, she'd work backward; she'd start with the mysterious Realist Trade Co. account and try to find all the deposits that had been sent to it. If anything other than the renovation invoices had been paid to the account, then that would give her another angle to investigate.

The sheriff's department had a constant drum of activity, and today was no different. Daphne wandered to the kitchen and grabbed the two slices of leftover pizza she'd brought for lunch. As she considered the microwave, she bunched her lips. Soggy crust, or cold pizza?

"I'll show you a trick," Shirley said, walking into the kitchen behind Daphne. She pulled the panini press away from the wall. "There's some foil in that drawer, there. Thanks."

Daphne watched as the other woman wrapped the slices of pizza in foil and stuck them in the panini press, not closing it enough to squish them.

"They'll come out good as new," Shirley said, then shot Daphne a glance. "Heard you're bunking with Sheriff Flint."

"He bullied me into it," Daphne groused.

Shirley barked out a laugh. "Wouldn't mind being bullied if it meant sharing a bed with a man like that."

Daphne bit back her protest. If she started denying that anything was going on between them, she'd lose her chance at getting her grandmother's pot back. "We're taking things slow," she said for what felt like the millionth time. "He just wanted to save me from having to hop up my apartment stairs multiple times a day."

Shirley didn't look convinced. "Uh-huh."

Daphne clicked her tongue, and Shirley laughed. Hank ambled in and sniffed the air. "Pizza," he said. "I'm jealous."

"Back off, Hank," Shirley warned. "Daphne needs her energy if she's going to save this department from ruin."

Hank threw his hands up and grabbed a container from the fridge. "Wife's got me on salads," he said. "If I come home smelling of pizza, she'll throw me out."

Shirley chuckled, then asked, "You hear about the break-ins last night?"

"Two in one night," Hank answered. "Unusual."

Daphne tilted her head. "You think they're connected?"

"According to Jerry Barela, it's someone trying to rob him." Hank speared a piece of lettuce and shrugged. "We're looking into it. None of his tools were stolen at Romano's, but the perp could have been interrupted. Didn't look like they actually made it inside."

"Would Barela have a reason to lie?" Daphne asked, frowning.

Shirley nudged her with her elbow. "Look at you, asking relevant questions. You'll be a deputy by the time we're done with you."

"No, thank you," Daphne said, gesturing to her face, then her ankle. "I don't think that would be good for my health."

The two others laughed, and Daphne retrieved her leftover pizza from the press. It was warm and crisp—nearly as good as it had been the night before. She sat at the table with Hank and Shirley, talking shop, feeling like she was part of something bigger than herself.

At her old job, she'd worked in one gray cubicle amid a sea of identical gray cubicles. Her coworkers had been quiet, studious accountants who kept their headphones in and seemed horrified when someone spoke more than three words in a row. The only noise in the office was the clack of keyboards, the clicks of mice, and the hum of the air conditioner system. She'd eaten lunch at her desk almost every single day.

It was nice to eat with other people, to feel like she was part of the team. To belong.

Daphne hadn't belonged anywhere on this island before. At eighteen, she couldn't wait to get away. Now she wondered if she'd been running away—and what she'd been running from.

When she got back to the interview room that served as her office, there was a small container on her desk. It was a tiny container of ice cream, but it was all-white cardboard—no logo. On top of the lid, a spoon balanced. Daphne glanced over her shoulder, but no one was looking her way. She crutched her way to the other side of the desk and popped the lid.

Mint-chip ice cream. Responsible Daphne would put it away, because pizza and ice cream were not a nutritious lunch, never mind not knowing who had left it here for her. But Responsible Daphne didn't seem to be in charge at the moment, because Daphne found herself grabbing the spoon and taking a bite. Her shoulders dropped as the ice cream hit her tongue, and she knew—she just *knew*—that this stuff was made by Rhonda Roberts.

Maybe the other woman wanted to apologize for spreading rumors about her, Daphne reasoned. It was an apology pint. That explanation was enough to satisfy her, so Daphne sat back in her chair and enjoyed the treat. Then she got back to work.

At five o'clock, there was a knock on her office door. Flint leaned against the frame. "Ready?" he asked.

"I've been thinking about it," she replied, "and I think I'll sleep at my place tonight."

"Oh yeah? How are you going to get there?"

She gave him a flat look. "I'll take a cab."

"And the stairs?"

"I'll manage."

"Am I really that terrifying?"

"Please," she scoffed and leaned back, crossing her arms.

The truth was, being in his presence was confusing. They could pretend to date each other for three more weeks without bunking together. It made more sense for them to pretend to take things slow to at least try to stem the tide of gossip. But the more time she spent with him, the more she liked him. And she didn't want to like him. She just wanted to do her job, get her feet back under her, and figure out her next steps. Dating—or fake dating—a high school rival wasn't conducive to achieving those goals. She needed to focus, and remember who she was.

She was Good, Responsible Daphne, who did things the way they were meant to be done.

Except when she planned covert heists with her batty grandmother. And when she almost-kissed the hot sheriff she was pretending to date.

The sheriff entered the space, and suddenly there was too much of him. His presence filled the room from wall to wall to wall. His energy snapped against her skin like it had that first night when he'd pulled her over on the side of the road. He leaned his knuckles against her desk, his body angled toward hers. Daphne fought not to lean back in her chair to make space between them. It felt too much like surrender, so she set her jaw and glared at him.

When he spoke, his voice was low and soft. "Do you always struggle to accept help from people, or is it just me?"

"Maybe I don't trust your intentions."

His answering smile was wicked. "That might be smart of you."

Daphne's feet were firmly planted on the floor, but she was off balance. Knowing it was a kind of surrender, she tore her gaze away from his and dropped it to her desk. She busied herself with shuffling her papers and closing her laptop. "I don't understand why you are so insistent on having me stay with you."

"Under my watch, you've been punched, tackled, and thrown across the room. You've had two black eyes and a sprained ankle. I don't like it. I don't trust you to make it through the evening on your own."

"And you care why?"

"I already told you, Cupcake. I don't want to have to find another accountant. We need to finish this work and give the people of Fernley a definitive answer before the election. The fastest way to do that is to keep our team safe, including you. That, and I don't want to find another date to my mother's vow renewal."

Glaring at the sheriff had precisely zero effect. He still watched her with those thick-lash-rimmed hazel eyes, challenging her.

It felt like she was seventeen again, being sent to detention for the first time in her life because of him. Infuriating, impossible man. The heat in her gut was anger, she was sure. The way her thighs clenched was a fight-or-flight response and nothing else. Though the pulse between her legs felt like white-hot lust, she knew she was mistaken about it.

"First of all, I told you not to call me Cupcake. Second of all, since when do you care about the election? I didn't think you were planning on staying."

"Maybe I like the job."

"Hmm."

"Come on, Davis. Either you're staying at mine, or I'm staying at yours. And I'd way rather sleep in my own bed. But if we have to share yours . . ."

"In your dreams, Flint."

"My dreams are none of your business, sweetheart," he answered, eyes alight, and Daphne's cheeks flamed.

She should have pushed him more when they'd left the medical center. Should have insisted that he leave her alone.

But as she gathered her things, Daphne realized that she didn't want to be alone. And more than that, she wanted to be with *him*. Yes, he infuriated her. He was still the arrogant, pushy jerk she'd known almost twenty years earlier, but the more time she spent with him, the less she hated him. She was playing with fire.

After spending so many years trying to do the right thing, it felt good to take a risk.

Daphne stood up, propped her crutches under her arms, and swung her way to the door. The sheriff held it open for her, flicking off the lights behind her. His hand drifted over her lower back as she wobbled over an uneven piece of ground. And when they descended the steps outside the building, the heat of his hand spilled over her lower back, sinking down lower in her gut.

If she was flushed when he opened the door to his truck for her and helped her in, it was only because of the exertion of using the crutches. Nothing else.

They drove to Flint's house, and as he parked in the driveway outside the small home, Daphne wondered what ties he still had to Fernley. The house wasn't a rental; she could tell by how easily he moved through it. It was an older home in need of a fresh lick of paint, surrounded by newer, larger houses on all sides.

"Where did you find this house?" she asked as he cut the engine.

Flint glanced at her, then at the house. It had off-white siding and brown trim. The rain was slicking the shingled roof, and it looked like the gutters were in need of a clean. "This is where I grew up," he said.

Daphne started. "What? Really?"

"My dad owned it and passed it on to me. I lived in it for a year or so after high school, before I moved away. By then, my mom had married her third husband, so I was on my own. Not that that was different from what I was used to," he added, almost like an afterthought. Giving her a tight smile, Flint slipped out of the truck and jogged around to open her door.

The rain was misting, but it felt like it'd get heavier before the evening was through. It had been raining off and on all day, with a few bouts of torrential downpour between clearer spells. As Daphne made her way up the path, one of her crutches slipped, and she teetered on her single healthy leg until Flint's hand gripped her elbow.

"This is why stairs are a bad idea," he growled.

Daphne tucked her chin in her chest to hide her smile. It had been a long time since someone had actually worried about her. She'd always been the one to take care of everything. The responsible one who managed schedules and kept on top of life's duties. Having someone at her back felt better than she'd expected.

Once inside, they stripped off their jackets and took off their shoes, and Daphne used a towel to wipe down her crutches. She made it to the guest room and sat on the edge of the bed, exhausted.

"I'm going to take a shower," Flint told her. "We'll figure out dinner after?"

"Sure."

He nodded and disappeared down the hall. A door opened, and a couple of minutes later, the shower turned on. Daphne looked at the pillows on her bed, knowing that if she laid her head on top of them, lifting it up again would be almost impossible. She heaved herself to her feet, leaving her crutches in the bedroom, and hopped toward the kitchen.

On the way, she passed a door. Glancing over her shoulder to make sure the bathroom door was still closed, she pushed it open to peek inside. Yes, she was snooping. But that seemed like a fair cost after being strong-armed into staying here by the island's sheriff.

A third bedroom lay beyond the door, filled with boxes of stuff. A junk room. She could see old clothes spilling from the tops of a few boxes, a clear plastic container filled with ancient electronics, and various old appliances and miscellaneous decor items stacked against every wall.

It was odd, since the rest of the house was militantly clean. Flint folded the throw blanket on the couch after every use, laying it over the arm of the sofa with its corners perfectly aligned. His kitchen was old but sparkling. The guest bedding had been perfectly pressed, with not a speck of dust in sight. Even the old venetian blinds had been wiped clean recently. His truck gleamed, and not just because of the constant rain.

But he had a junk room.

As Daphne made her way to the kitchen, she wondered about it. Was it a dirty secret? A room where he'd shoved all his past mistakes? She opened a couple of upper cabinets, looking for a glass. After finding one on the third try, she leaned against the sink and filled it. Her drink was halfway to her lips when she realized what that junk room really was.

It was his parents' stuff. It had to be. Maybe it was mostly his mother's, since he'd mentioned she was a pack rat. Was it possible she'd used this house as storage while Flint was away?

Heart thumping, Daphne turned to survey the kitchen cabinets. Did that mean Grandma Mabel's pot could be *here*? If that old pot in the corner cabinet of Eileen Yarrow's kitchen wasn't *the* pot, the only other place it could be was in this kitchen.

She could skip the vow renewal altogether. She wouldn't have to lie and pretend to be his date. She wouldn't have to be dragged into the old dragons' insane schemes, because she could present her grandmother with the heirloom pot without having to perform a complicated heist.

Daphne set her glass down, then hopped to the wall. She opened the lower cabinets, because surely, that's where heavy cookware would be stored. She found a cabinet full of mismatched Tupperware. The next cabinet had a few stainless steel pots, but nothing made of cast iron. The next one was used as a pantry, filled with spices and basics. Two cabinets remained.

She hobbled to the second-to-last one, wrenching the door open to peer inside. It was full of all types of cookware: baking sheets, cake tins, and . . . a cast-iron pan! Maybe . . .

Daphne pulled out a cake tin to peek behind it. Metal scraped and clattered as she snooped, pushing a pot aside to look behind it—

"What are you doing?"

Yelping, Daphne stood up so fast dizziness swept through her. Gripping the edge of the counter, she turned to face Flint on the other side of the kitchen.

"Were you looking for something?" he asked, frowning. Suspicion drenched his words.

"I was, um . . ." Daphne gulped. "I was trying to figure out dinner."

His frown deepened, and his eyes dropped to the open cabinet. "Right."

The beating of Daphne's heart was loud in her ears. She sucked in a long breath, mind spinning. He knew she was lying. He was angry. He didn't like her snooping. Had he guessed that this was about the pot? Her grandmother had all but broadcast her interest in the old Dutch oven; had he put two and two together? He was a cop, after all.

If he found her out, she'd lose her chance. She wouldn't be able to go to the vow renewal and get the pot back for her grandmother.

That thought shouldn't have induced such panic in Daphne. But she'd lived her whole life trying to do the right thing, and now she was at a crossroads. Restoring a family heirloom to its rightful owner *was* the right thing. But not only that, her grandmother had seemed so proud of Daphne for wanting to do it. She felt like a little bit of a rebel for planning to take it back, and that felt *good*.

For once in her life, Daphne felt like a Davis. She felt like she belonged in the family in which she'd been born. Until that exact moment, when Daphne realized that she could lose that feeling as easily as she'd gained it, she hadn't known just how desperate she was.

She wanted to belong. She wanted to come home and feel like people were happy to see *her*. She wanted to feel like she was a part of her family, and not just the one that people patted on the head and congratulated for being good.

She'd lost everything these past two years. She couldn't lose them too.

So when Flint opened his mouth to say something, Daphne knew he'd question her. She knew she'd crack under the pressure, and she might even blurt out the whole sordid tale. And then he'd think she was a pathetic liar who'd used him. She'd be humiliated, and she'd probably lose her job. Again.

Daphne couldn't let that happen.

There was a part of her—a small part—that hated the thought of Flint being disappointed in her. They'd reached a kind of truce. They were getting along. How would he treat her if he found out about her scheme?

She'd lived her whole life doing what was right. She'd gotten the grades. The scholarships. The degree. The fiancé. The mortgage. She'd planned to have a family. She'd wanted a perfect wedding.

Now what did she have?

She had a silly cast-iron pot that might not even exist. That was all she had to hold her to her family, to prove to them that she was one of them.

So, desperation nipping at her heels, Daphne played the only card she had.

Curling her fingers into the opening of her blouse, she wrenched the buttons out of their holes and let the garment slide off her arms, exposing her second-favorite bra to the man on the other side of the kitchen.

Flint's teeth made an audible click as his mouth closed. The blouse fell to the floor beside her injured foot with a soft whisper. Daphne forced herself not to cover herself up, because Flint's face had gone slack as his gaze had traced the shape of her demicup bra.

"Wh . . ." He blinked half a dozen times, then gulped. "What are you doing?"

That was a great question, and one that Daphne didn't quite have the answer to. "My bra is white lace," she said, which was a ridiculous thing to say because it was pretty obvious that Flint had been staring at her bra ever since she'd stripped her shirt off in his kitchen, and he was clearly able to deduce the color and fabric. "Do you . . . like it?"

His gaze snapped up to her face. "What?"

She'd never seen him this confused. He wasn't the confident man in charge. He wasn't the sheriff. He wasn't even the man who'd walked up to her in Jerry Barela's parking lot and found her holding the edges of her ripped shirt. The man looked like he'd lost all capacity to function.

They stared at each other for a second. Two. Three.

Then Calvin Flint *moved.*

CHAPTER 21

In the two seconds it took for Flint to cross the kitchen, Daphne wondered if she'd made a terrible mistake. Another terrible mistake. There'd been a few in recent history.

Then he was there in front of her, his hands sliding over her waist, and thinking became difficult. His thumbs traced the bottom of her rib cage in one hot sweep of skin against skin, and then he moved one hand to cup her neck and jaw.

She'd never seen his eyes so dark. They stared into hers, the length of his body pressed against the length of hers.

"You sure about this?" he rasped.

Daphne's hands had climbed up to curl into his shirt. His hair was wet from his shower, and he smelled like clean skin and soap. "Yes," she said, because what else was she supposed to do? She was the one running topless through the streets just to get his attention. She was the one who'd ripped a few buttons off her favorite shirt to distract him from her snooping.

Besides, it would be a lie to say she didn't want his hands on her body. She didn't *like* him. God, no. But he had this raw male energy that went straight to her head. And whenever they were in a room together, all that energy was directed at her.

She knew that most of what had bloomed between them was lust borne of convenience. He'd invited her to the vow renewal to save his reputation. He'd insisted she stay at his house because he didn't want the hassle of hiring someone new—or finding another date. And now he was looking at her like he wanted to devour her because she'd whipped her shirt off in his kitchen.

It wasn't anything real. How could it be? They were both unsure about their place on the island, and they had history. He was a bad boy who'd turned straight, and she was a good girl who was . . . confused.

Flint slid his fingers to her nape, then tightened them in her hair. He tilted her head back while his other hand swept up her side and over her breast. A tremor went through Daphne's body, and Flint let out a sharp breath in response.

"You have no idea how much I've wondered about your underwear since last week," he said, voice low. His thumb stroked the edge of the lace on the cup of her bra, and her nipple pebbled in response. "Wondered what color it is. If it had a little bow and a dangly charm in the middle. If I'd ever get the chance to see it again."

Daphne's breath staggered. She blinked at him, her own fingers finding their way to his neck. His stubble was rough against her fingertips, his throat bobbing as he swallowed.

"You sound a little bit like a deviant, Flint," she said, and it came out breathier than she'd anticipated.

He pressed his hips to hers, pinning her to the cabinets. His cock was a hard bulge as it pressed into the crook of her hip. "I'm not the one taking my shirt off at every opportunity."

Outrage sparked in Daphne's chest. He made it sound like she was desperate for his attention! "'Every oppor—'"

Flint silenced her with a hard kiss. His hand tightened in her hair as he bent her head back, lips devouring hers. It took less than a second for Daphne to melt like butter on a hot pan. She clung to him, her injured foot lifting up as she curled her leg over his hip.

Flint groaned, dropping his hand from her breast to hook it around her thigh. His hand skimmed the back of it, pinning her between his body and the cabinets. He ground himself against her as his kiss deepened, lips and tongue and teeth shredding every hope Daphne had of using rational thought and responsibility to get herself out of this situation.

She didn't want out of this situation. She wanted more.

"Flint—"

"You're not the good girl you pretend to be, are you?" His lips dropped to her neck, her clavicle, her chest.

Daphne leaned back, head against the upper cabinets, while Flint bent over to suck her nipple through the fabric of her bra. His hair was wet and cold when she gripped it to hold him there, his shirt damp around the collar.

It felt too good. Her mind was splintering. She'd never—

How long had it been since a man had *kissed* her? Really kissed her? Like nothing in the world existed but her lips and her body and her need?

Years. A decade. Longer?

Had anyone ever made her feel like this? Like she was one spark away from detonation?

He moved to the other breast, and Daphne let out a cry of complaint. With one hand still holding her thigh, Flint huffed a laugh against her skin and used his free hand to trace the lace edge of her bra. She watched him, chest heaving with every breath, as he slipped the lace down to expose her breast. Her nipple was hard, and Flint brushed his lips against it gently, gently.

"Flint—"

"Calvin," he corrected.

Tightening her fist in his hair, Daphne arched her back. She needed his mouth on her skin. "Calvin," she begged.

Warm breath gusted out of him, and he gave her what she wanted. He plumped her breast with his hand before taking it in his mouth, tongue teasing, teeth scraping, hand gripping hard.

Daphne was lost. She hadn't planned this, hadn't foreseen what would happen if she cracked open the door to this. It felt so much bigger than fooling around against his kitchen counter. It felt like turning away from the well-lit path of what Daphne should do and taking the first step into unexplored territory.

This man could destroy her. And Daphne didn't care.

He groaned as his kiss moved from her breast to her neck and over her jaw. Daphne turned her head and kissed him back, her hands dropping to the bulge in his pants. She was spinning out of control, and she wanted to wring every bit of pleasure from the moment that she could before her brain started working again. She wanted to *feel*.

Calvin leaned back and watched her palm his cock over his jeans, his lids low. "I used to dream of you doing this," he said, voice a bare rasp. His lips drifted over her shoulder as he pushed the strap of her bra until it fell over her arm. "Used to come home from school hating the way you made me feel, but I wanted you, Daphne."

"You—what?" Daphne asked, blinking.

The man whose body was pinning her to the cabinets let out a laugh that was little more than a sharp exhale of breath. "That surprises you?"

He reached between them to touch her the way she was touching him. The heat of his palm burned her through her work pants, the rasp of her panties almost too rough against her sensitive flesh.

"Yes, that surprises me," Daphne answered, licking her lips. "What do you mean, 'the way I made you feel'? You were the one who almost"—her breath caught when the heel of his palm ground into her clit.

"Long time ago," Flint replied, lids low as his gaze roamed from the movement of his hand to her bare stomach and all the way up to her disheveled bra. "Doesn't matter anymore."

"I think . . ." Daphne swallowed convulsively. The truth was, it was getting more and more difficult to think at all. Flint—Calvin—was sending heat spiraling through her core. All Daphne really wanted was to forget about the past—and the future—and see what happened next.

When his lips crushed hers, she didn't resist. She wrapped her arms around his neck, hooked her injured leg higher on his waist, and ground her hips against the movement of his hand. Her palms moved to his shoulders, then lower. She clawed at his shirt, tugging it up until she could feel warm skin and the hard pack of muscle under her touch. She traced the sides of his stomach, feeling the notches between his muscles. In the center of his stomach, hair rasped against her fingers. She followed it up to his chest, spreading her palms against his skin.

He groaned and pulled away, one hand reaching behind his head to pull his shirt off. Once it fell to the linoleum floor beside them, he flicked open her pants and pulled her zipper down with a harsh tug. His fingertips were warm as they pressed into her stomach and slid beneath the hem of her panties.

"White lace," he said, snapping the elastic.

"Uh-huh," Daphne agreed.

And that's when the doorbell rang.

They froze. Daphne looked in the direction of the front door, breaths jagged, blood on fire. Flint turned her head back to face him with the tips of his fingers and brought his lips to hers.

"Ignore it." He pressed little kisses on her lips, his hand moving lower. He was so close. So close it *ached*. She shifted, rolling her hips, needing—

The doorbell rang again. And again. And again.

Daphne groaned, her forehead falling to rest on his shoulder.

"They'll go away," he insisted, and his fingertips slid through her arousal to roll over her clit. They both hissed. Daphne's head jerked back up, her body bowing toward his touch. Flint's pupils were blown out, his irises the thinnest ring of honey surrounding them. "Fuck," he gasped. "Yes—"

"Daphne!" Grandma Mabel's voice called from outside the front door. "Daphne! We're all here! We brought dinner!"

Horror iced her veins. Daphne's head shot toward the sound of her grandmother's voice, and she shoved Flint's hand away. She scrambled to put her bra back on properly.

"They won't," she told Flint when he just frowned at her. "They won't go away. In fact, they might break down the door any minute, so I need to get some clothes on or I'll never hear the end of it."

Flint picked her shirt up and handed it to her, his jaw tight. He readjusted himself in his pants before facing the hallway that led to the front door, a muscle feathering in his cheek. "I'll tell them we're busy," he said.

"No!" Daphne said, despairing at the state of her mangled buttons. She'd need a fresh shirt. "No, they'll ask questions."

"I'll say you're in the shower," he said, glaring at her.

"They'll just come in and wait."

"This is *my* house, Davis."

"You don't know them like I do."

His jaw worked as he ground his teeth, but Flint finally dropped his shoulders. After picking his shirt up off the floor, he took one step toward the front door, then turned back to face Daphne. His finger came up to point at her. "This isn't over, Cupcake."

"For now it is." She said it to remind herself as much as him, because she knew her family. They were lovely, but they wouldn't go away.

And, selfishly, now that the scorching heat of her lust had been tempered, Daphne was grateful. She'd been a few seconds away from making a very, very big mistake.

CHAPTER 22

Calvin wrenched the door open and glared at the people on the other side. He didn't mean to be aggressive, but judging by the half step they all took away from him, he knew his face wasn't exactly friendly.

He couldn't help it. The softness of Daphne's skin still tingled against his palms. His scalp pricked where she'd fisted a hand in his hair. His lips burned with the need to taste her again.

He wanted to make her come undone. She'd gotten under his skin with her proper, buttoned-up exterior and wildcat heart. Truthfully, she'd always been intriguing to him. Always made him want more. It reminded him of how fiending for something felt, to want to lose himself in oblivion.

That sensation should have been enough to get him to pull back, to show him that pursuing Daphne was bad for his health. But Calvin couldn't help it. She was uptight and proper and a little Goody Two-Shoes, except she *wasn't*. And he wanted to strip away every bit of her armor until he knew her inside and out. Until all her secrets belonged to him.

But he'd been interrupted, the spell had been broken, and he didn't know if he'd get the chance again.

"What?" he barked.

"Well, I never," Mabel said, planting her hands on her hips. "Is that the way you talk to the constituents of this island, Sheriff?"

A deep, measured breath later, and Calvin was a touch calmer. "My apologies. What can I do for you?"

"We brought dinner," Helen said, lifting a silver pot. "Chicken-and-barley soup with fresh bread and butter."

"And a side salad," Ellie added. She carried a wooden bowl covered in plastic wrap. "We wanted to check on Daphne."

"We called," Mabel informed him, "but no one answered."

"If you guys are busy, we can come back later . . ." Ellie's eyes sparkled as a smile tugged at the corners of her lips.

"No," Daphne blurted out behind him. She was at the other end of the hall, leaning against the wall with her injured leg bent so she wouldn't put any weight on it. She was wearing a fresh T-shirt and jeans, but her cheeks were still flushed. "No, we're not busy. We were just talking about getting dinner started."

"I'm sure you were," Ellie said. Daphne shot her a venomous look, which Ellie answered with a smile.

"Good," Mabel said, and shoved her way past Calvin. After stepping into the living room, the old lady looked around for a moment before saying, "You do keep a clean house, Sheriff. I'm impressed."

"How's the ankle, Daphne?" Helen asked, walking past them into the kitchen.

"Getting better."

Ellie followed the two of them around the corner, and Calvin heard her ask, "Are you still going to be able to do the dance at the vow renewal?"

Wanting to follow them but feeling reticent about leaving Mabel unsupervised in his home, Calvin cleared his throat. "Can I get you a drink, Mabel?"

She paused in her inspection of the few photos he'd left on his mantel and met his gaze. "That would be wonderful. Have you got any wine?"

"I don't keep alcohol in the house," he said. "I can get you a soda or water, though."

"Water will be perfect." She smiled at him and turned back to her snooping.

It would be fine to leave her in the living room. She was an old lady, not a threat. But it was strange enough having Daphne in his space—hosting her family was another matter entirely. He liked his things to be kept a certain way. He relied on routine and predictability. His childhood had been marked by the chaos and desperation of having to fend for himself, and now his home felt sacred.

But he could deal with one dinner with a few locals. Daphne had always been close with her family; maybe it was time he got to know them better.

He made it to the kitchen in time to see Ellie hunting through his drawers and pulling out a serrated knife. She moved to the board, where a fresh loaf of bread waited. Helen opened two or three cabinets in search of bowls, which he retrieved for her on the far end of the kitchen. Daphne sat at the kitchen table, watching quietly.

"Tell us the truth, Sheriff—"

"Call me Calvin. Please."

Helen smiled. "Tell us the truth, Calvin. Is the dance at your mother's vow renewal as over the top as it sounds?"

He snorted, dropping a few ice cubes into a glass before grabbing the jug of cold water from the fridge for Mabel. "It's worse," he admitted.

Ellie snorted as she cut thick slices of bread and arranged them on a plate. Glancing at her sister, she said, "I just can't imagine you getting up in front of a room full of people to do a choreographed dance, Daphne. No offense."

Daphne rolled her eyes. "It's not that bad."

"You've always been my quiet, studious daughter," Helen cut in. "Always keeping to yourself. I think it's good for you to try new things. Get you out of your shell."

"As long as she doesn't get any more injuries," Mabel said, ambling into the kitchen. She slung an arm around Daphne's shoulders and squeezed. "You're more suited to a library than a stage, but you'll be all right."

Daphne's smile was tight. Calvin watched her force a laugh as she pulled away from her grandmother, and a pang went through his chest. How much of Daphne's image as the good daughter in the family was her own, and how much of it had been imposed on her?

He *knew* there was more to her than a geeky girl who loved numbers. He knew she had fire in her veins. How could she not, when she'd gotten in the way of Ryan Lane trying to steal a cashbox at the Winter Market, and the pickup truck driver trying to attack her grandmother? Even the way she'd questioned Barela had been proof of her spine.

And then there was the way she acted with him. She was the furthest thing from quiet and studious whenever they were in a room alone together.

A woman who tore her shirt off the way she had a few minutes ago wasn't the "quiet, studious" one.

"Maybe the rolled ankle is a good thing," Ellie added, dropping into a chair across from Daphne. "You can use it as an excuse to keep out of the limelight."

Helen hummed her agreement as she brought bowls to the table. "I just hate to see you hurt, honey," she said, leaning over to kiss Daphne on the head.

Calvin watched the exchange, noting the tightness in Daphne's shoulders. She thanked her mother for the food and said, "I should probably just focus on work instead of jumping into the thick of things. That's more Ellie's thing."

"You've been all off kilter since you got back on the island," Helen agreed. "Just look at your face, sweetheart."

There was a note in her voice that made Calvin's hackles rise. And when Daphne touched her bruises self-consciously, the pressure inside him became too much.

He'd always thought of Daphne's family as a tight-knit, *Brady Bunch* type of clan. In high school, he'd resented her for it. Her dad had been a beloved science teacher and her mom the kindhearted school nurse. Every day, he'd see their perfect little family in the hallways. She'd had it all—both parents, good grades, all the support she could ever need—and he'd had nothing. He'd felt bitter about all the advantages she'd been given, even if her family had a reputation for being lovable troublemakers.

She'd been the symbol of everything Calvin had wanted and could never have. He, who'd lost his dad, who'd been neglected by his mother from the time he was old enough to make his own breakfast, who'd had to pay for all his own clothes and food with whatever money he could scrounge, who hadn't had a single person make him feel like he mattered. He'd seen Daphne, watched her parents drive her home from school, envied the way she had every advantage, and he'd felt the sharp bite of jealousy.

But he'd been wrong.

Just as Calvin had been put in a box marked "Lost Cause," Daphne had been put in a similar one marked "The Good One."

Her family cared about her—that much was obvious. But did they really know her?

"Maybe you should stick to accounting once this vow renewal is over and done with," Mabel said with a laugh.

"Daphne's more than capable of doing whatever she puts her mind to," he cut in, voice harsh. The four women at the table looked up at him with wide eyes. He tried to temper his tone, but his chest was hot and he felt outraged on Daphne's behalf. "She earned those bruises with her bravery," he added. "The fact that she's also a talented accountant is something to be celebrated. It doesn't mean she can't be both."

Daphne blinked at him, straightening. Her eyes were wide and full of emotion. She swallowed thickly and gave him a tiny secret smile. Then she picked up her spoon. "Does that mean you expect me to be up there dancing with the rest of them at the vow renewal?"

"I expect you to teach me the steps, because last time I checked, I'm the one who screwed up and caused that whole mess on Sunday."

Daphne's smile widened until her whole face was lit with it. It was like the sun finally poking out from behind the clouds after a long, dreary winter. He felt the warmth of it from all the way across the kitchen.

Calvin grabbed his bowl and took the last chair at the table. "Besides, I'm pretty sure you've already memorized all the steps. Between you and Ceecee, you can teach me well enough that I won't smack anyone else in the face."

Daphne's laugh was like a balm on his flaring temper. She nodded. "It really wasn't that complicated," she teased.

"I wish I could see this dance," Ellie said. "You think you can sneak a camera into the event?"

For some reason, that made Mabel sit up and take notice. "That's not a bad idea."

Daphne groaned. "Grandma. Please."

Grunting, Mabel simply tucked into her food and ignored her granddaughter. Calvin flicked his gaze from the old woman over to Daphne, who rolled her eyes and shook her head.

"Where's Dad?" she asked, tearing her eyes away from Calvin to look at her mother.

"He and Hugh are fixing the fence on the northern pasture. Two of the sheep got out this morning, and we had to spend three hours looking for them."

"You should have just called me to bring Louie over," Ellie said.

"We didn't want to bother you," Helen replied, helping herself to salad. "I know you're busy with the wedding and the house plans."

"Still. Louie is literally a sheepdog, Mom. He would have brought them back in ten minutes."

Helen just laughed. "Maybe your father and I like the pain of doing it ourselves. It gave us something to do in our retirement."

Ellie snorted, and Mabel laughed. Calvin ate quietly, listening. Eating a home-cooked meal surrounded by people with this much easy comfort with each other was unfamiliar. He wasn't sure where he fit in, or whether he was enjoying himself or not. He still felt on edge on Daphne's behalf, but there was a pleasantness to the company.

"Heard there were two break-ins last night," Mabel said to him after a few moments. "The Deacons' new restaurant and down at Barela Contracting."

"Who'd you hear that from?" Calvin asked, brows arched.

"Who *didn't* I hear it from would be a shorter list," Mabel replied with a sly tilt of her lips.

"You forget that this is Fernley," Daphne chided. Her eyes were lit from within, and Calvin found himself staring at her for a beat too long.

"Right," he said, dropping his gaze to his food. "There was probably a game of telephone going as soon as the thief broke the glass on Romano's window."

"So you think there's only one thief?" Mabel prodded. "You think the two are connected? People are starting to worry, you know."

"As long as you lock your doors at night, I don't see why you should," Calvin replied. "We're still investigating, so I can't tell you anything more than that."

"Playing it close to your chest," the old woman said, arching her brows. "Very mysterious, Sheriff." She glanced at Daphne. "I can see why you like him so much."

"I do not *like* him," Daphne shot back, outraged.

Ellie laughed in her soup, and Helen just looked at her eldest daughter like she'd sprouted another nose. They, along with Mabel, laughed as a flush crept over Daphne's face. When Daphne puffed her cheeks out in embarrassment and began to chuckle, Calvin realized this was the image of her family he'd always envisioned. They were close, they cared about each other, but they teased each other too.

An old wound ached inside him. Growing up, he'd wanted so badly to be part of something like this. He wanted a big family around him. People who gave two shits if he hurt himself, who knew each other's business, who remembered his birthday. And all he'd had was a mother who cared more about moving on with her own life than taking care of him. He learned that he had to fend for himself or ruin himself in the process.

And ruin had been a real possibility.

"I don't *dislike* him," Daphne amended, not meeting Calvin's eye. Funny thing to say, considering what they'd been doing when the doorbell rang. "He's a competent sheriff."

"I might keel over from the praise," Calvin put in before biting off a piece of soup-dipped bread.

Ellie and Mabel laughed, and Helen gave her elder daughter an indulgent smile. Daphne's cheeks grew redder.

He wondered how Daphne had felt growing up with so many big personalities. Maybe she'd retreated into herself because they took up so much space. Maybe shrinking herself to fit the mold of the Good One had been easier than elbowing them out of the way so she could grow.

"I don't dislike you either, Cupcake," he said, and winked when her glare sliced across the table to him.

They finished their dinner, and Daphne's family lingered only long enough to clean up and leave his place as tidy as they'd found it. He helped Daphne totter to the front door to say goodbye to her family, and they both let out a long sigh as he closed the door behind them.

"I love them," Daphne said, "but they're a lot."

He laughed. "I'm starting to understand that," he said, and helped her to the sofa. They sank down into the cushions as the gentle patter of the rain falling on the roof filled the silence. Finally, they were alone again.

CHAPTER 23

Daphne wasn't prepared for Flint to lift her legs up and lay them across his lap. She fluffed the throw pillow behind her head and shot him a suspicious look. "What are you doing?"

"Checking the swelling on your ankle."

"Okay, Doctor," she teased, then closed her eyes as his warm hands slid over the joint. He slipped her sock off and ran a thumb up the arch of her foot. A groan worked itself up her throat before she could stop it.

"How's my bedside manner today?" he asked, voice a touch rougher than it had been a minute earlier.

She threw an arm over her face to stop herself from looking at him. If she saw anything close to the expression he'd worn earlier, when she'd whipped her shirt off in front of him, all bets would be off. "It's getting better," she admitted.

He huffed, hands gently stroking over her ankle. There was a long silence before he said, "Your family's nice."

"They're lunatics."

"They underestimate you."

Daphne dropped her arm and looked at him. Flint kept his gaze on her ankle, his hands sweeping down the top of her foot in steady strokes. It felt like heaven, but his words rang like a gong in her head. "What do you mean?"

He shot her a look she couldn't decipher. "They seemed pretty happy to see you as a mousy accountant who belonged in a library."

"Maybe that's what I am."

"Bullshit, Davis."

Daphne huffed. "And what, you know me so much better?"

"I know that you're brave and smart and complicated," he shot back.

"I feel like that's supposed to be a compliment, but it didn't sound like one."

He tilted his head as if to concede the point. "I just think you've shown yourself to be pretty competent in a lot of areas since you've started working for the department. I'm not sure they realize just how much you're capable of."

Daphne rubbed her hand over her chest, right over a spot that ached like an old bruise. "I've always been the black sheep," she admitted.

His thumb stroked around her anklebone. "Oh?"

"Once my sister came along, she sucked up all the attention and the light and the life in the room. I guess instead of fighting against it, I just decided to accept that I was the quiet one. They're not wrong about me being a mousy accountant who belongs in a library."

"You're far from mousy, Daphne," he said, hazel eyes flashing to hers. He blinked, his gaze returning to her ankle. His touch was gentle but firm, teasing the edges of her injury while stroking all the sensitive parts of her foot. It was intimate in a way Daphne didn't quite know how to handle, but she didn't want it to stop.

Heat curled low in Daphne's gut. "You know what I mean."

"I'm not sure I do."

"I just . . . I *like* being on my own, working quietly, doing things that other people think are boring. That's who I am. It's the reason my ex-fiancé broke it off."

"Because you were too smart for him?" Flint's brows scrunched as if it was the stupidest thing he'd ever heard.

"No," Daphne said, jerking as his fingertips tickled the base of her foot. A dart of pain went through her ankle at the movement, and she used it to clear her head. "No. Because I was the safe option, and he got bored of me."

The furrowed brow didn't go away. Flint stared at her. "The man got bored? Of *you*?"

Rolling her eyes, Daphne let out a scoff. "Come on, Flint. I'm an accountant."

"So?"

"So, by definition, I'm freaking boring!"

"I stay awake at night wondering what mess you're going to get yourself in when I have my back turned, Davis. You're not boring. A woman who wakes up and decides to wear red lace lingerie on a week-day morning is not a boring woman."

The heat that had sparked in Daphne's gut moved lower. "Well," she said, and then her words died. Her throat was tight when she said, "When he broke it off with me, my ex told me it was because I wasn't spontaneous enough. I didn't take enough risks. He felt like he was settling for me."

The movements of Calvin's hand on her foot stilled. He frowned at her. "He said that?"

She nodded. "I don't think he's entirely wrong. Up until a couple of weeks ago, I didn't take any risks at all."

"What changed?"

A gust of wind blew rain against the living room windows. Daphne stared at the darkness beyond the glass, watching the raindrops slicing through the cone of yellow around a streetlight. "I'm not sure. Maybe I got sick of feeling like my life was passing me by."

"For what it's worth," Calvin replied, his hands beginning to massage again, "it sounds like your ex was an idiot."

She snorted. "He wasn't that bad."

"Even after he did that to you, you defend the man?"

"Maybe I still think he was right."

Calvin's jaw tightened. He focused on the movement of his fingers as he said, "I don't." His thumb swept around her anklebone. "I don't think he was right at all. But I guess that's his loss."

Not knowing how to answer, Daphne sat there and stayed silent. Calvin slid her other sock off and began to massage her healthy foot. His fingers were strong as they dug into her arch, his thumb moving to run down between the bones at the top of her foot. Daphne sank down into the couch cushions, letting the tension of their conversation drain away.

No one had ever made her feel the way Calvin did. Not the way he poked and needled at her and made her crazy, but the way he *believed* in her. He didn't see a square peg when he looked at her. He didn't see an accountant who belonged in a sad cubicle with her soggy lunchtime salad and her precious spreadsheets. Daphne wasn't quite sure what he saw, but she knew she liked the way it made her feel.

In the silent house sheltered from the rain and cold outside, with his hands stroking her skin, Daphne wondered if, under different circumstances, things between them might have evolved into something real. Something without a ticking clock and a secret heist. Just honesty and attraction and connection.

It was Calvin who broke the silence. He looked at her and said, "You don't need to make yourself fit into the box these people make for you."

"'These people'?"

He lifted two fingers off her ankle in a dismissive flick. "Your ex." He paused. "Your family."

Heart thumping, Daphne met his gaze. It felt wrong to agree with him when her family was so important to her. When she believed, right down to the very core of her, that they were good people. "I've always felt like I never quite belonged in my family," she finally admitted. Even though it was obvious, it was a secret she'd never said out loud, and it felt like handing him a piece of her.

His hands kept moving on her foot, the weight of his arms heavy across her shins. As if he could sense that she'd just bared a part of herself to him and he wanted to give her something in return, Calvin said, "I was horribly jealous of you in high school."

Daphne tucked an arm behind her head, her lips curling into a grin. "What for?"

"I thought your family was this perfect unit. Thought you had it all. I'd lost my dad when I was eight and then been left to my own devices by my mom. I mean, she was young too. They were high school sweethearts, and she got pregnant at seventeen. She didn't grieve my dad like I did. I think she felt trapped by—by me. By her marriage to my dad. Being single after he died was her first taste of freedom."

His brow was furrowed as he concentrated on the movement of his hands over her foot, and a bit of the old ache in Daphne's chest unfurled. She'd never met a man who could read people like Flint could. Who could read *her* like Flint could. His pain was evident in the tightness around his mouth and eyes, but he still managed to speak about his mother's mistakes with empathy.

Emotion crowded Daphne's throat. It made it hard to speak. "Still," Daphne said. "You needed her."

His smile wasn't much of a smile at all. "I learned to do without." He stroked her ankle for a moment; then his eyes took on a distant look. "And then you were this beacon of a healthy family, bright, successful, pretty . . ." He shrugged, his gaze returning to the movement of his own hands. "It almost felt like a slap in the face."

"Is that why you hated me?"

When he glanced over at her, his expression was rueful. "I never hated you, Daphne."

The sound of her name on his lips was sweet and tender and intimate. She wanted to crack herself open and let him in, but that would mean opening herself up to the kind of hurt that could kill her. She gave him a flat look instead. "Bullshit."

He grinned, his hands moving from her foot up to her good ankle. He pushed her jeans up so he could massage the meaty part of her calf. His touch was firm but soft, and it made Daphne want to melt into a puddle of goo.

"I saw you as a worse version of all the things I resented in my sister," Daphne admitted. "A rebellious guy with a chip on his shoulder who went out of his way to try to be bad. Someone who had no consideration for how their actions affected other people."

"That's exactly what I was."

She traced the line of his clean-shaven jaw with her eyes, looked at his neat haircut, his tidy home. This man stood on his own and exuded strength and competence. When she was with him, she felt like nothing could go wrong. She'd been nervous to interview Jerry Barela, but his faith in her had never wavered. He made her feel like she could do anything.

This wasn't the boy she'd known all those years ago.

"What changed?" she asked quietly.

His jaw flexed, and it took a few long seconds for him to speak. When he did, Calvin's voice was low. "I had my first taste of alcohol when I was fourteen," he said. "By the time I failed senior year, I couldn't go a day without a drink. Took everything in me not to flunk out completely and forget about the whole thing, but somehow I managed to scrape myself together and show up enough to graduate a year late. I'd spent a decade fending for myself while my mom jumped from man to man. She'd marry someone thinking they'd fix her life, then divorce and move on to the next. I got lost in the shuffle, I think. Everything seemed hopeless. I didn't see the point of doing things the way I was meant to do them."

Daphne's heart ached. She held herself still as Calvin massaged one calf and then the other, his palms sweeping over her skin, his fingers digging into knots he found in her muscle, his thumbs making slow circles over her flesh as if the feel of her body calmed him. She wasn't sure if he was touching her for her sake or his, but she knew she didn't want him to stop.

"My mom always wanted a good life. She married men she thought would get her ahead. My dad had a steady job at the ferry terminal, but with me coming along so early and only one income, life was tough. He died, and she could move on easier, then. Now she's on her fourth husband, and she's finally made it." His lips twisted bitterly as he slid his hands back down to her ankles, touching the swollen, bruised skin of her injury with a tenderness that was at odds with the strength of his hands.

"I'm sorry, Calvin."

He blinked and turned to meet her gaze. A shadow of a smile tugged his lips. "Nothing for you to be sorry about, Cupcake."

The nickname didn't sound so mocking when he said it then. "Why do you call me that?"

His smile widened. "You don't remember?"

Frowning, Daphne stared into his honey-colored eyes. "Remember what?"

"Your birthday. We had your dad for chemistry, and—"

"He made me cupcakes."

Calvin laughed. "Your face got so red when he brought them out."

"I begged him not to mention my birthday. That was so embarrassing."

"They were good, though."

Daphne huffed, head lolling on the throw pillow. Her eyes lingered on Flint's features, and she loved the way his gaze softened when it met hers. When he smiled, he was so handsome it almost hurt to look at him. "I remember now," she said, braiding her hands over her stomach. "You were sitting behind me—"

"I always sat behind you."

Daphne stuttered, then recovered and said, "And you whispered 'Happy birthday, Cupcake' in my ear."

"I thought you were going to smash your cake in my face."

"I considered it."

Flint laughed, his hands still stroking her calves, ankles, and feet. "I was so jealous that day. No one had ever made me a birthday cake, and you didn't even seem to appreciate yours. It felt good to make you mad." His smile turned a little sad. "Sorry."

"I forgive you," Daphne responded, a wry smile on her lips. She opened her mouth to ask him about never having had a birthday cake of his own, but reconsidered. How was it even possible? A life without a family who showered her with affection, even if they didn't quite get it right all the time. Suddenly, she felt like an ungrateful brat for not appreciating her family. They only saw her through the lens of Responsible Daphne, but she'd never questioned their love for her.

She met Flint's gaze and found him watching her. "I can't believe you still speak to your mother," she said. "I'm not sure I would. My family members have their flaws, but I know in my soul I can count on them."

"I probably wouldn't speak to her if it weren't for Ceecee," the man whose hands touched her like she was precious admitted. "The only reason I took the job as Fernley's sheriff was to make sure my sister wasn't experiencing what I went through. I'm not sure how I feel about my mother. A big part of me doesn't care and just wants to let it all go, but she keeps trying to reach out. Another part of me hates the fact that she's happy."

"I'll sabotage the dance and smack her in the face with a feather at the vow renewal if you want me to."

He laughed, then, a full, deep sound. His eyes sparkled as he shook his head. "I appreciate it, but no. I don't think that'll make me feel better." He squeezed her good ankle for emphasis, then said, "To answer your original question, what changed is that I moved away from Fernley and nearly drank myself to death by the time I was twenty years old. I was working nights at a warehouse, and the foreman found me passed out on the job. Instead of firing me, he took me home. It was the first time someone gave a shit about what happened to me. The first time I felt like an actual human being."

Daphne's throat constricted. Her eyes stung, but she didn't want to cry. She didn't think the man baring his soul to her would appreciate it right now.

"He let me stay with him for months while I cleaned myself up and figured out what I wanted to do. His father had been a cop, and I spent a lot of time talking to both of them. I figured the best thing I could do was find a career where at least it felt like what I was doing had meaning."

Another crack formed in the armor that encased Daphne's heart. "I'm so sorry, Calvin."

His lips tugged. In a voice that was barely louder than a whisper, he admitted, "I like it when you use my name, Daphne. Sounds good coming from your lips."

When he lifted his gaze to meet hers, his eyes were dark and haunted. He'd dredged up his past and handed it to her on a platter, and Daphne couldn't figure out why. All she knew was that this man wasn't the arrogant, full-of-himself jerk she'd thought he was. He wasn't a bad boy with a chip on his shoulder who was all grown up and ready to cause more trouble. He was a complicated, honorable man who'd pulled himself out of his own personal hell through strength of will alone. He'd rebuilt himself, brick by brick, because that's what he had to do to look himself in the eye every day.

He was *good.*

And what did that mean for her—for them? She had no plans to stay on Fernley once the job ended, and the last thing she wanted to do was change her life plans for a man. The only reason she was here was to find a bit of steadiness before she could move on and chase her dreams properly.

But—what dreams? A gray cubicle in a sad office building? Wilted lettuce in a Tupperware at her desk? A man who settled for her because she was the safe option?

What had she *really* lost these past two years, other than shackles holding her back?

And how would he react when he found out she'd lied about the vow renewal? How could she possibly explain the fact that she planned on stealing back an old, worthless pot? She was using him to prove something to herself—to her family—and the more time she spent with him, the worse it felt.

She could admit it to him now. They'd opened up to each other; it would be the perfect time.

But what if she told him about the family heirloom and he pulled away? She'd lose him and any chance of retrieving her grandmother's Dutch oven. She might even lose her job if he took enough offense.

There was a slight chance he'd help restore the pot to Grandma Mabel. But was it worth the risk of losing it all?

"Talk to me," he said, torso leaning toward her on the couch.

Daphne bit her lip. There was *something* between them, but what if it was just the convenience of proximity, built on the shaky foundation of shared high school experience? Telling him about the pot would mean betting that this budding romance was real. It would mean trusting him to understand that it wasn't an old cooking pot. It was a precious family heirloom that contained her grandmother's childhood memories. It was Daphne's one chance at proving that she wasn't the boring, safe option that would inevitably be tossed aside when someone better came around. If she got her grandmother's pot back, that would mean she truly belonged in her family. It would mean Pete had been wrong about her.

Could she take the risk of telling him and losing her chance? She'd been taking more risks lately, but betting on this tenuous connection with Calvin Flint seemed like more than a risk. It was reckless.

Besides, she still needed that out. If she wanted an excuse to leave the island once her project with the sheriff's department was over, she couldn't mess this up with Calvin. As she sat on his couch and shared secrets with him, though, it was hard to think about leaving the island at all.

Blinking, Daphne met his gaze. She couldn't bear the thought of losing this thread of intimacy with him, even though she didn't have the courage to tell him about her harebrained scheme. Instead, she gave him another piece of her. "I'm ashamed of myself for thinking so badly of you," she finally replied.

His face softened, head leaning back against the cushions. His hand slid from her calf up to her knee, the warmth of it a brand through her denim. "Don't be. Whatever you thought about me, I can promise you I thought worse. And I'm sorry I got you in trouble with Mrs. Matthews."

Daphne snorted. "We're going there, huh."

His grin made it hard for Daphne to breathe. "I'll go anywhere with you, Davis."

It hit Daphne that she was in trouble. It was written all over the teasing smile on Calvin's lips, paired with the tenderness in his gaze. She felt trouble lurking in her heated blood, pulsing in her wrists and neck and core. The longer she spent with this man, the harder it became to resist him.

Even when he brought up the main reason she'd cursed his name for nearly two decades.

Halfway through senior year, Calvin had copied from her during a math exam. It should have been an automatic failure for both of them, and Daphne had had to beg and plead to be allowed to retake the exam, since a failure would have cost her a lot more than a bad grade. Her scholarships—at the time, her whole future—depended on top academic performance.

After teasing her relentlessly all year, Flint hadn't seemed remorseful in the slightest that he'd almost cost her everything. She'd hated him with a passion from then on.

As the memory resurfaced, a gust of breath left Daphne's nose. What had seemed so important to seventeen-year-old Daphne now seemed inconsequential. "I was so mad at you for so long. I cursed your name anytime I thought of you for years."

Interest sparked in his gaze. "Are you saying," he asked slowly, "that you kept thinking about me all this time?"

"Don't sound so smug," Daphne shot back, but her cheeks were flaming.

"I didn't know I'd left such an impression."

"I'll never hear the end of this now."

He laughed, his thumb stroking the inside of her knee. "'Daphne Davis was obsessed with me for years,'" he mused. "Sounds pretty nice when I say it out loud."

Clicking her tongue, Daphne reached over to pinch the underside of his arm. When he yelped and jerked back, she harrumphed. "'Obsessed' isn't the right word, Flint. More like 'extremely spiteful.'"

"Better than being forgotten." His smile was broad and unrepentant.

"You're the most annoying man I've ever met."

He beamed at her like she'd just paid him the compliment of a lifetime. Daphne's heart couldn't take much more of this. She swallowed past a lump in her throat, wondering what they were doing. What this meant. Tearing her gaze away from him, she fiddled with a stray thread on the seam of the couch. It took a while to start breathing properly again.

When Calvin finally spoke, his voice was quiet. "I'm sorry, Daphne. I shouldn't have copied off your paper. I'd studied, you know. I'm sure I could have passed on my own, but I was a bitter little shit who didn't care who I hurt. You didn't deserve to be taken down to the gutter with me."

All at once, Daphne saw him clearly. His strength. His spirit. His independence. It took bravery and humility to admit that he was wrong, and he did it without hesitation. Nineteen years later, he wanted to make sure that she knew he'd taken responsibility for his mistakes. He didn't just brush it under the rug. He owned up to it, even if it had only been a high school math test.

There was so much about this man that she admired. So much she wanted to discover. Not only that, but Daphne wanted to burrow into his heart and heal all the hurts that life had dealt him. She wanted to be the one he knew he could rely on when there was no one else.

For the first time since she'd broken up with her ex, Daphne wanted a man, and it wasn't only physical. She wanted to mean something to him. Wanted him to mean something to her.

And she was terrified.

CHAPTER 24

It had never felt this natural for Calvin to have someone in his space. His home had always been his sanctuary. He relied on the solitude and serenity of it to center himself every day. In a world that had showed him no one cared, home was the one place he could unwind the tension in his shoulders and just *be*.

But now Daphne was here, and he wondered if he'd been missing something all along. He'd found his way through his adult life mostly on his own, thinking it was the best way to keep his head on straight. After all, other people couldn't be relied on. His family had left him, either through death or neglect. His friends had been as troubled as he was. The only person who had cared had been his manager at the warehouse, and even with him, Calvin knew he'd overstayed his welcome after a few months.

It had never been more comfortable to be with someone than it would've been to be alone. Until now. Until he had the weight of Daphne's legs over his lap and the light of her smile shining on his face. His chest was tight as his thumb stroked the inside of her knee, a soft, insistent yearning growing in the pit of his stomach.

He wanted endless evenings like this. A lifetime of quiet moments, of jokes that would hardly make sense to anyone else. He wanted teasing and soft touches. He wanted to know that someone out there thought of him when no one else did.

The wanting took Calvin by surprise. It was so much deeper than sex. So much more than just companionship. He wanted something that he hadn't realized existed until now. It was like finding a portal to another world hidden in a house he'd lived in his entire life.

In Daphne's eyes, he saw an emotion he couldn't name. It looked like fear and longing and need all wrapped into one. Gulping thickly, he moved his hand an inch higher on her thigh, the denim of her jeans rasping against his palm.

"I should go to bed." Her whisper seemed to echo all around him, sounding louder than it should have.

Calvin froze, his hand still resting on Daphne's thigh an inch above her knee. "Of course," he said, but his voice sounded tight.

"I—I'm sorry—"

"Stop, Daphne," he interrupted gently. "Don't apologize."

Her teeth sank into her bottom lip, chin jerking down. "I'll see you in the morning?"

"Yeah," he said, and helped her to her feet. Once she'd retrieved her crutches, Calvin watched her move down the hall and disappear into her room. He sank back down onto the sofa, but it didn't feel as comfortable as it had a moment ago.

Maybe he was a fool for thinking he could have more. Hadn't he learned that in life, he always ended up alone? That he had to fend for himself, because no one would be there for him when it counted?

He was wishing for things that could never belong to him. He'd do best to remember that next time he thought he could make Daphne his.

The next morning, they made it to work without mentioning the kiss in the kitchen, even though Calvin found his gaze flicking to Daphne's lips whenever he thought she wasn't watching. No matter what he'd told himself the night before, he still wanted her.

By the time they made it to the station, his nerves felt stretched tight from being in the cab of his truck for the short ten-minute drive, surrounded by her scent and her voice and her presence. He was glad when Shirley told him that Chuck and Iris were fighting about the alpacas again, because it gave him an excuse to leave the building. Hank joined him, since the older man had a knack for calming the feuding neighbors.

As they drove out of Carlisle and toward the alpaca farm, the houses gave way to forest and the road began to wind.

"Nice of you to take Daphne in," Hank said, his eyes on the road ahead of them.

Calvin nodded, one hand on the steering wheel, the other drumming a beat on the door. "She's not a very difficult houseguest."

"That doesn't surprise me." Hank glanced over and smiled, his eyes crinkling at the corners. Then his smile faded, and he gave Calvin a long look. "Nice girl. Good family. Deserves the best, she does."

"Are you trying to tell me something, Hank?"

"I'm just saying, she's not the type of girl a man should toy around with."

Calvin stiffened. The muscles in his neck went hard. "What makes you think I'm toying around with her?"

Hank lifted his palms, his voice still calm when he said, "I'm just making conversation."

"If you have something to say to me, just say it, Hank."

"Daphne is a good girl, Sheriff. Always plays by the rules. Always does the right thing. That's all. I don't want to see her hurt."

"Is that all anyone around here cares about?" Calvin snapped. "How *good* Daphne is? How responsible? How many boxes she's ticked in life? How about you ask *her* if she feels like she's being toyed with, Hank. How about you ask yourself if there might be more to her than what she lets you see."

In the pause that followed, Calvin dragged in long breaths and tried to wrangle his temper back under control. He was on edge from last night. Frustrated at his own feelings, his own desires. And he was mad that everyone on this godforsaken island seemed to see Daphne as a one-dimensional person who was only good at accounting and doing the right fucking thing.

"I see," Hank replied quietly when Calvin's breathing had returned to normal. "I apologize for overstepping."

"And what's that supposed to mean?" Calvin's voice was still harsh. His knuckles were white on the steering wheel, his eyes glued to the road ahead. He was seething.

"I misread the situation, Sheriff. That's all. I didn't think this thing between the two of you was the real deal."

Calvin almost laughed. Was it real? What the hell was going on? They'd agreed to go to his mother's vow renewal because Daphne was trying to salvage her reputation, and Calvin . . . Calvin didn't know what he was doing. He was taking whatever scraps of attention he could get, even though he knew it would end badly.

A few minutes later, they pulled into Iris Whittaker's long gravel driveway. She was wearing rubber boots and an old winter jacket, glaring at two soggy alpacas who were munching on her grass. She was a short woman of about seventy, her head crowned in gray-and-white curls. Today, the shotgun was absent, which sent a little dart of relief through Calvin's chest.

Sneering at Calvin and Hank as they parked and got out of his truck, she thrust her arm at the animals. "You see what I have to deal with? They're worse than the deer!"

"Now, Iris," Hank said, ambling over to her porch. "We'll get this figured out. No need to get upset."

"'Upset. Upset'!" The woman's face went red. "You watch your tone, young man."

Hank propped a foot on the first step of her porch and gave her a respectful nod. Calvin turned at the sound of an engine. Chuck Rutgers came bouncing down the driveway in a rusty old Ford, glaring at Iris through the windshield. Sighing, Calvin turned to face the other man, lifting an arm to get him to stop.

Chuck had wispy hair that grew in a ring around his head just above his ears. He slammed a hat over his pate as he parked next to Calvin's truck. The Ford's door flung open, and Chuck stomped out. He glared at the woman on the porch.

"You've been taunting them, haven't you?" he accused.

"Get your filthy animals off my property!" Iris sneered as she spoke, pointing a gnarled finger at Chuck.

"Who're you callin' filthy?"

Hank sighed and exchanged a tired glance with Calvin. He held up his hands. "Let's just all take a deep breath, folks. Chuck, I'm going to ask you to take a step back. Iris, if you wouldn't mind going inside the house for a moment."

"Not while he's on my land, I won't," she said, blazing eyes glued on Chuck's face.

Chuck smirked, and Calvin wondered if the older man let his alpacas out on purpose to antagonize Iris. He wondered if he lived near Daphne for decades without being able to call her his woman, whether he'd resort to the same just to get her attention.

An hour later, the alpacas were back in their pasture, a heavy squall of rain had hit the island, and Calvin and Hank were on the way back to the station.

"I give 'em three days," Hank said. "You?"

"Maybe three hours," Calvin grumbled. "Did Chuck and Iris ever date?"

Hank laughed. "Married, divorced, then married again. The second divorce was messy."

"And now they live next to each other."

"Can't stand each other. Can't stand being apart," Hank agreed.

Calvin hummed. He slid into his parking spot and jogged into the station, jacket pulled up over his head to block the rain. As soon as he was inside, he noticed the clump of deputies standing by the kitchen hallway, sipping coffee, chattering animatedly.

He was sick of people. Sick of all the bullshit. Sick of never getting what he really wanted. He stripped his wet jacket off and hung it up just inside his office door.

That's when he heard his mother's voice.

CHAPTER 25

Daphne hadn't even been able to work through half a dozen lines of her spreadsheet before Eileen Yarrow appeared in the interview room doorway. The older woman had thrown a curious look around the room, then turned her bright eyes to Daphne.

"I hope you don't think a rolled ankle will get you out of the dance," she said by way of greeting, shifting the garment bag she held slung over one arm onto the other. "I heard you should be good to go within a week or so."

"Mrs. Yarrow," Daphne replied, blinking. "Good morning."

"Same to you," Eileen said, then lifted the garment bag. "Ready to try on your dress?"

Daphne blinked, then jerked back. "My dress?"

How, ten minutes later, Daphne found herself locked in the staff bathroom wearing a horrific eighties prom dress, she wasn't sure. Eileen had been insistent, and Daphne's protests went unheard. Eileen had a vision, she said. She wanted all the dancers, including her son's date, to look the part.

What part? was the question.

Daphne ran her hand down the iridescent-pink fabric that poofed out at the hips and fell in ruffly tiers to her midcalf. A sweetheart neckline was capped with the most gigantic puff sleeves Daphne had ever seen. On her left hip, a big floppy bow announced the beginning of the tiered portion of the skirt, as if anyone could miss it.

On the bathroom counter waited a sparkly pink tiara.

She looked like a little girl pretending to be Barbie for Halloween. Or an amateur ballroom dancer who'd accidentally stumbled into the wrong DeLorean.

She jumped when someone rapped on the door. "So?" Eileen called out. "Does it fit?"

"Um," Daphne replied, eyes glued on the reflection in the mirror. "Define 'fit.'"

"Come out. If we need to make alterations, I need to know now. We haven't got much time."

"Yeah, come out!" Shirley said. "Eileen has always had great taste."

Daphne glared at the door. There was a low hum of conversation outside the bathroom, and Daphne could only imagine the audience she'd have when she stepped out. Cops were the worst gossips, and today had been slow. They were desperate for entertainment.

Sighing, Daphne limped to the door. She was doing this for her grandmother. If she had to embarrass herself in front of a few people, who cared? This would all be worth it when she got her grandmother's heirloom pot back. Besides, it wasn't like she and Flint were actually dating. She could play along with this ridiculous outfit if it got her into the party.

Shoulders squared, Daphne flung open the door.

Only to see the sheriff walking across the office toward her, his mother beckoning with a hopeful smile on her lips. The group of deputies waiting by the bathroom door went deathly silent. Calvin's steps stuttered, his brows slamming down.

"Perfect," Eileen crooned when she saw the dress. "You look amazing, Daphne."

"You sure do," Shirley added, fingers doing a terrible job of covering her twitching lips. "I think I might have worn something similar to my homecoming dance."

"It's very . . ." Teri frowned as she took in the sheer volume of fabric. "Much," she finished.

"'It's very much'?" Daphne repeated, planting her hands on her hips.

"That it is," another deputy said.

She turned to face Flint, who had recovered from his stumble and approached the group. His frown was still firmly in place, his eyes slitted as they swept down Daphne's body and back up again. Turning to his mother, he asked, "Is this a joke?"

Eileen reared back. "Excuse me?"

"Is this a joke, Mother?"

"A joke! Why would I joke about my vow renewal? You know how much I care about this event. We've done fittings for all the other dancers. Ceecee loves her dress! She and Kathy helped me pick them out. Kathy said the flounces would look great when everyone twirls, and Ceecee picked the color. I told you we were doing hot pink, didn't I?"

His jaw worked, and he turned back to Daphne. "Would you have made Jenna Deacon wear this thing?"

"What kind of question is that?" Eileen said. "Calvin, this is for a *performance*. Kathy insisted we go for volume, especially for the big feather reveal."

"It definitely has volume," Shirley offered, fluffing the bottom hem.

"The proportions . . . ," Teri put in, nodding, failing once again to finish her sentence.

Despite the edge of embarrassment, Daphne found her lips twitching. Eileen was obviously a delusional maniac without an ounce of fashion sense, which was oddly endearing. And the look on Flint's face was a strange mix of horror and humor.

A few years ago, Daphne would have considered backing out. Back then, her life had been safe. Small. But now, what did she care? The only reason she was going to Eileen's event was to get a cast-iron pot back. She'd returned to the island at her lowest. What did it matter if she had to show up in a ridiculous dress?

She was doing this for her grandmother, and for herself. She'd wear whatever was required.

"Mother—"

Daphne's dress crinkled and swished as she twirled. The yards and yards of fabric spread out around her as she did, knocking into people's legs and the wall behind her. The weight of the fabric was enough to knock her crutches to the ground. She wobbled and caught herself against the wall, then met Eileen's gaze. "Thank you so much for thinking of me. I'd be honored to wear it to your vow renewal."

Eileen gave her a sharp nod. Daphne shifted to look at the sheriff. He had his hands on his hips and was staring at Daphne's dress like he wanted to burn it.

"Mom. Daphne. I'd like to speak to you both in my office." He gestured toward the opposite side of the room, and his mother squeezed his arm as she brushed past. Shirley picked up the crutches from the ground and helped Daphne squish the dress out of the way so Daphne could use them without tripping over her own clothing. Then she bit her lip to hide her smile and swung her way over to the sheriff's office.

She should've known the moment she saw Kathy directing their ridiculous choreography that there'd be costumes. Still, she couldn't have predicted this.

Slumping into one of the chairs, Daphne patted the fabric down so she could see over the top of it. Flint's face appeared, and she wasn't sure if he was angry or trying to hold back his laughter. Maybe both.

He turned to his mother, who sat in the chair to Daphne's right. "You never mentioned anything about a dress."

"You never asked."

"Daphne, you don't have to wear that thing."

"Of course she does!"

Daphne plucked at the fabric, watching how it shimmered under the fluorescent lights. "I think it's nice," she lied.

Eileen looked at her son and gave him a look that said *See? She thinks it's nice.*

"It looks like something from a Molly Ringwald movie, Mom."

"What's wrong with Molly Ringwald movies? Archie's favorite is *The Breakfast Club*."

Daphne fluffed one of the shoulder puffs. "Not *Pretty in Pink?*"

Flint pinched the bridge of his nose, then lifted his gaze to Daphne. "You're okay with this?"

Daphne shrugged, the fabric on her shoulders flapping like wings. "Sure."

Eileen patted Daphne's arm, then looked at Flint. "Calvin, look. If you don't want to do the dance, I understand. I know you and I . . . I know things haven't been easy. It was Ceecee that got excited about the choreography, and I . . ." Eileen touched the iridescent-pink fabric, feeling it between her fingers. "Maybe I've gotten carried away with it all. It's just a bit of fun, you know? Something to get people talking." She straightened her shoulders and looked at her son. "But I won't force you to do anything. I'm just glad you're coming."

Daphne watched the way Eileen smiled at Calvin and felt a pang of empathy. There was sadness in the older woman's gaze—and understanding. This wasn't a woman who felt good about her relationship with her son, but she looked almost lost as to how to fix it. Maybe it couldn't be fixed.

But a woman who was happy to have a silly dance with feathers and ridiculous dresses to mark her ten-year anniversary was a woman who liked to laugh, and who wasn't afraid to laugh at herself. It was a woman who took her nine-year-old daughter's opinions into consideration and didn't get hung up on appearances.

Either that, or she had awful taste.

Flint sighed, gaze sliding to Daphne. "It's up to you," he told her.

She heard what he didn't say: that he knew she didn't love to be in the limelight, and he'd listen to her if this dress was a step too far. He didn't think Daphne was the quiet, responsible good girl that everyone else seemed to see, but he still wanted her to be comfortable.

"Ceecee would be disappointed if we backed out," Daphne responded. "She lights up every time she mentions the dance."

"It was her idea," Eileen admitted, lips twitching. "Mostly, I'm looking forward to showing her the video when she's old enough to be embarrassed about it. And her father will do anything she asks," she added with a soft laugh. "'Wrapped around her little finger' doesn't even cover half of what she's done to him."

Daphne grinned. "She's a good kid."

Eileen smiled wide, then darted a glance at her eldest. "I'm just trying to do it right this time around." Her voice was quiet, but Daphne still heard her remorse and her pain. It wasn't her place to get between Flint and his mother, but she wondered whether there was any hope of forgiveness from him.

"You can change out of it after the dance," Eileen offered. "I think everyone else is planning to."

Daphne dipped her head. "Sounds good."

Flint's shoulders softened, and tenderness entered his expression when he lifted his gaze to Daphne's. "It would make Ceecee happy," he agreed.

"Worth it," Daphne replied, smoothing her hands down the fabric.

Flint escorted his mother to the exit, watched her walk out of the station, then prowled back into his office. He closed the door, threw the lock, and drew the blinds. When he turned back to Daphne, his eyes were dark as sin.

"Uh-oh," Daphne said a second before the sheriff hauled her out of her chair and dropped her on his desk.

"'Uh-oh' is right," he said—and crushed his lips to hers.

CHAPTER 26

Daphne's knees spread on instinct, but the dress had far too much volume to allow Calvin any kind of access. She laughed as he batted at the fabric, crushing the skirt and its many petticoats between them, a deep line carved between his brows.

"I hate this dress," he said, giving up on the skirt to wrap his hand around Daphne's nape. His lips were soft and giving, his tongue delving into Daphne's mouth with expert flicks.

Daphne pulled back and laughed, fluffing the fabric. "Can't imagine why."

"I've never wanted to undress you more, and that's saying a lot."

Heat sparked between Daphne's legs at the look on Calvin's face. She'd never seen such bare need. Not directed at her. So when he leaned over the pile of fabric to kiss her harder, Daphne didn't push him away. Instead, she wrapped her arms around his shoulders and held him tight.

Somewhere in the back of her mind, she knew they shouldn't be doing this. Not at work—not at all. She'd opened the door to it by stripping her blouse off the night before, and that had sent her tumbling off the edge of a tall cliff. She was falling through thin air, hardly able to breathe.

But Calvin's kiss was demanding, and Daphne's body responded like it had been made for him. Even with petticoats and iridescent-pink fabric separating them. Even with the hard wood of the desk digging into the back of her thighs and the knowledge that half a dozen employees were just on the other side of the door. With every touch, he was unmaking her defenses.

Besides, what was she defending against? Couldn't she enjoy the way his fingers dug into her hair? The way he groaned as his lips kissed along her jaw and nibbled below her ear?

No one had made her feel this good, not even—

Pete's face popped into Daphne's head, and she stiffened. How long would it take for Flint to get bored of her? How long until he realized that she was exactly the woman everyone said she was? That there was nothing special or exciting about her?

How much of this attraction was fueled by dredged-up teenage angst?

She'd planned her life with a man who'd tossed her aside like garbage. She couldn't go through that again. Not when she was starting to develop real feelings for Calvin, when she was seeing him as so much more than the bad boy he'd been before.

Calvin must have felt the shift in her, because he backed away an inch, eyes searching hers. "I lost you," he said.

"I just . . ." She shook her head. "This was just supposed to be the vow renewal. Maybe we're getting caught up in pretending."

His gaze flickered, throat bobbing as he gulped. "Is that what you think?"

"Either that or you have a fetish for awful dresses."

Calvin snorted. She was grateful when he took a step back, the tension of the moment dissolving.

Shoving a hand through his hair, Calvin backed away far enough that Daphne could slither off his desk. She turned to straighten some of the papers that her voluminous dress had knocked aside, grateful to have something to do with her hands.

The truth was, it didn't feel like she was pretending. It felt like she very much wanted Calvin, and she very much wanted Calvin to want her back.

But what if they fizzled and burned out? What if she opened herself up to a man once more, only to be told she wasn't good enough for forever?

It was better to focus on what she knew. Numbers. Work. Responsibility. She'd save up some money, keep her head down, and use this opportunity to figure out her next steps. Staying on Fernley Island—staying anywhere near a man as addictive as Calvin Flint—wasn't part of the plan.

Her hands gathered up a stack of papers that had fallen over, lining up the corners of the documents. She bent over to pick up a photocopied document from the floor, shoving her skirts out of the way to reach it.

"Have I made you feel uncomfortable, Daphne?"

Standing, Daphne held the document in her hands as she turned to face Calvin. "Sorry?"

"I thought . . . I'm sorry if I misread what was going on between us."

That was the problem. He very much hadn't misread it. It was Daphne who was falling too fast and too hard. She shrugged one shoulder, the puff sleeve exaggerating the movement. "No. It's not that. I just . . . I'd rather just stick to the deal."

"Even though you're attracted to me and I'm attracted to you."

She tried to give him a flat look, but her cheeks were warming from the admission that he found her attractive. She dropped her gaze to the document in her hands. "I think you've made assumptions about me that aren't entirely accurate," she said.

"Like what?"

"Like the fact that I'm not boring," she said, frowning at the page.

"You're not boring."

"This company name is interesting," she said.

"Daphne, I'm trying to be serious right now," Calvin said, frustration lacing his words. "You're underselling yourself, and I don't understand why."

She shook her head. "No, look. Rated Retails Co. It's an anagram of the account name where the funds for the renovation went." Her skirts swished as she hopped to cross the distance between them, turning the paper to face him. She pointed to the company name. "See? 'Rated Retails' and 'Realist Trade' are anagrams of each other."

Dragging his gaze from her face, Calvin frowned at the paper. He took the sheet from her and stared at the account number. "An anagram is when all the letters are shuffled around, right?"

Daphne knew that they needed to address whatever was going on between them. They needed to lay some ground rules, at least until the vow renewal. Were they pretending to be together? Were they casual? Was any of this real?

But Daphne was a coward after all, because she clung to the company name on that piece of paper like it was the last door floating on the North Atlantic after her ship had hit an iceberg. It was work, and work was safe. Besides, it was the first sniff at that company she'd gotten since they'd spoken to Jerry Barela.

"Yeah. Here." On a scrap piece of paper, she jotted down one company name above the other, then drew lines between the letters.

Calvin approached, the warmth of him pressing into her shoulder. "You saw that in one glance?"

"You have no idea how many times I've stared at the words 'Realist Trade Co.' and the account number associated with the company," she answered, lips tilted. She tapped on the document. "What's this quote for?"

"This is a copy of the contract for the renovation at Romano's. The original is in the evidence locker. We found it at Barela's office the day of the break-in and took it because of the footprint."

Looking past the numbers on the page, Daphne noticed the muddy shoe print on the corner of the sheet for the first time. Her heart thundered. "I need to look something up," she said, and grabbed her crutches.

CHAPTER 27

Daphne's dress sounded like plastic garbage bags rustling as she hurried to get her crutches. Calvin watched the fabric shimmer in the light of his office, wondering if there was anything this woman could do or wear that he wouldn't find attractive.

He'd felt such a rush of emotion for her when she'd agreed to wear it for Ceecee's sake. That she *cared*. And all he'd wanted to do was make her his.

Meanwhile, she'd taken one quick glance at a spare sheet of paper and might have uncovered an important clue. The woman was intelligent and caring and kind. She was sexy and funny and perfect.

He didn't think he could live without her.

But she'd pulled away.

Calvin helped Daphne wrangle the ridiculous fabric, opening the door for her as she hurried to her desk. His heart pounded as he followed her in, watching her sit behind her laptop and bat her skirts out of the way. In a flash, her computer was awake and she was navigating to the Washington Secretary of State Entity Search.

"This has been on my to-do list since we spoke to Barela, but I wanted to finish categorizing and sorting all the transactions first," Daphne explained, her fingers flying over the keyboard. "I like to work methodically; otherwise, things get missed."

Calvin's lips twitched. "Why does that not surprise me?"

She glanced at him, the pink of her dress reflecting on her chest and neck. It was truly a hideous garment, but it was growing on him. "If you want to make a joke about me being a nerd, go ahead. I've heard them all before."

"I don't think you're a nerd."

"That's a good one," she said, mouth curving into a smile. Her brows drew together as the screen loaded in front of them. "Okay, Realist Trade Co. isn't coming up. Let me try the other one."

Calvin leaned one palm on her desk and the other on the back of Daphne's chair. His thumb slid across her back, teasing the skin between her shoulder blades. He couldn't help himself. He wanted to touch her, always. And when she was like this, lit with inner fire, with none of the self-doubt that sometimes crept into her expression, she was magnetic. Irresistible.

"Hmm," Daphne said. "Not that either. Let's check the Department of Revenue website. If they have multiple DBAs registered under the same LLC, we'll be able to find it there."

"DBAs?"

"'Doing business as,'" Daphne answered. "Basically, the customer-facing name of your business."

"And that could be different from the name the business is incorporated under?"

Daphne nodded. A new site popped up, and Daphne typed in "Realist Trade Co." A fraction of a second later, they had the business name, the legal entity name, and the unique business identifier. "Bingo," Daphne said, a tiny triumphant smile curling her lips. "Let's check Rated Retails."

Calvin leaned closer, and the scent of her shampoo rose up to meet him. He looked over her shoulder as she did a second search, both of them exhaling sharply as the screen loaded. Both companies had the same LLC as their legal entity name: BDT, LLC.

Daphne flicked back over to the first website and copied the name into the search box. She didn't even touch the mouse. Her fingers moved faster than Calvin could track, making information flash on the screen like magic. Then it was right there: a name and an address.

Daphne leaned back in her chair as she frowned at the screen. "Robert D. Troy." She turned her head to meet Calvin's gaze. "Why does that ring a bell?"

"Bobby Troy is the man who loved his truck so much he almost took your head off for insulting it just outside the station," Calvin said.

Eyes widening, Daphne glanced at the screen. "The guy who crashed into the convenience store?"

"Bobby D. Troy," Calvin confirmed.

"BDT, LLC," Daphne read, breathless.

"I'll check our records, but I'm pretty sure that's his address." Calvin pointed to the registered business address still glowing on the screen.

Even simply watching her in profile, he could tell that Daphne's mind was working a mile a minute. She flicked over to a new tab on her computer and pulled up a social media site. Within seconds, she had Bobby Troy's picture up on the screen. "The owners of this company trust *this man* to handle their legal obligations? They listed *him* as their registered agent?"

Calvin hummed. "You don't think he runs the company."

"The man cared more about his precious truck than anything else. I can't see it."

"We should go check his place out. See if we can spot anything suspicious."

Daphne straightened, and her eyes grew bright. Then she looked at her ankle and grimaced. "I'll slow you down," she said. "I can do more here. I'm almost through all the financial records, and then I'll be able to work backward and check if I've missed any other suspicious payments going to different businesses registered under the same LLC."

Disappointment washed over Calvin. He liked having her at his side. He enjoyed the bright spark of her mind and the way she made connections so quickly. But she was right. She could do more good here, and she'd be safer too. He was forgetting himself.

"You should get back in your own clothes," he said, touching the gigantic puff sleeve floating in space beyond her right shoulder.

Daphne glanced down at herself with a faint look of surprise. "Right. Good call."

Helping her to her feet, Calvin cleared his throat. "You sure you're okay with wearing it and doing the dance and everything?"

Daphne smiled at him, her hand sliding onto his forearm to give him a squeeze. "We've come this far, Flint. I won't let you down."

Her words were half-joking, tossed out to make him laugh. Instead, they hit Calvin right in the chest and nearly made him stumble. She was ready to face embarrassment for him. He told himself it was just because she was true to her word and she'd made the commitment, but when she looked at him like that . . .

It felt like she cared. Like she was putting him first. Like, maybe, she *wanted* to go to a torturous event with him, because being by his side was better than being alone.

But that was crazy. She'd pulled away from him every time they'd gotten close. She'd been more than clear that she only wanted him to save her reputation from vicious gossip on the island and give her a reason to leave when she was done here. Sure, she was intent on fulfilling her end of the bargain, but it wasn't because she wanted to share some secret joke with him as they went to a ridiculous family event together. They might be attracted to each other, but none of this was real.

Calvin did his best to remind himself of that fact—until Daphne's expression softened and she said, "Be careful, Flint."

"You think Bobby Troy'll start tackling again?"

"I'm just saying, I'm injured enough for the both of us."

Unable to resist, Calvin leaned forward and placed a kiss on the edge of the healing bruise on her cheek. "I'll be careful."

"Good," she said, and gave him a nod that said *Go on*. He watched her hobble toward the bathroom where her abandoned clothing was stashed; then he strode to his own office to double-check Bobby Troy's address. Once he'd confirmed that it matched the registered business address, Calvin grabbed his jacket and headed for the door.

Twenty minutes later, he was pulling up outside a run-down house in the central part of Fernley Island. The houses were relatively close together here, and they were all small and in varying states of disrepair. It was a far cry from where his mother and sister now lived, and it reminded him of his own neighborhood growing up.

He slowed as he approached the front of Bobby's house, looking at the chain-link fence encircling the small yard, the various bits of rusting machinery, the children's toys that looked to be at least a decade old. Overgrown weeds poked their heads out all along the gravel pathway, and the two concrete steps leading to the front porch were cracked right through.

After driving down to the end of the block, he turned and made a loop around the street, checking the back fence. Bobby Troy's precious truck was parked on a patch of gravel at the back of the house, its hood up. Calvin lifted two fingers off the steering wheel in casual greeting when Troy glanced up from the work he was doing on the engine. A scowl marred Troy's brow. He stood still as Calvin drove on and away, watching the whole time.

Calvin could park his vehicle and question Bobby, but that might tip him off. Better to wait until they had more information.

By the time he got back to the station, it was nearly time to pack up and go home. Daphne leaned against his door as soon as he sat down behind his desk, eyes questioning.

"He was home. Mean-mugged me as I drove past."

She hummed, frowning.

Calvin combed a hand through his hair, watching the way the fading light from the overcast sky diffused over Daphne's features. She was beautiful. And strong. And smart. And—

"Better to stay away," she said. "Otherwise whoever owns the business will know we're onto them." Her eyes were far away, clearly having no idea of the direction of Calvin's thoughts.

"Have you made any progress?"

Daphne tilted her head from side to side. "I've requested a copy of the original renovation quotes from Jerry Barela," she said.

"Oh?"

"I was checking the paperwork over again, and the documents almost looked like they'd been tampered with. Thought it wouldn't hurt to cross-check our copies against Barela's records."

"You've got a knack for this," Calvin told her, feeling a rush of pride and—and—something else. Something that ran deep and fast like a river hurtling toward a fall over a cliff.

Daphne smiled. "I'm just thorough. Most people get annoyed with me."

"Most people are dense."

Laughing, Daphne tilted her head to the door. "You got more work to do, or should we head out?"

Calvin glanced at his desk, at the mounds of paperwork he had to get through. Then he stood. "Let's head out. I'm starving."

She rewarded him with a brilliant smile, and Calvin knew he was lost.

CHAPTER 28

The days passed. Daphne felt the urgency of the investigation, sensed the fact that they were closing in on some real answers. She still had a lot of work to do to prepare her report for the sheriff's department, and most of it detailed the mismanagement and banal overspending she'd anticipated.

Everything except the failed renovation that lurked at the back of the building like a monster in the dark. Through that plastic-covered doorway was evidence of something that had gone wrong in this place. The more Daphne dug into the details, the more clearly she saw that something criminal had occurred.

Outside work, Daphne and Calvin circled each other. She'd backed away from him three times: after their kiss in the kitchen, then on the couch, and finally in his office. She knew, from the way he kept himself at a slight distance, that he was giving her space.

The problem was, she didn't know if she wanted it. She fell asleep wondering if she'd taste his kiss again. She woke up needing to slide her hand between her legs to ease the pulsing ache he'd caused there. She stole glances at him every chance she got.

But taking that final step toward him required more courage than she possessed. It meant baring her soul in a way that terrified her. It meant trusting that he wouldn't toss her aside when he got bored of her. If he got bored of her.

He'd never *actually* said that he wanted something beyond the vow renewal. What if he was just running out the clock on their attraction too?

But as the tension wound her tighter every day, Daphne wondered if he was simply responding to her cues, and if that's what her family had done her whole life. Did they treat her like the Good One because that's all she showed them? Was Calvin handing her the reins because he could tell that's what she needed to feel safe?

"Barela's quote was different," she told Flint almost two weeks after they'd discovered Bobby Troy's involvement, on a Monday evening, when the contractor had finally responded with the documents. "Nearly twenty percent lower than what the department ended up paying for the renovations."

Calvin glanced at the papers she presented him, laying them out on his desk side by side. Daphne had ditched the crutches over the weekend, her ankle now able to bear her weight with the help of a soft wrapping. Still, it was a relief to sit down across from him as she watched him study the two documents.

"Renovations that never happened," he said, knitting his dark brows. The sun had set only a half hour ago. The days were getting longer. The fluorescent lights above cast Calvin's face in harsh shadow, but he still looked like the most handsome man Daphne had ever seen.

The sheriff lifted his gaze to Daphne's. "What does this mean?" He pointed to the documents.

She blinked down at what she'd found. "My theory is that the company, BDT, acted as a middleman. Money goes to the business, they skim some off the top, and the rest goes to the contractor. I don't know why they never paid Barela. If they had, and the renovations had been completed as planned, I never would have caught it."

Calvin rubbed his jaw, a long exhale slipping through his nose. Daphne wanted to lean across the desk and run her thumb down his furrowed brow to ease the worry from his expression. The urge to touch him had only gotten worse in the days that had passed. They ate together, drove to work together, spent their evenings together. But since she'd shied away from him the day she'd tried on his mother's dress, Calvin hadn't pressed her.

And she hated it.

She wanted his hands on her body. Wanted his kiss. Wanted his cock. The longer they danced around each other, the more unbearable it became to not have the right to be with him. Truly *be* with him.

But how could she think that, when what they had was based on fakery? Sleeping with him would complicate everything. It was better to keep her distance, to focus on doing her job, and get this vow renewal out of the way. She was only Daphne Davis. She wasn't the one who was chosen in the end. She wasn't good enough, or exciting enough, or spontaneous enough.

She was only good at doing what she was meant to do. Work. Save. Plan for retirement. Make good decisions that somehow never ended up as good as they were supposed to be.

Except . . .

There was Calvin, who looked at her with eyes that said she was special. He made her laugh. Made her feel like she'd discovered none of life's secrets before he showed them to her. When he watched her the way he was watching her now, Daphne saw the world brighten. His focus was all she needed to feel beautiful and important and worthy.

It was folly. Of course it was. He was just a man, and she was just Daphne. They'd struck this stupid deal, and she hadn't told him the truth about the heirloom she'd decided to retrieve from his mother's house, if it even existed. But they'd worked together, eaten together, lived together, and Daphne felt like so much more than she'd been before.

She was sick of holding back.

The change within her happened quietly. One moment, she was terrified of letting him get too close. Then he glanced up, and the frown on his brow cleared. His eyes went soft the way they sometimes did when he looked at her, and Daphne wondered how she'd ever managed to hold out this long.

This man was everything she'd ever wanted. She'd be a fool to let him go.

"You have a funny look in your eyes," he said.

Her throat was dry. "I think I want to go home now."

Eyes flickering, he licked his lips. "Your home or mine?"

He was giving her an out. Leaving her the space she'd requested, even though the desire was written plainly on his face. She knew that if she told him she wanted to go back to her sad little apartment, he'd offer to drive her there. And it would be the end of something they hadn't ever defined. They'd go to the vow renewal—and? Then what?

Despite everything that had happened over the past few weeks, Daphne was tempted. The big slice of her that wanted to curl up in her shell where she was safe and warm begged her to take the lifeline he offered. She could be responsible. She could do what was best in the long run.

Finish her work here. Find a new job. Start her life. Work. Save. Meet and marry an accountant or an actuary who understood her need for fail-safes and safety nets.

The urge to keep herself small and safe was an anchor chain wrapped around her waist, dragging her down below the surface. The longer she spent in Calvin's presence, the more her shell felt like a prison.

She'd been punched, tackled, and challenged. She'd taken a risk on agreeing to the date. And she'd survived. She'd *belonged*. For the first time in her life, Daphne didn't feel overshadowed by the people around her. She didn't feel like the square peg. Her sharp edges were being worn down, and she *fit*.

She fit—with him.

"Your home," she croaked.

Calvin didn't leap out of his chair. He didn't vault over the desk and ravish her where she sat. He hardly moved at all. But a slight tension stole over his shoulders for a moment. His eyes grew sharper as he watched her. Then he nodded and stood.

Extending a hand toward her, Calvin helped her out of her chair. His fingers stroked the inside of her wrist and sent delicate shivers racing over her skin. He stood half a foot away from her and let his gaze drop to her lips, and Daphne trembled with the need for him to kiss her.

Weeks. *Weeks* of this torture, and she'd reached her limit.

Calvin's lips quirked. "Let's go, Cupcake," he said, and in Daphne's addlepated mind, the stupid nickname actually sounded good. His hand traced down every bump of her spine to rest on her lower back, the heat of it blazing through the layers of her clothes.

They walked out of his office, leaving the documents and the computer and all their work behind without a glance. All Daphne's focus remained on the hand at her lower back, the brush of his chest against her shoulder, the sound of his breath, steady and calm.

The more unruffled Flint was, the more Daphne felt herself unravel. She sat in the passenger seat of his truck and watched him close her door. She followed his unhurried movements as he circled the front of the vehicle and got behind the wheel. His hands, broad, strong hands that Daphne was desperate to feel on her skin, gripped the steering wheel and the keys as he started the truck. Every movement was deliberate and composed.

It was torture. Sweet, awful torture. Her thighs clenched and rubbed together, and other than the flicker of Calvin's gaze to catch the movement, there was no reaction. They pulled up outside his house and looked at the low roof, the dark windows, the scraggly bushes on either side of the front door. The engine rumbled and turned off.

And Daphne had had enough. She waited long enough for both of them to unclip their seat belts; then she had two handfuls of Calvin's shirt gripped in her white-knuckled fists, and she was pulling him to her where he belonged. He let out a short sharp grunt of surprise when her lips collided with his, and then those big hands were cupped around her face as he kissed her back exactly the way she needed.

His tongue slid against hers the moment she opened her mouth to taste him. He traced her cheek with his thumb while his other hand dove into her hair and loosened the bun at the nape of her neck. His groan lit a fuse in her veins. She clawed at his uniform, needed to feel skin. Needed *him*.

"Daphne," he said, kissing her jaw, her neck. His stubble was rough enough to abrade, and she wanted to feel it against her inner thighs. With one hand gripping her nape, Calvin let the other slide down her chest. He squeezed her breast before feeling her waist and stomach, rough and needy as he touched her. When he slid his hand between her legs, Daphne spread her knees and rolled her hips toward him. He squeezed her there, over her pants, and Daphne moaned.

"Now," she panted. "Right now."

He huffed, kissing her jaw, her neck. His teeth closed over her earlobe. "All this time, I waited for you. And now you try to rush me?"

Her veins were full of fire. His fingers rubbed against the seam of her pants as Daphne found his lips and kissed him. Her fingers trembled as she slid his buttons free, greedy hands clawing at the expanse of chest she exposed. She'd never felt like this. Out of control. Needy. Desperate.

Something had snapped. Or maybe it had broken, like a dam bursting. All her tightly held control, her careful walls, her responsibilities. They'd rushed out of her, and now she was left with ragged edges and grasping need.

Calvin pulled back. His eyes were dark as midnight, lips wet from her kiss. Between her legs, his fingers teased her clit with far too many layers of fabric between them. "What changed?" he asked, his voice rough.

"When?"

"Why now?"

She huffed. "Do we need to talk about this right now?"

He hummed and squeezed between her legs. A dart of white-hot pleasure streaked through her. "Yes, sweetheart. We do."

Frustration burned her from the inside. She'd succeeded in unbuttoning Flint's uniform, and her fingers were sliding through the coarse chest hair between his pecs. His skin was warm, stretched taut over his muscular frame. She wanted more than a slice of chest. She wanted him naked beneath her, so she could enjoy all of him. Never had Daphne felt so ready to reach out and grab her own pleasure.

And, she realized with a start, never had she felt so safe to do it.

She met his gaze and said the only words that could come close to explaining the seismic shift that had happened inside her. "I'm sick of being good."

CHAPTER 29

Calvin didn't think his heart had ever beat this hard. His entire focus narrowed to the feel of her lips on his. The taste of her mouth. The softness of her skin. The blazing heat between her legs. A lust like he'd never experienced burned through his veins. He wanted this woman desperately. Completely.

Another emotion lurked beneath his desire. Something deeper and more complicated that might have been growing ever since the moment she'd glared at him when he'd pulled her over that first night. Maybe the seeds had been planted nineteen years ago, and all it had taken was one bat of dark eyelashes over furious blue eyes to make them take root.

He was hurtling over a cliff with death waiting at the bottom, and he didn't care because she was finally here, ready, willing, and his.

He should've taken her inside. Should've looked away from her to make sure none of the neighbors were watching. Should've treated her like a gentleman was meant to.

The problem was, he wasn't feeling like a gentleman at all.

When he popped open the button of her pants and slid down the zipper, Daphne's chest trembled with anticipation. Her hands slid over his chest and up to his shoulders, pushing his uniform out of the way. He loved the way she touched him. It was soft and sweet and desperate. She touched him like she never wanted to stop. Like there was something about his skin she couldn't get enough of.

He knew the feeling.

Because the moment he slid his hand into her underwear, Calvin knew they weren't going to make it inside until she came on his fingers. "You're so wet," he marveled, his voice rough as gravel as he touched her. "So wet and hot, Daphne."

She let out a breath that might have been a laugh, her fingers tangling into the hair at the nape of his neck to pull him closer. Her nails dug into him, drawing a groan from his lips. He loved the way she kissed him, with an edge of wildness, a stubbornness, like she'd demand her pleasure from him if he held back.

This was the iron will he'd glimpsed in the flashes of her eyes. The side of her she kept well hidden, lest anyone think she was anything other than the perfectly responsible, perfectly good Daphne they saw.

But she'd demanded this from him the moment they'd pulled up outside his house. She'd kissed him like she'd craved it. And now she rolled her hips into his touch and panted out his name like the sweetest music he'd ever heard.

Her panties were lace. Again. Dark blue this time, so he could see the contrast of his skin beneath them as he touched her. He watched the movement of his fingers, studied the trembling of her stomach. He wanted to memorize this woman. All her moods, her shape, the sounds she made when she came for him. Calvin wanted to drink in every little detail, every reaction, every sigh, and store it away to examine later. He wanted to know all the ways she came undone. Wanted to be the man who learned every secret she kept locked away.

She felt perfect in his hand. Wet and soft and warm and so fucking perfect he couldn't think of anything else. He stroked her until she trembled, fingers finding that bud of pleasure that made her pant. She looked so good when she was flushed and needy and desperate.

Sliding his finger inside her, he watched the flutter of her lashes against her cheeks. His cock was hard as stone, the pressure an aching reminder of what this woman did to him. It was impossible to stop the moan from escaping his lips when he felt the soft clasp of her on his finger. Daphne's lips fell open as he touched her, her chest heaving when he pumped his fingers, then moved to circle her clit. The nails were back, then, little points of pain in his shoulders as she clung to him.

"You feel so much better than I imagined," he rasped, nose tracing her jaw, the shell of her ear. "And I imagined you'd feel like heaven. Can't wait to get inside you."

If he could do that without moving from this exact position, he would. But he dropped his gaze to the movement of his hand, dark lace against his hand, soft, soft skin beneath his fingertips—

"Oh!" Daphne cried on an exhale, hips jerking. "Calvin—" Her hands scrambled for his own pants, but he clicked his tongue and slid another finger into her warmth.

"Stop touching me," he said, curling his fingers until her mouth fell open.

Her eyes were hazy as they met his, the tips of her fingers hooked into the waistband of his pants. She licked her lips as he touched her, then shifted her gaze to the movement of his hand beneath the navy lace.

Nothing existed except her body, her breath. Time lost all meaning as Calvin's attention narrowed to the woman sitting beside him. He felt dizzy with the feel of her, the scent of her, the taste of her. His own need became a feverish thrum inside him, the kind of insistent pressure that felt like it was too much and not enough all at once.

His will was ruled by her soft commands, whispered in the close heat of his car: *Like that, don't stop, softer, harder, yes.*

He'd run headlong into hell if she told him to do it with that voice.

And then she let go. Her cry was a sweet surrender. The arch of her back an image Calvin would remember always. He drank in the line of her neck, the harshness of her gusted breaths, the feel of her hands gripped around his biceps, the jerk and roll of her hips as she chased the pleasure of his fingers.

Her eyes were hazy when he finally slid his hand free. He couldn't resist pressing another kiss to her lips, loving the way she softened at the barest brush of his mouth against hers. Then he was furtively checking the windows to make sure they were alone as he haphazardly buttoned his shirt, and once he was sure they hadn't been seen, he got out of the car and circled around to Daphne's side. She wrapped her arms around his shoulders and let him pick her up. Her cheeks were a soft shade of pink, her eyes the blue of a clear summer sky.

"I can walk now, you know," she told him as he brought her to the front door, her voice still pleasure-drunk and sultry. "There's no need to carry me."

"I know," he said; then he unlocked the door, picked her up again, and carried her across the threshold.

CHAPTER 30

Being in Calvin's arms made Daphne feel drunk in that giddy, effervescent way at the start of a good night. Her fingers trailed over the hair on his nape as he kicked the door closed and carried her down the hall to his bedroom. She'd never been inside it, and even her curiosity about the room couldn't drag her gaze away from his face.

Giggling as he tossed her on the bed, Daphne watched as he tugged his shirt out of his pants and undid the buttons he'd fastened crookedly before bringing her inside. His hair was a mess, his eyes were dark and full of desire, and his movements had lost their fluidity. He looked impatient as he took in the sight of her on his bed, and Daphne felt powerful and beautiful and precious.

The voice in her head that protested about this course of action had gone silent, locked away in a corner of her mind that wasn't accessible here. Instead, her own clumsy fingers worked her blouse open, excitement making her fumble over the tiny white buttons. When she'd finally gotten the last one open, she felt Calvin's fingers curl over her waistband. A breathless laugh slipped through her lips as she lifted her hips to help him shuck off her bottoms, panties and all.

His pants were still on, but her protest died before it could be voiced when he fitted his shoulders between her thighs and brought his mouth to her core. Her hips lifted to meet him, but Calvin's hands clamped over her hip bones to hold her down for him to devour.

"Calvin," she gasped, fingers tunneling in his dark hair.

He hummed against her flesh, tongue and lips exploring every inch of her. With any other man, she would've been self-conscious. Hell, with her ex-fiancé, she'd never been able to relax enough to orgasm like this. But Daphne was untethered. All the threads of her that kept her safe inside her shell had been snipped, and now she was floating on a current of pleasure.

She came again with a cry, body arching as the sensations splintered through her. Limbs heavy, skin flushed, and eyes at half-mast, she looked at the man framed between her thighs and felt a rush of emotion so strong her lungs suddenly felt too big for her chest. He met her gaze as he kissed the inside of her right thigh, his hands stroking her skin like she was something to be cherished.

They moved as if in a dream. Daphne slipped her arms from her blouse and unclasped her bra under Calvin's hungry gaze. His hands worked his belt open, and she found herself fascinated by the movement. The tendons moving under his skin. His deft fingers. His broad palms. A quiet, insistent pulse rose in her, a need to have those hands on her body once more.

And when he pushed his pants and underwear to his ankles, the need grew to a feverish ache. His cock jutted out, its tip glistening. Daphne licked her lips.

"I've imagined this moment," Calvin said, voice rough, as he reached into his nightstand for a condom. "I thought I'd have more control than this."

Daphne huffed. "You seem pretty calm to me."

The bed dipped as he joined her, calloused palms sliding over her knees to spread them. "I'm not," he said. "All I can think about is getting inside you. All I want is to feel you come on my cock, Daphne."

"That can be arranged."

His exhale was shaky. Cock sheathed and ready, Calvin pressed a palm to the bed above her shoulder and dipped his lips to hers. Daphne's body ached for him, and she rolled her hips toward his. He smiled against her lips and nipped at her.

As he settled atop her, Daphne let out a long sigh. His weight pressed her into the mattress, his hips spreading her thighs wider. She could feel him, hot and hard and ready against her folds. All he had to do was shift his body a few inches, and she'd feel the stretch of him pushing inside.

Anticipation clawed at her like a beast scrabbling to get out. Now that she was here, in his bed, she wondered how she'd managed to resist him for weeks. Wondered how she'd possibly survived without the weight of his body on top of hers, without his kisses for sustenance.

"That night you called me," he said, lips tracing her ear, "after I asked you to be my date . . ." He rocked his hips against her, and Daphne's lids fluttered shut.

"Mm?"

"I hung up the phone and jerked off to the thought of you right here, like this," he admitted, grinding his cock over her clit.

Daphne exhaled a weak laugh, hands tracing the muscles of his back and shoulders. "Really?"

"You were so snippy with me, but it didn't matter. I wanted you then and I want you now. You drive me crazy, Daphne. Everything you do turns me on."

It was a heady feeling, to have a man like Calvin Flint admit that she affected him so. To think that he looked past her drab clothing and her love of numbers to notice the woman beneath it all. Or maybe, Daphne realized as he rose up on his forearms to meet her gaze, maybe he appreciated those parts of her as much as the ones she kept hidden. The lace and silk under the boring office clothes. The bravery behind the mousy exterior.

Pleasure darted through Daphne's veins. She felt empty and full all at once. She wanted him to stop looking at her like that, because the depth of emotion in his gaze terrified her—and she also never wanted the moment to end.

"I'm glad you pulled me over," she told him, loving the way his lips curled in response.

And when he shifted his hips and reached between them to fit himself into her opening, Daphne knew the ground was unsteady beneath her feet. She knew something was changing, but she wasn't afraid. She drank in the sight of him, the feel of him beneath her palms, the weight of him on top of her.

He pushed his cock inside, and they exhaled together. Calvin's lids fluttered as a rough groan was ripped from his throat, his forehead dropping to the pillow beside her. Daphne was stretched and filled until it felt like she'd never get her breath back. She wrapped her legs around his waist and rolled her body for more. Her nails carved lines in his hard back. Her teeth sank into his shoulder.

Their movements became frenzied. Nothing existed except him and her and unending pleasure. His lips devoured hers in a clumsy kiss, his hands framing her face as their bodies moved.

"Mine," he said against her mouth, hips snapping to drive himself deeper. "You're mine, Daphne."

She'd regret it later, probably, but the words made her feel like she was lifting off the bed, floating away from all that had kept her small and scared and safe. "Yes," she panted, clutching him closer, kissing him harder, taking him deeper.

Calvin's movements were jagged, his breaths rough. Daphne could sense that he was close, and she wanted to give him as much pleasure as he'd given her. But when his hand reached between them to press at the spot that drove her wild, she was lost.

She saw the triumph in his gaze as her muscles locked up. Heard the rough, broken words of encouragement he gave her. Felt the way he hardened inside her as she came. But it was all distant. Mostly, she felt a rush of pleasure so intense all she could do was cling to him and hope she survived the aftermath.

He shouted her name, hands clamping on her hips to hold her where he wanted her. Boneless and limp, Daphne enjoyed the aftershocks of pleasure as she watched his face go slack, his hands tightening briefly before letting go to soothe the ache of his grip.

Hazel eyes met hers. He looked stunned.

Daphne reached up toward him with heavy arms, coaxing him to drape his body on top of hers so she could feel the weight and heat of him. With his head nestled against her neck, his lips pressed a kiss to her pulse. They stayed there for long heartbeats, adjusting to a world that had suddenly been rearranged.

CHAPTER 31

That night, Daphne got very little sleep. She and Calvin existed in a cocoon of tenderness and pleasure, speaking in touches rather than words. Rain pattered on the roof through the night as their cries filled the room, exhaustion finally overtaking them only a few hours before dawn.

Waking up next to Calvin filled Daphne with sweetness. She ran her fingers through his chest hair and nuzzled at his neck, loving the way his hand trailed up and down the dip of her waist. Her knee was slotted between his legs, the scent of him embedded in her skin. She was happier than she remembered ever feeling.

"Morning," Calvin mumbled, pressing a kiss to her forehead. His hand slid from her waist down to her ass, squeezing her curves before stroking back up to her ribs. He touched her like he couldn't get enough of her, and Daphne never wanted him to stop.

"Morning," she replied. She pressed a kiss to the soft skin just below his stubble, embers of desire flaring to life despite her tiredness.

Maybe once she wasn't in the same room as him, she would regret taking this leap. Maybe when his scent and touch and kiss weren't drugging influences on her rationality, Daphne would be able to think about the consequences of jumping into bed with the man who'd unraveled her so easily and so completely.

But his fingers trailed over her skin, and his chest rose and fell with his breaths, and with slow, gentle coaxing, he nudged her legs apart so he could feel what he did to her, his fingers already knowing the patterns of her pleasure as they slid to where she needed them most.

She'd lost her mind, and she didn't care.

They made it to work only fifteen minutes late, and Daphne hoped their night together wasn't stamped on their faces. She scurried to the fluorescent lights of her interview room and buried herself in financial records to clear her mind of more pleasant things.

For the first time since she'd started this job, Daphne struggled to focus. She couldn't find that state of flow where her mind latched on to numbers, where finding patterns became easy. Her gaze kept drifting to the open doorway to catch glimpses of Calvin. Her ears perked when she heard the rumble of his voice.

She had it bad, and it should have made alarm bells ring in her mind.

Unfortunately, her mind was occupied by dreaming of the moment she'd get to go home with him.

Those daydreams were interrupted by the arrival of Grandma Mabel. Daphne glanced up from her work when she heard her grandmother's voice, and a moment later, the old woman herself appeared in the doorway. With a crafty grin, Mabel glanced over her shoulder and shuffled inside. She closed the door to Daphne's office and came around to give Daphne a tight hug. "Look what I got," she said, and she pulled out her phone and turned it toward Daphne.

A photo from Eileen Yarrow's kitchen stared back at Daphne. Specifically, it was the blurry photo she'd originally sent of the corner cabinet—except it was now crystal clear. Taking the phone, Daphne zoomed in. "How?"

"The magic of artificial intelligence!"

Daphne blinked and glanced at her grandmother. "Okay. But . . . how?"

Mabel's grin was self-satisfied, her eyes gleaming with mischief. "Our tech guy did it. He explained how the computer uses complicated algorithms to restore images. He said it might not be entirely accurate, but Daphne! This is it! This is my mother's pot!"

There were so many things Daphne wanted to clarify in her grandmother's statement, so she started at the beginning. "Tech guy? What tech guy? You haven't been poking around the dark web, have you?"

"Don't be ridiculous," Grandma Mabel said, then pulled a chair from the corner and plopped herself down on it. "I'm ninety percent sure this is the pot, Daphne. Eighty percent, minimum. The shape, the size, even those little ripples on the lid and the shape of the handle—it's got to be! And in just a few more days, we're going to get it back. All thanks to you."

Daphne huffed a laugh as she pushed the phone away. A needle of discomfort pierced her breastbone at the thought of performing a heist for an old cooking pot after what had happened between Calvin and her. She should tell him about it, shouldn't she?

But her grandmother was looking at her with bright eyes, and Daphne couldn't disappoint the older woman. It was so rare that Daphne got this type of attention, that she felt seen in a way that wasn't related to drudgery or responsibility. She had gotten lots of praise for getting good grades and doing her chores. She'd been patted on the head for being her boring old self her whole life. But she'd never been included. She'd never belonged. Not like this.

She'd gone out on a limb for Calvin, and now she wanted to do the same for her grandmother. It wasn't good enough to hide all the messy parts of herself away. She wanted to show Grandma Mabel that there was more to her than being good.

Calvin never had to find out . . . did he? Or she could find some way to explain about the pot if it came up. Besides, how smart would it be to tell the island sheriff that she was planning to steal something from his very own mother?

Telling him was the right thing to do. But wasn't she sick of always doing the right thing? Ellie got away with all kinds of mischief just because she had the guts to try. Couldn't Daphne be like her sister this one time? Didn't Daphne have the right to be the hero for once?

She cared about Calvin—probably more than she should. But at the back of her mind, she knew that this tryst between them had to end. He'd realize that she didn't always get in the way of cashbox thieves and feral pickup truck aficionados. He'd realize he'd been wrong about her, and he'd walk away. They always did.

But her family loved her. They always had. Getting her grandmother's heirloom back was a small rebellion that would finally make her feel like she was part of the Davis clan.

"Are you ready, honey?" Grandma Mabel asked, her eyes still shining as she smiled.

Daphne ignored her discomfort and nodded. "As ready as I'll ever be."

"Good. Let's go over the plan."

There wasn't much of a plan, but Daphne sat with her grandmother for a few minutes, talking about escape routes and drop zones for the pot. It was ridiculous. She knew it was ridiculous. The whole thing was absurd. She'd either succeed in getting her grandmother's cast-iron pot back, or she'd humiliate herself in an ugly dress.

But for the first time in a long time—maybe ever—Daphne felt close to her grandmother. The true closeness of a shared secret. It was almost as addictive as Calvin's presence, and Daphne had already indulged in her whims once; why not do it again?

Half an hour later, Grandma Mabel winked at Daphne and poked her head out the door as if to check if the coast was clear. Daphne couldn't help her smile as her grandmother shuffled out, offering cheerful greetings that were meant to distract from their clandestine plans.

"What was that all about?" Calvin asked, his shoulder propped against the doorframe.

Daphne leaned back in her chair and let her gaze trail over his shoulders and chest, ignoring the guilt of her secret. He didn't *really* know her. Didn't really care about her. How could he, when he thought she was so much more than she was? It was better for Daphne to do this for her family. "Just Grandma being Grandma," she said.

He huffed, a soft smile teasing at the corners of his lips. "Got you this," he said, moving his hand out from where he'd hidden it behind the doorframe. He held out a pint of ice cream, identical to the one that had appeared on her desk two weeks earlier.

Daphne straightened. "It was you! You're the one who left me ice cream the other day."

His eyes crinkled as he smiled. "Who did you think it was?"

"I thought Rhonda Roberts was apologizing for spreading rumors about us."

Snorting, Calvin crossed the distance to her desk and set the pint on top of it. Daphne cracked it open and smiled. "Mint chip. How did you notice the flavor I was eating in the dark on the side of the road?"

"I didn't," Calvin said, heading for the door again. "But you told me it was your favorite once in senior year." He glanced over his shoulder to grin at her, then disappeared around the corner.

She stared at the pint until her fingers were numb with cold from holding it. He'd remembered an inconsequential detail about her from a couple of decades ago. What if . . .

What if he *did* care? What if this thing between them wasn't as doomed as she'd thought?

Then her grandmother sent her a text that said Love you, honey, and Daphne set the ice cream aside.

Daphne was able to complete her report by Friday afternoon, the day before the vow renewal. She'd checked all the financial records and found nothing suspicious, apart from the renovation payments. Now it was up to the police to root out whoever was behind the lost money and falsified invoices. Daphne had done her job.

As she emailed her report to the man she couldn't wait to be alone with, a wave of sadness washed over her. She was finished. Unless she had loose ends to tie up, or the department decided to hire her to do more work, there was nothing more for her to do here. The job was over.

She wouldn't get to see her coworkers every day, or enjoy the buzz of energy in the building. She wouldn't get to have those leaning-in-the-doorway chats with Flint, because pretty soon, they wouldn't be working together.

No more commutes together. No more detective work. No more pit-of-the-stomach excitement at being trusted with something bigger than herself. No more Calvin Flint.

Her feet carried her to his office, where she found him frowning at his computer screen. She watched him for a few moments, an ache building in her chest.

What now? After the vow renewal tomorrow—what would happen? Did she stay on the island? How? With what money?

She'd built up her savings and gotten her feet back under her, but she hadn't anticipated the fact that those feet might decide to grow roots. Could she really stay here and try to make it work when she wasn't even sure that this thing between the two of them was real?

It was based on a lie, after all. And no matter what had happened between them in the privacy of his bedroom, they hadn't talked about a future. For all Daphne knew, Calvin might be treating this as a casual bit of fun while they had to pretend. He was a good man, but that didn't mean he was in love with her. She was the one who had gotten carried away—again.

He glanced up, the frown clearing from his brow as he saw her. "Just reading through your report. No other bombshells," he said. "That's good news."

"As long as you can figure out what's going on with the lost payments."

He nodded, then tilted his head. "You okay?"

Daphne forced her lips to stretch into a smile. "I'm good. I might head out early, if you don't mind. Stretch my legs." She nodded to the windows behind him. "First bit of sun in weeks."

"Sure," he said. "See you at home?"

"Yeah," she replied, then ducked out of his office and fled. As the exit closed behind her, Daphne couldn't help glancing back. Her gaze caught on her own reflection in the glass door, the room beyond obscured by the glare of the sun, as if whatever happened inside that building was no longer for her eyes.

For the first time in many weeks, Daphne wished for stability. She wished she had a plan. She wished she knew what she was supposed to do.

She walked through Carlisle, all the way down to the water, and watched the waves lap at the rocky shore. The afternoon ferry was already gone, and the harbor was quiet. She listened to the cries of gulls and inhaled the scent of salt and seaweed.

Her feelings for Calvin had taken her by surprise, but she couldn't let herself get swept out to sea. The last time she'd done that, the breakup had nearly crushed her. What she needed was some sort of lifeline.

So she took out her phone and emailed her old manager in Seattle, asking if he knew of anyone who was hiring. She didn't want to leave. Not now. Not yet.

But she needed to be responsible and figure out her next steps. It didn't hurt to have some kind of plan. After all, she didn't know what would happen at the event tomorrow. Once it was over and he didn't need her anymore, would Calvin change his mind about her? Would he decide that she was too boring, after all? Would he turn around and tell her that he needed more excitement and spontaneity and passion when the fire between them eventually guttered out into something less illicit?

She hit the send button and slid her phone into her pocket. A gust of wind teased a strand of hair from her bun, and she tucked it behind her ear as she turned toward the hill that would lead her back to Flint's place. Guilt swarmed her gut like a flood of angry hornets at the thought of the email hitting her former manager's inbox, of the job offers that might or might not come from it.

But why should she feel guilty? She needed a job. Tapping her network for a backup plan was the smart thing to do. The responsible thing.

And Daphne was nothing if not responsible. Once tomorrow's event was done, she'd have no reason to pretend she was anything other than exactly what she was.

CHAPTER 32

Calvin didn't like the shadows lurking in Daphne's eyes. She'd been weird ever since she sent her final report through, and now, as she slid earrings in her ears and smoothed her hands down the tiers of her fluffy pink dress, it felt like there was something she wasn't telling him.

"You okay?"

She met his gaze in the mirror. "You keep asking me that."

"And you keep dodging the question," he said, pressing a kiss to her shoulder. His hands slid down to her waist, and he sighed as she leaned her back against his chest. They fit together so perfectly. It didn't matter that this date had started as a silly agreement. Calvin was all in. This was the woman he wanted. She was everything he dreamed of and so much more than he deserved.

After tonight, he'd ask her to move in with him. His house was lonely, and he was ready to lay new, happy memories over the old. He'd clear out the spare room of his mother's junk and make it into an office for Daphne. She could start a business. People always needed accountants, and she was good enough at her job that she'd always find work.

A future unfurled before him, one without loneliness or neglect. One where the woman he'd chosen decided to choose him back. As he inhaled the scent of her perfume and ran his fingers over her stomach and ribs, watching the way Daphne's eyes fluttered shut in the mirror, Calvin dreamed of wedding bells and babies. Milestones that even a couple of months ago had seemed both wildly improbable and entirely mundane. Other people's dreams and realities—never his.

But she was here, and she'd come to him when he'd waited, and he knew in his heart that they belonged together.

"You look beautiful," he said, because she did. She'd looked as perfect with black eyes and messy hair as she did in her buttoned-up accountant's uniform and her racy lingerie. She was beautiful when she wore a ridiculous dress, when she wore jeans and a T-shirt, when she wore nothing at all.

But Daphne opened her eyes and gave him a flat look. "I look like an eight-year-old girl's bed skirt," she said.

He huffed and pressed another kiss to her shoulder, then turned her around and nudged her chin up so he could kiss her lips.

The woman made a fool out of him, and he couldn't help begging her for more. She always had, and he suspected she always would. She was the most beautiful thing that had ever happened to him, and all he wanted to do was make sure she stayed his forever. He pulled away from the kiss and looked into her sky blue eyes, wondering how it was possible to love someone this much. The emotion felt too big for his chest, like if he inhaled too deeply, his ribs would crack from the pressure.

"Maybe we should skip the vow renewal," he said, hands sliding down to her ass. He could lay her down on the bed and show her what she meant to him, even if he couldn't yet put it into words.

Daphne surprised him by stiffening and pulling away. "Don't be silly," she chided. "This was the deal. I intend to hold up my end of the bargain."

He blinked, surprised. Sourness coated the back of his throat as he tried to think of something to respond with. She was still talking about their deal? For the first time since they'd spent the night together, Calvin wondered if he'd completely misread the situation. Was it possible she didn't feel the same way he did?

This wave of feeling that threatened to drag him under suddenly seemed dangerous. How could he open up to her when she could easily decide to turn around and walk away? She could leave him, just like everyone else. Except it would be worse, because she'd made him believe in a life he'd never thought would be his.

He forced some cheer into his voice as he said, "I'll let it slide, I promise."

If they stayed home from the vow renewal, it would mean this thing between them was real. It would give him the chance to tell her all he felt for her without risking his own sanity—his own heart.

Daphne threw him a little side smile and fluffed her skirts. "Can't let an outfit like this go to waste. Come on. We're going to be late."

She marched out of the bedroom and down the hallway, no sign of a limp in her confident gait. Calvin watched her disappear, and his world tilted. What if this had just been sex to her? What if he'd been completely delusional to think that a woman like Daphne would actually choose *him*?

He followed her more slowly, looping his tie as he tried to shake the bitterness from his thoughts.

Their exchange of favors would be over after tonight, but that didn't mean Daphne would leave. All it meant was that from tomorrow onward, he'd have to be honest about what she meant to him. Just a few hours, and this charade would be finished. He'd know whether or not Daphne felt the same way he did.

When the doorbell rang, they both headed toward it. Daphne opened the door and paused while Calvin came to a stop behind her.

Mabel grinned wide, cheeks carved with deep wrinkles as her blue eyes sparkled with mischief. "Big night," she said.

Daphne glanced over her shoulder to meet Calvin's gaze. "Yeah," she said to her grandmother while staring at him.

Suddenly, Calvin felt the same current of tension he'd felt in Helen Davis's living room. There was something here he didn't understand. Doubts echoed in his mind, even louder than they'd been a moment before.

His mother had left him to fend for himself while she jumped from man to man. Virtually every responsible adult had written him off and tossed him aside. Why would Daphne be any different?

She was a magnetic, intelligent, beautiful woman. She was meant for bigger things, and no matter what insecurities she might have shared, she knew that Fernley wasn't the end for her. That's why she'd wanted an exit plan with their bargain. Hell, it's why she'd been so mad about those scholarships back in high school.

Why would she settle for Calvin? He was just the screwup who'd pulled himself together against all odds. He wasn't the type of guy that women chose in the end. He'd learned that lesson young.

History had taught him that the only person he could rely on was himself. Over the weeks, he'd lost sight of that. He'd let himself get caught up in a woman who could easily decide to walk away, just like everyone else.

What if he'd been wrong about Daphne all along?

CHAPTER 33

"Excuse us," Grandma Mabel called out while her fingers wrapped around Daphne's forearm. She towed Daphne down the porch steps and across the front lawn, where Greta's beige clunker of a car idled by the curb.

"Grandma, is this really necessary—"

"Hush, honey," her grandmother replied. "We're all here. We just want to go over a few details."

Daphne frowned as she bent over to peer into the car windows. Greta waved cheerily from behind the wheel, her thighs twitching as if with anticipation for the pedal-to-the-metal getaway she probably hoped to make later. The passenger seat was free, with Grandma Mabel's purse in the footwell.

And in the back seat, Ellie beamed at Daphne as she lowered her window. Beside her, another person was hunched over a laptop.

Daphne squinted at her sister, then at the laptop user. She started. "Ryan?"

Pushing his hoodie back from his face, Ryan Lane glanced over to lift his chin in greeting. His laptop screen illuminated his face in an eerie white glow. His bruised temple had healed from the beating that Daphne had delivered with her purse. "Sup," he said.

"What are you doing here?"

"He's our tech guy," Ellie announced.

"On that note, what are *you* doing here?" Daphne demanded. "You're supposed to be cured of your deviant ways. You're getting married and everything."

Ellie's smile was unrepentant. "One last job," she explained. "I couldn't let Grandma handle this one on her own. I'm here as an extra set of eyes in case something goes wrong."

Daphne shot a furtive glance over her shoulder. Calvin sat on the small bench by the front door, tying his shoes as he watched them. She forced a smile before turning back to her sister. "The probability of things going wrong just skyrocketed with you being here." She glared at her grandmother. "You all should go home."

"No can do. We've paid Ryan for his time, and we intend to get value for our money," Mabel explained.

"Paid him for what?"

"I have access to the Yarrows' security system," Ryan said absentmindedly, fingers flying over his keyboard.

"You *what?*"

"He's very good," Mabel said.

"He's our eyes and ears," Greta explained. "We'll be able to see everything that happens inside and guide you."

"Here," Ellie said, shoving something at Daphne. "Wear this."

Daphne took the bundle Ellie had dropped in her hands and recoiled. "I'm not wearing an earpiece. No way. What do you think this is? We're not executing a bank heist."

Ryan's fingers stilled. He squinted at the earpiece, then shrugged at Ellie. "We'll go with plan B."

Daphne planted her hands on her hips. "What's plan B?"

"Group text," Ryan said. "The five of us plus Harry. I'll text her at the optimal time for her to cause a distraction, and that'll be your cue to head to the kitchen to make the grab."

"This is a disaster," Daphne mumbled.

"Not yet," Ellie replied brightly. "Right now it's only a *potential* disaster. Nice dress, by the way."

Daphne glared at her little sister.

"Right," Grandma Mabel said, "Ellie and I will wait for Ryan's signal, and then we'll meet you by the eastern side of the backyard fence. There's a gate, so you should be able to either open it or drop the pot over the fence. We'll grab it and go."

"I'll keep the car running," Greta supplied. "I've got my route planned out."

"We did a dry run this morning," Grandma Mabel explained.

"You did a dry—" Daphne bit off the end of her sentence as a headache bloomed behind her temples. Why had she agreed to this? How could she ever have thought this was a good idea?

Now she was hooking up with a man who would drop her as soon as he got bored of her. She was once again out of work with few prospects, and about to put her reputation at risk—for what? What was the point of all this?

Grandma Mabel's hand slid over Daphne's forearm, drawing Daphne's gaze. Mabel's eyes softened as their eyes met, her warm fingers squeezing Daphne's wrist. "I'm so proud of you," Grandma Mabel said softly. "I'd lost hope of ever getting that pot back, and if it weren't for you, that piece of my history would be gone forever."

Just like that, Daphne's uncertainty vanished. She'd go through with this plan, no matter what it meant for her relationship with Calvin. Her throat constricted, and she cast another quick glance toward Calvin, who had disappeared from view.

Whatever happened between the two of them didn't really matter in the end. Daphne would always be the diligent worker bee, the one who read the terms and conditions, who had a color-coded schedule. She would always be the opposite of spontaneous.

A man like Calvin Flint would forever be out of reach. He'd end up with someone like Jenna Deacon, because he'd soon realize that all this chaos and excitement whirling around Daphne wasn't the normal state of affairs. When the dust settled, he'd see that she really was the boring good girl everyone thought her to be. He'd realize that he wanted excitement and spontaneity, just like Pete.

He hadn't made any promises, and neither had she. Maybe it was better to treat this as a temporary tryst.

Daphne would be left to fend for herself, with her to-do lists and retirement forecasts. She knew that, in the end, that was the only possibility available to her. No man would truly want boring old Daphne Davis once he realized that passion didn't last forever.

But just this once—this *one time*—Daphne could be something more. She could do it for her grandmother. She could do it for her sister. She could do it for herself.

Nodding at her grandmother, she turned to Ellie. "If anything starts looking hairy, you get these guys out of there," she said.

"I promise," Ellie said with a solemn nod. Then she reached out through the open window and squeezed Daphne's hand. "I didn't know you had it in you, Daphne. I have to say, it's pretty awesome to see this side of you."

"Enjoy it while it lasts," Daphne replied, then squared her shoulders and marched back to the house.

Calvin was waiting on the couch. He slipped his phone into his pocket when she walked in, his brows arching. "Everything okay?"

"That depends on your definition of 'okay,'" Daphne quipped, then let her lips curl into a smile. "You ready?"

"As ready as I'll ever be." His gaze dropped to Daphne's legs, then to her feet. "You going barefoot?"

Daphne glanced down. A few blades of grass clung to her toes, and her skin had gone pink from the chill outside. She hadn't even realized she'd gone out without shoes on. "No," she said. "Of course not."

Calvin exhaled as he stood, his hands sliding over Daphne's arms as uncertainty clouded his gaze. "Are you sure you're okay, Daphne? You look like you're about to go to war."

Lips twisting, Daphne let her gaze slide away from his. "Maybe I am."

Calvin's warm chuckle settled into Daphne's bones and made her wish for things that would never belong to her. She trembled as he curled his finger under her chin, his lips brushing hers in a tender kiss. When he pulled away, his eyes were intent, like he was trying to read something in her expression, or trying to tell her something with his.

"I've got some fresh mint-chip ice cream in the freezer for tonight," he said softly. "Once this event is over, we'll come back here and eat the whole thing. Just you, me, a couple spoons, and that couch."

It was ridiculous to want to cry at those words. Patently absurd. But Daphne felt like Flint was dangling something in front of her that could never truly belong to her. Her perfect date night was a comfy couch, a warm blanket, and a pint of mint chip. Her perfect man was someone who was happy to be right there with her.

And she knew that once the shine wore off, once they were no longer sneaking around, pretending and not pretending, once Flint realized that Daphne really was as dull as everyone said, Daphne would have to take all these moments and tell herself they'd meant nothing.

The problem was, to her, they meant a whole lot more.

CHAPTER 34

The house glowed with a thousand twinkling bulbs. Fairy lights lined the steps leading to the front door and shone like beacons on the A-frame roof. Through the big front windows, Daphne could see guests milling as they drank and laughed.

She jumped when Calvin's hand landed on her thigh.

Brows arched, he stroked the crinkling fabric of her dress. "You're on edge."

"I'm fine."

"We'll stay long enough to make it through the ceremony, and then we can leave. If anyone bothers you, including my mother, I'll talk to them. I know last time we were here wasn't the most pleasant time for you."

His kindness made Daphne's heart ache. She swallowed back her protests and forced a smile. "I'll be fine, Flint," she said. "I'm tough."

His smile was soft and sweet. "That you are," he said, then exited his truck and jogged over to her side. The evening was cool, but hints of spring were in the air. Daphne huddled in her jacket and watched where she stepped in her high heels, still slightly unsteady on her ankle. Calvin was there like a pillar at her side, and she let herself lean on him, just this once. They were supposed to pretend to be together, anyway. She might as well enjoy it while it lasted.

They walked up the steps, and Calvin slid his hand to her lower back. His warmth surrounded her as they rang the doorbell and waited for the big timber door to open. She wondered how many other moments they'd have like this, how many casual touches they'd be able to exchange under the guise of meaning something to each other?

Daphne straightened. Best not to think about that now. She had a cooking pot to steal. An heirloom to return to its rightful owner.

The door opened. Eileen and Archie Yarrow stood in the opening. Eileen threw her hands out like she wanted to hug Calvin, then pulled back and clasped them at her breast. "You came!" She beamed at them, gaze flitting to Daphne. "Thank you for wearing the dress. Come in. I'll take your jackets."

"Thank you," Daphne said, shaking out her nerves as she shed her outerwear. The house was warm and bright, with music and laughter filling the air. Down the hall, caterers milled through clumps of guests, bearing trays of finger food and flutes of champagne.

Behind them, the doorbell rang again, and Eileen shooed them down the hallway toward the party.

"Just long enough to stay for the ceremony," Calvin murmured, his hand sliding over her upper back, fingers warm against the bare skin between her shoulder blades.

Daphne smiled at him. "Unless we accidentally have fun."

"I won't hold my breath."

Grinning, Daphne let the sheriff lead her deeper into the home. He was greeted by half a dozen people within moments, and Daphne found herself swept up into small talk and polite smiles as she stood at his elbow. Her gaze darted around the room until she spotted Harry, sitting on a two-seater couch next to Dorothea, the two of them like queens holding court over their subjects. Harry's eyes slid to Daphne's, and her chin dipped the slightest bit.

Game on.

"Have you made any headway with the break-ins?" an older woman asked, and Daphne turned her attention back to the conversation.

"It's an ongoing investigation," Calvin replied coolly. "I can't comment on it at the moment."

"Oh, come on, Sheriff. Give us a little hint." The woman winked at him, swatting his arm.

He flashed a charming grin at her as he said, "You know I can't, Christine."

"You're no fun," the woman replied, pouting.

"I can say that Daphne has been integral to the investigation. If you're looking for a diligent and talented accountant, she's the woman for the job."

Daphne straightened, glancing at Flint in surprise. The praise sent warmth spreading through her chest. It didn't sound like the usual dismissive kind of compliment, where people said she was smart as if it were a mark against her. It sounded like he truly believed what he said.

Daphne smiled at the woman. "He has to say that because I'm his date," Daphne demurred.

Christine laughed. "And we're all jealous of you for it, dear. Although I'm not jealous of that dress, or the fact that you have to dance in front of us all."

A warm palm on Daphne's upper back drew her gaze to Calvin's, whose eyes were twinkling as he stared down at her. "We were both more than happy to do what we could to make my mother's event a success," he said.

Christine hummed. Calvin extricated them from the conversation with ease, but they were soon accosted by another couple, and another, and another. Daphne tried to keep up, but she very much felt out of her element. Then her clutch buzzed, and she excused herself.

A text in a newly formed group chat. We've got eyes and ears, people, Ryan wrote.

Yesssssssss, Ellie added. Then, a moment later, she wrote, Daphne, you look like you're ready to puke or run away or both.

Daphne huffed and slipped her phone back into her bag without answering. Calvin's gaze found hers. He raised his eyebrows, and she smiled at him. Shuffling back to his side, she did her best to be a good, unobtrusive, unnoticeable date. This was the whole reason they'd struck their silly bargain, after all. She might as well hold up her end of it.

Until someone barreled into her legs. She looked down to see Ceecee's face enveloped in bright-pink ruffles, her hair pushed back with a headband, her cheeks rosy with excitement. "Daphne," she whispered as if she were about to impart an important secret, "your dress is *amazing.*"

Pulling back, Ceecee fluffed the iridescent-pink tiers of her own dress and twirled so the fabric flared out and glittered as it moved. Daphne had to admit, the style looked pretty good on a nine-year-old.

"Don't know if I'd say 'amazing,' but it's growing on me," Calvin muttered.

"Like a mushroom," Daphne confirmed.

When Calvin and Ceecee laughed, Daphne couldn't help but join them. For a few precious seconds, she felt nothing but happiness. It was right there in the sparkle in Calvin's gaze and the sound of Ceecee's snorts. Daphne's heart sent out a soft whisper that said *Don't you want this for yourself?*

Hot on the heels of her joy was a wave of grief and longing so strong she had to turn away from the two of them to hide her reaction. Yes, she wanted it. She wanted to get to know Ceecee better. She wanted to spend her days and nights with Calvin. She wanted to be the woman he thought he saw in her.

But she was just Daphne.

Her melancholy thoughts were interrupted by the tapping of a microphone. All eyes turned to Kathy, who wore a dazzling navy gown studded with sequins. She looked like a pillar of dark glitter with spiky blond hair plonked on top to give her a few more inches of height.

"We have a special treat for you today," Kathy announced. "Would our performers please follow me?"

Ceecee hooked her hand in Daphne's elbow and vibrated with anticipation. "Have you been practicing?" she whispered.

Daphne tilted her head from side to side. "As much as we've been able."

"Hopefully Calvin doesn't punch anyone this time."

"I didn't *punch* your grandmother, Ceecee."

Ceecee shot Daphne a mischievous glance, and the crowd parted to let them through. They were joined by other dancers, the ladies dressed in hot-pink ruffles, the men in black with pink ties. Kathy used her powers as lead choreographer to clear the dance floor, which encompassed a third of the room by the French doors that led to the backyard. The pink feathers had already been stashed on the perimeter.

With a squeeze of Daphne's arm, Ceecee shot across the dance floor to take her place. Calvin's hand slid down Daphne's spine in comfort or commiseration or both, and he took his spot on top of a mark on the floor. Across from them, just outside the circle, Jenna Deacon arched her brows at Daphne's dress, then flicked her gaze to Calvin and smiled.

Daphne tried not to let it bother her. What use was jealousy? She had no claim over Calvin Flint. Sure, they were together now. But would they be together tomorrow?

She was used to being overshadowed by people who were more charming, more beautiful, more spontaneous. Prodding the old wound didn't feel good, but it was familiar.

She shifted her gaze away from the other woman and focused on Kathy, who stood over them like a drill sergeant assessing the latest batch of new recruits—and finding them lacking. Her hands were clasped behind her back, her eyes were narrowed, and her lips were pinched in a thin, disapproving line.

Some unseen signal passed from Kathy to whoever was manning the stereo. The music started, and Daphne's feet began to move. There was a slight ache in her injured ankle, but she made it through the turns, the shimmies, and the steps. The gasps and titters of the audience fell away, and all that existed was pink fabric and movement. It was utterly ridiculous and amateurish, and Daphne couldn't help the smile that bloomed over her lips. Across the circle from her, Ceecee looked like she was having the time of her life.

Daphne glanced at Calvin, who laughed as they spun and shimmied like their lives depended on it.

She dove for her feather, then turned and tented it over the middle of the dance floor, shoulder to shoulder with Calvin. Ceecee's face was beaded with sweat as she shook her feather, and the drama of the moment cranked tighter. Behind them, the French doors opened, and two people sneaked inside and crouched under the feathers. The music swelled, a crescendo of crashing cymbals.

Once the music had reached its peak, all the feathers lifted. Eileen and Archie Yarrow stood in the middle of the dance floor as their pink-clad dance troupe circled away to the beat of the music. They smiled at the clapping crowd and then put their arms around each other and began to slow dance.

Daphne leaned against the wall and blew out a harsh breath. Beside her, Calvin dropped his feather and leaned his shoulder against hers. She glanced up to find him watching her, his cheeks flushed, his hair in beautiful disarray.

He smiled at her, wide and bright, and Daphne knew she was in love with him. Pain and pleasure twined around each other as she held his gaze, her breaths heaving, her heart galloping, her mind certain that she could never have him.

"Thank you," he whispered.

Caught in the storm of her emotions, Daphne didn't understand what he was talking about. "For what?"

"For being here," he said. "For being you."

It should have been the best compliment anyone had ever paid her, but it felt like he'd just punched her in the gut. She hid her reaction by turning toward Harry, who'd stumped her way over to them, leaning heavily on her cane.

"That was the most ridiculous thing I've seen in my life," she said while Eileen and Archie twirled on the dance floor. "I wish I'd gotten it on tape."

"Eileen promised to save the recording to torture Ceecee with when she's a teenager," Calvin told her. "I'm sure we can get you a copy."

Daphne forced a laugh, but it came out as a hiccup. Harry narrowed her eyes at Daphne but said nothing. On the dance floor, Eileen and Archie took a bow as the music faded to nothing.

"Eileen and Archie, everyone," Kathy announced into a microphone. "Ten years of love. Ten years of commitment. Let us all come together and join them in renewing their vows to each other."

"Have you lost your nerve, girl?" Harry asked quietly as she leaned close to Daphne's ear.

Daphne shook her head, eyes darting to Calvin, who was staring at his mother in the center of the dance floor. "No."

"After the ceremony is when we make our move. Meet me by the kitchen when Ryan gives the signal."

Daphne straightened and focused on the happy couple. She glanced at Calvin, but he seemed lost in his own thoughts as he watched his mother recommit to her husband. In another world, Daphne might ask him what he was thinking. She might coax the truth of his emotions from him and let him know that she was here for him. In another world, that would be her place, her responsibility.

But their agreement was coming to an end. Her job at the department was over. She didn't have the right to ask about the investigation into the shady BDT, LLC, and she didn't have a right to ask Calvin to lean on her if he needed to.

It had taken all her courage to close the distance between them and finally spend the night with him. It had felt like a leap into the unknown, as terrifying as it was thrilling. Now Daphne wondered if she'd made a mistake. It would've been easy for Calvin to tell her that he didn't want their arrangement to end, especially after she'd taken the first step. But he hadn't. His promises had ended with ice cream on the couch when his mother's event was over.

No one had ever looked at Daphne and said, *I choose you.* Pete had tossed her aside and made her feel boring and worthless. He'd used her for stability, for emotional support, for the mediocre sex they'd shared throughout their relationship. Then he'd decided that he was happy to turn his back on her without a second glance and without a thought to what Daphne had invested in their life together.

She didn't want Pete back, but she wanted to be someone's first choice. She wanted to be worth the risk. What had Calvin risked so far? A bit of gossip that would always be more favorable to a man compared to a woman. The inconvenience of hosting her in his guest room. His dignity during a silly dance.

Was that all she was worth to him? How long until he saw her through Pete's eyes and decided he'd rather have someone better?

After she got her grandmother's pot back, Daphne would be done with high-stakes heists. She'd avoid getting punched in the face by runaway thieves. She'd focus on getting a steady job and doing what needed to get done.

She wasn't the woman he thought she was, and she had no right to pretend anymore.

It was better that their agreement was nearly over. She'd gotten too close. She'd slept with him—repeatedly—which had been a critical mistake. But she could finish this right here, tonight, and then crawl back into her shell and return to the life she was meant to lead. One of safety, stability, and responsibility.

She *knew* it was better this way. She knew herself. At the end of the day, Daphne was a coward. She'd fallen for Calvin, but she didn't have the guts to see if he'd love her back once he remembered who she was when the dust settled. His rejection would hurt far, far more than Pete's ever did, because Calvin had looked at her like no one ever had. He didn't see Good Girl Daphne Davis. He saw a figment of his imagination. He saw the woman Daphne wished she was in reality.

Tonight was the end, and that was a good thing.

When applause filled the room, Daphne murmured something about finding a bathroom and ducked away from him. Her eyes stung, and she took deep, shuddering breaths to pull herself together.

Harry waited for her near the hallway that led to the kitchen. Nodding to the older woman, Daphne glanced over her shoulder.

Jenna Deacon had made her way to Calvin's side. Her hand was stroking his arm, and she batted those beautiful eyes up at him. A dagger twisted in Daphne's chest; they fit together better than Daphne and Calvin ever had. Two beautiful people who made sense, side by side.

Yes, it was better for this to end. And tonight, it would.

Her clutch buzzed at the same time as Harry's phone let out a loud ding. They exchanged a weighty glance, then pulled out their phones.

It was time to get Grandma Mabel's pot back.

CHAPTER 35

"I can't tell you how grateful I was to see you pull up to Romano's that night," Jenna said, fingernails digging into Calvin's arm.

He tried to shake her off, but the woman had a grip of steel. He grimaced at her. "Just doin' my job, Ms. Deacon."

"Jenna," she corrected.

Inclining his head, Calvin glanced over the room, looking for—there. Daphne stood next to Harry, the two of them staring at their phones. Daphne's shoulders were tight. She looked miserable.

Guilt gurgled in Calvin's stomach. He'd gotten caught up in self-pity as he'd watched the ceremony, thinking of all the commitments his mother had failed to keep with him. But as he'd watched, he'd seen true happiness light his mother's face. He wanted to be the type of man who could forgive her, who could be happy for her.

Ceecee loved her mother, and from what Calvin had witnessed, Eileen doted on her like any loving mom would. There was none of the neglect or pain that he'd experienced.

She was young when she had him. She'd failed him, yes, but she was human. Just like him. He'd failed plenty of times, and now he was here, trying to be better.

As he'd watched his mother sway in her husband's arms, Calvin remembered the way his father would sweep her around the kitchen when he got home from work. The memory slammed into him and rocked him onto his heels. His mother would laugh and laugh; then she'd turn to Calvin and pick him up. His father would wrap his arms around the two of them, and the house was a place of joy and comfort and family.

He remembered the way she'd held him after the funeral, the way he'd heard her cry through her bedroom door for weeks afterward.

And, as Archie Sr. twirled her in his arms and beamed at his wife, Calvin remembered the way he'd hated her for it. She'd always emerged from her room with dry eyes and a too-bright smile on her face, and Calvin had resented it all—her secret grief and her attempts to pretend it didn't exist. He'd resented the way she held him, because she wasn't Dad, and she wasn't being honest with him. He'd pushed her away. He remembered tense car rides. Slammed doors and shouted words.

Their family had fallen apart, and his mother had sought solace elsewhere. She'd flitted from man to man, married and divorced, and Calvin's bitterness had crowded out every other emotion. But when she'd stopped trying to reach him entirely, he'd hated that most of all.

Maybe her many olive branches were just that. Offers of peace. A fresh start.

If only he could let go of the last of his resentments and accept it.

It would feel good to forgive his mother. A weight would lift off his shoulders, that heavy burden he'd carried with him for close to thirty years. They'd never have a normal mother-son relationship, but maybe they could have something else. They could care for Ceecee and get to know each other. There could be mutual respect.

If he could just trust that Eileen was being honest. That she really had changed as much as he had.

Consumed by thoughts of the past, he'd missed what was going on with Daphne. And now she was across the room, and he was being held in place by a woman who had a bionic claw for a hand.

"You know, even though we didn't speak much in high school, I always thought there was something special about you," Jenna said.

Her perfume was cloying, and Calvin breathed through his mouth as he nodded. His gaze was still on Daphne, who was speaking to Harry.

There was a wrinkle between Daphne's brows, and she had that look on her face like she was overthinking. "Hmm?" Calvin said to Jenna, his entire attention focused on the other side of the room.

"I knew you'd do big things," she crooned.

Daphne took a deep breath, deep enough that even from a distance, Calvin could see her chest rise and fall. Beside her, Harry straightened, thumping her cane on the ground once as she faced Daphne.

Calvin's instincts screamed. It was like a million ants crawling over his skin. A claw raking down his spine.

Something was happening, and he didn't know what it was.

Daphne had hidden something from him, just like his mother had hidden herself away in her room. There was a fracture between them he hadn't noticed before. A thread of panic wound its way through his chest, circling his lungs in tighter and tighter bands.

"And I was just so sad to hear that you'd left the island," Jenna continued, shuffling so close that her breast pressed against Calvin's arm.

Frowning down at her, he tried to shake her off. "It was a long time ago," he said.

"Still. I'm happy you're back." Her free hand came up to rest on his chest, and Calvin tried to move out of the way. His back hit the wall, and Jenna shifted in front of him. She smiled. "I know you're here with Daphne, but maybe—"

A crash shattered through the air, and all heads turned toward the sound. Calvin's head snapped up to where Daphne had stood a moment before, but both she and Harry had disappeared.

That's when the screaming started.

CHAPTER 36

Daphne blinked at the shattered vase in the hallway, Harry sucking in a hard breath beside her to recover from her scream. The end of her cane crunched against a piece of aqua-streaked glass. The old woman let out another yell as bodies appeared in the kitchen door.

Two caterers jumped out to help, and Daphne hooked her arm around Harry's shoulders. "She needs to sit," she said.

"You!" Harry demanded, pointing her cane at the first wide-eyed caterer. "Clean this up before someone cuts themselves. And you, stop anyone else from coming down here. Someone could be seriously hurt."

The command in Harry's voice left no room for argument. The first woman jumped and rushed back into the kitchen to find a broom. Daphne followed close behind, towing Harry along. They entered the kitchen and waited for the broom-carrying caterer to shuffle past. As soon as the caterer had gone out to the hallway to clean up the mess, Harry got a wicked glint in her eyes.

Just like she'd done a moment ago, the old woman wound up with her cane and swung at the nearest glassware. Wineglasses went flying against the wall and exploded into a thousand shards, raining crystal over the kitchen floors.

"Oh!" Harry said. "Clumsy me." She poked her head out the kitchen door to where the caterers had jumped. "Stay out there until we've cleaned this up. It's not safe in here!"

"But the broom—"

Harry closed the door and leaned against it, her eyes bright. "Go on, girl. Get the pot and get it over the fence. We haven't got much time."

Daphne cast a quick glance at the shattered stemware. Distantly, she wondered how and when this would all blow up in her face.

But there were more important things to attend to. She darted to the corner cabinet where she'd spotted the Dutch oven the first time, hauling pots and pans out of the way to get to it. Cookware clattered and banged as Harry hissed at her to be quiet. Her hands closed around the rough, cool handles of the cast-iron pot.

Calvin had been right. This thing was horrendously heavy.

It let out a loud clatter as Daphne dropped it beside her feet, the lid banging against the pot and the pot banging against the floor. She was making too much noise. Way, way too much noise. And she was way, way too slow.

Someone pounded on the door.

"There's glass everywhere!" Harry called out. "Give us a minute." She gave Daphne a loaded look and mouthed, "Hurry!"

Daphne nodded, her hands trembling as she stuffed the pots and pans back onto the lazy Susan in the corner cabinet, metal clanging, lids flying, pot handles jamming themselves into every corner and crevice. After kicking the corner door closed, Daphne watched it bounce back open a couple of inches. She shoved it again, to no avail.

"Leave it," Harry said. "Get that thing out of here. I can't hold them much longer."

"Harry? Is Daphne in there with you?" Calvin's voice called out through the door.

Panic shot down Daphne's spine.

"We're cleaning up the glass that broke," Harry said, and thrust her pointed finger at the side door. "Give us a minute. It's like a crime scene in here."

"Let me in," Calvin said, and he didn't sound like nice, kind Calvin Flint. He sounded like the Fernley County Sheriff. "Daphne? What's going on?"

"Just trying to keep everyone safe!" Daphne said as she hurried to the side door, and Harry swept her cane through the broken glass so Calvin would hear the tinkling of the shards against each other.

Her arms were already aching with the weight of the pot, but Daphne was in too deep to turn around now. Calvin would open the door and see the pot. He'd know she'd lied to him.

After putting the pot on the edge of the counter, Daphne opened the door and held it with her hip, then grabbed the pot again and stepped outside. Through the window cut into the top half of the door, she exchanged a deep nod with Harry, then shuffled out of sight as quickly as she could.

She stood in a narrow walkway between the fence and the side of the house. The A-frame roof went all the way to the ground, cedar shingles releasing a pleasant scent in the space. Concrete pavers lined the walkway, with moss and weeds growing between them. Creeping flowers had begun to bud in spots between the moss, waiting for their moment to bloom. The side fence was warm timber, about six feet tall, with half-inch gaps between the vertical slats. To Daphne's left was the side gate that led to the front yard, held closed by a hook latch. Near the other end of the walkway, leading to the backyard, a few terra-cotta pots sat gathering rainwater, accompanied by a rusty rake.

"Over here!" Ellie hissed.

Whirling in the direction of the voice, Daphne spotted her sister's eyeball through a gap in the fence. Ellie lifted her arm and wiggled her fingers over the top.

"Toss it over," Grandma Mabel directed. "We're ready."

Daphne glanced at the side gate, then back at the kitchen. She could hear Calvin's deep voice, and there was no time to wrestle with the gate. She had to get rid of this thing. "Either catch this or stand clear," she said, and lifted the pot lid over the fence. "It's heavy."

"Got it," Ellie said, and the pot lid's weight disappeared from Daphne's hands.

"This is it! I remember this scratch. Oh, it's *gorgeous,*" Grandma Mabel murmured, which was patently untrue. It was rough and old and probably worthless to anyone other than Grandma Mabel.

"This thing weighs a ton," Daphne said, hauling the pot up to her shoulder before resting it on top of the fence. "Be careful."

Grandma Mabel let out an excited squeal as Ellie's hands wrapped around the pot's handles. Daphne watched it disappear over the fence, then hurried back to the kitchen door.

"She's *fine,*" she could hear Harry saying. "She just went out to toss the first bag of broken glass. Now, shoo! Get out of here before you cut yourself. We've got this under control."

Daphne peeked around the edge of the window to see Harry closing the door on Calvin's face. Nearly there. All she had to do was go back inside, clean up the mess they'd made, and pretend nothing had happened. Easy-peasy. She was almost home free.

A bright flame of excitement finally flared in the pit of Daphne's stomach. She wanted to cackle and pump her fists. She'd done it!

"Daphne!" Grandma Mabel whispered, her fingers poking through between the fence slats.

"I'm here," Daphne said, crossing the small space to stand in front of her grandmother.

"Thank you, honey. I never thought I'd get my mother's pot back. Never thought I'd touch it again. I'm so proud of you, and I love you more than words can say."

Eyes stinging, Daphne shoved her own fingers through the fence and gripped her grandmother's hand. "I love you too, Grandma."

"No one could have done this except for you," she responded, emotion thick in her voice.

"I'm just glad you've got your pot back," Daphne whispered. She peeked between the wooden slats to see the tears in her grandmother's eyes.

It was only a half truth, because retrieving the pot wasn't the only thing that made Daphne glad. Dizzy elation bubbled through Daphne as her grandmother's eyes misted on the other side of the fence. Grandma Mabel had never looked at her like that before.

For the first time, Daphne was a true Davis. She was just like Ellie, her mother, and her grandmother. She belonged.

Had this been a silly plan? Of course. Had she put her own heart on the line by letting herself get close to Calvin Flint? Definitely. Would she want to do this regularly? Absolutely not in a million years, no.

But was it worth it for this moment?

A hundred percent, without a doubt, *yes*.

Daphne smiled, then turned back to the house. There'd be time for celebration later. For now, she had to get back inside, clean up, and pretend that nothing at all had happened here. She crossed the few feet of space between the fence and the house, placing one hand on the shingled roof as she headed for the kitchen door.

Inches from her destination, with her fingers reaching for the knob, Daphne heard voices.

"What are you doing here?" a man demanded in a low hiss. "Get out of here, Bobby."

"You've been dodging my calls."

"I figured you'd get the message," the man repeated.

The voices were familiar. Daphne frowned, fingers on the cool metal of the doorknob, her heart pounding. *Go back inside,* she told herself. *This is none of your business.*

She gripped the knob and turned it.

Then the second man said, "That damn sheriff drove by my house again last night. That's the third time since I first spotted him when I was working on my truck. He knows something, Archie."

"He doesn't know shit."

Daphne's blood turned to ice. Archie Jr. and Bobby D. Troy were just around the corner, and neither of them were happy. Daphne's mind whirled.

If Bobby Troy was here, complaining about Calvin keeping an eye on him, the only logical conclusion was that Archie Jr. was the head honcho behind BDT, LLC. Which meant that the break-ins, the discrepancies between the invoices from Barela . . . all of it pointed back to Archie. The mayor of Fernley Island.

Archie Jr. was behind Realist Trade Co., Rated Retails Co., and BDT, LLC. She thought back to the last time she'd seen him, when he'd been his usual arrogant, sniveling self. He'd stormed off . . .

Daphne's eyes went wide. Archie had stormed off when she mentioned going to see Barela, and *that very night*, Barela's offices were broken into.

Coincidence?

Lungs so tight she could barely breathe, Daphne stood rooted to the ground and tried to parse all the information while Archie and Bobby hissed at each other. Her mind made connections faster than she could blink, but she still couldn't decide what to do.

Was someone else involved? She needed to tell Calvin what she'd heard. But what if they said something else incriminating? Wouldn't it be better to hear the rest of their conversation?

Releasing her grip on the kitchen door, Daphne eased toward the backyard. Their voices sounded close, so she moved slowly, wishing her dress weren't made of this plasticky material that rustled like sacks of dry leaves. To make matters worse, her phone was inside her zippered clutch. She couldn't get it to record their conversation without making noise.

"He *knows*, Archie."

"You shouldn't be here. We're not supposed to speak at all. Now get out of here, and I'll call you when I have time."

"I want out."

A dark silence followed, and Daphne held her breath.

"You want *out*?" Archie repeated, violence lurking at the edge of his tone.

"You heard me. I don't want my name on any of your shit anymore. We almost got found out with Sheriff Jackson, and now this."

"Bill Jackson didn't squeal," Archie pointed out, and Daphne heard the words he left unsaid: *And neither will you.*

"I'm no snitch, but I'm sick of looking over my shoulder. I'm out, Archie."

"We made a deal. All you had to do was tell me when you got mail for me, and you'd get that nice envelope of cash in your mailbox on the first of every month. Has that money ever failed to appear?"

"A thousand bucks a month isn't worth as much as it was when we started this."

"So this is about money. You're extorting me. Have I got that right?"

Daphne nearly rolled her eyes. That was rich, coming from a man who, by the looks of things, had been embezzling funds for years. Archie Yarrow Jr. wasn't exactly a paragon of virtue.

New, hurried footsteps approached. Archie said, "Not now, Jenna."

"What's he doing here?"

"I want out," Bobby repeated.

"Since when?" Jenna asked. "Never mind. I don't care. Archie, there's no point. He doesn't want me."

Archie grunted, and it sounded like pure frustration. "He's been driving by Bobby's place. He might be onto us. If you could've just gotten close to him—"

"He doesn't *want* me," Jenna complained. "I *tried.* It's like he's in love with her or something."

Daphne frowned. In love with who? Jenna couldn't mean Daphne, could she? They were obviously talking about Calvin driving by Bob's place, so what other "her" could there be?

But Calvin wasn't in love with her. They'd come up with this stupid fake date plan, and now it was over. They had gotten too close in the process and became confused. That was all.

Right?

"I don't get why you broke into Romano's anyway, Archie."

"I *didn't*," the man hissed.

"Someone did," Bobby put in.

Daphne's eyes widened. If Jenna was asking about the second break-in, did it mean Archie himself had been responsible for the one at Barela's? What had he been trying to steal?

"Go back inside. Keep Flint occupied. We're done here."

A pause, and Jenna's footsteps retreated.

It was Bobby who spoke next. "We're not done until you tell me we're *done*, Archie. I'm not doing this anymore. There's too much heat. And if you don't even know who did the second break-in, what if someone else is onto us?"

"No one is onto us," Archie insisted. A foot scuffed on pavement, and Daphne strained her ears. There was a grunt. Were they fighting? Archie whispered something, but it was too low to hear. She needed to get closer. It sounded like they'd moved away from the corner of the house.

In the brief moment before Daphne shifted closer to the edge of the walkway, she wondered if she was doing the right thing. A month ago, Daphne wouldn't have been in this position. She would never have agreed to come here with Calvin. She never would've kissed him. Never gotten punched in the face. Never done a silly dance in a gigantic dress.

She'd been playacting ever since she got back, pretending to be someone she wasn't. Except she felt like herself. Right now, as she inched closer to the edge of the walkway, it felt like she was following her principles. Sure, she wasn't exactly being responsible. And her comfortable, warm shell had been left somewhere to gather dust without her.

Maybe there were parts of Daphne that could be impulsive. Maybe it wasn't playacting; it was just opening herself up to another side of herself.

On the island where she'd grown up, where she'd always been known as the good, responsible sister, Daphne was able to see herself in a new light. She stole family heirlooms back. She shacked up with hot men. She followed her instincts.

Sure, she was still 90 percent sure it would all blow up in her face, but didn't it feel *good?*

Well. It did, up until the voluminous tiers of her dress nudged up against the rusty rake, which proceeded to slide down the angled roofline of the home to crash into—and shatter—half a dozen terra-cotta pots.

The noise was deafening. Daphne froze, shoulders hunched up near her ears, breath trapped in her lungs.

Four quick footsteps sounded, and Archie Jr. appeared at the end of the walkway. He took in the smashed pots leaking old rainwater, the rake, and Daphne in her dress, standing there like an absolute dolt.

"Whoops," she said. "Thought the bathroom was out here. I'll just—" She jabbed a thumb over her shoulder toward the kitchen door.

The lie was an obvious one. Within seconds of it coming out of her mouth, Archie's face twisted, and he lunged toward her. His arms circled her biceps as he spun her around and trapped her against the fence. Behind him, Bobby snarled.

"You've been eavesdropping," the mayor accused.

There was one rule Daphne had learned from watching Ellie weasel her way out of trouble their whole lives: When faced with incontrovertible facts, double down on your preposterous lie. It worked at least 70 percent of the time. "Me?" Daphne asked, blinking. "No. I was just looking for the bathroom."

"Quit playing stupid. I know it was you who sicced the sheriff on us. If you hadn't started sniffing around, he never would have found out about Barela."

"The contractor? What about him?"

Bobby frowned. "Maybe she doesn't know anything."

"Shut up, Bobby," Archie spat out. "Daphne Davis is a nerdy little good girl who can't help herself from sticking her nose where it doesn't belong. Isn't that right? She's the type to tell a teacher when they've forgotten to collect homework that was due."

"Okay, that was *one* time, and I'd worked really hard on my essay—"

"You'll regret the day you stuck your nose in my business, Davis," Archie said, a strange light entering his eyes.

Daphne wanted to put as much space as possible between them. The back of her head hit the fence. There was nowhere to go. She'd have to fight her way out of this, which would mean more injuries—or worse. She wouldn't be able to go back inside and pretend everything was okay.

This was the moment everything blew up in her face. There was no getting out of this. Archie wasn't going to let her go.

As if she wanted to make sure of it, Daphne's mouth started moving before her brain caught up. "You've been embezzling public funds for years, haven't you?" she asked.

Still looking at her with those strange eyes, Archie smiled. "No one figured it out. No one until you." Threat laced his words. Real, ice-cold fear began to skate along Daphne's nerves, and she worried that the "or worse" portion of her "injuries—or worse" prediction would come true.

"You used Bobby to set up the shell company, and you falsified invoices for work that was paid for by public funds," Daphne guessed. "Skimmed what you could off the top. Pretty smart," she said, knowing the Archie she'd grown up with thought he was the smartest person in any room he happened to walk into.

"Of course it was smart," Archie snarled, nails digging into her biceps. "It was a flawless plan until you came along."

There was scratching at the side gate, and Daphne forced herself not to glance over. The last thing she needed was Grandma Mabel and Ellie to come barreling in, guns blazing. Then again, she needed backup. The man currently pinning her to the gate squeezed her arms, his eyes flicking to Bobby, then to the gate, then to the backyard. He was going to make a move.

Daphne had to keep him distracted. Flattery seemed to work, so she kept going. "You set it up perfectly," she said. "But why didn't you pay Jerry Barela?"

Archie Jr.'s lip curled. "That worthless father of mine spent all his money on his new wife. Nothing left for my campaign. And it turns out people were sick of Mayor Archie Yarrow by the time I came along, so I had to campaign harder than Dad ever did."

Daphne resisted the urge to roll her eyes. It was more likely that Archie was a sniveling little punk who'd run the island's local government into the ground if it suited his whims, and everyone knew it. Case in point, the embezzlement.

The gate's lock rattled.

Daphne cleared her throat to hide the sound. "How does Jenna fit into it?"

"My office has been handing out grants like candy," Archie said, laughing. "The expansion of tourism on the island was a major part of my election platform. If a few of those grants go to friends of mine, well . . ."

Daphne feigned admiration. "I never could have come up with that," she told him.

"That's because you aren't as smart as you think you are, Davis."

Judging by her current predicament, Daphne figured he was probably right about that. But the only thing she could do was keep him talking. "So, you wanted Jenna to get close to the sheriff as . . . insurance?"

"She would've wrapped him around her little finger if you hadn't come along and messed it all up."

Of all the mistakes Daphne had made lately, getting in the way of a yearslong embezzlement scheme hadn't been on her bingo card. It almost made her laugh. She'd been so worried about an old cast-iron pot, when real crimes had been going on right in front of her. "So you broke into Barela's office to try to steal documents back, and then you broke into Romano's . . ."

"I didn't break into Romano's," Archie Jr. snarled. "And when I find out who did, they're going to be thrown into the same shallow grave you end up rotting in."

Daphne tried to take a deep breath, but her lungs were shutting down. Her fear was slowly freezing her muscles, and she was running out of things to say. Archie was antsy; she could tell by his darting gaze and the way his grip on her arms kept tightening. She'd have pudgy hand-shaped bruises at the end of this. More injuries to add to her collection.

The old Daphne, the one who played it safe and did what she was expected, wouldn't make it out of this. But Daphne had mined the depths of her own self over the past months—maybe the past years, ever since her ex had insulted her and left—and she knew there were deposits of strength inside her that she could use.

She wasn't going to let Archie Yarrow Jr. hurt her. She wasn't going to let *any* man hurt her.

She'd learned that about herself. And she'd learned another thing too. Wisdom from an older generation all those weeks ago at the Winter Market.

Without much space to work, Daphne had to forego a full-on kick and settle for a well-placed knee. She exploded into movement, the tiers of her dress flying up in front of her as she angled her knee at Archie's balls. Air exploded from his lungs when she made contact with the soft flesh, a wheeze of pain not far behind. He doubled over and Daphne stumbled away from him, just in time to see the gate at the end of the pathway fly open.

Grandma Mabel brandished the lid of her precious pot, her face a mask of fury. Ellie wasn't far behind, the main body of the pot dangling from one hand. The two of them ran down the walkway toward the men, who gaped at them.

"Don't just stand there," Archie gasped at Bobby. "Do something!"

Bobby Troy took one step forward. His foot landed on the tines of the rake Daphne had knocked over, flipping the handle up in the process. It hit him square in the face and caused him to stumble back and fall on his ass in a puddle of dirty water and broken terra-cotta.

With a garbled yell, Archie straightened and reached for Daphne. She set her shoulders and faced him, fists bunched, ready to punch.

Her grandmother flew past her and got there first, cast-iron lid held overhead in two white-knuckled hands. She brought the lid down on Archie's head and watched as he crumpled to the ground, staring down at him with a look of pure disdain.

Archie Jr. groaned, one hand cupping his crotch, the other splayed out at his side. His eyes were hazy and unfocused, but at least he wasn't dead.

Daphne glanced at her grandmother and gulped.

Grandma Mabel admired the lid. "This thing is *great*," she said, then turned her eyes to Daphne. "You okay, honey?"

Daphne nodded. "I think so," she replied, then glanced up when she saw movement in the backyard.

Calvin Flint stood at the end of the walkway, hands dangling at his sides, muscles tensed for action. His gaze flicked over Daphne first, then the men on the ground, then over to Ellie and Grandma Mabel. When his eyes landed on the Dutch oven, understanding dawned in his expression.

It only took one look at his eyes for Daphne to know that he'd guessed the real reason she'd accepted this date with him, and it hadn't been to save her reputation. What she hadn't expected was for him to look so utterly devastated.

The emotion cleared from his face in a blink, and the sheriff, stone faced, told them, "You're all under arrest."

STEP FOUR: EXECUTE A CLEAN BREAK

CHAPTER 37

Tiredness dragged at Calvin's eyelids. It weighed down his bones and made it hard for him to think. Even after everyone had been brought to the station and dealt with, after the district attorney had been notified of the arrests, after the first round of interviews had been completed, after he'd gone back home for a couple of hours' sleep, he still couldn't shake the feeling that he'd never feel rested again.

His mother and her husband had provided security footage that included video and audio of the altercation outside. Archie Yarrow Jr. wouldn't be able to wriggle his way out of this one. Calvin had watched the video at least twenty times, and each time he'd been rocked by a riot of emotions.

He hated seeing Daphne at Archie's mercy, but he couldn't help but admire her for staying calm. He was hurt and angry that she'd lied to him about her reason for attending the vow renewal, but in doing so, she'd handed him this case on a silver platter. He didn't know whether to be grateful, relieved, or furious—so he let himself be all three.

What kept circling in his mind was the fact that he'd been right; Daphne hadn't really wanted to be with him at all. She'd used him. It really had all been a bargain to her, an exchange of services. She'd be his date, and she'd steal her grandmother's pot back. That weird instinct that had been triggered when he'd sat on the Davises' couch had been trying to warn him from the start. Mabel really had been asking about half-century-old cast-iron cookware.

How much had Daphne faked? Was any of it real? The laughter, the long evenings on the couch, the way she softened against him? Had she used sex as a way to distract him from what she really wanted?

It had hurt to grow up without a dad and with a mom who didn't care about him. It had hurt to realize that he was on his own.

But this?

To think that he'd finally found someone he loved, someone he could build a life with . . . and all she'd wanted was a worthless bit of cast iron? Calvin didn't even measure up to a *cooking pot*?

She'd used him to get the pot back, and she'd planned to use him as an excuse to leave the island. Calvin had been the fool who'd thought he deserved something more. He'd never deserved a thing.

The reality was that Calvin wasn't worth fighting for. He never had been. His mother had let their relationship deteriorate when it should have been her responsibility to be there for him; he hadn't been a priority to Eileen, even as a hurting preteen and definitely not as a troubled young adult.

And now he wasn't a priority to Daphne; she'd told him so from the start. He felt so stupid for falling for her. A woman who had the world in the palm of her hand, who accomplished everything she set her mind to. She'd been a brilliant investigator, of course. She was brilliant, period.

And Calvin? Calvin had scraped by with a high school diploma, and his greatest achievement was being handed the reins of a department in shambles, probably because he'd make a good scapegoat if he messed it all up.

No one went to bat for the kid who'd always been bad news. Daphne had probably seen that from the start.

Now back in his office with a cup of coffee as dawn tried its best to lighten the clouds to gray, Calvin stared at the black cauldron sitting on the end of his desk.

All this for an old cooking pot. It wasn't like Daphne—but then again, what did he know? He'd been fooled by her. He'd actually thought she cared about him.

Teri walked in while he rubbed his temples to try to ease the headache that had only increased in strength over the past several hours. She dropped into one of the chairs across from his desk. "Just got done with Jenna Deacon," she said. "Claimed to not know anything about anything, then asked for a lawyer."

Calvin sighed as he nodded. "Fine."

Teri hummed. She was silent for a few moments before she said, "We can't keep them here much longer, Sheriff, and we've already interviewed them all. They've cooperated. The DA was pretty clear about which cases he was willing to prosecute and which ones he wasn't."

He didn't need Teri to say who "them" was referring to. Jerking his chin down, Calvin pushed himself out of his chair and braced himself. Interviewing Bobby Troy and Archie Yarrow Jr. had been easy compared to who he'd have to face next.

For the duration of the walk to the holding cells, his stomach churned. Acid burned up his throat, and his muscles twitched all over. Then he turned the corner, and he saw them. Saw her.

Ellie and Mabel had their arms around Daphne, who was holding a paper cup full of coffee between her knees. The three of them looked up when he approached. He saw the way they curled their arms protectively around Daphne, how their eyes narrowed on him. The perfect family, circling the wagons against a threat.

Once again, Calvin was on the outside. Alone. Once again, he was reminded that he'd always stand apart, because everyone who mattered let him down.

He'd actually fallen in love with her. Even now, the dark smudges under her eyes and the watery tears clinging to her bottom lashes made his ribs tighten uncomfortably. He wished he could wrap his arms around her, but she'd lied to him. It really had been fake for her all along, and he'd been the fool who'd seen things that didn't exist.

It felt like he was seventeen again, seeing the perfect girl with her perfect family, skipping off into the sunset of her perfect future. It didn't matter that they were looking at each other through the bars of the Fernley County Sheriff's Department's holding cell, because Daphne had people to stand beside her, even when she was locked up.

Calvin didn't have anyone to stand beside him at all. He never had and likely never would. He'd learned that years ago, so why did it hurt so much to realize it all over again now?

She wanted a clean excuse to leave the island, and she'd get one. Calvin wasn't going to stand in her way.

His keys jangled as he took them out, and he tore his gaze away from Daphne's. The three of them stood in unison, and even that rankled because they did it together.

All he'd wanted was one person—*one* person—who might care about him the way he cared about them. One person to give a shit.

But that had been too much to ask.

He didn't recognize his voice when he rasped, "You're free to go."

Daphne blinked, and Calvin hated that he still found her beautiful. Tired and rumpled and dirt streaked in that horrid dress, she was still the most stunning woman he'd ever seen. And she didn't want him back.

"We are?" Daphne finally asked, then shot a quick glance at her grandmother.

Calvin said nothing and stepped aside as he held the cell door open. Mabel shuffled out first with Ellie for support, Daphne following behind. She paused as he locked the holding cell again, wringing her hands in front of her stomach.

"Calvin—"

"I don't think there's anything else to say," he told her, hooking his keys back onto his belt. He forced himself to meet her gaze. "I've reviewed your statement. We'll call you if we need any more information."

Daphne's throat bobbed as she swallowed. "I'm sorry—"

"I don't care."

It was a lie, of course. He cared a hell of a lot. But what did it matter in the end? It wasn't like she cared in return.

"I never meant to hurt you," she pleaded. "I just wanted to do this for my grandmother, and it all kind of spiraled out of control."

"Was any of it real?" Calvin heard himself ask, his voice cold and distant. He held her gaze and arched a brow.

Daphne gulped. "I . . . yes, Calvin. Yes, it was real."

He couldn't listen to more lies. Not when he wanted so badly to believe them. What did it matter what she said? If she truly cared about him, she would've put him first. She would've treated him like a decent human being and told him the truth.

He jerked his head toward the exit. "Just go, Daphne. We had a deal, and it's over now. We should just leave it at that."

She lingered for another moment, then ducked her head and walked past him.

Just before she turned the corner, Calvin called out her name. She turned, brows lifted, something like hope creeping into her expression.

"I'll pack your things up and leave them on the front porch. You can come by and grab them while I'm at work tomorrow."

The flash of hurt across her features made Calvin feel like he'd just driven a nail into his own heart, but what was he supposed to do?

They'd had an agreement. It was over. He knew where they stood, and now she did too.

CHAPTER 38

Daphne's mom and dad were waiting outside the station, which meant the three troublemakers had to squeeze in the back seat. Daphne ended up in the middle, shoulders hunched up near her ears, thighs pressed against Ellie's and Grandma Mabel's.

Her mother turned around to look at the three of them. "Where's the pot?" she asked, as if that was the most important thing.

"That no-good, stick-up-his-ass sheriff confiscated it," Grandma Mabel grumbled.

"You did bonk Archie Jr. on the head with it," Helen pointed out.

"Only the lid!"

"Besides," Ellie added, "Archie was acting like a violent psychopath. Grandma saved Daphne's life."

Daphne shifted to grab her seat belt, shoving her sister's hip out of the way so she could buckle it. "It was all for nothing," she said.

"Oh, honey," Grandma Mabel replied, wrapping her arms around Daphne's shoulders. "We had fun, and I got to hold my mother's Dutch oven one last time. It was worth it just to see you stand up for yourself."

Eyes prickling, Daphne nodded. She didn't have the heart to tell her family that it absolutely had not been worth it. She'd broken all the rules that she usually lived by. She'd acted recklessly, and now she was facing the consequences. Total humiliation, the loss of a good professional reference by the sheriff's department, and a surprise breakup as the cherry on top.

As her father put the car in gear and drove away from the station, Daphne kept her eyes on the road ahead. All she could see was Calvin's face when he'd spotted that stupid cast-iron pot. The recognition, quickly followed by a horrible, hollow look in his eyes. She'd watched him realize that she'd lied to him.

In that moment, Daphne knew she'd been wrong about him. She'd thought he would toss her aside as soon as he tired of her, the way Pete had done. Calvin would see that she wasn't the brave, impulsive woman she'd pretended to be, and he'd grow bored. But she'd had it all wrong.

That brave, impulsive woman was real. She came out when Calvin challenged her, when he made her feel like she could be anything she wanted. Daphne had hidden from herself, had kept herself small, but the bad boy from high school who'd been driving her nuts for the better part of two decades had seen what was beneath the veneer of responsibility she wore.

Calvin had cared. About her. About what might be growing between them.

As they left the Carlisle town limits and drove north, Daphne had the horrible, sinking feeling that she'd hurt him in a way that couldn't be fixed.

She should've been honest with him from the start, this good man with a big heart and a history full of hurt. There were deposits of courage buried deep inside Daphne, and she should've mined them when she still had the right to speak to him. Daphne had wanted to take risks, but she'd shied away from the one gamble that might've actually paid off. Now it was too late.

Calvin deserved better. He deserved a partner who saw that core of gold and valued him for who he was, not a cowardly little mouse who thought she was brave because she ran around stealing old cookware to make herself feel like she belonged.

At her parents' house, Daphne sank onto the couch and remembered the Monopoly game they'd hastily set up on the coffee table. She remembered the couch dipping when Calvin sat down beside her, the way his eyes had sparkled when he looked at her.

He made her feel like she could do anything, and she hadn't had the decency to return the favor. She'd taken the confidence he'd given her and thrown it back in his face. She hadn't trusted in his affection, because her own insecurities had gotten in the way.

And now it was over.

"They could do with better coffee at the station, I'll tell you that much," Mabel said, sinking into her usual armchair with a fresh cup.

"Believe it or not, it's better than it was the last time I was there," Ellie replied. She glanced up when the side door opened, and Hugh strode in. His shoulders dropped in relief when he spotted Ellie. She beamed at him. "I'm back!"

"I thought you were done getting arrested."

"It was Daphne's first time," Ellie protested as she sprang up to her feet and spread her arms toward her husband-to-be. "I was there for moral support."

Hugh shook his head and wrapped Ellie in strong arms. He ducked his face into her neck, and the two of them swayed slightly as they hugged. Daphne watched, her heart squeezing when she heard Hugh say in a quiet, private voice, "I missed you last night."

Ellie pulled away and pressed a kiss to Hugh's lips. "Me too," she told him, then turned to Daphne. "But you should have seen us! Daphne kneed the mayor in the balls!"

Hugh gave Daphne an appreciative nod. "Nice."

"I don't think he'll be mayor much longer," Grandma Mabel said, "what with the embezzlement and all."

"And the concussion," Daphne added, shooting her grandmother a sideways glance.

Grandma Mabel sipped her coffee, smiled, and said nothing.

When her father came to sit next to her, Daphne leaned her head on his shoulder. He wrapped an arm around her shoulders and held her, and for a moment, she felt like a little girl again, safe in her father's arms. As her mother went around to refill everyone's cups, then sank down in a chair of her own, Daphne listened to the excited chatter and realized that she'd been wrong about something else.

She *did* belong here. She was just as much a part of this family as anyone else. Not because she had decided to be brash, but because they would always be here to support her. Her parents had encouraged her to leave the island for college. They'd cheered on her academic dreams, even when tears had streamed down their faces when it came time to say goodbye. They'd been there for her when Pete walked out; all she'd had to do was tell them, and the whole family had rallied around her.

Yes, she was different. She liked numbers and got a special kind of thrill when using complicated queries and pivot tables in her spreadsheets. Her family couldn't relate, but they accepted it. Encouraged it. Celebrated it.

She'd never been on the outside of the Davis clan. The only person who needed to accept Daphne for who she was was herself.

"I saved you the heel of the bread I made this morning," her father said, his cheek pressed against the top of her head as he held her. "How do you feel about having it with butter, maybe a little jam? We picked up the rhubarb stuff you like so much."

It was ridiculous that an offer of bread, butter, and jam would mean so much to Daphne, but her eyes still prickled. Even though everyone in the family liked the heel, her dad would always save it for her when he could—even when she'd spent the night in a Fernley County Sheriff's Department holding cell. No one else in the household liked rhubarb jam, but her parents had gone out of their way to stock it for her.

How could she have thought that they didn't appreciate her for who she was?

"That sounds really good, Dad," she croaked, throat tight with emotion.

He kissed the top of her head and got up to move to the kitchen. A second after he'd vacated his spot, Helen took it and wrapped Daphne in another hug. "I love you, Daphne," she said quietly.

Brushing tears off her cheeks, Daphne nodded. "I love you too. I'm sorry."

Helen laughed as she pulled away, pressing a kiss to Daphne's forehead. "Nothing to be sorry about, sweetheart. I'm just glad you're here, and you're okay."

Daphne nodded and wiped her cheeks again, and her attention was drawn by Hugh's voice.

"So, wait, Archie's been embezzling money? Those break-ins were him? Why?"

Daphne explained everything she'd learned about Archie Jr.'s schemes. "Not sure about the Romano's break-in, though," she noted.

"I'm sure it'll all get figured out soon," Grandma Mabel said, then brightened when the doorbell rang. "That'll be Harry and Greta. They said they had something to show us."

"I'll get it," Ellie said as she got up. A moment later, she came back, trailed by Harry, Greta, and Ryan Lane.

The teen had his laptop under his arm, and he gave everyone in the room a little wave. He held up a USB drive. "Got all the recordings from yesterday. You guys want to see them?"

"Hot damn!" Mabel said, jumping up. "Do we ever!"

"Shouldn't you be giving those to the police?" Daphne asked.

"They already have them," Ryan said, taking a seat on a rickety wooden chair and setting his laptop on the coffee table. "I figured you'd want your own copy."

"Whatever we're paying you, I'm doubling it," Mabel announced. "Let's start with that ridiculous dance."

Ryan glanced at Daphne, a grin twitching at his lips. "Sure," he said, and Daphne groaned. For the next while, the whole gang watched and rewatched the footage from the night, dissecting every interaction, laughing at every replay of Daphne kneeing Archie Jr. in the testicles, and going through the fight frame by frame.

Once her mortification had died down, Daphne actually enjoyed herself. She watched herself fight and dance and scheme, and knew that the woman on the recording wasn't a stranger. It hadn't been an aberration of her character caused by temporary madness. She was that woman who retrieved family heirlooms and defended herself in the face of danger.

And Calvin had known it all along. He'd seen her, even when she hadn't seen herself.

CHAPTER 39

Calvin threw himself into his work; it was all he had. Two days after the arrests at his mother's vow renewal, he gave a press conference to the island's media, explaining that a long-term embezzlement scheme had been uncovered.

Along with the video of Archie Jr.'s confession, Bobby Troy had given them the entire story. Ready to wash his hands of the whole thing, he'd cooperated fully, explaining that he'd been taking payments for being the registered agent of the company. He had years of texts and emails that proved Archie Yarrow Jr. had been the leader of the scheme, siphoning public funds into his pockets via the companies.

There were falsified invoices leading back close to a decade. The most egregious of them had been the sheriff's department renovation.

Daphne had spotted the inconsistencies as soon as she'd started looking into it. He wondered if someone else would have been able to untangle the old records. She popped into his head constantly. When he walked by the interview room that had been her office. When he had to approve work expenses for his team. Whenever he opened his freezer and saw that lonely pint of mint-chip ice cream.

Burying himself in work didn't seem to help the way Daphne lingered at the edges of his consciousness day in and day out, but it was the only thing he had left.

A week after the vow renewal, Calvin drove to his mother's house to pick Ceecee up for their hangout day. The weather was nice, so they'd planned to go for a hike around Fernley National Park. He mounted the steps that led to the front door, trying not to think of the moment Daphne had nearly fallen and he'd reached out to catch her. It was the first time he'd had her in his arms.

He'd thought it meant something. He'd thought he'd finally found the missing piece.

He was a fool.

Shaking his head, Calvin made his way to the front door and rang the bell. Ceecee's running footsteps announced her arrival, her smiling face appearing in the doorway a moment later.

"Hi!" she said, and let him in.

"No running in the house, Ceecee!" his mother's voice called out. She appeared at the end of the hallway and smiled when she saw Calvin standing there. "Oh, good! You're here! I packed you guys some food and a thermos of hot chocolate for your hike."

Calvin's first instinct was to refuse his mother's offer, but Ceecee closed the door and slipped her hand in his. He made his way to the kitchen, glancing around the room as he remembered the shattered glass and the panic he'd felt when he hadn't known what Daphne was up to.

"You still like turkey clubs?" Eileen asked, glancing over her shoulder as she wrapped a sandwich in foil. "I wasn't sure; I can make something else if you prefer."

"Turkey club's fine," Calvin responded, frowning. "You remember what kind of sandwich I like?"

Eileen's eyes filled with a flash of sadness, and she turned back to the food, fingers moving in deft, practiced motions as she wrapped the sandwiches and slid them into a bag. "Of course," she answered, her voice artificially bright.

"I like ham and cheese," Ceecee announced.

"Classic choice," Calvin said with a solemn nod, and his little sister grinned.

Eileen packed their lunch, moving periodically to the stove to stir the hot chocolate warming in a saucepan. She poured it into the thermos and fit the lid before packing it in the same lunch bag. Calvin felt like he was watching a stranger. She hadn't packed him a lunch since he was eight years old. He'd survived on peanut-butter-and-jelly sandwiches, cereal, and crackers for years.

Now, decades later, she was packing him a perfect little lunch with hot chocolate and apple slices like it was the most normal thing in the world.

"Ceecee said the two of you had fun at the driving range on Wednesday," Eileen said.

"We were both terrible at it," Ceecee said with a big smile on her face, "but I was better than Calvin."

"Golf isn't my strong suit," he conceded, a smile finally curling his lips. He relaxed into a chair as his mother worked and Ceecee chatted, trying to ignore the ache in his chest. Ceecee jumped up from her chair when Eileen asked for help putting the sandwich fixings away, the two of them moving in the kitchen like they'd done it a thousand times.

He watched his mother bend down to kiss Ceecee's head when they were done, a soft "Thank you, honey. Have fun with your brother" whispered into her hair, and wished he wasn't so bitter. He wished he could see the efforts his mother had made to make amends, wished he could forgive her for all the ways she'd failed him.

When everything had exploded with Archie Jr., Calvin's first instinct was to look at his mother with suspicion. Had she known about the embezzlement? Had she been involved? What about her husband?

So far, he hadn't been able to find any evidence of culpability pointing to either of them. From what he gathered, their relationship with Archie Jr. had never been close. It should have been a relief, but as he sat in her kitchen and watched her be a mother to his half sister, he realized a part of him had wished she were a criminal. He wished he could point to her and say, *See? I knew she was rotten.*

Instead, he had to face the reality that his mother wasn't the evil, neglectful, selfish monster he'd thought her to be. She was human. She'd gotten pregnant with him at seventeen. She'd had to struggle her way through her young adulthood; Calvin knew exactly how that felt. He'd come out the other side. Was it so unbelievable to think that his mother might have done the same?

Now they were both here, dancing around the edges of a relationship neither of them knew how to approach.

Like they always did, his thoughts turned to Daphne. Outside the holding cell, she'd told him their connection had been real for her. Maybe that wasn't a lie. Maybe, just like his mother, she was a complicated, messy person who couldn't always see through the tangle of her own emotions. She made mistakes, just like they all did.

Just like Calvin did.

He knew what her ex had said to her, how deeply that had hurt her. When Calvin was hurt, he lashed out and self-destructed. When Daphne was hurt, he bet she retreated to the safety of her comfort zone.

He'd never told her how he felt because, he realized now, he was waiting for her to take that leap, just like he'd waited for her to come to him physically. Wasn't she in a better position to put her heart on the line than he was? With her family and her privilege and all the support she took for granted? Intelligent, determined, dependable Daphne who could take the world on and win.

Wounded, lonely, tentative Daphne who worked so hard to live up to sky-high expectations.

Had he expected too much of her?

If he had, why did it feel so impossible to forgive her?

"Here," Eileen said, handing the lunch bag over to Calvin.

He took it and thanked her, then followed Ceecee to the front door. Ceecee had her hiking boots on in minutes and was out the door like a rocket, but Calvin found himself lingering on the stoop. He turned back to his mother and watched the way the spring sunshine lit the tired lines of her face.

"Thanks again for this," he said, lifting the food.

The smile she gave him reminded him of Ceecee. Bright as the midday sun. "I'm just glad you're here," she told him. "Ceecee lights up every time you guys make plans together." She hesitated, brows drawing together slightly, then said, "If you wanted to come for dinner sometime during the week, we'd all love to have you—"

"I'll think about it," he said, knowing he was being rude for interrupting her but not able to accept yet another peace offering. Not right now, when he was confused and hurt and alone.

"Sure," Eileen answered, painting another smile on her face. This one trembled at the edges, and it didn't reach her eyes. It was familiar, that smile, and it still hurt to see it on his mother's lips all these years after his father's death. "You just let me know, and we'll put out another plate."

"Come on!" Ceecee called out, waving from the bottom of the hill. "Let's go!"

Calvin snorted, nodded to his mother, and followed his little sister to the truck. They spent the day looking at moss and mushrooms and centuries-old trees. Ceecee talked so much they didn't spot a single animal, but Calvin didn't care. They sat on a bench overlooking a cliff with waves crashing at their feet, ate their sandwiches, crunched on apple slices, and sipped warm, rich hot chocolate.

Ceecee wiggled over on the bench so she could lean against him, then said, "Why does Mom always get sad when you come over?"

Calvin jerked. "What?"

"She tries to hide it, but I can tell. Is it because you're mad at her? She told me she wasn't a good mom to you when you were my age."

Calvin kept his eyes on the San Juan Islands in the distance, tracing the hazy horizon as Ceecee's words sank in. "She said that?"

"Yeah. Is it true?"

Not knowing what to say, Calvin took a sip of hot chocolate. Finally, he admitted, "It's true."

"And it hurt your feelings?"

A huff slipped through his lips. It was funny how a nine-year-old could distill years of pain into one simple sentence that encompassed it all. "I'm trying to forgive her," he admitted, "but it's hard."

"My dad once told me that the hardest thing is to let go of bad feelings. But then he said that when you're mad, you hurt yourself more than the other person, and that kind of made sense. Like one time, I was mad at my mom because I didn't like this one girl on my soccer team and I didn't want to go anymore, but she wouldn't let me stop until the end of the season. But then my dad made me see that the madder I got about it, the less I enjoyed practice. So I tried not being mad anymore, and it worked. And then we won the championship." She kicked her legs out on the bench, her gaze on the cold, crashing water below. "Being mad for the sake of being mad doesn't help anything."

She looked up at him and gave him such a hopeful smile that all Calvin could do was laugh. "That's very wise of you," he told her.

Ceecee nodded. "Yeah. I know."

That evening, Calvin took the pint of mint-chip ice cream out of the freezer, grabbed a spoon, sat on the couch, and ate the whole thing in one sitting.

CHAPTER 40

Daphne read the email from her old boss for the sixth time. The job offer was right there in black and white, the screen glowing in the darkness of her drab apartment.

She should've felt relief. A job offer was a lifeline. It was a way forward, a safety net, another step in the direction of responsibility. Two months ago, her bags would have been packed the moment the email landed in her inbox.

Now it felt like a trap.

It would be another monotony of gray cubicles. One with a great 401(k) match and the promise of safety. But her last "safe" job had ended in a layoff. Was there such a thing as job security? Maybe she'd been lying to herself about more than just her risk tolerance.

Maybe all the years she'd spent chasing stability had really been Daphne running from who she was, looking for safety outside herself, when she should have been working on her own confidence. If she accepted this job, what would she really gain, other than enough money to scrape by in the city?

Besides, leaving the island meant leaving her family. It meant leaving Calvin.

She'd seen him twice over the past two weeks. Both times were at the station, when she'd gone back in to give statements about the goings-on at the vow renewal. Calvin had sat across from her, stone faced, peppering her with questions as if she were a stranger.

Both times, she left feeling drained and ashamed. She'd hurt him by lying about her reasons for agreeing to go to the event. She'd put distance between them with her cowardice. She hadn't believed their budding romance had been real.

But how real could it have been if he wouldn't even speak to her? He was eager to turn his back on her without so much as a conversation about what had happened between them. Wasn't that evidence that they were doomed to fail from the start?

Sighing, Daphne tossed her phone aside and rubbed the heels of her hands against her eyes. She hauled herself off the couch and grabbed the garment bag from where she'd laid it over the back of a dining chair, iridescent-pink fabric visible through the plastic viewing window at the front.

Twenty minutes later, she pulled up outside the Yarrow residence. She made her way through the gate and trudged up the stone stairs, then waited patiently after ringing the doorbell.

Eileen opened the door a few moments later. Her brows shot up. "Daphne," she said.

"I brought your dress back," Daphne said. "Dry-cleaned and mended. There was a small rip in one of the petticoats, but they did a good job fixing it." She unhooked the big reusable shopping bag from her shoulder and pulled out the box within. "And these finally made it to the island. I wasn't sure about the brand of your old wineglasses, but these were the closest I could find. I also went to the glassblowers' workshop down by Barela's yard and asked if they could make a vase. If you've got a picture of the one we broke, they'll try to re-create it as closely as possible."

"Oh," Eileen replied, taking the garment bag and the wineglasses. "Thank you. That glassware actually belonged to the caterers, but I appreciate the gesture. It's very kind of you. Don't worry about the vase. It was Archie's mother's." Her eyes glimmered as she smiled. "We'll just call it collateral damage."

Daphne laughed, then sobered. "I'm sorry about everything that happened. I didn't mean to ruin your event."

"That stepson of mine is the one who ruined it. I thought he was up to something for a long time but convinced myself I was imagining things. He and his father never really saw eye to eye about politics on this island, but when my Archie retired, he had to take a step back and let his son run the place. And look how that turned out." Eileen set the dress down on the foyer bench, then looked at Daphne. "Would you like to come in? We're just about to sit down for dinner."

"Oh no, thank you," Daphne said. "I should get going." She turned to do just that and paused when Eileen asked, "Have you spoken to Calvin lately?"

Daphne stopped with one foot on the porch's bottom step, the other on a concrete paver. "Not since the last time I went down to the station to go over my statement."

"He's been working himself to the bone. I thought maybe . . ." She smiled sadly. "I thought maybe you'd be the one to settle him back down. He seemed so happy when the two of you were seeing each other."

Bitterness twisted in Daphne's gut. "I think I ruined any chance I had at doing that," she admitted. "I . . . never told him about . . ."

Eileen arched her brows. "About that old pot and your plan to get it back?"

Cringing, Daphne let her gaze slide to the side. "I'm so embarrassed."

"Why didn't you talk to me? I had no idea the thing belonged to your great-grandmother. I thought it was my mother's. She said she got it at a flea market. I kept it because it's the perfect size for making stews."

"That would've been a better idea, huh?"

Eileen leaned a shoulder against the doorjamb and laughed. "I was told you were the responsible daughter."

Daphne groaned and slapped her hands over her face. "I don't know what I am anymore. I just came here to work on the sheriff's department's accounts. None of this was supposed to happen."

"You got any more burglaries planned, or was it more of a one-and-done thing?"

This was the most excruciating interaction of Daphne's life, but she deserved it for bringing chaos to this woman's home. "One and done," she replied, meeting Eileen's amused gaze. It surprised Daphne that Eileen had such a good attitude about it all—then again, a woman who'd choreographed a ridiculous dance and let her nine-year-old act as costume designer for the sake of a few laughs at her party wasn't the type of woman who took herself too seriously.

"Shame," Eileen said, grinning. "People have been talking about my party for weeks. I've been basking in the attention. I thought maybe you'd be open to do a repeat performance."

Shaking her head, Daphne admitted, "My old boss just offered me a job, so I don't think I'll be hanging around for much longer. This island is bad for my health."

Eileen snorted. "I know the feeling. Wasn't until I met my Archie that I started thinking I could make Fernley Island my home, and I was born here."

"Thank you for being so gracious, Eileen," Daphne said. "I wouldn't blame you if you slammed that door in my face instead of inviting me in."

The look on Eileen's face was soft and almost fond. "I get why Calvin likes you so much," the older woman said. "Nothing like someone who stands up for what they believe in, isn't afraid to own up to her mistakes, and is intelligent and beautiful to boot."

Daphne could hardly stand to continue this conversation. She'd wanted to return the dress and run away. It was the last tie she had to this family, and she was ready to move on from the most mortifying experience of her life. "He's not such a big fan of me at the moment."

"He does know how to hold a grudge, that son of mine."

Chest aching, Daphne tried to force a smile. "I'll let you get back to your dinner. And let me know if there's anything else I can do to make up for what I did."

"Talk to Calvin," Eileen said in a voice echoing with sadness. "That's the only thing I'll ask of you. Don't make the same mistakes I made and stop fighting for him."

Boulders lodged themselves in Daphne's throat, making it impossible to voice a reply. How could she fight for a man who didn't want her? What was there to fight for? She nodded at the woman in the doorway, then waved her goodbye and headed back to her car.

CHAPTER 41

It was an overcast, chilly day in mid-April, one of many when the spring sunshine struggled to break through the clouds. Calvin woke up and got dressed as usual. Went to work. Found out what, if any, shenanigans had happened overnight on the island. Days just like that had begun to blend into each other, an endless stream of monotony, work, and rain.

Around ten o'clock that morning, Shirley knocked on his office door. Glancing up from the report Teri had put together about the Romano's break-in, Calvin arched his brows at the other woman.

"You got time to come to the kitchen for ten minutes?"

He closed the folder with the report and nodded. "Sure," he said, not really wanting to leave his desk. Teri had found a witness who'd told her that the renovation at Romano's had partially been funded by a local government grant for the expansion of tourism on the island. A grant that had been approved and disbursed by Archie Yarrow Jr.'s office. The former mayor had admitted it on tape, and now they had concrete evidence to prove the embezzlement.

With his romance with Daphne dead in the water, the only thing Calvin had to cling to was the hope that everything that happened would be worth it in the end. And that would mean beady-eyed Archie getting exactly what he deserved.

But Shirley held the door open for him and smiled, and Calvin knew part of his job was keeping this department together. He'd grown fond of Shirley and Hank and Teri and all the other people who made this place function. The thought of staying and putting his name on the ballot for the election in the fall was more attractive than it had been when he'd first arrived.

And then there was Ceecee. His mother. The more weekends he spent with his sister, the more he saw the way his mother cared. An old, deep wound had begun to knit itself shut, and despite his best intentions, Calvin found himself growing roots here.

"Chuck and Iris called this morning," Shirley told him. "No shotguns today, thankfully," she added with a grin.

"Alpacas jumping fences again?"

"Chuck has accused Iris of deliberately spreading acorns along her property line. Poisonous to alpacas, apparently. Can you believe it? This is the milkweed incident all over again, with the Davises and Jason Brownlow." She clicked her tongue. "Iris denied it, of course. I had half a mind to send Ellie Davis over there to remind them what happened last time someone tried this."

Grunting, Calvin tried and failed not to let the mention of Ellie send his thoughts careening toward Daphne. Now wasn't the time to start wallowing.

They made it to the kitchen, where all the deputies and staff on duty began to sing the "Happy Birthday" song. Calvin tripped over his feet and caught himself on the wall, stopping short as Shirley presented him with an oversize card, signed by every one of his coworkers.

On the table was a store-bought sheet cake with the words *Happy Birthday, Sheriff Flint* written in cursive. He blinked at all of them as the song came to a close, throat tighter than it should have been. No one had wished him a happy birthday in years. Up until this moment, he'd forgotten it was his birthday at all.

"Thank you," he told them, trying to hide the emotion in his voice.

"We just wanted to let you know we appreciate all the work you've done since you got here," Shirley told him, smiling. "Now. Who wants cake?"

Calvin ate a slice and enjoyed a few minutes' break with his colleagues. The cake was a touch too sweet for his taste, but he still couldn't fault it. Someone—multiple someones—had come together to mark the day as something special, and that felt good. It made those roots a little thicker. Made him feel a little less alone.

The work cake probably softened him up for the phone call he received from his mother that afternoon.

"Happy birthday, Calvin," she said, and he could hear the smile in her voice. "How's your day been?"

"Good," he replied, and it wasn't exactly a lie. There was still an echoing emptiness in the pit of his heart, but he didn't feel quite as hollow. Loneliness still nipped at his heels, and he didn't have much in the way of deep friendships, but someone had remembered him. Someone had thought of him.

"I know you're busy at work," Eileen said more tentatively, "but Ceecee was wondering . . ." She let out a breath that sounded half-embarrassed and half-frustrated. "*I* was wondering if you were free for dinner tonight. Ceecee made you a card."

"Oh," Calvin said.

"Listen, you don't have to stay for dinner. Just come by and let Ceecee wish you a happy birthday, or maybe we can come to your place—"

"No, dinner sounds good," Calvin heard himself say, shocking himself in the process. "I can come to your place."

His mother sounded equally as surprised, but there was excitement in her voice too. "Really?" she asked. "Oh, good! Six o'clock? Six thirty?"

"Six thirty will be fine," he said.

"We're doing a barbecue. Burgers. Nothing fancy. Just wanted to have a meal together."

"That's fine, Mom," he said.

"Oh," she sighed. "Good. All right, I know you're at work. I'll let you go." Emotion rang in her voice, and Calvin himself wasn't quite immune when he bid his mother goodbye.

After setting his phone aside, Calvin stared at the dark screen for a beat, wondering why this felt like such a momentous occasion. It was one dinner. Nothing special. His mother had said it herself.

But it was the first time he'd accepted one of her olive branches without hesitation, and Calvin found himself relieved for it. He *wanted* to go to his mother's house and see if they could turn over a new leaf together. He wanted to see if these new roots were worth digging in deeper, if this was a place he wanted to call home again.

He could run for sheriff, and he knew he'd probably win. Live in his house. Get to know the people on the island through his work. Have a purpose.

It sounded good—and it made him sad.

Because he could live and work and serve on this island until he died, and it would never feel as good as those moments snuggled under a blanket with Daphne's legs on his lap. A birthday cake in the staff kitchen warmed his heart, but it didn't light him up the way Daphne's smile did.

He missed her. She'd made him ache for something he hadn't even known existed. The type of companionship that felt effortless, as if being with her had been the natural way of things.

He could try to mend the relationship with his mother. He could build a relationship with his sister. He could be the best sheriff Fernley had ever seen.

But he couldn't have his heart broken.

Calvin couldn't put himself at risk of being neglected again, not when being with Daphne had felt like carving his own heart out and handing it over on a platter.

Then again, hadn't he been quick to point out whenever Daphne was playing it safe? When she was making her life smaller than it should've been because she was afraid of taking a chance?

She'd hurt him, and it was a struggle to let go of the ache. All these years, he'd lugged his pain around like a useless extra limb. Why? If he could have dinner with his mother, why couldn't he reach out to Daphne?

The dark phone screen drew his gaze. His fingers twitched. His pulse pounded.

Maybe . . .

What if she *didn't* leave Fernley Island? What if Calvin could convince her to stay?

Then Teri poked her head through the doorway and asked him about the case, and he told himself he'd think about Daphne later, when he had time to make sense of his emotions.

At six thirty, Calvin reached for the doorbell beside his mother's front door. Before his finger could make contact, the entrance flew open and Ceecee launched herself across the threshold.

"Happy birthday!" she yelled, her voice muffled in Calvin's stomach.

He laughed and hugged her back. "Thanks, kid."

"Mom is so excited you're here, but don't tell her I said that."

Calvin's lips curled, and he looked up to see his mother shooting Ceecee a sardonic smile. She pretended to roll her eyes, then gave him a genuine smile. "I am happy you decided to come," she said. "Happy birthday, honey."

"Thanks, Mom."

"We put up decorations," Ceecee told him, sliding her hand into his. "Come see! I blew up so many balloons my head got all woozy and my dad had to tell me to sit down."

Laughing, Calvin let himself be towed deeper into the home. Twisted garlands had been strung up in the living room, where the vow renewal dance had occurred, with a banner wishing him a happy birthday tacked to the wall. Balloons were taped to the wall and left loose on the ground, and Ceecee ran at a clump of them to kick them into the air. Her laughter made Calvin smile.

"Can I get you a drink?"

Turning to meet his mother's gaze, Calvin nodded. "You got soda water? If not, regular water's fine."

"Sure," she said, and ducked into the kitchen.

A moment later, her husband appeared and gave him a strong handshake. "Glad to see you, Calvin," Archie Sr. said. "Eileen couldn't stop smiling all afternoon."

Calvin's heart gave a twist. He'd been so closed off with his mother, harsh and angry. What was the point? Their past wasn't magically going to disappear just because they'd both grown up, but they *had* both grown up. Couldn't this be the start of a new relationship between them?

"I wanted to thank you for how you've handled things with my son," Archie Sr. said as he watched Ceecee rub a balloon on her head to make her hair a staticky mess. He glanced at Calvin and gave him a sad smile. "If I'd known what he was up to, I would've stopped him years ago. But I appreciate you being thorough and as discreet as you can on this island. I know you're probably sick of telling people you can't comment on an ongoing investigation, but I wanted to tell you how much it means to me."

"It'll all come out at some point," Calvin said. "Once the legal eagles take over, there'll be a lot more information for people to dissect."

Archie Sr. let out a long sigh. "After so many years running this place, my son goes and tarnishes our family name. Decades of public service, and now this." He shook his head. "The only consolation is that you're the one who uncovered it all. We might not be a blood relation, but I'm happy you're part of this family, Calvin. Your mother has made me so happy, and she's given me my only daughter."

"Your *favorite* daughter," Ceecee corrected, hair clinging to the balloon she held to the side of her head.

"My favorite daughter," Archie confirmed, spreading an arm so Ceecee could give him a hug.

Calvin's first instinct was to back away and give them their moment. But Archie had just offered him something he'd never had—to be part of the family. To belong here, with these people.

His heart thumped. A bit of the hollowness inside him receded.

Archie smiled at Ceecee, then turned to Calvin. "I can only hope that we can all move on together."

"Here you go," Eileen said, presenting him with a crystal tumbler full of sparkling water, with a perfect, juicy slice of lemon perched on the edge. Calvin took it, then watched his mother caress Ceecee's hair before leaning in to kiss her husband's cheek. "Let's put the burgers on," she said, her hand squeezing Calvin's arm as she walked by.

She touched him as easily as she did her daughter, and Calvin felt another pulse in his heart. There was lingering awkwardness between them, an uncertainty about the exact bounds of their relationship, but for once, Calvin didn't focus on it. He let himself enjoy the intimacy of the evening, not realizing that with that soft, almost unconscious decision, he'd begun to forgive his mother.

They ate burgers and talked about sports, the weather, Ceecee's schooling, and old war stories about Archie Sr.'s time as mayor. By the time his mother brought a cake out, Calvin's shoulders had fully relaxed, and he was able to smile as he listened to the "Happy Birthday" song for the second time that day. His mother had gone to one of the fancy bakeries in town and gotten a three-tiered beauty of a cake, complete with perfectly piped icing and delicate chocolate decorations. It looked incredible.

"Make a wish!" Ceecee commanded, wiggling with excitement in her seat. Calvin closed his eyes and blew out the candles. As he cut Ceecee a piece, she grinned at him. "What did you wish for?"

"I can't tell you, or else it won't come true."

Ceecee grinned. "That's true." She accepted the piece of cake he handed her across the table and scooped a glob of frosting onto her finger. Then, with the kind of abrupt change of topic that only children are capable of, Ceecee announced, "Daphne was here last night."

The knife froze, hovering above the cake. "Daphne Davis?"

"Your girlfriend," Ceecee confirmed.

"She's not my girlfriend." He turned to his mother. "What was she doing here?"

"Returning the dress after getting it dry-cleaned and fixed."

"And she gave us new wineglasses. She's nice," Ceecee said.

All the lightness that Calvin had felt over the course of the evening collapsed into a leaden ball in his gut. "Yeah," he said, not meaning it at all. He glanced at his mother and, not sure what, precisely, he was wondering about, he asked, "Did she say anything else?"

"Only that she got a job offer off-island," Eileen replied, shrugging.

Calvin blinked, attention returning to the knife he still held over the cake. He cut another slice and gave it to his mother. "She's leaving?"

"I guess so. She said her old boss offered her a job."

"I see," he said, and passed a slice to Archie. Serving himself last, he stared at the chocolate cake on his plate and thought he might throw up if he ate it.

Daphne was leaving Fernley. That was a good thing. There was nothing between them. They'd gone their separate ways, just like they'd planned. She was free to go, confident in the knowledge that the gossip about Archie Jr.'s crimes would overshadow any talk about the two of them. Everything—well, almost everything—had gone according to plan.

So why did the thought of never seeing her again make him feel so cold?

CHAPTER 42

It was late by the time Daphne pulled up outside Calvin's house. The clock on her car's dash said a few minutes past nine. Late enough that she hesitated, glancing at the lights shining from behind the living room curtains, wondering if he'd think she was horribly rude for showing up like this.

Ever since she'd left Eileen's house the night before, Daphne had felt like life was running away from her. She was on a conveyor belt, being carried out to a destination without her conscious input. Another cubicle. Another step in her life plan, her foot positioned exactly where it should be.

But things had changed.

Her internal pendulum had swung too far in the other direction. Her body had been bruised and battered; her heart hadn't been safe from injury either.

She'd read her old boss's email about a hundred times, and every time, the feeling of dread got stronger. A life of cubicles and traffic, a series of safe decisions that got her nowhere.

Huffing out a breath, Daphne cut the engine and got out of her car. She circled around to the passenger side to grab a box from the front seat, then closed the door with her hip as she faced the house. Calvin was in there, and he probably didn't want to see her.

But she had to do this.

If anything, she had to apologize. Maybe he'd slam the door in her face and she wouldn't get the chance, but she had to try.

Calvin was the one who'd jarred her out of her stupor of safety. He was the one who'd shown her that there was depth to her she hadn't plumbed before. He was the one who'd seen it and appreciated it. He was strong and kind and good, and he didn't deserve to be lied to.

Even if he told her he never wanted to see her again, she had to stand up, put her hand on her heart, and tell him he deserved better than to have been misled.

Being a planner at heart, Daphne had rehearsed her speech. She'd visualized it a thousand times over the course of the day, ever since she'd seen the post on the sheriff's department's social media about Calvin's birthday. She'd written down all the reasons she wanted to tell him she was sorry, and all the ways that he'd made her life better in the short time they'd been together.

All those carefully practiced words flew out of her head as soon as Calvin answered her knock. He stood in the doorway, surprise lifting his brows, and Daphne forgot everything she was meant to tell him. He was so beautiful, standing there in a soft tee and faded jeans. She ached to be allowed to fall against his chest and feel his arms come around her.

Maybe this was her penance. To see him this last time and know that she loved him while being absolutely certain that she'd messed it all up.

Grief and longing and need formed a writhing ball of snakes in her gut, and all Daphne could do was look up in his hazel eyes and wish she'd realized how much she felt for him earlier. She wished she hadn't been so afraid.

"Daphne," he said, breaking the silence stretching between them.

She blinked, then blurted out, "I made cake."

His gaze dropped to the box she held between two trembling hands. "Cake?"

"I didn't know what flavor you liked so I made vanilla, but then I worried you'd think that was boring, so I made a red velvet one with cream cheese icing. And, actually, really I made you twenty-four cakes because I decided to do cupcakes, because . . . well . . . I . . ."

In her panicked need to make amends, Daphne had thought of the silly nickname she used to hate. Now, the twenty-four treats lined up in the box with perfectly piped swirls of icing seemed like a presumptuous way of demanding that Calvin forgive her.

His brows furrowed as he glanced in the box. "I see."

"For your birthday," she explained, feeling stupid. "I saw the sheriff's department post about it online, and I thought . . ." Gulping, Daphne shook her head. "It's probably silly. I just thought about what you said, about no one ever making you a birthday cake, and I figured . . ."

His eyes lifted to meet hers. She couldn't read what was written there, and her anxiety mounted. He deserved so much better than a bumbling apology from a woman who didn't know herself. She'd thought a few cupcakes would fix what she'd done?

"I'm so sorry," she said, blinking back tears. "We made that silly deal, and I lied to you. I caused a scene at your mother's vow renewal, and I wasn't honest with you."

"About what?"

"About how I felt!" Daphne cried, clutching the box closer as she sucked in a hard breath. "You were so strong and good and, and . . . and just *everything*, and you made me feel like I could do anything. You made me feel special, Calvin, and I just—got so scared. I thought you'd get bored of me and toss me aside, so I didn't tell you the truth about the pot. I should have told you. I should have told your *mom*. God, I made such a fool of myself, and now . . ."

She thrust the box of cakes at him.

"Take them," she said, then hesitated. "Unless you don't want them, in which case, don't. But—happy birthday. And I'm sorry. And you're the best man I've ever known, and even if you tell me you never want to see me again and slam the door in my face, I'm still glad I got to spend time with you."

Calvin still hadn't moved. He had a strange expression on his face, and Daphne was having trouble meeting his gaze. Her heart began to thump, and she knew that once again, she'd made a mess of the situation. Panic and embarrassment and heartbreak wound themselves around her ribs, squeezing so tight it became hard to breathe.

When Calvin made no move to take the cakes from her, Daphne did the only thing she could. She gave him a no-nonsense nod, set the box on the ground between them, and hightailed it back to her car. Her pulse pounded so hard that she heard nothing but her own rushing blood and the breaths sawing in and out of her lungs. Her eyes were blurred with tears. Her hands trembled as she clawed at her purse for her keys, needing to escape.

She'd made a fool of herself—again. Cupcakes as an apology? In what world would that fix anything? He'd made it clear he didn't want to speak to her over the past month. She shouldn't have come to see him. It was stupid to think she deserved forgiveness.

Her keys slipped through her fingers in her purse until she finally gripped the fob. Feeling for the right button, she unlocked her doors and reached for the handle.

And a broad palm landed on the door to hold it closed.

Daphne froze. Her shoulders were hunched up near her ears, her breaths panting as if she'd sprinted from the door to the car. Hell, maybe she had. The last ten seconds were a blur.

"Is this goodbye?" Calvin asked in a low voice.

Daphne glanced at the distorted reflection of his face in the curved window of her car. Her heart splintered at the question, because of course this was the end. She gulped. "If that's what you want," she whispered.

"Look at me."

She didn't want to. All Daphne wanted to do was get in her car and run away to somewhere she was safe. But she'd come this far, and he deserved to see her face to face. If she was honest with herself, Daphne might have admitted that she wanted to look at his face one last time, since he'd just confirmed that this was the end.

Squaring her shoulders, Daphne turned. She knew her eyes were watery when she lifted her gaze to meet his, but she worried that if she tried to blot her tears, he'd think she was being dramatic.

"I heard you got a job offer," Calvin said.

Daphne nodded. "I emailed my old boss a while ago. We both got laid off at the same time, but he's got an opening at his new company."

A muscle twitched in Calvin's jaw. "I see. When do you leave?"

Daphne blinked. A tear escaped, and she brushed it away, then shook her head. "Oh, I'm not." Her gaze slid to his shoulder as she let out a bitter laugh. "I turned him down. I still don't know if that was a mistake, but hey. I've made a lot of those lately, so what's one more? At least my family's happy I'm sticking around."

The sour twist of her lips faded when she lifted her gaze to meet Calvin's. His eyes were intense, blazing as they circled her face. "You turned down the job?"

Daphne nodded.

"Why?"

"I . . ." Words stuck in her gullet.

Calvin shifted closer, the scent of him sweeping over Daphne as she inhaled a trembling breath. The hand he'd kept pressed against her door moved to her shoulder, then to her neck, thumb brushing her jaw as he tilted her face up so he could study her expression. "Why did you turn it down, Daphne?"

Maybe it was the feel of his skin against hers that broke down the last of her defenses. Or maybe it was the shivering hope in his gaze, or the simple fact that he was chest to chest with her, and Daphne had never been able to resist him.

Of all the reasons she could have given him—all the logical little blocks she'd lined up in her head about career progression and living costs, about being close to her aging grandmother and working on her family relationships—there was only one that came to mind.

"Because I'm in love with you," Daphne whispered.

Breath gusted out of him, and his grip on her neck tightened, his other hand reaching for her waist. Suddenly he was closer, the whole world contracting to only him. To that first brush of his lips against hers. The trembling breath that slipped through his lips as he shifted to press a kiss to her nose, then her cheek. The way his hands softened as he held her, drawing her tight to his chest.

When Calvin finally kissed her—really *kissed* her—Daphne clung to him like he was her only salvation in a raging storm. She wrapped her arms around his shoulders and kissed him back, the length of her body pressed to his. He pulled away to wipe his thumbs against her cheeks, and she realized she was crying.

"I'm sorry," she said.

He smiled. "Stop apologizing."

"I can't."

Huffing, Calvin kissed her again. It was tender and soft, but it held a thread of promise. The promise that this was real and enduring and everything Daphne had been so terrified to face.

Leaning his forehead against hers, Calvin let out a long sigh as his fingers stroked her cheeks, her jaw, her neck. "I'm sorry too, Daphne."

She jerked back. "For what? You haven't done anything wrong."

"I never told you how I felt, and I should have, and then I let you walk away and never reached out. All because I was afraid of what you meant to me."

Daphne's lip wobbled. "And what's that?"

His smile was sweet and warm, his thumb stroking her jaw. "I want to show you something," he said, and reached down to thread his fingers through hers. He tugged her to the front door, then leaned down to pick up the box of cupcakes and carry it inside, depositing it on the bench next to the entrance. Then he led her to the bedroom.

On the bed was a suitcase, half-full of neatly folded clothes. At the foot of the bed was her grandmother's cast-iron pot.

Calvin wrapped his arms around Daphne, his chest pressed to her back. He braided their fingers together and clasped them against her stomach so she had no choice but to lean against him.

"I don't understand," she said, looking at the suitcase and the pot.

"I had dinner at my mother's house tonight," Calvin explained. "She told me you'd gotten a job off-island. As soon as I got home, I started packing my bags."

"For what?"

He leaned down to press a kiss to her shoulder, lips curving against her skin. "To run after you and drag you back here," he said. "Obviously. Plan B was to run after you and move to Seattle together. Whatever you preferred, as long as I got to be with you."

Spinning in his arms, Daphne worried that her ribs would break from the pounding they were taking from her heart. She slid her hands up his chest, feeling the prickle of his coarse chest hair through the thin fabric of his tee. "And the pot?"

"Grabbed it from the office on the way home. I figured the first thing to do before I followed you to wherever you were going was return it to its rightful owner."

If she hadn't loved him already, Daphne would've tumbled headlong in silly, besotted adoration at that confession. Her cheeks ached as she smiled wide, more tears spilling from her eyes. "This is a dream," she said.

"I hope not," he replied, touching his nose to hers. His hands swept down her sides and dove under her shirt, and they both sighed at the feel of his palms on the bare skin of her back. "I love you, Daphne. I think I loved you at eighteen, and it didn't take me long to fall for you almost two decades later. I love your grit and your brain and your smile. I love how stubborn you are and how you light up at the promise of ice cream."

Daphne laughed, choking on her happy tears.

"You make me feel like I have a home," he told her. "You make me want a future together, when I've never dreamed beyond the next couple of weeks before. I love you so much I didn't even know it was possible to feel this way, like my entire world revolves around someone else. Like I need to see you and kiss you and touch you just to survive. For the first time in my life, I feel like I'm not alone."

Breathing was difficult; speaking was impossible. The only words Daphne managed to squeeze out through the grip of her emotion were, "Kiss me."

Calvin's lips curled into a smile. "That I can do."

It was close to midnight when they came up for air. Giddy and exhausted, Daphne slumped over Calvin's chest as he trailed his fingers through her hair. She'd never been so comfortable in her life.

"Did you ever figure out who broke into Romano's?" she asked, voice muffled against his skin.

Calvin hummed.

With a superhuman effort, Daphne lifted her head. "Is that a yes?"

His eyes sparked with barely hidden mirth. "It's a yes."

She rested her chin on her hands, his skin warm beneath her palms. "What aren't you telling me?"

"You want to go for a drive?"

"Right now?"

His smile was irresistible; Daphne would follow this man anywhere. She rolled off him and pulled her clothes on, and ten minutes later, they were passing Romano's dark windows and then turning down the alley that ran behind the restaurant.

Calvin stopped his truck a few feet from the dumpsters and leaned his forearms on top of the steering wheel.

Daphne stared at the alley, all harsh lighting and dark shadow. "I don't follow."

"Give it a minute," Calvin said, eyes on the big steel container.

Sure enough, within moments, movement made Daphne lean forward. Two glowing eyes reflected the truck's headlights a moment before an enormous raccoon clambered out of the dumpster and trotted away.

Daphne glanced at Calvin. Calvin arched his brows.

"A raccoon?" she asked, incredulous. "How? It's way too small to reach the window."

"There was an old mop on the ground when I came out here the night of the break-in," Calvin explained. "I had a theory, and I tested it out last night by shoving a broomstick in the corner of the dumpster. It took about an hour for the raccoon to shuffle around enough to knock it over. I figure the garbage was at just the right level—pretty full of all the construction junk—and the mop was at just the right angle. The raccoon must have nudged it, and it smashed against the window to trip the alarm."

Daphne let out an incredulous snort. "You're sure?"

"There was nothing to steal. No one on any security cameras. No evidence of anyone actually getting inside, which they couldn't have done from that window in the first place. No reason for Archie Jr. to break in here if he was trying to steal records to cover his tracks. This is the only thing that makes sense. And besides, there was a handprint that was too small to be a full-grown human's, other than one belonging to a very tiny woman. Raccoons have opposable thumbs."

"A raccoon," Daphne repeated.

"I've let Animal Control know. They'll trap her and move her out of town."

"This island," Daphne said, shaking her head.

Calvin laughed. His hand slid over Daphne's thigh, thumb stroking along her leg as his eyes softened. "You want to go home?"

Daphne's heart thumped. She could get used to Calvin Flint looking at her like that, asking her that exact question. "Yes," she told him.

He didn't move from his position, his thumb caressing her thigh once more. "You want to move in with me?"

There was only one way to answer that question. As a bright smile bloomed over Daphne's lips, she reached over to curl her hand around the nape of his neck. "Yes," she said. "I definitely do."

"Good," Calvin said, and he kissed her so thoroughly she knew that when they got home, there wouldn't be any sleep happening for a long, long while.

EPILOGUE

Nine years later . . .

Daphne's hands were sore from clapping as she watched Ceecee cross the stage for her high school graduation. Beside her, Calvin let out a sharp whistle to add to the ruckus. He grinned when Ceecee glanced over at them, her cheeks red and her eyes shining. She threw them a little wave, then accepted her diploma.

"I'm so proud I could burst," Eileen said, leaning her head on her husband's shoulder.

Daphne slid her hand in Calvin's elbow as they took their seats again to watch the last few graduates accept their diplomas. When the ceremony finally ended, the audience filed out into the June sunshine outside, clumping in small groups to wait for the graduates and staff to emerge once they'd returned their gowns.

Calvin did his usual routine of shaking hands and acting like the competent, respected sheriff he was. Daphne watched him as she waited for Ceecee to appear, her love for him still managing to grow every day. Sunlight gilded his dark hair, now dotted with more silver, and his eyes crinkled at the edges when he smiled. Last year, he'd won his third election and continued to serve as sheriff of Fernley County. He'd grown into the position over the years, dutiful and fair, and it was hard to imagine anyone else leading them the way Calvin did.

Daphne had built a small but loyal client base for her own accounting business. She hadn't sat in a cubicle—gray or any other color—in over a decade. She'd embraced the relative instability of running her own company, and had been rewarded with a flexible schedule and a steady, growing income. The chaos that happened after her arrival on Fernley Island taught her that chasing stability could include some risks—as long as she stayed honest with herself and the people she loved. She hadn't lied to Calvin about anything since the pot.

Archie Jr. had been convicted and spent nearly two years in prison. He moved away from Fernley, and contact between him and his father had dwindled over the years. Ceecee once told Daphne that she'd lost one brother but gained a better one in the process. Their family had ragged edges and complicated relationships, just like any other. Daphne figured she fit in just fine.

Jenna Deacon had cut a deal with the state and gotten away without any prison time. When Romano's folded shortly after the unraveling of Archie's schemes, she'd left the island too.

"Will the kids be joining us for the barbecue?" Eileen asked, drawing Daphne's gaze. The kids had arrived not long after Daphne and Calvin had tied the knot.

"Of course," Daphne replied with a smile. "I'll text my parents to let them know we're heading to your place soon."

Calvin shook one last hand and crossed toward them. He slid his hand across Daphne's shoulders and tucked her against his chest, lips pressing a soft kiss to her temple. Daphne leaned against him, soaking in the quiet peace his arms provided.

"How are you feeling about Ceecee taking off for college in the fall, Mom?" Calvin asked as Ceecee emerged.

"I'm so proud of her," Eileen said.

"She's heartbroken," Archie Sr. corrected.

When Daphne and Calvin laughed, Eileen clicked her tongue. "Just you wait until your youngest takes off," she chided.

Ceecee barreled into them, throwing her arms around her parents before moving to hug Daphne and Calvin. "Thank you for coming!"

"Wouldn't miss it for the world, kid," Calvin said, squeezing her shoulders. "I'm proud of you."

Ceecee beamed at him. She was a gorgeous girl with long brown hair who had never lost the limitless energy that drove her. She was an accomplished dancer and the valedictorian of her graduating class. She'd had her pick of colleges, and chose to stay relatively close to home by committing to the University of Washington. She had a bright future ahead of her. Daphne had watched her relationship with Calvin deepen over the years, and it had made the decision to have children with him that much easier.

The kind, loving competence with which he approached his job was amplified at home. Even now, when he threaded his fingers through Daphne's and tugged her toward the car, she knew he was looking forward to being reunited with their two little ones.

They piled into their cars and drove to the beautiful A-frame house where Archie Sr., Eileen, and Ceecee still lived. The gardens had grown over the years, and in the summer, they looked like a woodland dream. Her parents were already waiting outside the house. Helen was inspecting flowers with Caroline, their four-year-old, and Claude had Benji, their six-year-old, thrown over his shoulder.

"Got a potato delivery," Claude announced as Daphne and Calvin approached. "Where should I drop them?"

Benji squealed. "I'm not potatoes!"

"Hmm. How fresh are they?" Calvin asked, squeezing Benji's arms and sides until the little boy squealed and squirmed his way out of his grandfather's arms.

"Who's hungry?" Eileen called out as she exited the car, herding the little ones inside. It was hard to imagine Eileen as a neglectful mother; she was a doting grandmother to Caroline and Benji, and a loving mother to Ceecee.

"I brought bread," Claude answered with a wink. Daphne smiled, knowing it had been baked in *the* pot. All their special-occasion baked goods had been ever since Calvin and Daphne returned it to Mabel's grateful hands.

Some days, after visits to the Yarrow residence, Daphne saw lingering tightness around Calvin's eyes. She knew he still experienced pain from childhood memories, but it didn't stop him from showing up and trying. He'd had many conversations with his mother over the years. They'd mended their relationship and reached a place of mutual respect. As their family grew, those bonds had strengthened.

It was one of the things that Daphne admired most about him. He was a man who wasn't afraid to do the right thing, even if it was difficult. It was what made him a good sheriff, a great father, and the most perfect husband she could have asked for.

A short while later, Ellie and Hugh arrived with Grandma Mabel in tow, along with their daughter, Maisie. Kathy burst through the door and started shouting commands at Archie as he manned the grill. Friends drifted through the door to congratulate Ceecee, and the party went late into the night—with no arrests, no stolen cookware, and no cast iron–induced concussions. In other words, it was a success.

That night, once the kids were passed out after the excitement of the party and tucked in their beds, Daphne climbed under the blankets beside Calvin. He spread his arms and pulled her close, and she rested her head on the bare skin of his chest, her fingers running through the coarse hair growing between his pecs.

His fingers trailed over her side, rucking up the silky fabric of her nightgown. "I like this," he said, feeling the fabric between his thumb and forefinger.

Daphne smiled. "I figured you would."

After rolling her onto her back, Calvin propped himself above her. "You're still the most beautiful woman I've ever seen, you know," he told her, nose coasting over her jaw. His hand slid up her thigh to squeeze her hip.

"Am I?"

He hummed. "Even when you fish for compliments."

Daphne laughed and curled her hands around his shoulders. She kissed him deeply, then lifted her knees so he could settle his hips between them. "I love you," she whispered.

"Love you more."

"Not possible."

She felt him smile against her cheek a moment before he dipped his head and bit her earlobe in response. A shiver went through Daphne's body, fire lighting in the pit of her stomach. She turned her head to kiss her husband, knowing that in his arms was exactly where she was meant to be.

Turn the page to see a preview of Lilian Monroe's *Four Steps to the Perfect Revenge!*

Four Steps to the Perfect Revenge

CHAPTER 1

Ellie Davis needed muscle. Ideally, she'd find great, ambulant slabs of it attached to a frame that didn't ask too many questions.

"What are we doing here again?"

Ellie scowled at the scrawny blonde woman crouching in the bushes beside her. Wynn Howard had been Ellie's best friend since the first day of first grade, but she was not made for sitting in foliage under a steady, gray drizzle. Wynn pulled a leaf off the bush and hunkered down under her black rain jacket, a grumpy tortoise uninterested in important covert operations. "I'm hungry."

"You're a terrible accomplice is what you are." Ellie turned back to the fence looming ten feet away, pushing a branch aside so she could see what she was up against. The fence was timber and about eight feet tall. It had a gate secured with a metal chain and a solid padlock. Ellie knew it was solid because she'd failed to slice through it earlier with the only tool at her disposal. The bolt cutters in her hands were slick with water, the red duct tape wrapped around the handles warm beneath her fingers. "As to what we're doing, we're getting Louie so I can get off this island for good."

"Oh, come on, Ellie. You're not serious about that, are you? Where are you going to go?"

"I'll figure it out once I'm on the mainland." She'd crash on her sister's couch, cuddle her dog, and move on from this place.

Wynn let out an exasperated noise, peeking around the side of her hood to meet Ellie's gaze. "It was *one* mug shot. Your mom has, like, a hundred mug shots from the seventies and eighties. It's practically a family tradition. Your grandmother was *proud* of you."

Ah, yes. The illustrious family legacy. How could Ellie forget? She'd lived in the shadow of her parents' misspent youths her entire life. Her mood grew darker than the oppressive cloud cover draped over her head. "Is this supposed to be convincing me to stay on this stupid island? Because it isn't working, Wynn."

"Fernley is your home."

"*That* was my home." She pointed the bolt cutters at the cedar shingle roof poking above the nearby trees. "Now it's the building I'd burn down if I had any desire to commit arson."

Wynn lifted her head, pushing the hood of her rain jacket back an inch so she could stare at the house through the scraggly fir trees. She seemed to mull over Ellie's words, tearing the leaf in her hands into teeny, tiny pieces. Then she glanced at Ellie and gave her a thoughtful look. "Your mom got arrested for arson once, right? Didn't she burn down the mayor's house when she was fifteen?"

Ellie didn't dignify that with a response. She'd worked hard to rise above her parents' reputations so the people on this island would give her a chance. She'd built a business, put everything she had into gaining the respect of her peers. And now—

But never mind that. Ellie had only one thing to do before she could be free of this place. Her dog was behind that fence, and she wasn't leaving the island unless Louie was by her side.

Six months. *Six months* was how long she'd spent trying to get Louie back the right way, the legal way. She wasn't waiting one minute longer.

With one last look left and right, Ellie dashed to the padlocked gate and tried her might against the chain once more. Her first attempt hadn't yielded any results, but now she was desperate. Desperate women were dangerous—and effective.

The chain holding the gate closed was thick, galvanized steel, and it didn't even dent in the jaws of her stupid bolt cutters. Fergus O'Hara had sold them to her out of the trunk of his car in exchange for an extortionate three hundred dollars, and he'd been a damn liar about how sharp they were. The patina of rust and the duct-taped handles should have been her first and second clues as to their effectiveness, but Ellie hadn't had many options in the bolt cutter department. Buying new ones at the hardware store moments before breaking and entering would have won her another mug shot and a second lifetime's worth of humiliation.

She squeezed until her muscles gave out.

The chain held, clinking gently against the timber fence, laughing at her. She scowled.

If she were staying on the island, Ellie would give Fergus a piece of her mind. These bolt cutters might not get through steel, but they'd probably work on human toes—and other body parts. Luckily for Fergus, she'd be on the next ferry out of here when he rolled out of bed at the start of the next century.

Grunting and growling with effort, Ellie put all her weight into squeezing the handles one more time. She needed to break this chain, *needed* to get Louie out of there . . .

She fell back, panting. Stumbling forward again, she wiped raindrops from her eyes to see if the chain was any closer to yielding.

Nothing. Not even a scratch on the metal link she'd thrown all her weight into snapping.

"I'm going to kill him," Ellie grumped. *"Best bolt cutters on the island,* my ass."

The thick padlock shackle didn't yield to Ellie's efforts any more than the chain did, so she resorted to whacking it with the pointy end of her useless tool like it was some kind of felonious version of a strongman carnival game, where the prize was not getting arrested. Or, more accurately, not getting arrested *again*. The sound of metal hitting metal echoed around the forest, sending a nearby bird flapping in outrage.

"Let me try." Wynn held out her hand, pink nail polish perfect as always.

"Your arms are twigs."

Wynn pursed her lips. "I've been working out, Ellie. Plus, it's about technique more than brute strength."

Ellie wasn't so sure about that, but she handed the cutters over.

After a short struggle, Wynn let out a frustrated huff and started whacking the padlock too. Once she'd exhausted herself, she let the bolt cutters dangle from her fingertips and met Ellie's gaze. "We need someone with lots of brute strength. Technique is not important."

Ellie snorted, slipping the bolt cutters into her backpack before hiking it up on her shoulders and clipping the chest strap. She frowned at the chain, then backed up a few steps and studied the top of the fence.

"Um . . . Ellie?" Wynn took a step closer. "You're not going to—"

Ellie took off at a sprint, channeling her inner Jackie Chan as she lifted her leg to try to propel herself up the fence with a powerful kick. She'd never run up a vertical surface before, but today was her day. She leaped, hanging in the air as time stopped around her. Then her fingers brushed the top of the fence and slipped off, and she landed on her back on a bed of wet ferns.

Note to self: ferns do not provide for a soft landing. Especially when her backpack was full of lumpy tools and sharp edges.

Groaning, she clutched her tailbone. The chain knocked merrily against its gate while the muddy imprint of her shoe stared back from the surface of the fence, taunting her.

So far, Ellie's career as a criminal had been pathetic. She wasn't even living up to the family name she'd tried so hard to outrun.

Wynn appeared above Ellie's head, hand extended. Accepting her friend's help, Ellie clambered to her feet and set her jaw.

"I can jump that fence. Then I'll grab Louie and go out through the front."

"The front is padlocked too," Wynn pointed out.

"I'll go through the house."

"What about the alarm? I'm sure the code has been changed since you moved out. And you know it probably connects directly to Sheriff Jackson's phone. He'll be here within minutes if it goes off."

Damn Wynn and her stupid, faultless logic. Ellie stared at the barrier separating her from her dog. "So I'll jump the fence, grab Louie, then . . . then . . ."

"I'll give you a boost," Wynn suggested; "then you pull me over with you, and we can lift Louie back over together. He'll be fine jumping down from the top. Then I can boost you over again, you pull me up, and hey presto, we're gone without a trace."

Ellie grinned. "This is why I keep you around, Wynnie. That's genius."

"You keep me around because everyone else thinks you're a crazy person who's going to snap and attack them with a baseball bat."

Ellie would never live that mug shot down. "Low blow, Wynn."

Wynn grinned and scampered away. She knelt near the fence and braided her fingers together, lifting her head awkwardly so she could see Ellie under the hood of her rain jacket. "Ready."

Ellie blew out a breath and joined Wynn at the fence. A moment later, propelled by Wynn, she pulled herself up onto the top of the timber fence, swinging one leg over to straddle it. The fence had a flat piece of two-by-four across the top, just above the foot-tall privacy lattice. It was wide enough to sit on but not exactly comfortable.

Wynn cheered. "See? I'm strong." She jerked her chin toward the yard. "Any sign of Louie?"

Ellie scanned the space. It was just as she remembered. A hot tub sat dormant near the back door, on the left side of the big deck. The fire bowl at the bottom of the deck's steps was filled with wet ash and charred wood, surrounded by concrete pavers and new patio chairs. Green, lush grass was edged with weeds and the carcasses of last year's flowers. New blooms wouldn't get planted this year because Ellie didn't live here anymore, not that she was bitter about it or anything. And on the far side of the yard, a yellow doghouse with a red roof shone like a beacon of light in an otherwise soggy, dismal world.

A snout poked out of the opening, followed by Louie's black-and-white head. Her happy, loving, beautiful, smart, loyal border collie.

"He's here," she breathed, unbelievably relieved. "He's okay." Even though he'd been left outside in the rain. From the reconnaissance Ellie had done over the past six months, her ex-fiancé kept Louie outside almost all the time. The dog was fed and watered and had a comfortable doghouse, but Louie deserved better. That he'd been banished from the house was enough to make Ellie's blood boil, but now wasn't the time to get angry. Now was the time to get even—and get out.

"Good. Help me up." Wynn extended her arms. "Let's be quick. We've wasted enough time. Jason will probably be home soon."

"In and out," Ellie confirmed. Seeing her ex-fiancé while she was trespassing in his yard was not on her agenda for the afternoon. He'd probably have the police cuffing her in no time, and one item on her rap sheet was more than enough for a lifetime.

She tried to reach Wynn's hand by bending to the side, using her thighs to anchor her to the top of the fence. Even at full stretch, their hands were still a foot and a half apart. Wynn made a pitiful jump and didn't come close to grabbing Ellie's outstretched arm.

"Um. Hold on." Ellie braced her hands on the top of the fence and lay flat across it, letting her legs dangle down. The timber was slippery and wet, and it dug in uncomfortably at her chest and hip.

A whine from the far end of the yard caught her attention. Louie was out of his house, watching her. He barked once, tail wagging so hard it whacked the yellow corner of the doghouse in a steady *whump-whump-whump.*

"Hey, buddy," Ellie called out, throat tight. "I'm coming for you."

Louie barked again, tongue lolling, then came bounding across the yard toward her. He jumped up on the fence, his front paws a few inches below her dangling foot. He snuffled and yipped, then dropped down and zoomed in a circle on the lawn, overcome with doggy joy.

"Good to see you too, Louie."

The dog panted, then yawned and sat down, watching her. He'd wait patiently, because he was a good boy—and he could probably smell the treats she'd stashed in her backpack. They were Louie's favorite, homemade by the local veterinarian. She doubted her ex had gone out of his way to buy them, which meant Louie had suffered six months without.

Ellie blinked hard to clear her eyes, then returned her attention to Wynn. They had to both get over this fence and somehow get Louie and each other back out again, and time was running out. Tears would only slow her down.

She clung to the fence with her knees and extended her arm down, wiggling her fingers. "Try now. We should be able to reach."

Wynn stepped up to the fence and reached up, stretching onto her tiptoes—

"Yes!" Ellie wrapped her hand around Wynn's wrist. Their skin was slick from the rain, but that shouldn't be a problem for a simple lift. All Ellie had to do was haul Wynn up high enough that her friend could pull herself the rest of the way.

Easy-peasy.

"Jump on three, Wynnie. One, two, thr—"

Wynn jumped early, a half second before Ellie could brace herself against her friend's weight. She immediately pitched to the side, scrabbling to grab the slick wood with her opposite hand.

But it was too late.

Between Wynn's hard yank, the awkward position on top of the fence, the weight of the backpack shifting, and the water drenching absolutely everything, Ellie slipped off the top of the fence and came crashing down on top of Wynn.

The ferns failed to soften their landing once more. Wynn cried out in pain, Ellie groaned, and they writhed around on the wet forest floor like beached whales until they could untangle their limbs and sit up.

"Argh!" Ellie slapped the ground with both hands. Frustration singed her chest, burning against the inside of her rib cage. She just wanted her dog back. Was that too much to ask? Louie wasn't even supposed to be here. All his papers had Ellie's name on them. Every vet visit, every toy, every treat, every kibble had been bought with Ellie's money.

Jason had no right to keep him, but he was the heir to the Brownlow fortune. He was the director of the Brownlow Foundation, a stupid, celebrated charity that purported to fight for environmental sustainability on the island. She'd glimpsed some of the paperwork, and she knew that the upper echelons of Fernley society donated *generously* to the cause. Yet, in addition to the charity, Jason was building a luxury resort next door to Ellie's parents' property, which involved clear-cutting a huge swath of virgin forest.

Nobody seemed to notice this obvious conflict of interests. The only uproar was from people like her parents who had no political or economic weight to throw around.

Jason, on the other hand, had the whole damn island in the palm of his hand—including Sheriff Jackson, who'd refused to intervene when she'd complained about Louie. The dog was a civil matter, the sheriff had said. Nothing he could do.

Yeah, right.

After Ellie's arrest, the sheriff had given her the runaround for *five months* before recently admitting that he wouldn't help her get her dog back. The Brownlow-nosing jerk. (The first month after her arrest had been spent wallowing. It was a bad time. Ellie preferred not to think about it.)

Well, Ellie was done relying on other people. She wiped her eyes to clear the raindrops and the tears of anger that clung to her lashes. She'd cry when she was on the mainland with Louie by her side, once she was off this island and away from these people. She looked at Wynn. "You want to try again?"

Wynn leaned against the fence, using her hands to gingerly lift her calf. She winced, then met Ellie's gaze. "I don't think I can, Ellie. Something's wrong with my ankle."

Get exclusive free bonuses, including three red-hot novellas, by signing up for Lilian's reader list:
www.lilianmonroe.com/FourSteps.

About the Author

Lilian Monroe writes swoon-worthy contemporary romances with a dash of mystery, a sprinkle of suspense, and an always-satisfying happily ever after. She is the author of multiple series that go from heartwarming to heart pounding, including We Shouldn't, Unexpected, Manhattan Billionaires, and the Heart's Cove Hotties. When she's not writing, she's daydreaming about which story to tell next.

Keep up with Monroe's latest releases, freebies, and more by visiting her website at www.lilianmonroe.com.